Recusant

Book 2 of the Brin Archives

by

Jim Cronin

Solstice Publishing - www.solsticepublishing.com

Dedication

This book is dedicated to all my friends and family. I need
to give each of you fair warning, and a challenge. I was at a
loss for character names for this story, so I borrowed and
altered many of your names. I hope you have fun locating
your character. I promise, cross my heart, and everything,
that I in no way made any effort to match a character's
personality to yours.

Prologue

(Approximately 1,200 years ago)

"Skae High Command, this is Kolandi Raj Ansus, please respond, Skae High Command."

Static echoed in the Raj's ears as she gripped the com link in a white-knuckled desperation. Her royal robes and long brown hair showed the neglect of long hours in the war room. Ansus rose only recently to the position of High Raj. She fervently hoped it was not her destiny to be the last Raj.

Her nose became insensitive to the stench of bodies during her confinement in the dim bunker long ago. The deep space images on the screen before her revealed the devastation of their fleet in their encounter with the Gorvin. Two hundred top-of-the-line war cruisers had been completely destroyed, another three hundred fighters were out of commission. She watched as the overwhelming forces of the Gorvin plowed through their defenses like an energy blade through a cloud, and were now aimed straight at Kodut, their home world.

On the displays, a second line of vessels, the laser launch ships, took up their attack formation. A cloud began to grow ahead of the ships as they deployed their weapons.

"Raj Ansus, Raj Ansus, this is Skae High Command. We are receiving you."

"Praise the gods." Ansus let out a sigh of relief, realizing she had been holding her breath in anticipation. The Skae had their own difficulties with the Gorvin and communications were unreliable at best. "High Command, we need your help. Our fleet is gone. The Gorvin are preparing to attack Kodut. Their light sail probes will enter our atmosphere in a matter of hours. Our planetary defense satellites cannot handle so many small devices traveling at those speeds. Please, we need help."

Technicians monitoring the long range sensors continued to report the enemy's progress. "Probe light sails are open, launch ships are powering up their laser cannons." In moments, tens of thousands of light sail devices, each a package no more than ten centimeters across, and filled with millions of microscopic nanobots and micro-encapsulated genetically enhanced viruses, leapt forward toward Kodut at half the speed of light, powered by photons fired from hundreds of laser cannons on the launch ships.

Static filled the room for what seemed an eternity. Ansus heard quiet sobbing from one of the attendants huddled behind her. Her own mind filled with rising panic as time passed without a response.

"Skae High Command, come in. Are you receiving us? We need your help. Come in, please."

A deep, resonant voice answered. "Raj Ansus, this is Imperial Commander Tac. I regret to inform you that we have nothing in your sector to send to your aid. All of our forces were sent to the Keldon sector in response to Gorvin threats there. It will be three days at best before our ships can reach you."

"We won't survive three days, commander Tac. You must send immediate help."

"I'm sorry, Raj Ansus. There is nothing we can do. We simply do not have the resources to send you until then. Take shelter as best you can, preferably deep underground in well-filtered bunkers. The Gorvin weapons are biological and technological. Your people will survive, but you must shield your technology from the attack. We will send our fleet as soon as we can, but we are too far away to reach you at this time."

"There is no *time*, commander. We don't have the time to shield our systems. We barely have time to get ourselves into shelters. Are you certain the filters will keep out the virus?"

"They are the best we have. Far superior to previous versions, but test results are marginal. I wish you the best. Have faith. Get your people to safety. We will come as quickly as we can. Commander Tac out."

Four hours later, deep underground in the royal bunker beneath the capitol city, Raj Ansus, her court, and many of the government officials sat in tense silence as monitors revealed the sky ablaze with streaks of fire as the Gorvin probes entered the atmosphere. Similar reports of the attack came from outposts across the planet. The light sails, each one a meter in diameter and manufactured from enhanced graphene nanotubes now acted as atmospheric brakes. Heat and drag forces broke open the probes, releasing the viral and nanobot weapons into the atmosphere.

"Our only hope now is the filters." General Dorn, leader of the Kolandi military forces, nodded as he assessed the dispersal patterns. "If they fail, the nanobots will seek out and shut down all our technology, down to the simplest devices."

Raj Ansus nodded in agreement. She sat in her padded chair, hands folded in her lap as she conferred with her military experts. "How severe will the damage be, General? How soon will we be able to rebuild?"

"Without our tech, life in the cities will be unsustainable. We must be prepared for planetwide pandemics, starvation, rebellion, in other words, the end of our civilization. Save those we can, but then the virus will infect us all."

"But all the reports say it isn't lethal. The Gorvin weapons rarely cause death."

"Yes, but in cases like ours, when they have attacked the closest allies of the Skae, those races are trapped on their planets. The virus alters their physiology setting up a biological resonance with a planet's natural gravitational field. Any attempt to return to space and rejoin the Skae as an ally results in their death. No cure has ever been found, despite all the efforts of the Skae and other allies."

The lights began to flicker and static filled the monitors. Technicians fought to maintain their panels. "All systems are failing, communications are down in sectors twelve, twenty-six, and twenty-nine. Massive overloads are building across the globe."

Raj Ansus started to ask another question, her mouth opened to begin, but she could not find the words. The horror of her people's future was too great to comprehend. She gathered her will in an attempt to project courage to those around her.

Four days later, the Skae fleet arrived. The first unmanned scout ships lost all power as they attempted to enter Kordut's atmosphere. The majority of the fleet held back and orbited Kodut between the twin moons. Early attempts to communicate with the Kolandi proved useless. The Gorvin nanobots had nearly eliminated all electronic wavelengths planetwide. Only when a very high intensity beam pierced the barrier could communications with the surface take place.

"Yes, Commander Tac, we can read you, but barely." Raj Ansus stood outside the entrance to the royal bunker. The communications officer worked furiously at a panel of knobs and switches trying to eek the last bit of power from a rapidly draining battery pack. "The filters were unsuccessful against the virus. We regained consciousness yesterday with only minimal fatalities, but medical tests show we are definitely infected. The Gorvins have destroyed all electronics. Can you provide any information on the expected life of these devices?"

"Our best estimates, you must realize these are only preliminary, indicate the devices are replicating and will remain active for a minimum of five hundred years. Our readings also show the virus has established itself in your biosphere and shows signs of growth. It now has the ability to infect the DNA of all life forms on the planet. The virus works so quickly it could invade our technology, and us as well, as soon as we enter your atmosphere. We cannot assist you without risking ourselves."

Ansus felt her heart sink. She slumped into a nearby chair, her mind desperate for any sign of hope. "There must be something you can do. You can't abandon us. We have supported you for generations. We have bled and died for you. Help us."

The silence which followed lasted long enough to convince the Raj communications had been lost until a crackle from the speaker broke the stillness and commander Tac's voice, barely audible now, pronounced their sentence. "My most profound apologies, Raj Ansus. There is nothing we can do. Rest assured, though, our scientists will never stop looking for a cure to the virus, and our technicians will find a way to break through the dampening field. We will not abandon you. One day we…"

The communications officer checked his instruments, looked up at his Raj, threw his hands up in defeat, and shook his head. "That's it. The battery is gone. We're on our own for now. Those blue-skinned devils are going to let us die aren't they?"

"There is nothing they can do for us. We must survive, or die as best we can. Gather the rest of the officers. We must begin preparations for evacuation of the city and learn to become farmers." Raj turned and strode off to be alone and gather her thoughts. *We must survive. We will survive.* A tear ran down her brown cheek as she straightened her shoulders and lifted her face toward the sky. *This will not be the end of us.*

Chapter One

The desert sun beat down on Maliche Rocker's prostrate body like a microwaver set to rapid bake a Tirpit roast. Lying down on his belly as he gingerly laser-picked the matrix away, one grain at a time, from a new discovery of some engraved metallic shards among some ancient pottery had his heart racing. The life of an archaeologist was ninety-nine percent drudgery spent in a damp cellar or lecturing in a broken down classroom, but the one percent times like this were thrilling and made the rest, as well as the ridicule of his family, all worth it.

"I can't be sure, but if my suspicions are correct, we have just made the discovery of the century, Aras. Take a look at these engravings." He adjusted the settings on his laser-pick so a broader beam swept away dust from the surface.

Aras, the enthusiastic grad student scooted in closer to get a better look. She held her broad-brimmed hat above them to help shade the artifact and give them a glare-free view. The thin epidermal scales of her bare arms glinted in the sunlight. "I don't recognize the language, professor. What are they?"

Maliche laughed, puffing up a bit of dust in the process. "If my memory is correct, nobody has seen anything like this in over two hundred years. This may be an artifact of the Kolandi."

Aras's eyes shot open as she rolled onto one side looking at her mentor. "Wait, the Kolandi? What makes you say that? All Kolandi artifacts recovered so far are pottery, some rough metal farming implements and such. These are too advanced to be Kolandi."

"Most others would probably agree with you. But you forget my ancestry. Being a direct descendant of the original Rockers gives me a few advantages. I know I've seen these markings before, and on something similar. I just can't place it right now, but when we get back I'll be able to confirm my suspicions."

After taking holographic photos to show the exact placement of the artifacts, making detailed notes, and clearing away enough of the matrix, Maliche reached out to pull the fragment free. "Ouch! What the phalk?" He pulled back his hand and sat up to examine his fingers, certain to find a bad burn. "Huh, not a scratch. It felt like I stuck my hand in a power generator when I touched it."

"Let me try, professor." Aras pulled on her gloves and slowly extended her hand toward the artifact, wincing in anticipation, as her fingers got closer. At her touch, she relaxed. "It seems okay now, professor. I'm not feeling anything." As Maliche watched, she pulled off her glove and carefully touched it again. "Nothing. It feels fine. Hold out the box for me and I'll pull it free."

Examining the engraved shard in the container, Maliche again attempted touching it, but pulled back, shaking his hand in pain as he absorbed another shock. "How can you not feel that? It wasn't as bad as the first time, but still stings like a quetzal." He handed the box to one of the nearby laborers. "Put this thing on the artifact table in the tent. And be careful with it. I'll be there in a minute."

The worker accepted the container and headed toward the tent. Out of curiosity, he tried touching the piece of metal with one gentle talon, only detecting the warmth of metal sitting in the sun. He glanced back over his shoulder, shrugged, and carried the object to the artifact tent, handing it to one of the preparers.

The research assistant sitting at the long wooden table dropped his pen when he saw the engravings. He jumped up, grabbed the laborer by his sleeve, and pulled him to a far corner of the tent. "Where did you get this?"

"The boss found it over there." He pointed in the direction of Maliche and Aras, still focused on the remaining pieces of pottery in the new site. "He told me to bring it to you."

He pulled the smaller man close, whispering nose-to-nose. "All right, go about your business, but don't tell anyone about this. Understand?"

The man glanced around nervously, but nodded in agreement. "No problem, sir. It's just a piece of metal out of the desert. No need to get so upset. I'm simply here to do my job and get paid."

The preparer glared at the man for a moment, tossed him loose, and waved him off. He examined the artifact again, glanced around the room quickly to make sure he was not being observed, and stashed the metal in his pocket.

Later that evening, the camp was in an uproar once Maliche discovered his potentially historic discovery was missing. None of the workers had seen or heard anything, and the one he entrusted it to swore he did exactly as told and turned the item over to the preparers in the tent.

Aras burst into the tent, breathless from her running. "It's true. One of the research assistants took a shuttle a few hours ago. Probably the one we thought was the supply ship heading back home. No flight plan was filed, so we have no way to track where they actually went."

"Phalk. Get on the communicator and alert the authorities that we have a stolen shuttle. Maybe they can track it down for us."

Aras approached Maliche, placing one hand on his shoulder. "Don't worry, professor. We'll find the artifact. It can't be too difficult to trace. There's nothing else like it, so our people will know the minute it shows up on the black market."

Maliche leaned heavily on the table, his head hung low. "I hope you're right. That piece was the discovery of a lifetime. We need to close up camp early and get back to try to find it. The rest of this site was pretty common anyway. We can come back next year if we need to."

"I'll see to it, professor. Keep your hopes up. It's bound to turn up soon. You'll see."

***

A week later, back at First Town, the capital of Brin civilization on Raince'to, the streets radiated out from the center of the city where the Savior's Memorial stood. Maliche set his mag-lev to auto pilot so he could gather his thoughts. The sight of the Savior Memorial always stirred deep and reflective emotions within Maliche Rocker. *I've spent my life chasing after their memory. This new artifact may have answered all my questions. How could I have been so careless? I never should have left it out of my sight. Dr. Neywa certainly seemed anxious about the sketches I made when we talked last night. Maybe he found the key to the writing on them. Could it finally be proof of the Kolandi?* He slammed his fist on his knee. *Maybe this will be the discovery to wake up those feather-fluffed quetzals in The Assembly and force them to listen to someone other than the guilds and provide some decent funding for our research.*

The vehicle came to rest in his reserved parking spot, and Maliche stepped out to wander among the familiar story of his ancestors. The imposing structure with its polished pink granite exterior and tall columns housed a museum as well as the ancient tombs of Jontar Rocker, Maripa, and Karm; The Saviors. A shuffling of feet and hushed whispers disturbed his thoughts.

"Can anyone tell me the significance of these holographs?" The teacher smiled as dozens of eager hands shot into the air. "Marita, what can you tell us about them?"

The girl, her school uniform immaculately pressed for this trip, and bursting with pride, proceeded to describe the scenes before the class. "This one shows our ancestors transporting the DNA samples across the galaxy in the Hegira II. And these others show how Jontar and Maripa Rocker built first town and saved the early colonists from starvation."

Maliche smiled as he strode passed the group. Elsewhere in the shrine, endlessly smiling docents, dressed in period accurate attire, told the stories to hushed and reverent groups.

The security guard at the entrance to the holy of holies smiled and nodded at Maliche as he passed.

"Good morning, Professor Rocker. Nice to see you again."

Karm's Obelisk stood in the very center of the rotunda. Flanking the obelisk to the left, Maripa's simple marble headstone and inscription only added to her mythological status as The Mother Savior. Of course, Jontar Rocker's marker stood over an empty grave, but that mattered little to those who stood silently, often wiping back tears paying their respects. These were the ultimate ancestors of Maliche and Selan, eight generations removed. This accident of birth gave rise to the exalted position of all direct descendants of The Saviors, each one taking the name of Rocker once their genetic markers tested at the accepted level of relatedness.

A while later, back in his mag-lev, Maliche sat in another ground traffic jam. He watched wistfully at the free flowing commute of the air vehicles traveling in six separate layers above him. *One of these days I'm going to give in and let Selan buy me one of those. The mag-lev ground lanes are always the worst. Good thing my classes don't start until the afternoon.*

A light drizzle began as Maliche finally pulled into his parking spot on the outskirts of the university campus an hour later. *Maybe I should have stuck with genetics instead of the desolate backwaters of archaeology. A spot in the parking garage would almost be worth it on days like this.* He set the controls to lower the support pads, turned off the magnetics, and gathered his gear as the vehicle settled onto its extended landing legs. Maliche lifted his jacket over his head and jogged the quarter mile to his office.

Cutting through the main genetics department building allowed him to get out of the rain momentarily. There were five other buildings devoted to the study of anything and everything to do with DNA, but this four story building stood as the crown jewel of the school. Maliche paused to listen in to a counselor talking to a batch of new students as they gazed at the murals of his ancestors on the high stone walls.

"Each of you will play an important role in the eventual discovery of a cure for our desperate situation. You will soon take a battery of aptitude tests to determine which field of research you are best suited for. Each of the five buildings devoted to this worthy profession is dedicated to a different area of research. When you receive your results, you will be assigned to a lab in one of these buildings." She paused for a moment, slowly gazing at each of her charges and breaking into a broad smile. "Who knows, but one of you may go down in history along with the revered Rockers as a new savior."

Due to a mysterious set of circumstances related to this planet's environment, The Brin faced a desperate situation. Each succeeding generation's life span was becoming shorter than the previous generation. As a result, the study of genetics was the most noble and vital profession any Brin could aspire to, especially if one's name was Rocker. Maliche's choice of archaeology proved to be an embarrassment to his family, and a never ending source of ridicule from his father and brother.

A guard scowled at Maliche as his wet shoes squeaked on the granite floor. The rainwater dripping from his jacket marked a long trail behind him. Maliche simply smiled at the guard as he passed by the desk, flashing his ID badge. The blue and green border with gold helix declared his rank as a pure Rocker.

The guard snapped to attention. "Sorry, sir. I'm new to this building. Haven't seen you here before."

Maliche waved off any concerns, reading the name off the man's badge. "No problem, Officer Tagut. I've been away doing some field research for a few weeks. Just got back in town. Keep up the good work."

Taking the corridor to his left, Maliche maneuvered through crowds of students on their way to classes, eventually reaching the exit door at the other end.

After using two more buildings as temporary shelters, Maliche arrived at the entry to the archaeology department. Actually, the building belonged to the music department. Archaeology rented out the basement and a couple of classrooms on the second floor. As he passed the displays of various artifacts in the hall, Maliche slowed his pace, eventually stopping completely to examine the specimens contained within the glass cases. Small cards with his name on them as the discoverer flanked several of the pieces. He grinned as his thoughts danced over memories of past expeditions to remote regions of the planet. He tapped the glass and sped down the hall toward his office.

"Hello, Professor," called out Maliche as he opened the door at the bottom of the stairwell. He wove his way through one of the narrow, dimly lit aisles amid the tall metal shelves. Half of the ceiling panels either flickered randomly, or were completely black. Hundreds of boxes and assorted pieces of pottery, fabric, utensils, and other artifacts filled the dozens of shelves. The smell of dust and mildew permeated the air. In the back of the room hunched the figure of Professor Neywa, peering through a hand lens as he read one of the books piled around him, a threadbare shawl covered his shoulders. Maliche heard the steady plink of water dripping into a puddle from one of the overhead pipes. A small service robot hovered nearby with suction tubes trying to deal with the mess.

"Haven't they come to fix that leak yet?"

"Sometime next week, they tell me," answered the elderly head of the department without looking up from his reading. "Better go check the service bot before it overflows. That thing is so old, its sensors don't always register when it is full."

"Maintenance has been saying that for two weeks now. You'd think they could spare us an hour." Maliche hung his jacket on the wall hook and set his valise on the floor by his chair at the only other desk in the room. He tapped the controls on the rusted robot, checking the panel readout. "It looks okay to me, but I'm going to call maintenance again and tell them to get out here today."

The old man chuckled as he looked up from his work. "Now don't go and do something foolish like that. If we make too big a stink over a dripping pipe, the board may decide we're not worth the expense after all. Then where would you be?"

"You mean without this fine office and the prestige of a professorship at this outstanding university?" Maliche dropped heavily into his chair and nearly toppled over backward, catching himself at the last second. "Kak mag-supports again! I'm surprised they keep us around at all. If they got their way, the board would require two courses of genetics instead of one every semester and dump us, along with history, philosophy, art, and a few other less than prime departments to make room. It's probably only a matter of time before they start calling it the theology department and make my phalking ancestor's stories their book of holies."

"My, aren't we in a grand mood today," the old professor said, placing his hand lens carefully on the book. "What's happened this time?"

Maliche opened his mouth to start his rant, but changed his mind when he looked into the calm, wrinkled, gentle face of his mentor. He rubbed his talons through his disheveled crest in an attempt to preen and straighten some of the rain-soaked feathers back into shape. "Nothing, professor, just another argument with my brother over my work here. I wish he would, at least, be a bit more understanding and helpful. You would think he might be able to use his influence on The Assembly to help his brother a little, instead of treating me like an embarrassment to the family."

"Don't waste your time wishing for the impossible. I learned long ago to keep my crest feathers down and my opinions to myself. The more we can fly under their radar, the better off we are. We may be the only ones who truly appreciate the importance of our work, but one day, others will see it as well."

"And what am I then... chopped grendel bait?" Aras stood a few feet away with feet firmly planted and arms folded across her chest. Her knee length dress, worn over torn canvas pants and high black boots, hung gracefully on her curves. A faded and well used pack slung negligently from one shoulder.

Dr. Neywa never noticed her approach and jumped at the sound of her voice. "Sorry, Aras. I should have said the three of us. Can you forgive an old man his inexcusable forgetfulness?" He bowed his head and reached out with upturned hands to the pretty graduate student.

She held her stance and maintained her reproachful stare. Maliche suppressed a smile.

"This department, and myself especially, would crumble and wither into oblivion without your invaluable assistance, my dear. We are eternally indebted to you and your tireless efforts." He gave Aras the most pitiful look of remorse he could muster.

"And don't either of you ever forget it!" Aras smacked one of the flickering wall light panels shocking it back to life, smiled, and grabbed her microelectronic reader pad, stylus and hover-desk pane from the nearby shelf. She tossed her pack onto a dry section of floor and sat gracefully in her chair under the now functioning light panel.

"Are your notes for next week's labs ready for me to look over yet?" asked Maliche.

"Yes, professor, but I wanted to look them over one more time to make sure I didn't leave anything out."

"I'm sure they're fine. Your work is meticulous. Get them to me as soon as you are ready."

A bright smile lit up her face as she glanced at her mentor. "Thank you, professor. I should have everything ready in less than an hour."

Maliche allowed his gaze to linger on the shapely figure of the young girl before returning his attention to professor Neywa. "Have you had a chance to review my notes on that lost artifact from my last expedition to the desert? I hoped you could answer a few questions about it."

The elderly dean of archaeology lifted his glasses as he rubbed his pale blue eyes. Letting out a long exhale which was half grunt, he slumped back in his chair. "I knew this day would come. I was beginning to lose hope of ever seeing it with my own eyes, though. Are you certain your drawings are accurate?"

"As close as I can remember. I made the sketch as soon as we learned the piece was missing. I got a close look at the markings, so it's as good as I can make it."

Neywa exhaled heavily and slapped his hand on one knee. "Hang on a minute. I have something to show you." He punched a command into the keyboard on the arm of his chair, causing it to hum and lift slowly off the ground.

Placing his talons into the directional sockets he guided the chair down the hallway.

Maliche and Aras looked at each other. Aras hunching her shoulders in response to Maliche's raised eyebrows as he rose to follow the dean into the dark recesses of the shelf maze.

As Aras tapped the on switch of the overhead light panels, Neywa blew the dust off the label of several boxes before proceeding to another aisle. "Been a long time since I looked for this one," he said as he continued the search in another aisle.

As the accumulated dust of years of neglect revealed another label, professor Neywa's eyes lit up and he pointed to the container in front of him. "Aha! Here it is! Be a good lad and grab this one. Bring it back to my desk for me."

Maliche hefted the filthy box, coughing as he inhaled some of the dust rising from the lid and set it on one of the few float trays still in operation.

Aras, no longer content to eavesdrop from her desk, joined her mentors. "What's in the carton, professor?"

Maliche caught her eye, displaying his own confusion with a shrug. Professor Neywa, a glint of mischief in his eye, wagged a talon at the two. "Patience. You must learn patience to be an archaeologist."

Returning to their office space, Aras cleared a section of the professor's desk for Maliche to put the box. : Neywa shifted his weight in the hovering chair, causing his left knee to creak almost as loudly as the chair.

"Before I open this, the two of you must swear you will never reveal to anyone what you are about to see. If word of what's in here gets out to the wrong people we could all spend the rest of our days driving levi-cabs."

Maliche and Aras gave each other startled looks, but said nothing.

The old professor's gaze did not waver. "I'm very serious. I need your promises."

Maliche and Aras shared a brief look, nodded, and then Maliche spoke for both of them. "All right, you have our word. Nothing said to anyone outside this room."

The department head scratched the back of his neck, preening a few gray feathers, then reached down, opened the carton, and pulled out a metallic box. "I haven't thought about this in decades. The markings on your artifacts jarred my memory, so I dug this out to be sure."

The old man set the box on his desk. The surface was smooth, except for a name; Rocker, and some strange carvings underneath.

Maliche stared for a moment. "What are you doing with something belonging to my family? What's inside?"

Neywa smiled, tapping the box with his talons. "I have no idea what is in here. Fifty years ago, I found this box and have never been able to open it. My isotopic measurements told me it was somewhere around two or three hundred years old. Other matters interrupted my investigation, so I hid it, thinking I might be onto something and didn't want anyone else to get the credit. From time to time, I tried to get it open, but nothing ever worked, so I set it aside. Maybe an electro-torch would do the trick, but I didn't want to destroy anything fragile inside. Frankly, I had forgotten all about it until you showed up with those new discoveries. I needed to make sure I was correct about the marking, though, so I dug it out again. I'm sorry I never told you about it, but I truly forgot about it until now."

"What about the markings? Let me see..." Maliche reached out to take the box. As soon as he touched it, he felt his palms grow warm, heard the whirring of gears turning and a loud click. Startled, he stepped back, eyeing the container with suspicion. "What's going on here, professor?"

"I suspected as much. Somebody locked this box with your family biometrics. Only another Rocker could open it. Go ahead, look inside."

Maliche nervously lifted the lid and carefully removed a package. Unwrapping it revealed an old, leathery book. On top of the book sat a metallic medallion. "Those are the same marking as I found on the lost artifact. What's going on here?" He picked up the medallion and turned it over in his talons. A strange buzzing grew in his auricles; the world lurched and went black.

As a gray light grew in the darkness, Maliche felt disembodied. Hazy figures took shape before him, becoming nearly solid. He recognized them, but this was impossible.

***

Jontar Rocker sat; shoulders slumped, staring at the flower draped coffin. Tears streamed from his bloodshot eyes, his mind numb. He felt Karmito's grip on his shoulder.

"It's time, father." Karmito tightened his grip, then released it with a gentle pat and walked slowly to the podium. He stared out at the hundreds of mourners gathered to pay their respects. He tightened his hold on Tari's talons.

His daughter returned the clasp. "I'm here, father. I've got you."

"Welcome friends and honored guests. It is truly humbling to see such an outpouring of love for my mother. I know she would have been deeply honored by your presence, but, knowing her, she probably would have asked what all the fuss was about and told you to go home and quit wasting your time with such nonsense." A quiet laughter rose from the nodding heads in the audience. He continued the eulogy for another ten minutes, first extolling Maripa's virtues, and contributions to this new society, and her heroism in helping to bring it about, followed by a lengthy exaltation of her commitment to peace and prosperity for all on the planet; Brin and Kolandi alike. All of this barely registered on Jontar. His thoughts relived the final years on Dyan'ta and the nearly disastrous beginning to their new life on Raince'to. The emptiness inside ached to hear her voice one more time, or to feel her warmth at his side again.

The gentle voice of the biocomputer spoke in his mind. *"I can let you hear her, or feel her touch again, if you wish it. A few simple adjustments to your system are all it would take."*

"No," he replied in silence. *"She would not want me to continue on that way. I need to learn to live with my grief. I have Karmito and the grandchildren. I must let them grow to fill my life now."*

"I know. I'm glad you realize this, too."

More dignitaries took to the podium, each praising the woman who helped save them from extinction and led them through the difficult days in the early years. Each speaker had a tale of how Maripa guided his or her guild, sometimes by force of will or threat of bodily harm, but successfully through each crisis even after the brothers arrived.

"Come father, we need to thank our guests." Karmito's gentle grip brought Jontar back into the present and, with Tari on the left, helped raise him to his feet.

"I'm all right, children. Just an old fool reminiscing." He raised a talon to wipe the tears from his face. "I miss her."

Tari wiped the tears from her own face as she held on to her father's arm, supporting him. "We all do. But we still have each other. She would not want us carrying on so."

Jontar looked up into the afternoon sky. Not a cloud disturbed the intense blue. The warmth of the mid-summer day felt good on his wrinkled skin. He gave a weak smile.

"Especially on such a beautiful day as this. She loved to go for long walks on days like this. Or maybe a good game of Rings." He hesitated, the smile broadening. "I never could beat her at Rings. Kak she was a great player."

The family, Tari and Elarc, Karmito's wife flanking Jontar and Karmito, took their positions to greet the guests. The procession of well-wishers continued for over an hour, each person giving a kind word or a simple hug.

"I can't believe you have the gall to show your face here, Deshro." Jontar startled at the vehemence in Karmito's voice as he addressed the leader of the mining guild. "Haven't your people done enough harm? Since when did you ever show my mother the slightest respect?"

Deshro held his hand out for another moment before dropping it to his side. "Now, now, we must keep up our appearances, mustn't we? I know we have never seen eye to eye on matters, but I have always respected Maripa as a worthy adversary in the affairs of state. We are here to pay our final regards."

"More likely to gloat, now that she is not around to obstruct your schemes. Go away before I call security to remove you."

The large miner shook his head and clasped his taloned hands behind his back. "Yes, well she was a thorn in our crest even after you won the elections, but still, I had hoped we might get off to a fresh start."

"Not likely. Now go and let us mourn in peace."

"Very well. I'll see you soon in the central hall." He turned and gave a slight bow to Jontar. "My sincere condolences on your loss."

Jontar simply stared blankly, not acknowledging Deshro's gesture. As the receiving line drew to a close, Jontar flinched as the flash of cameras sparkled from the edge of the gathering. A few reporters approached.

"Let's go," Karmito said to his family. "I don't want to deal with them now."

Jontar stood firm and embraced his son. "As the leader of this community you need to talk to them. Your mother and I understand. Go, talk to them. Or would you rather let Deshro fill the void?" He gestured in the mining guild leader's direction. "You know your mother and I shared your suspicions about the guild's activities. I promise to keep her research safe where only we can access it. Now go and take care of your public responsibilities. We will have time to grieve together soon enough."

Mayor Karmito Rocker took a deep breath and sighed. "Of course… you're right. All of you go ahead. I'll catch up in a few minutes." He strode off to speak to the reporters.

Jontar took Tari's talons in his and smiled. "You, too. You and Elarc go to the mag-lev. I need a few minutes alone."

Tari studied her father's face, gave Elarc a quick glance, and then nodded. "All right, father. We'll wait for you by the transport."

He looked back over his shoulder at Maripa's casket. Stands of flowers surrounded the gravesite in a rainbow of color. He raised two talons to his chest, then to his lips as the tears flowed again. Turning aside, he walked the few steps to Karm's memorial obelisk. Maripa chose her burial site as close to Karm's as possible, despite her disgust at what she referred to as an obscene monolith. Giving in to immense public pressure she had finally given permission to build the structure, but never grew used to its presence. Jontar approached the marble monument and sat on one of the benches.

"Take good care of her, old friend. She missed you terribly, you know." He sat for several minutes, remembering the struggles against Brach and their final triumph, their abandonment here on a new world, nearly joining the rest of their race in extinction. After a long while, Jontar stood up and stepped forward to the base of the monument. The ache of loneliness returning, he reached into his pocket and pulled out a brightly colored feathery lure. He held it in his grip, then knelt down and placed it atop the attached plaque. Rising, he sighed and strode off to rejoin his family.

***

"Wake up, son. Come on now… there you go."

"Maliche, are you all right?" Aras handed him a glass of water as he regained consciousness.

"Aras? Professor? What happened?" He sat up, took a sip from the glass, and tried to gather his thoughts. "I saw Jontar Rocker… at Maripa's funeral." He looked up into their worried faces. "Everything was so real, as if I was there."

"Take it easy, son. You took a pretty hard fall. Let me help you up." Neywa and Aras hoisted Maliche into a nearby chair. He felt the dizziness fade and clarity return to his thoughts. A chill crept through his pants through a wet spot where he had fallen into a puddle from one of the leaky pipes.

Aras retrieved the medallion from the floor where it dropped and started to hand it back to Maliche. He saw the concern on her face, her hands shaking as she held the medallion out for him. "That was worse than when you first touched the artifact back in the desert. It only shocked you then. This time you were unconscious for several minutes."

The professor intercepted the artifact before Maliche could reach it. "I'd wait a bit before touching that again. Especially since this isn't the first bad reaction you've had with these things." He set it on the table and picked up the book. "You might want to look at this first."

Maliche took the book and leafed through the pages, stopping occasionally to read a passage. He looked up at Neywa and Aras, his eyes filling with tears and his voice choking. "This is Maripa's journal."

"*The* Maripa?" Aras leaned in to get a closer look.

"All the old family stories are in here. They're actually true." Maliche gently closed the book placed one hand protectively on the cover and, keeping a safe distance, pointed at the medallion. "That must be hers, too. I recognize that medallion from an old portrait of Maripa in our family archives. She is wearing it, or at least one with the same sort of engravings." He slapped his forehead suddenly. "That's why the artifacts engravings looked familiar. They're the same as in the portrait's image of her wearing the medallion. I knew I had seen them somewhere before."

Professor Neywa nodded, gathered the book and medallion, and placed them back in the metal box. "That would seem to agree with my date measurements. For now, though, you need to go home and get some rest, young man. We can investigate this further tomorrow."

Chapter Two

Jontar sat at his desk, reading his final entry to Maripa's journal. Only three weeks since her funeral, but his resolve to leave only grew stronger. He had to learn why he had not heard from the brothers, and why they had not come for the funeral. Closing the leather bound book, he sat with one hand gently stroking the cover.

"It's done, my love. Everything is prepared. Our son will soon be in a strong enough position to take on the guild and reveal what we have discovered about them. You can rest in peace. Now I must go and find our friends."

He took up the book, along with the Kolandi medallion, and placed them into the security vault. Touching the surface, he fed the metal container with his biometrics. With a silent command, a blue glow spread from his hand and surrounded the box.

"Now only a Rocker can unlock it. Time to get moving."

At the sky port, mechanics and flight crews busied themselves at the half-dozen shuttles standing on the tarmac. Apprentices rushed mag-lev carts from one pad to the next. Overhead, the sun shone bright with only a scattering of puffy clouds dotting the blue sky. The fresh scent of spring filled the air. One shuttle in particular attracted special attention as preparations for its departure came to an end. Amid the hum of solar-powered electric motors and the rising whine of the shuttle's enhanced mag-lev engines the ground crew added the last of the cargo to the storage bins, checked the security straps one last time and closed the hatch.

The crew chief handed the manifest to Rocker, saluted, and strode off to his next task. Rocker returned his attention to Tari, Karmito and their families. Rocker hugged each of his grandchildren, ruffling their top crests.

"Behave yourselves while I'm gone. Make your grandmother and me proud. If you do, I just might have some presents for you when I return."

The children, vibrated with excitement at their first visit to the sky port, listened to him briefly before running off to explore, their father in tow. Turning to Tari, he gathered her into a strong embrace, and then held her at arm's length.

"You are so much like your mother. Beautiful, intelligent, strong… we couldn't have been happier with you."

"I love you, too, father. Do you really have to go so soon?"

"Yes, sweet one, I have to know what happened. I need to know if we were the cause of their disappearance, or if something more sinister forced them away. I only hope my suspicions are wrong." He took her face in his hands and smiled. "You go take care of those fledglings."

The two embraced one last time and Tari strode off to gather her family for the take-off.

Rocker turned to face Karmito and his family now, but focused first on his daughter-in-law. "Elarc, my second daughter. Maripa and I have been so happy with you in our lives. Karmito chose well." He took her talons in his, and then held her close.

Returning the embrace, Elarc smiled brightly from behind tear-filled eyes. "Be well, Papa. I hope you find what you are looking for. And don't worry, we'll visit Mother's grave often during your absence." Squeezing both his hands in hers again, she leaned in, kissed him on the cheek, and then went in search of the others.

Jontar embraced his son, fighting off the memories of life with him and his mother in the early years. "Goodbye, Karmito. I want to get out of here before any crowds start to gather."

"Are you sure you're ready to leave now? Mother is only gone a month. You are still more than welcome to stay with Elarc, me, and the children. There's plenty of time yet."

Rocker hugged his son again and placed an arm around his shoulder as they walked toward the shuttle. "No, it's time to go. I've imposed on you and your family long enough. Plus," he held up his glowing palm, "my friend in here tells me we need to go now if we are to have any chance of finding them."

Karmito reached out to grasp his father's shoulder. "Do you have everything you need?"

"Everything this old bucket can carry." He embraced his son one last time and climbed into the shuttle. Before closing the hatch, he looked back at Karmito. "You know how proud your mother and I are of you, don't you?"

"Yes, father, I do. And I love you, too. Come back to us as soon as you can."

Rocker stood for a moment, and then touched the contact to close the doorway. He strapped himself into the pilot's seat. He waved out the window at his family, punched the controls, and soon the craft soared over the eastern hills. He forced himself to keep his eyes ahead and not look back toward the disappearing city; the life he knew he had left forever.

***

"Maliche, what is your problem? What are you muttering about? It's bad enough when you start rambling on about ancient history, but this is too much. Do we need to call the doctor?"

Maliche realized he was sitting across the breakfast table from his younger brother. His head swam with the collision of two realities struggling against each other. "Selan? What are you talking about? Why would I need a doctor?"

Selan massaged his temples, wincing as if in pain, as he frequently did whenever he had this discussion with his brother. "You're my brother, and I love you, but you drive me crazy with all this talk of ancient civilizations and our ancestors. Your obsession is getting worse." He plucked another bread roll from a tray in front of him. "You were telling me about some new book or something you found, and then drifted off. You started muttering all sorts of nonsense about Jontar Rocker and those extinct Kolandi. For a few seconds there, you seemed to be in some sort of trance, just muttering nonsense."

Maliche's head cleared as he chewed a mouthful of fried eggs. "I'm fine, Selan. Just a little tired. Things at work are getting a bit tense with the front office lately, and now there have been some exciting new discoveries. Guess I'm just exhausted is all."

"Why can't you practice a more respectable profession? I mean really... archaeology? Why do you insist on bringing ridicule to our family? With your markers and intelligence, you could have developed a magnificent career in genetic research or any other path more suitable to our station. But this crazy obsession about our ancestors forces the family to set you aside and give me the responsibilities which should be yours."

Maliche snorted as he reached across the table to pluck another bright blue mondelberry from the polished silver bowl. "Why should I do what everyone else wants me to do?" Light from the tall windows along one wall of the dining hall reflected rainbows around the container. "There are thousands of others researching why each generation's life span is getting shorter. The last thing anyone needs is for me to get in the way of such vital work."

Selan tossed up his hands and snorted. "Don't give me those old excuses. You're a Rocker. Everyone expects us to lead the way. It was our ancestors who saved us in the beginning, and now they expect us to save them again. Everyone believes you are deserting them."

"And who is 'everyone'? You are the one with the highest level of Rocker-genes, not me. Once you were born all that responsibility fell into your lap and I couldn't have been more relieved." He slouched back into the chair, plopped his feet up onto the adjacent chair, and brushed a pile of crumbs from his stained and wrinkled silk dressing robe.

"My markers are only two points higher than yours," Selan said, pointing a gold fork at his older brother. "Yours were the highest in recorded history. You should be doing something more worthy of your status. Your scores at the university more than qualified you for a position in any of the most prestigious genetic research labs on the planet."

Maliche took another bite of his breakfast, spilling half of it on himself in the process. "Selan, I have no interest in researching radiation levels or atmospheric conditions. And don't get me started on how boring nutritional components of native foods would be. All of you are better off letting those who are interested in being confined to a sterile laboratory solve the problem. Besides, now your genetic link to our grand ancestors is the greater, so all the glory, and position in government affairs belong to you, dear brother. And I praise the Eternal every day for my good fortune. Every member of our family has gone into genetic research or politics. We don't need another geneticist; the world is full of them. The Eternal knows we have enough assemblymen... too many if you ask me. Nedia and the children are treasures, they adore you, and our family's future is secure with them. You have freed me from a dreadful fate of responsibility and boredom. I thank you for that. Now, since nobody looks to me as the next Head Minister, I can pursue my whims and fancies."

"How can you call yourself a Rocker? Doesn't our family mean anything to you?"

Maliche paused halfway as he reached out to stab another piece of fruit with a talon. "Of course our family is important to me. Why do you think I travel into those remote areas and spend all my time digging through ancient records? I want to learn about our history... especially the original Rockers three hundred years ago. I want to know if all the stories we grew up hearing are true, or just some mythology grown out of the retelling of tales over the centuries. What motivated them? How did they build that first settlement into a thriving society? Did they really meet Kolandi? Did those indigenous people really go extinct, or are there some hidden remnants buried in the still unexplored regions of the planet? Or are they nothing more than mythology? I'm finding some intriguing artifacts concerning their existence and possible fate you know."

Selan threw his arms in the air, jumped up from his chair and stomped across the room to pour himself a stronger drink. "Not those old tales again. Wives tales and legends told to children. Nothing more. Do you realize what a laughing stock you are making of us in the legislature? I spend half my time there trying to dispel the stories circulating about your ridiculous exploits. If we belonged to any other family, one of the Cloners, your antics would have brought us to ruin and disgrace long ago. Father and I have enough trouble with the guilds and their demands. The miners and that leader of theirs leap at every opportunity to weaken our position, and your exploits provide them with plenty of ammunition." Returning to his chair, he downed the yellow liquid in one long gulp.

"Then it is a good thing we *are* Rockers, and not one of the Cloners. Because I do not intend to cater to the ideals anyone else wants me to conform to."

The sound of metallic footsteps resounding on the polished marble floor interrupted Selan's terse response. The android house-bot, a newly developed luxury servant only the wealthiest clans such as the Rockers could afford, approached the brothers with accustomed formality.

He halted a respectful distance from the table and addressed Selan. "Your driver is here, sir."

"Thank you, Jerek. I'm on my way." Selan waved a hand dismissively.

Maliche laughed at his brother. "When are you and father ever going to get rid of your drivers? That old anachronism only serves to flaunt your position in everyone's face and helps blind you to what the people really need."

As he stood and straightened his tailored and brightly embroidered suit, an indication of his elite status among the legislators, Selan picked up a roll and tossed it at his brother. "You are probably the most aggravating person on Raince'to. Have fun with your scrolls and broken pottery."

Maliche dodged the roll and laughed. "It would be easier if you could convince those pirates in the capital to loosen up the purse strings and provide us with a few more grants. See you tonight, little brother. Try not collapse the economy."

Maliche continued to nibble at his breakfast a while longer, contemplating how best to approach Dr. Neywa. *Another black-out? And what's with these insane visions... if that's what they are? It all seems so real. I hope the professor can shed some light on all of this today.* He stood to leave and shook the small crystal bell in the center of the table. At the tinkling sound, a cleverly disguised electronic signal, a bevy of kitchen and cleaning service bots entered the hall and attended to their duties.

***

Neywa sat lost in thought as he considered the medallion in his hand.

Maliche stood up, and paced the floor, preening his crest in frustration. "That's what's so confusing about it. I can't translate any of those markings. They appear to be some sort of pictographs, but there's nothing like them anywhere. Frankly, I'm stumped."

"There's more you need to know, Maliche. I had planned on showing you this as well yesterday, but after your episode, you were in no condition to deal with it." He laid one hand on the carton which had held the medallion and Maripa's journal, but hesitated. "You both remember your promise to keep all of this secret?"

Aras nodded as she approached her mentors. "Of course, professor. You can rely on us to keep your secret."

"All right, then. All of our careers are in your hands now." He reached out and removed the container's lid, setting it aside.

Aras and Maliche leaned in closer to get a better view. She rested a hand on Maliche's shoulder as she came closer. Her hand felt warm and soft. Her hip brushed lightly against his. Maliche shuddered slightly at the touch. *For love of The Eternal, you really are an old pervert. Get ahold of yourself.* He refocused on the notebooks professor Neywa lifted out of the box. Aras took the empty box with her free hand and tossed it onto the floor. A service bot scurried from its holding bay and picked up the lid, placing it neatly on a shelf.

"Sixty-five years ago, I was a first year student here at the university. I needed to complete an elective credit, so I signed up as an assistant in the archaeology department. I figured not much happened there, so I would probably have a lot more time to study. A month after I started, all strix broke loose."

Maliche nodded in recognition of the significance of the date. "The demolition of the ancient city ruins. Some believe it was an alien city, others say it was once the ancient home of the Kolandi, before some disaster struck them."

Neywa stared at the stack of papers, his eyes closed as he told the story. "Yes. A group of children were killed wandering among the ruins, so the government decided to tear it all down. Public safety was the excuse. Anyway, the archaeologists went berserk and demanded time to collect anything of value or historical interest before it all vanished. The authorities granted two months to get whatever they could, but only under close supervision of government security forces. You can imagine the chaos that created around here."

Aras waved both hands in front of her, calling a halt to the revelation. "Wait...what ancient city? You mean the one in those children's fables about the Kolandi?"

"That's the one," Maliche said. "The government has done an amazing job of covering up the truth of the matter. They label anyone foolish enough to talk about it a conspiracy theorist and the public dismisses them. For two centuries The Assembly has forbidden any large scale study of the site. Everyone *knows* it is just a myth."

"You mean it was real? I thought it was just some story to frighten us kids."

"No, it was very real. But even by my time, the government spent a great deal of time and effort to wipe out any mention of it. All public records were seized, very quietly of course, and all teaching of its existence was gradually removed from the curriculum at every level. A few of my professors still talked about it from time-to-time, but they retired or stopped when the ridicule became too much for them. History and archaeology joined the ranks of the lesser sciences so almost nobody has even heard of the ancient city anymore."

"But why? Didn't people wonder about it?"

Professor Neywa shook his head, waving one hand negligently. "Not really. They completely obliterated the ruins of the city and plowed it over so nothing remained. The older generations gradually died out and the younger folk just figured it wasn't worth much. Especially with all the money going into other areas of research."

"So, what does this have to do with your secret here?"

"I'm getting to that. Anyway, everyone frantically tried to gather as many relics as they could. Photographers ran all over recording images of anything they could find. A dozen heavy lifters brought in material every day. I spent my days sorting and organizing everything as it came in. The important thing was to get the artifacts collected as fast as possible. Cataloging and analyzing the artifacts could occur later, after completion of the salvage work."

I'm sorry, professor," interrupted Aras. "None of this makes sense. If so many artifacts were collected, what happened to them? And why doesn't anyone remember the city anymore?"

"The time for the city's final destruction came. It was quite the spectacle. Security forces kept most people away, but a few of us snuck to the top of a hillside and watched. The destructor beams activated, causing all of the structures to glow. One-by-one they collapsed and fell apart into piles of dust. They plowed under the once great city of the ancients, losing it forever. The mining guild got the permits to open up one of their underground mining operations, so everyone thinks of it as the old mine now. Back in the labs, we began the incredible task of cataloging and analyzing the collection. Before long, rumors started circulating of evidence indicating a civilization preceding the Kolandi. We always assumed they built the city, but then, through some catastrophe that led to their eventual extinction, they abandoned technology and lived the desperate lives of the poor destitute our ancestors tried to save."

Maliche raised up, stretched his back and began pacing. "I've always had trouble with that story about them. I grew up with too many family legends telling something quite different from the official line. I don't think we were the ones who saved them... at least not at first. It's one of the reasons I got into Archaeology to begin with."

Neywa grinned shaking a talon in Maliche's direction. "I wouldn't be surprised in the least. Your family legends may be more accurate than you think. Now where was I? Oh, yes, the rumors. A few of the linguists were attempting to translate some of the inscriptions found on the walls of the city and on some of the relics. Pictographs really, but more intricate and organized into complex patterns unlike any others we've ever seen. Some of the artifacts showed a level of sophistication and technology far beyond anything we have ever encountered, even today. It was immediately after a meeting with some government officials that everything went wrong. To demonstrate our need for greater funding, we showed them the progress we were making with the translations. That afternoon soldiers burst into the warehouse and confiscated everything. All the relics, all our notes, everything was taken. Our people were taken into custody and interrogated."

Aras turned pale and her mouth dropped open. "How is that possible? What right does the government have to interfere with scientific research?"

"They gave us an official notice, signed by the Premier and several heads of the legislature, heads of the mining and manufacturing guilds topped the list. It said we were in violation of state security."

Aras trembled, talons tapping rapidly on her knees. Her eyes blazed. "State security? How dare they!"

"Oh, they dared, all right. When they were finished nobody even mentioned the city again. Everyone transferred into different departments or to other universities. Some took early retirement. I was a lowly student clerk, so they left me alone after learning I didn't know anything—at least until later."

Professor Neywa sifted through the notebooks sitting on his desk. "Praise the gods these old records never made it into the computer data banks. No money to hire anyone to transcribe them. Ah, here it is." He opened one of the books and held it up for his protégés to read.

Aras gently took the notebook from him, examining it closely as she turned it in her talons. "It's amazing. Are these inscriptions the same kind as the ones on the medallion?"

"Very observant, Aras, you may have the makings of an archaeologist yet. Yes, they are almost identical, in fact."

"Is this what I think it is?"

"A record of the language of the Kolandi, or at least what we assume it to be, as transcribed form artifacts collected in the old city," confirmed the professor. "Some of the professors hid these records as soon as the purges began for fear of losing them."

He ran his hand lightly over the inscription. "And the medallion? Is the writing on it in the same language?" Aras was asking as a momentary wave of nausea passed over him.

"Are you all right?" Aras grabbed Maliche's hands to help steady him.

Maliche shook his head to clear it. The dizziness vanished as quickly as it came. "I'm fine. Must have been the excitement."

Dr. Neywa watched Maliche for a moment, and then returned his attention to the writings. "They are the same. My work with those artifacts ignited a passion in me, despite the dangers they obviously possessed. I was hooked on archaeology. I eventually graduated and the dean awarded me a position in the department here at the university. We were barely hanging on even back then and the authorities properly chastised me any time I even mentioned the ancient city. We stuck mostly to Brin history from then on. Then came the day of my discovery. While searching down here in the dungeon for some piece of information I can't even remember now, I tripped over a loose stone in the floor far in the back. When I tried to reset the stone I found that metal box with your family name on it, and these papers. Nothing I tried could open it. I didn't want to risk damaging its contents, so I kept it safe, hidden in the same crate as these papers. I assume someone from your family, Maliche, wanted the information kept secret and hid the container here. I tried making a few discrete inquiries, but no one seemed to know anything."

"And you have kept them hidden away ever since? Weren't you afraid someone might discover them?" Aras asked.

"Did you read the label on the box they were hidden in?"

Picking up the carton, Aras turned it around until she could read the writing.

Neywa
Personal supplies: The Legislature: An Historical Analysis

"Nobody would ever disturb my personal notes on the most hated and boring course offered by this university."

Maliche looked up from the notebook. "So what does this have to do with my medallion?"

"Just this... the two are almost identical. Same pictographs, same syntax, everything is identical, except... yours is roughly three hundred years old. These notes record samples of a culture over two thousand years old."

Maliche stood stunned, unable to even process this news.

"So, how can two languages be so similar if they are thousands of years apart?" asked Aras.

The aged, furrowed face of the old man brightened into a smile as he raised one talon. "Now that, is an excellent question."

Chapter Three

Hours later, after making certain they were ready to make a proper investigation of the phenomenon, Maliche set the crate of notebooks on his desk and retrieved the metal vault containing Maripa's journal and medallion from the bottom drawer.

Aras took his elbow, turning him to face her. "Are you sure you want to do this? You scared the mutes out of me yesterday."

"I have to. We need to know what's going on here. I need to know why I'm having these hallucinations." He held her talons in his as they sat down. "Just don't let me hit my head on the floor again. Are you ready to record anything I say?"

Professor Neywa checked the connections on his equipment and held up the microphone. "We're ready."

Maliche picked up the silver medallion and gripped it hard in his fist. He then began to read the first lines of his ancestor's journal.

My name is Maripa Rocker. I am one of the last survivors of the race who escaped the planet Dyan'ta before its destruction. I have decided to set the record straight and tell the story of our lives and how we came to this world. The journey across space to our new home was nearly brought to ruin by The Monarch and members of The Faith. Karm proved more than equal to the task and it was they, not us who perished.

I suppose I should start with the story of the two brothers. Despite the efforts of many to credit Karm, myself

and my husband, Jontar with our survival, it is they who saved us from perishing on an alien world...
***

The world began to fade again, swirling into mist as if a fog filled the room. Maliche tried to speak, but the others vanished as a new reality appeared before him.
***

The wounded grendel charged. The hunting scythe missed its mark barely slicing the hairy beast's shoulder blade instead of smoothly gutting the creature. The man recovered his balance, twirled the curved blade, a grendel claw tipped and edged with sharpened metal and attached to a long handle, and turned to face his prey again. Sunlight flickered through the green canopy of the forest, highlighting the blood flowing from the wound. Howling in rage the great black brute snapped at everything in its reach. Branches shattered in the massive jaws that ripped them from the trees. The beast's monstrous curved claws tore at the ground leaving long deep trenches in its wake. Rising on its haunches, the creature stood to its full eight-foot height and roared a deafening bellow.

The two men back among the trees watched the incredible display of power and rage, circling around for the opportunity at another clear shot. The grendel's shaggy dark head swung from side-to-side, stopping to face the enemy as they stepped into the narrow trail to the watering hole, and attacked. The beast attacked the men before they could raise their weapons.

"Jump, Neas! Get clear!"

Vidad shoved his brother to the side behind several trees and dove to his left. Neas felt the rush of air on his bare arm as the grendel's tusks missed his flesh by inches. The brute snarled and sent great globs of foam flying from its massive, frothing jaws. When it snapped at them, it found only empty air. The beast ran forward for several more strides before coming to a stop.

"Vidad, are you okay?" Neas lurched to his feet searching the thickets for his brother. Their clothing, made from the reflective scaly skin of a mordu, provided excellent camouflage in the forest.

"Where are you?"

Vidad wiped a mixture of torn leaves, dirt, and saliva from his face as he called out. "Over here to your left. Are you hurt?"

Neas checked himself for injuries and, not finding anything more serious than a few scratches, patted his forehead and pointed skyward with the sign of thanks to the gods. He looked toward his brother's voice and saw him nearby; barely visible as his reptilian-skin clothing reflected the greens and browns of the foliage almost perfectly, crouched low behind a large tree. "No, I'm fine, but we need to get out of here."

"Not until we slay this creature. It will feed our people for many weeks. We cannot stop now. Hurry, before the beast returns. Get your blowpipe ready to slow it down with another dart so I can approach from behind and kill it."

Neas signaled his agreement with a wave of his hand and moved off to find a better location from which to stick the beast with another poisoned blow dart. Howls of the enraged beast filled the air, muffling the sound of footsteps among the broken branches on the ground. The dirt and leaves covering Neas added to his camouflage in the patchy light of the jungle floor.

Wiping sweat from his brow, Vidad returned his attention to the grendel. The creature thrashed about in the underbrush growling and wreaking havoc on anything within reach. Raising his blowgun, Neas carefully loaded a heavy dart, poisoned with the venom of three species of vipers, and aimed down the length of his weapon. The monster let loose a deafening roar as the dart found its mark in his neck.

Neas jumped into the air, flailing his arms to attract the grendel's attention. "Come on you ugly beast! Come and try to kill me! Let us see who the master of these forests is."

Neas yelled and jumped as the creature zeroed in on him. The ground shook with each stride, but He held his ground and prepared to dodge the monster, hoping his brother was in position. The grendel closed, leaped high into the air, claws, and curved teeth closing fast on the hunter.

Suddenly, the beast let out another deafening roar. Blood spewed from its mouth, its eyes wide in surprise. Vidad, leaping from a low-hanging branch, swung his hunting scythe in a powerful arc. Neas leapt to the side just in time as the grendel crashed to the ground, rolled on its side, clawing at the long gaping wound in its side. The long claws tore at the spilling internal organs, but only succeeded in opening the wound further. As his life's blood flowed onto the ground, the grendel's cries, and efforts to fight against his foes grew weaker, until only the gasping sound of its breathing remained. Only then did the two brothers approach.

"Spirit of the grendel, we thank you for the food and hides you provide us. We honor the warrior you were and pray the Sky gods accept you into their midst." With that, the elder man took his knife and sliced the main artery in the beast's neck, ending its life.

Quiet returned to the forest. No breeze stirred the broad, pointy tipped leaves. Dust specks glittered in the beams of light stabbing through from the sky above. Within moments, life returned as well. The sounds of cardis and blutons crying out as they flew among the branches grew louder and the squeaks and chitters of dits and various other creatures soon filled the air. The brothers sat on the ground next to their conquered adversary breathing hard, arms draped over their bent knees, heads, dripping sweat in the sweltering heat, hung low.

Vidad eyed the forest carefully. "Let's get this done, before this young one's mother returns."

Later that evening, after butchering the grendel and packing the meat and a number of bones which would make useful tools onto their burden beasts, the brothers sat around their campfire in the small glade. The gentle trickling of a stream nearby joined with the incessant buzzing of the night insects. Distant growls of predators or shrieks of some hapless prey occasionally penetrated the peace. The night also brought a calm breeze to the jungle, adding the groaning of tree trunks to the night's symphony. The clear night sky showed bright with myriad stars twinkling above their campsite. A thin grey tower of smoke rose above the flames. The scent of roasted grendel wafted on the breeze. They savored the taste of fresh meat, a welcome relief from the dried rations and tough, stringy portions of small game comprising their meals of the past three days.

"Caeri will be very proud of you," said Neas. "You hunted well today, and your kill will bring much needed relief to our people." A small carving knife cut carefully into one of the pieces of driftwood Vidad always carried. The image of a woman took shape with each new stroke. He smiled across the campfire at his younger brother as Neas tore another bite from the dripping haunch, wiping his hands on his pants.

Vidad's dark eyes sparkled in the firelight. "It was you who stood in the grendel's path as he charged. You are the one who took all of the risk. Ila will be very angry at you for being so foolish."

"We don't have to tell her everything, do we?" asked Neas. He searched for something to change the subject. "Is that another figure of her you're working on? The resemblance is remarkable even now."

Vidad laughed at the obvious attempt to distract him. "Yes, it relaxes me to whittle these figurines. I don't miss her so much when I carve her face. Don't you want your wife to hear another tale of your bravery?" Vidad pounded his chest to poke fun at his younger sibling. "The great hunter is afraid of his own wife? Say it is not true!" His laughter echoed through the night forest.

Neas could not help but join in his brother's laughter. He shook the blade at Vidad and tried, with little success, to sound stern. "You know she'll tell her sister and then both of them will skin you alive too when she hears how close you let the beast get before killing it. I think for both our sakes the High Priestess and her sister should hear a much less dramatic story of our victory tonight."

"Perhaps you are right... Caeri and Ila would be very upset with us. Perhaps it would be best if we told them we found the beast with a broken leg and speared it from a safe distance."

Vidad tossed his leftover bones into the fire and wiped off his knife before returning it to the leather scabbard on his hip. He shook off the pile of wood chips collecting on his shoes. He nearly fell off the stump he sat on when Neas gasped and jumped to his feet.

"What is that?" Neas pointed at a bright light moving across the fixed field of stars.

Vidad stood and followed Neas's gaze. The light grew bright enough to cast shadows in the forest as it crossed the familiar constellations.

"It is not a falling star," said Vidad as he stared at the object, his eyes adjusting to the radiance. "Look, it is not burning as it falls. And it has more the shape of a spear than a star and does not waver in its path."

"By the gods," whispered Neas, wiping his hand over his face in the ritualistic gesture used in the tribe's prayers, never taking his eyes off the strange incandescent object. "Are the legends true? Are the Sky People returning to us?"

"I don't know what to think," said Vidad as he, too, wiped over his face. "But we need to return to the village and tell Caeri of this sight. She may be able to understand its meaning. We will leave at first light."

The brothers watched, transfixed in wonder, as the glowing cylinder continued its journey, slowing as it descended across the sky until it vanished below the jagged mountains on the western horizon. An hour before sunrise they awoke. The chill morning air condensed their words into small clouds as they spoke of the strange traveling star, and their route home. They ate a hasty meal before packing their supplies onto the pack animals, so the sun measured barely a finger width above the horizon before they pulled on their fur cloaks and started on the trail heading for home.

Two days later, the pair crested a low grassy hill and saw their small village in the distance under the brilliant blue sky. The distant mountains showed hints of the orange and scarlet foliage signaling summer's end. Overhead, flocks of Blutons on their annual migration flew in row after row of V-shaped groups. The small settlement contained about two dozen family huts, one room, adobe walls with one or two windows and a single door in which hung colorful woven fabrics. Smoke rose through the holes in the center of the thatched roofs. A large central building, its walls covered in ornate ceremonial drawings, served as a meeting hall for the council and various other tribal rituals.

Outside this gathering of structures stood the blacksmith shop, open front to allow the forge's heat to escape, and living quarters behind. Split rail stock yards contained the few drunges, sturdy burden beasts with horns and long thick fur, owned by the village. A scattering of low thatched roofs covered the below ground storage shelters shared by everyone in the village. Downwind stood the village smokehouses where they preserved half of every hunt or catch for the long winters.

"Neas! Vidad! What did you kill? Was it something ferocious? Will you tell the story tonight?" The children danced around the returning heroes, climbed on the backs of the plodding drunges, searching through the packs for some hints of the adventure.

Yes," said Neas. "The greatest and most awful grendel you have ever seen." He raised his arms and imitated the animal's stance on its hind legs. "But, I don't know. The story might be too much for you to stand. I wouldn't want to give you all nightmares and send you screaming to your mothers." He waved his arms and growled as he stepped toward the children pretending to be the grendel. The children squealed in delight and ran around Neas, attacking him from all angles as if they themselves were mighty hunters.

Vidad smiled as he watched his brother play with the children. *He has always been a child at heart. He will make a good father someday.* "Did any of you think to tell Caeri we have come back?" he asked the children. "Quickly now, go and tell her we are home."

The mighty hunters stopped their game, looked guiltily at each other, turned, and ran back to the village. The shouting attracted the attention of everyone in the village. They all stopped what they were doing and came out to greet the returning hunters. Vidad handed the drunges' leads over to a couple of the older boys.

"Take them to Sedhor. The meat needs to be prepared before it spoils. Then feed and water the animals and put them out to pasture. We will be by later to pick up our supplies." The boys bowed obediently and led the drunges away.

Vidad turned to one of the women. "Where are Caeri and the elders? Why have they not come to greet us?"

The woman bowed as she responded. "They are still in the council chamber, Vidad. A terrible omen appeared in the sky the other night and the elders are meeting to discover its meaning."

"Then you all saw the light in the sky as well?"

"Yes, Vidad. Everyone saw it and is afraid for what it may foretell. Some people whisper of the return of the Sky People."

Vidad considered this for a moment. His voice rose as he addressed the gathering. "We, too, saw the light and have returned to learn its meaning. I will go to join the elders and we will pray to the gods to reveal the truth of this mystery to us."

Vidad removed his hunting scythe from his shoulder, and handed them to Neas. "I will go to speak with Caeri and the elders now. I will be by later to get these and talk with you. Go on home now and be with Ila."

Neas nodded and grabbed his brother's arm. The two stood looking at each other without speaking for a moment. Vidad smiled, reached up and ruffled Neas's hair then turned in the direction of the council chamber. The most important structure in the village, the council chamber was a round hut surrounded by thick stone walls and topped by a tall conical thatched roof with a small hole in the center to allow smoke to escape. Decorating the outside of the walls a variety of colorful images depicted the history and religion of the people.

Tonight, everyone was particularly aware of the image depicting a shining pointed cylindrical object flying across the sky, an image from their deep past known only as The Sky People. Legends told of great and magical deeds performed by the Sky People and how the Kolandi were their friends. Ancient tales also told of The Great Calamity, forcing a separation between the Kolandi and the Sky People, and how the Sky People would someday return.

The Princess sat in the only chair of the chamber. Surrounding the fire sat the village council, consisting of six women and four men. Caeri was the current descendant of a long line of matriarchs whose ancestors ruled this village for centuries. A small metal circlet sat atop her long black hair glowing in the firelight. Her scarlet feather robe flowed regally from her shoulders beautifully offsetting the fine golden fabric of her ankle length dress, worn only during high council. Samej, the Homsan, stood behind Caeri, leaning heavily on his ceremonial staff, the symbol of his office as advisor to the Princess, every inch covered in colorful carvings depicting important events in the tribe's history. Disheveled tufts of grey hair sprouted from his nearly bald head, but a magnificent long, silvery grey beard hung from his brown and weathered face. The elders sat in circle surrounding the fire pit in the center of the room. Vidad pushed aside the decorated hide covering the entrance to the chamber and stepped into the room.

"We have no proof of your claims the Sky People have returned, Joxmae," said one of the elderly women in the circle. Her long grey hair framed a wrinkled and time-worn face, but her blue eyes were bright and unwavering.

"What else can it be, Sechrid?" replied Joxmae. "This was no natural event."

"Just because we cannot explain something is no justification for jumping to religious claims, Joxmae. Besides, who needs them? They abandoned us long ago. Why would we want them now? Who is to say they would not betray us again, if they even exist? These are legends, Joxmae. The Sky people may be nothing more than stories to frighten children. We are better off without them." Sechrid crossed his hands in front of his face, pulling them apart in a sign of dismissal as the others shouted in outrage at his heresy.

The unexpected light from the entrance caused Caeri to look up from the heated discussion. "Vidad!

You've returned!" She rose from her chair and walked around the circle of elders, and reached out to greet her husband.

The elders stopped their arguing and joined their voices to the greeting. "Welcome, Vidad." Each one grasped Vidad by the arm or clapped him on the shoulder amid the clamor of welcome.

"Not a moment too soon."

"Are you aware of what has happened?"

Vidad, ignoring the elders momentarily, embraced his wife then stood back a respectful pace and bowed, wiping his face in honor of her position and as ritual dictated inside the chamber. He then turned and bowed to the elders who returned to sit in their circle.

"Yes, I have seen the light in the sky. Neas and I returned as quickly as we could to discover its meaning." He held Caeri's hand a bit longer, and then took his place as chief hunter among the elders. The Princess returned to her chair.

Joxmae picked up where he left off before Vidad's interruption. "It is written in the scrolls after the fall from grace and our people's separation from the gods, when the Sky People abandoned us, they would one day return."

Rilanta, youngest of the women present and newest member of the council closed her eyes, lifted her face, and searched her memory for the quotation. "And in the fullness of time, the Sky People would return. Their silvery chariots will light the night sky, but with a light not from fire. They shall descend and unite once again all which was torn asunder."

Sechrid shook his head. "Then where are they? The ruins of their great city are only three days walk from our village. Why would they pass so far if it is truly them? And why would the gods let their city be left to fall into ruins? Samej has told us he believes the light landed far to the west, beyond the sea. If they are going to unite us again, why would they not return to their home? I say the light was no returning god. We are wasting our time chasing after myths and old religious nonsense. Even if the legends are true, they speak of gods who left us to save themselves. Why would we search for gods such as them?"

More shouts of indignation ensued, many of those gathered threatened violence if Sechrid continued his denial of the Sky People. The Princess raised her hand and the Homsan stamped the ground with his staff to quiet everyone.

"We have been over this a dozen times now." Her voice, though calm, carried the full weight of her authority. Her dark eyes narrowed only slightly as her gaze met Sechrid's stern, weathered glare. "The time for talk is done. We need to know more before we can arrive at any conclusion as to what the light means. We must send an emissary to the west to seek out the source of this mystery."

"How do we send an emissary across the sea?" asked Joxmae.

Vidad sat up taller and looked toward the Princess, bracing himself for the argument he was about to instigate. "I will go. I know of a tribe on the coast who travel far out to sea in their boats. They tell stories about ships caught in storms and lost for months only to return, claiming discovery of lands on the far side of the sea. I will convince them to take me across the sea to that far away land, and I will search out the Sky People, if they exist."

"No, not you, Vidad," said the Princess. "We will find another. We cannot risk losing you, our best hunter. How would we survive without your skills?"

"Who else would even have a chance? There are plenty of young hunters who can feed the people while I am gone."

Caeri lowered her face and her shoulders slumped. "And what of our children? This expedition could take years before you return. You would be but a faded memory to them before you returned to us."

"You know I am the only one for this journey, Caeri. How could I look my children in the eye if I were to send another to do my job just so I might stay home and be safe? They would never respect a father who placed others in danger rather than risk himself."

Caeri slowly nodded her head, then lifted her eyes and stiffened her back. She turned to face him, her eyes full of authority as she assumed the full demeanor of her position as Princess.

"But you may not leave until the lake thaws in the spring and you have worked with the young hunters. Winter is no time to travel and they must be trained well before you can leave us."

Vidad bowed his head in respect, surrendering to the will of his Princess, and beloved wife. "Agreed."

The counsel murmured their agreement and concluded their proceedings, documenting and announcing to the entire village the decision to send Vidad on the mission to find out if the Sky People had indeed returned.

"But tonight," Caeri announced, "will be a celebration. We will rejoice in the return of our hunters and their success."

The people cheered and went off to gather the supplies for feast. Vidad and Caeri retired to their home.

"Father! Father," shouted Rahnoa as she leapt into Vidad's arms her arms grabbing him in a death grip. "You're home at last! I missed you so much!"

"And I missed you, too, little one," Vidad told his youngest daughter as he spun her in dizzying circles, her long tan legs swinging wide, losing one sandal in the excitement. "My, how you have grown." He placed the smiling girl back on the ground, held her at arm's length, admiring her. "And such a beauty, too. It won't be long before I will have to sharpen my blade to warn off all of the young boys."

"Oh, father. Don't be silly. Boys are just stupid." The seven-year-old blushed anyway, and then scrunched her face in thought as she considered her declaration, smiling quickly as she resolved her dilemma. "Except for you and uncle Neas, of course."

Vidad laughed, turned Rahnoa around, and pushed her toward the door. "Go gather your sister and brother. Tell them it is time to come help prepare the dinner. Off with you now!"

"Don't think this discussion is over," Caeri warned her husband as soon as their daughter was outside. "I'm not happy with the way you maneuvered me into agreeing with you in front of the council."

Vidad smiled, reached into his pouch, and produced the new figure he sculpted during the hunt for the grendel, presenting the gift to his wife. "Do you like it?"

Despite her irritation, the Princess smiled as she accepted the gift. "It's lovely, Vidad. You know I love your carvings." Tears began to well up in her eyes as she examined the small figurine depicting her surrounded by their three children. A flash of mock anger quickly replaced them. "And don't try to distract me with another of your presents. You aren't getting off so easily."

Turning to place the statue on the mantle with the others, she gazed lovingly at the collection. Looking back over her shoulder toward Vidad, a slight smile grew on her lips and a teasing glint sparkled in her eyes

"Just one thing. You might want to try carving something besides figures of me. People who visit might get the idea I'm growing vain."

***

The winter passed slowly. Snow piled high and the lake froze thicker than in recent memory. The hunters, joined by several older children, played furious games of Togash on the ice. Sticks with nets tied to the end allowed players to hurl egg shaped rocks, wrapped in strips of leather, between teammates. Each team scored by tossing the rock at a four-foot-tall post stuck in the ice, defended by the other team. This helped keep the hunter's skills sharp, toughened the muscles of the boys, and kept the Homsan busy by requiring his frequent attention to all manner of gouges, lumps, and other minor injuries.

Fresh food was scarce, but the stores they laid up would be plentiful when portioned wisely. The young hunters learned quickly and soon became experts at tracking and snaring all manner of smaller game. Tikla continued to impress the elders with her skill as a tracker and hunter. The boys of the village competed for her attention as she approached the age for her to choose a mate. Nosaj showed particular talent in organizing and leading the others in productive hunting parties. The larger animals roamed far and wide, but Vidad and Neas found enough small game to teach their students many new skills. By late spring, when the snow finally melted and the large herds returned, Vidad trusted his apprentices enough to let them attempt hunts without him while he evaluated their technique from a nearby hill. Almost no one returned with injuries any longer, at least anything serious.

"The lake is almost free of ice these days," Vidad told Caeri one evening after a successful hunt. "I am thinking it is time to allow Nosaj the opportunity of leading the next hunting party on his own. He has shown great promise." He stood by the fire as she sat at her polished brass mirror preparing for bed.

"Yes," she replied, "and the weather is so much warmer and more pleasant now. I am sure the boy's parents will be very proud of him."

Vidad lowered his head, peered sidelong at his wife, took in a deep preparatory breath and broached the topic they both dreaded. "It is time we discussed my mission to find the Sky People."

Caeri sat silently combing her hair, a dark emptiness growing in her heart.

"We cannot delay any longer. If I do not leave soon, then I will never reach the coast before next winter arrives. It is a very long journey."

She lowered the comb to her lap, fighting the wetness growing in her eyes. "I know. When must you leave?"

"I can make all the necessary arrangements and gather my supplies in a week's time."

Caeri rose up from her chair and joined her husband at the fire, placing one arm around his waist. "Come back to us." She kissed him, walked slowly away, crawled back into bed, and burrowed under the heavy furs.

The week passed quickly. Vidad held one final meeting with the newly trained hunters, double checked his supply list, and retightened the loads on the pack animals. Samej presided over a brief ceremony of parting in the council chambers, invoking the gods favor on Vidad's quest to find the Sky People. He said his goodbyes to Caeri and the children and headed off with the morning sun at his back.

"And just where do you think you're going without me?" Neas asked from his perch on the pile of firewood at the edge of the village.

Lost in thought as he walked, the sudden intrusion of Neas's voice startled him. "What are you talking about? You've been helping me plan this for months. And the answer is still no. You are not going." He shook the reigns and started to move on.

"Okay, fine. You go back and tell Caeri, the Royal Princess herself who commanded me; you are overriding her decree and refuse to let me accompany you on this journey." He jumped off the wood pile and took a few steps back toward the center of the village.

"Wait, Caeri commanded you to do this with me?"

"Well, not exactly. More like she thought my idea of this being a two-man job was wonderful. She knew you would object so we agreed to keep it a secret."

"What about Ila?"

"Oh, she is upset, of course, but she understands. And she knows my traveling with you will calm her sister's fears, at least a little. She's a lot stronger than you give her credit for you know."

Vidad glared at his brother for a moment, but the smile Neas was flashing him quickly dissipated the anger. "There's no way I can talk you out of this?"

"Not a chance." Neas walked behind the woodpile and reappeared with a string of pack animals of his own. "Shall we get started?"

***

His chest heaved, gasping for air. Maliche released the medallion, setting it clattering on his desk. He let Maripa's journal fall from his grasp as he braced himself against the onrush of reality.

"I saw them, professor. I saw the Kolandi. It was as if I were a spirit floating among them, observing their lives without them knowing. This is insane. How is this happening?"

Professor Neywa glanced at Aras, his brow furrowed. "I cannot say, Maliche. I've never encountered anything like it."

Aras took Maliche's face in her hands, examining him. "You were only unconscious for a few minutes. You rambled a few things we didn't understand, and then you woke up. We barely had time to do anything."

She went to the sink and brought back a glass of water. As Maliche drank, she pressed a portable med viewer to his chest and watched as the display provided his health vitals. Despite the readings confirmation of his suffering no more than a burst of adrenaline, Aras took his wrist, measuring his pulse.

Maliche shook free of her hold. "Only a few minutes? It had to be more. I felt like I was gone for hours, possibly days."

"Perhaps you should tell us what you saw. Maybe that will help unravel some of the mystery." The professor picked up his notebook and a pen, waiting for Maliche to begin.

Chapter Four

The center of government on Raince'to resided in First Town. This burgeoning metropolis would be unrecognizable to those who first settled the small village so long ago, where Maripa once held court in a one room town center, also the site of weddings, funerals, and a variety of other community events, elected officials now held seat in the towering Assembly Building. Rising up twenty stories, this cylindrical monument of steel and glass was visible for miles. By law, no other building could be taller. Here were the offices of every major guild and county representative on the planet.

Selan Rocker stood at the window of his office watching the traffic fly by. Six levels of mag-lev vehicles flew above the heavily congested ground lanes radiating out from the Assembly Building. The higher the level, the more expensive the vehicles became, and the less congested the traffic. Selan chuckled as he noticed two drivers on the ground level gesturing wildly at each other, pointing to the damage caused by their collision. "Maybe we should pass some legislation to abolish all ground level traffic. Too many wasted resources are spent dealing with the problems created there."

Selan's aide jotted the suggestion on his ever-present note pad and swiped the note into a folder titled *Possible Future Legislation*. "Perhaps replacing the ground roads with parks would make the idea more attractive." He appended the note in the folder and glanced at the clock in the upper corner of the device. "Time for today's session, sir."

Selan nodded and tapped the control panel on the wall turning the glass opaque as he headed toward the main assembly room.

Today, on this final day of this session's legislature, several important votes were on the dockets, including the eighth proposal put forth by representatives of the mining guild. Inside the main assembly chamber, everyone was anxious for the long day to come to an end.

"The final vote on the matter of a 0.2% increase to the mag-lev vehicle tax to support increasing mining guild exploration on the continent of Mariposa will now begin." Fejf Rocker, Premier of the Assembly, called out to the assembly of legislators. As the highest ranking Rocker, at least until the next election when everyone expected Selan, his son and heir to assume control of the government, Fejf was head of the assembly as was his father and grandfather before him. Selan occupied the center chair among the leading members of the assembly. As head of the committee for guilds, Selan held the second most powerful position in the legislature, outranked only by his father.

All members of the assembly with voting privileges pressed their talons into the slots in their desks marked VOTE. Once connected, small panels lit up with the choices YES, NO, and ABSTAIN. A slight pressure towards their choice highlighted the vote in green. Increasing pressure into the slot cast the desired vote. Computers tallied the votes and displayed the results on a screen in Selan's desk. At the same time, a holographic projection broadcasted the tally above the officials for all to see. Once the vote was completed, Selan touched the TALLEY button and received a print out of the votes. After a quick perusal, Selan selected SEND and highlighted the Premier's name, sending the totals to Fejf.

The Premier leaned in toward the microphone and announced the results. "Four hundred sixty-three in favor of the resolution, twenty-six opposed, and two abstentions.

The resolution passes." The result was a forgone conclusion, given the power of the mining guild, but a smattering of applause broke out in any case.

Fejf rapped his gavel stone on his desk to call for quiet. "This concludes all business for the current session. All rise and be dismissed." With a final crack of the stone he exited the chambers.

Selan opened the door to his office and stopped dead as he recognized Nedia sitting at his desk. "Hello, dear. To what do I owe this rare pleasure of your visit today?" He walked over to her, and she raised her cheek for him to kiss.

"I was in the area and stopped by to see if you might want to see a play tonight. The children are with my mother, so I thought we might take advantage." She closed the open drawer of the desk as she stood. "I was getting tired of waiting for you, so I was about to leave you a note, but here you are."

Taking her talons in his, he helped her to her feet and pecked her forehead. "I am sorry, my dear, but I have an important meeting tonight with several Guild members. Perhaps another night."

"Of course, dear. I understand how busy you are." Her eyes dropped a bit and her smile faded slightly, but otherwise, Nedia maintained her composure.

Selan walked Nedia down to the lobby of the Assembly building where they embraced and parted.

Back in his office Selan was nearly finished packing up for the day when the buzzer on his intercom sounded.

"Yes, Ditan, what is it?" he asked.

"Raencert, from the mining guild is here to see you, sir."

Feathers and quills, he was supposed to be here hours ago. What is that old bird up to now? Probably trying to put me in my place again, the old mutes. Selan took a deep breath and grimaced as he considered the ramifications of that particular thought. "Send him right in, Ditan."

The door opened and in strode one of the largest Brin Selan ever saw. Raencert began his career at age twelve as a silver miner across the ocean in central Mariposa. He earned his reputation as a hard fighting man one did not trifle with and rose quickly through the ranks during the next forty years. More than one opponent met with accidents over the years if they did not learn when to get out of Raencert's way. No one could ever prove his connection to the accidents, but no one doubted it, either.

These days he wore the suit and collar of a guild representative. The crossed pick, double jack, and sledge overlaying a miner's helmet embroidered in gold on his sleeve indicated his particular guild and rank. Raencert ran the mining guild. In only three long strides, he crossed Selan's office, holding out his gnarled and massive hand in congratulations.

His booming voice reverberated throughout the room. "Well done, Selan. All eight measures passed with ease. Just what we need to expand our interests in Mariposa. Any difficulty from the other guilds?"

Selan expected the question, knowing it was a formality. "Nothing we couldn't handle. Here are the vote totals." Selan handed over a sheet of paper with the name and actual vote of every legislator in the assembly. "As you can see, the lumber guild offered the expected resistance to any incursions into their lands, but there were a few stubborn opposition votes as well."

"Yes, I see. Don't worry, Selan. You did very well. I can handle this from here. I doubt we'll have any trouble from them next time."

"All right, but keep me out of it. I can't have any ties to whatever happens to them."

Raencert towered over Selan, a dark scowl grew on his face. "You worry too much, young man. I just want to send someone over to politely persuade them to our point of view. I haven't had to take any truly drastic action in years." Raencert paused, eyeing the young Rocker as if he were an undertaker measuring a body for a coffin. "Not that I won't do whatever is necessary to get what we want accomplished. So don't you start getting brittle talons on me now."

The implications of that statement shook Selan to his core. "You know I have always supported the cause of the mining guild, Raencert. I just can't afford any scandals. Not with my father preparing to retire after the next session."

The hulking figure smiled, knowing his control over the next Premier was solidly in hand. "Nobody will ever be able to uncover anything. You should know that by now. We've been at this for two hundred years. So relax, and enjoy your recess. I will be back in touch sometime before the next session to lay out our strategies for future legislation."

They hooked talons again, and he turned to leave. Stopping abruptly, as if suddenly remembering something he returned to Selan's desk. "I hear your brother is writing a proposal for another expedition into the desert again. Have you discussed the reasons for this with him?"

Selan knew better than to let anything Raencert said or did shock him, but could not prevent the look of surprise on his face. "No, I didn't know anything about it. We almost never talk about his work, since it usually ends up in a loud argument. Father disapproves of such things at home."

"Maybe you better control yourself and look into it. I don't want him snooping around any of our operations over there."

"No need to be concerned. Maliche has no interest in mining or any of the other guild operations. The deepest deserts and ancient artifacts are all he cares about. His last expedition was hundreds of miles from anything remotely associated with your work. I expect he wants to return to the same location. He mentioned something about a mysterious artifact he found there last time."

"What sort of artifact?" Raencert asked, suddenly alert.

"I'm not sure. As I said, we got into another argument at the time and besides, he said someone stole it from the site so he wasn't sure exactly what it was. It's probably nothing, though. You know how he gets about his broken pottery and such."

"You may be right," Raencert said, tapping the talons of one hand together in loud clicks, a brief grin appeared on his face, but it vanished into a scowl before Selan could be sure he really saw it. "But keep an eye out just the same. We don't want any surprises that would slow down operations. And we certainly don't want him getting anywhere near our new facility"

"His permits only allow explorations into the fringes of the desert, a few dozen miles or so. Our mine is hundreds of miles away. I think now you're the one worrying too much."

"I'm not worried about your brother at all, Selan," Raencert replied pointing a huge finger toward the young man. "But you know the risks as well as I do. I just like to be well informed. The more information I have, the fewer surprises there are—I hate surprises."

A shudder ran up Selan's spine. "Okay, fine. I'll find out what I can."

"Good. Let me know whatever you learn. I'll be in touch." Raencert turned and, this time, left the office. The room itself seemed to relax once he was gone.

Chapter Five

Maliche sat up in his bed, sleep eluding him after the events of the day. Doubts about his sanity grew stronger as he recalled the vividness of the visions. He could still smell the stench of the grendel as if he had actually been on the hunt with the brothers. No, not actually there; this vision had a somewhat different feel. It was like the sensation he got when he was completely absorbed in a favorite story book, but much stronger.

"I must be losing my mind." He climbed out from under the blankets, pulled on his tattered brown robe, and paced the floor mumbling to himself. "Maybe everyone is right about me. Maybe something is broken in me. Why in the world would I choose a life of digging up relics in the most miserable locations on the planet instead of my rightful place in society?" He stopped in mid stride, tilting his head as if listening to some inner voice. "No. I cannot accept that view. This does not feel crazy. Well, it does, but not in that way. Something is driving me to learn the truth about our history. I have to know why."

He stomped to his armoire, flung it open, and recovered the journal and medallion from a drawer. Returning to his bed, he tapped the control for lights. In response, a small lamp rose silently up from his night stand and hovered steadily over his left shoulder. The lamp turned on to a pre-programmed brightness and adjusted to project precisely onto the pages of the book. He stretched out, held the medallion in his left hand, and began reading again.

Our lives on Raince'to, as we named our new home, began well enough. The cloning process worked remarkably well and, with help from the Skae, our population grew steadily. Even Karm's biocomputer seems to be evolving. He claims the device now speaks to him with an actual voice.

As the months progressed, though, the virus proved too much for us. Our crops and livestock were devastated. With our food supply in jeopardy we grew desperate. To come so far through space only to die on this alien world would have been a tragedy for the ages...

***

Maripa stirred when she heard the baby crying. "Jontar, it's your turn. Go check on little Karm."

"MmmHmm," mumbled Rocker as he turned over, pulled the blanket over his head, and fell back asleep.

"I'm not kidding, Jontar, go check on the baby." Her voice carried the icy warning of her warrior persona, but the gentle snore from under the covers told her she needed to take more direct action. A well placed elbow between two ribs delivered the right effect.

Jontar bolted up rubbing his side. "Ouch! What was that for?"

"Oh, thank you, dear," cooed Maripa, fixing him with her most deadly smile. "It's so nice of you to volunteer to check on the baby, so I can get a good night's rest for a change." She patted her husband's arm, curled herself into a ball, and buried herself further under the blankets.

"Okay, no problem." As his feet touched the cold floor, he shuddered and stared numbly into the moonlit room. Stretching, he hauled himself up from the bed, ran his talons through his top crest, pulled on his robe, and shuffled stiffly down the curved hallway toward his son's room.

"What is so important? Did you really need to call this meeting tonight?" Jontar asked his son as he approached the child's basket. The round sleeping basket swayed gently as it hung from the ceiling. The child, now a year-and-a-half old, sat smiling and watched his father enter the room. Jontar unlatched the basket's safety-bar lid and picked up the squirming boy.

"Tirsy... want dink."

The boy's father smiled at him. "You do realize it's two in the morning, don't you? Of course you do. Oh well, if you insist, young man. Guess I might as well join you. I wasn't exactly enjoying my dreams, anyway."

The two sat in the kitchen, both with their drinks. The architecture of this, and all buildings they constructed on Raince-to, retained the somewhat circular shape and gentle curves of walls into floors and ceilings of their lost home world. Jontar stared out the window into the night as his son, nestled into his father's lap, slurped noisily at his cup.

If we don't solve this problem soon, I'm not sure we can survive another two seasons. This is one stubborn virus facing us. I just can't seem to find its weakness. At this rate, none of the crops will survive for long. Maybe the teams working on the native plant species will find a way to make enough of them edible. We might have come all this way, only to die of starvation on an alien planet.

Dr. Jontar Rocker, head Geneticist and Leading Citizen of Raince'to, the name of their new home world, felt a warm trickle flowing down his leg.

"Oh, great!" he said to his son. "Now we both need to get cleaned up."

He held little Karm at arm's length as he carried him back to his room and placed him on the bowl-like changing table. After a flurry of well-practiced diaper artistry, the baby was ready for bed. With his son safely latched back in the sleep basket, and quick wash of his leg,

Jontar returned to his own bed to try to salvage at least a few more hours of sleep. The heavenly scent of frying meat, toasted bread, and aromatic tea greeted his waking.

"Good morning, dear," said Maripa as he joined her in the kitchen for breakfast. "Thanks again for doing the honors last night. I really needed the rest." She brought him a plate of eggs and sausage, kissing him on the forehead as she set the plate on the table.

"No problem," he replied. "I wasn't getting much sleep, anyway."

He grabbed a slice of bread, piled some eggs on top, and took a bite. The sun felt warm on his back as it shone brightly through the window. He watched Maripa as she gracefully maneuvered around the room, and he thought again how beautiful she was and how lucky he was to have her in his life. Her top crest glowed brilliantly in the morning light and her face reflected her inner peace and happiness. Hers was the grace of a predator stalking the night—a fact which she frequently reminded him of whenever he challenged her to a Rings match.

Suddenly, the back door slammed open and Karm burst into the room. "Good Morning!" Where is my favorite namesake?" He slung his ever-present fishing vest over a chair and propped his fly rod in the corner. "I thought we might go tackle the pond again today while you two were off taking care of business." His eyes twinkled from behind his tanned and wrinkled face.

"Good morning to you, too," replied Maripa. "Little Karm was up half the night, so he's sleeping in, but I'm sure he's up now, if you want to go get him. His breakfast is almost ready, anyway."

"No sooner said than done, Mrs. Mayor," said Karm. He bent down to kiss his diminutive niece's cheek, stealing a slice of toast in the process, and strolled out of the kitchen toward the nursery, whistling some random old tune.

Rocker scratched at his crest again, yawning loudly. "Well, at least somebody is in a good mood these days. Are we absolutely certain he is my clone? It seems very unnatural to me for anyone to be so chipper this early in the morning."

"You know he is just trying to keep everyone's spirits up. With his status as The Savior, he feels an obligation to be an inspiration and symbol of new possibilities. It's killing him to see us in such trouble, especially when he can't do anything about it, but he won't show his anxiety to anyone. He thinks if he keeps up a positive and energetic front, then others will be comforted and not so worried."

Rocker smiled at his wife and took the last bite of his breakfast. "I know. And he's succeeding, too. Not sure what we would do without him."

Karm returned, laughing and spinning the young Karm in circles as they sailed into the kitchen. He plopped the child into his seat at the table as Maripa brought the bowl of boiled grains. Karm picked up the small spoon and handed it to the boy, keeping a damp cloth at the ready.

"Just don't let him fall in the lake and get soaked," she warned her uncle. "I may no longer be a bodyguard, but you know I'll kick your ass if he catches another cold."

Karm narrowed his eyes as he turned to look at Maripa. "Yes, I bet you would," he laughed. "Okay, I promise to keep the little prince safe and dry… as much as possible." He winked at the boy who giggled again, spitting out a blob of grey mush.

"I have to get going," said Rocker. "The new test results will be in this morning and I need to take a look at them."

"Anything promising?" Karm asked, his demeanor suddenly losing its gaiety.

Rocker shrugged and gave the old man a half-hearted smile. "We're always hopeful, but we're grasping at straws lately. Don't hold your breath just yet."

"Don't give up hope. We've gotten out of some pretty nasty situations before. You'll figure it out." Karm waved farewell and returned his attention to cleaning up little Karm's latest mess.

Maripa took another bite from her own plate and put the dish into the sink. "Let me grab my bag and I'll meet you at the mag-lev." She crossed the room to give Karm and her son a hug.

"We have another day of fielding complaints from desperate farmers ahead of us again. I just wish the labs knew something to give them some hope."

Karm turned to face Maripa. "You're doing a great job, my dear. I couldn't be prouder of you and what you have accomplished these past two years."

"You want your old job back? It's yours any time you want it."

Karm's shoulders drooped; sadness appeared in his eyes. "If only I could, my dear. No, the weight of office is yours to bear now."

"She smiled and hugged Karm again, ruffling his greying crest with her talons. "We'd all be dead if it wasn't for you. I just hope it wasn't merely a delaying action. I'll never understand why you resigned from the mayorship. Why turn the reigns over to me?" She grabbed her coat and kissed little Karm on the back of his head, the only spot not covered in mush.

"I'm not as young as I used to be, my dear. The stresses of getting us all here safe and sound took a great toll on me. Remember, the processes which cloned me were not as sophisticated as the rest of you. The Skae learned a great deal about the techniques and fixed some of the problems before starting on you, and then your brilliant husband solved the remaining problems. But I was their first attempt, not everything works quite as well as it should." He smiled and stroked her crest with a talon. "I have all the faith in the world you and Jontar will figure it all out. You'll see. Besides, I have plenty to keep me occupied being your eyes and ears out there among the people. Some of the guilds need a firm hand to keep them from running amuck and you need as much intel as you can get. Now get on to your work and let us get started on our adventures." He gave Maripa his best smile and waved her on her way.

Maripa took a seat next to Karm and leaned in close. "Speaking of the guilds, I've heard rumors of the farmers trying to organize some sort of campaign to join forces with the machinists. And those phalking miners are pressing to explore across the ocean again. Their reports are all in order, but I don't trust them. They're up to something they don't want any of us to know about. Can you look into it for me?"

"I wish we had overturned the regulations giving them sole responsibility for extended exploration. It was a bad idea, in retrospect. We definitely need some sort of oversight of their activities. I'll get back to you on them."

Maripa joined her husband as he finished packing the mag-lev vehicle with the last of their provisions for the day. They hooked talons as they sat next to each other, gave each other a crooked smile, and started off down the road. The roads were still dirt, or mud depending on the season, but there were many more of them now than at the start. Two thousand citizens filled the growing town. Stone and wood buildings lined the streets. Shops and offices filled the center of town; the cloning facilities still held a prominent position and occupied the largest two story buildings. Private homes spread out on the edges. The solar power station stood at a distance to the south. Its gleaming panels captured the suns energy providing electrical power, heating and cooling for the town. Each building retained the rounded edges and curved walls of their former homes on D'yan-ta, but without the majesty of the steel and glass towers of old. Bolt and his Skae companions provided the basics to help the Brin establish a foothold on their new planet, and then vanished without a word only three months after the landing.

Everywhere people waved as the Rockers passed. They all smiled, but without joy. It wasn't long, though, before they drove out of town and out among the dying farms. Wilted crops, small and brown stalks sparsely scattered along furrowed rows of dust sat on both sides of the road. Even small breezes lifted clouds of thin topsoil into the air as whirling dervishes. The occasional herds of domesticated hodak and other large animals brought with the settlers were nearly gone. Those few remaining creatures searched endlessly for some sprouts of nourishment, but their protruding ribs and staggering gait gave stark proof of their inability to use the native grasses as feed.

"Don't worry so much, honey," said Maripa. "We all know you and your team will lick this problem soon. You didn't bring us all this way just to die here. You found a way to save us then, and you'll solve this one, too."

"I wish I had your faith, Maripa. I just don't know. Karm's biocomputer is clueless, or at least not willing to give us an answer yet. Even Karm can't tell which. I sometimes wonder if that device is really our friend. If his miracle device can't find a solution, where does it leave us?"

"You figured out the SCNT stabilization process back on Dyan'ta, not Karm's biocomputer. And you can do it again. Don't be so hard on yourself. All these nerves are just getting in the way. Have a little faith." Sipping on her tea from the thermos, she smiled at him reassuringly, her eyes shining with absolute trust in her husband's ability.

"At least I was working with familiar genetics and gene sequences back then. This alien virus is a totally new bug with some awfully strange stuff going on in its DNA. The triple strand and extra base pairs are next to impossible to unravel. Each time we think we are close to an answer; the bug finds a way to mutate around us. The first season it was just playing with us when it took only ten percent of the crops. Last season, we found out it meant business when it took half. If we don't crack this soon, there won't be anything left to plant."

Taking a left turn at the next intersection, they approached the entry to the first farm on today's schedule. A team of agricultural lab techs, dressed in the blue coveralls denoting their guild, walked toward them from behind the farmhouse.

Rocker banged his head into the back of his seat as he watched the lab techs come closer. They carried containers of grey-green wilted plants and each one walked with stooped shoulders and limp top crests.

"Kak. Not again."

***

Maliche tossed and turned, kicking off the heavy blankets. He fought to wake up, but a heaviness settled in his mind and he drifted back to sleep as the vision shifted its focus and texture. The smell of salt water filled his nostrils.

***

"Land at last!" cried Neas. "I thought this ocean would never end!" their ship rolled with the gentle waves as its great cloth sails billowed and snapped in the wind. Dark grey clouds gathered to the west as the ship creaked and groaned with each movement. Sailors clung precariously to the ropes high above the deck as the captain shouted orders. On deck, additional crew pulled in unison on more ropes changing the angle of some sails, and furling others. The navigator and first mate conferred with each other over the charts.

Staring into the distance, Vidad watched as the billowing clouds and brown strip of land on the horizon signaled the end of their long sea voyage. He kicked away the latest pile of wood chips surrounding his feet and turned to small wooden figure in his fingers, deciding where next to sculpt.

"I always thought of the crossing as a matter of days, not weeks. I imagined the Govayaer exaggerated the distances to drive up their price for bringing us across."

"Their knowledge of the stars and sea currents is unbelievable," said Neas. "Even your skills as a tracker pale in comparison to what these people are capable of. I talked to their navigator. He showed me how he felt the currents to tell our location when clouds covered the sky. I thought he embellished his stories to impress me with his importance, but now, I'm convinced he treated me as if I were a child on the first day of lessons."

Vidad nodded in agreement. "Who could believe anyone capable of traveling for weeks without a single landmark arriving at the exact location and time they predicted. I wish I could spend a year learning from them. Maybe after our task is finished I can return."

"Good luck convincing Caeri. She probably won't let you out of the village for twenty years after this expedition. Not even if you brought her a hundred new carvings."

"Yes, you're probably right. Let me think about it for a while. Maybe I can come up with a believable argument."

"Not in a million years. Look, the coast is approaching fast. We'd better get the gear packed up."

In a matter of hours after their first sight of land, the sturdy reed boat slipped through the surf and came to rest on the sandy beach. A small village, more of a trading post than a town, sat on pillars several feet above the soggy, seaweed covered ground. The smell of rotting fish and decaying vegetation assaulted them. About fifty people moved about the hamlet carrying bundles of furs, pushing wagons of fruits and meats, repairing boats of various shapes and sizes, conducting the business of a vibrant settlement. More individuals displaying a wide range of statures and skin colors from light tan to nearly pure black manned the storefronts hawking their wares. Arms flew and voices shouted in a never ending barter. The sounds of commerce, ringing anvils, saws slicing through lumber, voices of numerous hagglers filled the air. Vidad and Neas followed their companions up a set of rickety steps and into the bustling community.

Their friend, the navigator, led Vidad and Neas to a dark back room behind the tavern where the headsman of the station conducted business. The man sat in a rope sling hung from the ceiling. Two functionaries sat on barrels, one on either side, carefully writing figures in their account books. After a brief introduction, the headsman called for two more barrels moved over for the brothers to sit on as they determined their next course of action.

"Yes, we saw the light in the sky you speak of," said the headsman. His grey eyes narrowed and his brow furrowed as he sized up the strangers. "In fact, there were many strange lights back then. They came and went for a few months and then vanished. Nobody has seen them in over a year. But our business lies to the east, not the west so we never investigated. There are no mystics living in this village. We can't afford to lose anyone for such useless endeavors." He turned his grizzled head and spat on the ground as if to emphasize his point.

Vidad was incredulous. "How can you not be curious? What if the light signaled the return of the Sky

People? Doesn't fulfillment of prophecy justify sending someone to investigate?"

The headsman shook his head in disagreement, waving a gnarled, weathered hand in dismissal. "Our interests are in profit. Prophesy is the job of a Homsan, not traders. Life on the frontier is difficult enough without the added burdens of religion."

"Can you tell us anything at all about the lights?" asked Neas. "The sole purpose of our journey is to track down those mysterious lights and discover their meaning."

The headsman rubbed his stubbled chin and gazed at the ceiling of his office for a moment, then cast a discerning eye on the travelers. "Our best estimates suggest the lights made landfall about two months' journey to the west. Too far for our interests, but not an impossible journey for those willing to attempt it. You might want to talk with some of the local hunters to learn more about the terrain along the way. I will arrange for you to meet with a few of them… for a share in the fee, of course."

"That would be helpful," replied Vidad. His experience with traders on his side of the ocean prepared him for the negotiations to follow. "We also require supplies and pack animals for the trek. With your help we can be on our way in two or three days."

Two nights later, consulting a rough map based on information gathered from the hunters and trappers, at the cost of only a few coins, Vidad and Neas plotted their path through the wilderness toward the most probable location of the Sky People. At sunrise, the pack animals loaded and strung together, they headed down the muddy trail into the unknown.

Behind the brothers, hidden in the shadows, lurked two hooded figures. The secretive pair followed the brothers for a couple of hours before they stepped to the side of the trail. They appeared to argue over something, and then ran off back down the trail. Turning left along a side path, they pushed through the brush. A low hanging branch caught the hood of one of the individuals, pulling it free from his head, revealing a shimmer of feathers. Taking off the cloak to untangle it, a beam of moonlight stabbing through the trees reflected off a pin on his right breast. A crossed single jack and hammer, the emblem of a Brin miner.

"You know this is absolutely crazy," said Neas.

Vidad grinned, but kept marching forward. "Just think of the stories you will have to tell when we return… some of your old material was getting stale."

A medium-sized dirt clod exploded harmlessly on Vidad's back. The brothers laughed, pleased to be together for this daunting journey.

Chapter Six

Maliche, late as usual, slunk to his place at the elaborately set dinner table. A bevy of mechanical servants lined the far wall awaiting the signal from Fejf to begin serving. Ceila, Maliche's mother, Nedia and Selan sat silently; eyes focused intently on the silverware in front of them. Fejf's expression carried all the pent up anger of a thundercloud before the storm is let loose. The imperious head of the household picked up the crystal bell, touched the appropriate button, and shook it, activating meal service. The tone set the immaculately polished and elaborately equipped domestic bots into a flurry of activity. Meats, fruits and vegetables of all sorts, far more than the five present could possibly require, soon filled the table. Then additional hovering trays circled the table offering choices to the family members, carving and ladling to each as they indicated their preferences. All in tomb-like silence.

"Do you have to leave tomorrow, Maliche?" Ceila, unable to contain her sorrow any longer, risked breaking the stillness. "I will never understand what could possibly be so important out in that desert of yours. How can a bunch of broken pots and unreadable scraps of paper interest anyone?"

Maliche sighed, took a bite of meat he held in his silver talon clips and, taking a quick glance toward his father, decided against trying to explain his occupation again. "Yes, mother, I really do need to leave tomorrow. Everything is arranged. And what I am learning out there may have great importance not only to our family, but to all of us."

Ripping off his talon clips and tossing them onto the table, Fejf shoved his chair back, nearly gouging the marble tiles. "Great importance indeed! More likely you'll be the ruin of this family. You've always been a disappointment, but now you are bringing the anger of some of the most powerful guilds down on our heads with this talk of wild dreams. It was bad enough all those years trying to explain your obsession with ancient myths, your head always in the dust somewhere, but now... you need to wake up, fledgling, before you take things too far." He stormed out of the room, slamming the heavy carved doors behind him.

Ceila stood quietly, gently removed her talon clips and placed them carefully next to her plate. "I apologize, Maliche... Selan, Nedia. This was my fault. I never should have said anything in front of your father." With a sad smile, she nodded toward each of her sons and daughter-in-law and slipped out of the room. Nedia rose quickly, nodding at Selan, before following after Ceila.

"The two of you never learn, do you?" Selan skewered another bite of meat with his index clip, swallowed, chasing it with a long draw of sweet wine. He used the dripping clip to point across the table at his older brother. "Father will never accept your choice to abandon his ambitions for you as his first born. He always dreamed of you being the next Rocker to solve our aging crisis and save the Brin. He feels you have betrayed him."

"I know, Selan. But I have different interests and goals for myself. I refuse to buckle under father's unreasonable demands—regardless of his threats. I can't be the next Jontar Rocker. What I am doing is vitally important."

"Too bad so few others agree with you."

"Followers don't make one right, Selan. Besides, if I'm right, I may just overturn everyone's opinion of archaeology." Maliche leaned in conspiratorially toward his brother, checking the room for eavesdroppers, and lowering his voice to a whisper. "I may be on the verge of finding out what happened to the Kolandi—if anything happened at all."

Selan's brow furrowed as his crest fluffed. His eyes darted around the room as if checking to see if anyone was listening. "What do you mean 'if anything happened at all'? They all vanished hundreds of years ago. It's all in the histories. What are you up to, Maliche?"

"It's too early to say with any certainty. I only have a few artifacts to support my hypothesis, but I am hopeful this expedition to the Great Southern Desert will provide me with the evidence I need."

Selan's visage grew darker. He leaned in, pointing a talon at Maliche. "What are you talking about? And what do you mean, the Great Southern Desert? Your permits only allow you access to the western perimeter. You've been there several times and never found anything to set you off like this."

"Nothing I've shared publicly, anyway. I don't want to compromise your position in The Assembly, Selan, so I have not said anything, and I won't, until I get definitive proof." He hesitated, eyes shifting upward and left trying to decide, and then reached across the table to place his hand on top of his brother's. "Selan, the Kolandi may not be extinct. They may just be hiding from us."

Selan's jaw opened and closed several times in stunned silence. He grabbed his goblet, took a long drink, and sat back in his chair staring at Maliche. He wiped his face with his empty hand and took another gulp of the wine. "Now I must agree with father. You've gone completely feather-fluffed. Your type has been searching the perimeter of that desert for centuries without discovering so much as a hint of the proof. They are extinct."

"And there you have the crux of the problem. We're only allowed to search the perimeter. My permit allows me to go further than ever before into the interior. I have always taken some liberties as to where the 'perimeter' ended, and I'll admit I have stretched that boundary a bit. Fortunately, the authorities have, so far, willingly looked the other way, but now I have written permission to search a previously unexplored region. All strictly gridded and mapped out, but precisely where my previous finds would suggest something significant."

Tossing his hands in the air, Selan stood up and headed toward the door. "Only you could look at a broken shard of some ancient cooking utensil and see natives wandering the planet. You are a hopeless dreamer, Maliche." The door opened abruptly as he reached for the handle and he nearly collided with Nedia.

"Why must you always fight with your brother, Selan? You know how it upsets everyone." Her chin lowered to her chest, eyes downturned.

Taking a deep breath, Selan placed one hand on her shoulder as he passed. "You know how exasperating he can be. I just need to go for a walk."

***

The Guild's section of town proved to be more sinister than Selan ever imagined. The streets teemed with miners who dwarfed him, male and female alike. Glaring lights and blaring music advertising the many amusements available to the passerby assaulted his senses. The smells were none too pleasant, either.

The public mag-lev's automated announcement indicated this as the location of the Double Jack, the bar Raencert owned, and dropped him off at the corner pointing down the block. But the barrage of sound and the smell of garbage, cheap drinks, and unwashed bodies made the walk difficult and unpleasant as he pushed his way through the crowd. At last, he noticed the old fashioned mechanical sign with two figures, one swinging a large hammer while the other held a spike, above a red metal door. The sight of the monstrous doorman caused him to regret agreeing to this meeting. Taking in a deep breath, one he regretted immediately, and marshaling his courage, Selan approached the establishment.

"I have an appointment with Raencert." Selan tried to look as important as his title would indicate.

The guard eyed him up and down, consulted his communicator, and then opened the door. "Up the back stairs. The boss is expecting you."

The interior of the Double Jack proved to be precisely the opposite of its exterior. A string quartet played beautifully on the tastefully decorated stage. Several dozen tables complete with tablecloths, china and crystal filled the floor, each occupied by well-dressed couples of obvious wealth. Plush carpeting covered the floors and several works of art decorated the walls. The Maître d' approached and directed him toward the stairs leading to Raencert's office.

Raencert met him at the door hooked talons, placed a powerful arm around Selan's shoulder and led him into the sanctuary. "So what do you think of my place?"

"Not at all what I expected." Selan realized this sudden honesty may have been a mistake, but it was too late now.

Raencert laughed as he seated himself behind his desk, its surface inlaid with polished stone. "Elegance amid the common. Precisely the image I intend to convey. Here in this district, I can be in close touch with the common worker and still cater to the upper crust whose favor I need to court from time to time."

"How do you convince your customers to come into this region? Aren't they likely to get mugged or something?"

His voice took on a note of iron as he leaned forward. "Anyone foolish enough to threaten one of my guests would not be tolerated. Everyone you see on these streets depends on the mines, and the mines depend on me. The last such incident was ten years ago. I ordered the idiot shipped off to one of the Eastern Continent mines with a stern warning to never return to this side of the ocean. Of course, rumors of much direr consequences grew, with my help, and so business continues undisturbed. Now, what is of such grave importance that you couldn't wait until tomorrow to discuss?"

Selan sat upright in the small chair trying to make himself larger. The impatient glare on Raencert's face and his reddening crest convinced him it was best to tell everything.

"It's my brother… somehow he managed to obtain a travel permit to explore portions of the interior of the Great Southern Desert. He plans to leave tomorrow."

"I am already aware of that. Nothing happens in the desert without my approval… or did you think I was completely incompetent? I have set very specific and narrow coordinates, far from anything we would be concerned about, for him to dig for his artifacts. This way, we can satisfy his curiosity, and the interest of many others, about the desert. Too much secrecy breeds too many questions we don't want being asked." Raencert folded his well-muscled arms across his broad chest, daring Selan to continue.

"You know me better than that, Raencert, I'm here to make sure we are both together on this. I don't want anything to go wrong any more than you do."

Selan's eyes shifted nervously from Raencert to the doorway and back again. The lump in his throat felt as big as a grendel as he swallowed. Even for one of his authority it was never wise to upset someone like the head of the mining guild. High ranking officials have mysteriously vanished before and Selan did not relish the thought of being the next.

"There is more. My brother hinted that he often uses his status as a Rocker to sometimes ignore the limits of his permits and I know he plans to go beyond the limits you have set for him."

"I would not have expected anything less from him. We know all about his taking liberties and using his influence to go places he is not supposed to be. In this case, however, we have set certain precautions in place to make sure his extracurricular endeavors go nowhere near our secret mines."

"What precautions? He may be an embarrassment to the family and a feather-fluffed idealist, but he is my brother. I wouldn't want him hurt just to protect a few hidden profit sources. At least, not unless we had no other options."

"You let me worry about that. Is there anything else before you go?"

"Nothing for now. I wouldn't worry about him turning up anything. He just has some harebrained idea about the Kolandi not being extinct. He thinks they may just be in hiding somewhere in the desert. He won't be concerned about locating any of the mines."

Raencert paled noticeably for the briefest of moments, his voice took on even greater ominous tones as he leaned forward, arms crossed on the desk. "What, exactly, did he tell you about the natives?"

Chapter Seven

Thank The Eternal for the brothers. Despite the efforts of many to credit Karm, Maripa, and myself with the saving of our people, the truth lies in the teachings of those kindly strangers. They showed us how to work the land to make the vegetation palatable. It was they who taught us the proper techniques of treating the meat of the native animals, so we did not poison ourselves. We should have raised monuments to them, not ourselves...

***

Maliche nodded as he sipped from the glass of water. The visions always left him feeling drained. "That's as far as I got before blacking out?"

Aras set the journal back on the desk. Her face contorted as she sat staring at the book, she folded her arms across her stomach, and looked back at Maliche. "This contradicts everything we're taught. It was your ancestors, Jontar and Maripa who saved everyone, not the Kolandi." She slammed her personal note processor on the desk, jumped to her feet, and stormed off to the far corner of the room, arms hugging herself in a tight grip.

"Everything my visions are telling me says our version of history is wrong... at least on this account. The Kolandi did and were capable of more than we know. My visions have made that clear. Their legends seem to indicate they are descended from a culture more advanced than our own. Only a great tragedy, one lost in antiquity, reduced them to a non-technological society."

"This is why I authorized your new expedition to the desert. Maybe you can find some new corroborating evidence in the areas we've picked out based on what you've told us of the Kolandi village." Professor Neywa turned off the imaging recorder and leaned back in his chair, rubbing his chin. "Again, your mutterings were somewhat incoherent for the most part, and this episode was only a minute or two longer than the last. We need to hear your recollection of exactly what you saw before you take off this afternoon. It may be the last opportunity I have to gather some data from you for quite a while."

"It's more than simply something I see, professor. It's like I'm living right alongside them all. Time has no meaning in the visions. You tell me I'm only out for a few minutes, but it feels like weeks, sometimes months to me. It's very disorienting when I wake up."

"I believe you, son, and I sympathize with your anxiety over it all. If we are to be of any help, please, tell us what you can." He waved for Aras to take her seat at Maliche's side.

Maliche took a deep breath, felt his heart racing as Aras reset the med viewer on his chest, double checking the readings were all within acceptable parameters. He closed his eyes, trying to recall the experience. "I was in Jontar Rocker's laboratory. The mood was desperate... everyone on edge. Crops and livestock were dying due to some unknown virus which attacked the Brin species they depended on."

As the memories surfaced Maliche relived the vision.

***

"Doesn't anything kill this phalking virus?" Dr. Rocker paced the aisles of his lab shouting at the ceiling. "Over two years and this thing still hides its secrets. I can't fail. There must be another way."

The latest printout detailing another failed experiment littered the floor around the former Professor.

Not even the explorers returned with good news. Oh, they found mineral deposits, rivers, lakes, even the remains of an ancient alien city according to one report, all valuable for the future if anyone survived, but nothing to help solve this current crisis. At first, the city ruins held great interest for everyone, but nobody discovered anything to indicate who built the once magnificent structures or where they went, so the pressures of survival returned relegating everything else to secondary status. In another hour, the rest of his team would arrive, but for now, Rocker was free to vent his anguish.

"Some brilliant geneticist I turned out to be," he barked at the walls. "There must be an answer. What am I missing?"

The door burst open and in rushed a breathless young intern. "Dr. Rocker! Come quick!"

Now what? "What's the matter? Is anyone hurt?"

The intern leaned heavily on the nearest desk as she caught her breath, her eyes wide in excitement. "No, Doctor, everyone is fine, but you need to see this, it's unbelievable. There are humans here!"

Before he could reply, the girl was running back through the door and down the hall. *What the hell does she mean, 'There are humans here'? Stories from the Skae said something about a long-lost race they called humans, but they can't be real. Certainly not something that would pop up out of thin air in town. This better not be some juvenile prank.*

Lost in his thoughts, the doctor never saw where the young woman ran off to. Stopping to look around once he reached the street he saw the large crowd gathered at the edge of town.

***

Oh great, she must have meant there's a fight here. Rocker picked up his pace, and then stopped dead in his tracks when the mob parted. Standing there with his arms dropped to his sides, jaw hanging open he watched two humans walking down the street in the middle of a crowd of agitated onlookers. Long black hair, not feathers, covered their heads. Something about their skin was startlingly strange. Yes, it was darker than most he had ever seen, but there was something else. Then, as the sunlight shined through a gap in the clouds, he realized the human's skin lacked the transparent scales of the Brin. Except, that is, for the tips of their talon-less fingers which appeared to have a single thick scale on each. They were uttering strange sounds, some sort of communication he thought, but even the gestures they used to accompany the sounds were too unfamiliar to make any sense of.

Even their clothes were unusual. Not synthetic at all, but some sort of scaly animal skin sewn into trousers and a sleeveless vest which appeared to change color as the two walked passed different structures The weapons they carried caused Jontar to pause. Both men used tall curved-blade weapons, part animal claw and part worked metal, as walking sticks, and both had long knives hanging from sheaths on both hips. Bone handles of smaller knives protruded from their boot tops. The shorter of the two also carried a long and intricately carved hollow wooden tube and a quiver of foot long darts slung across his chest.

I hope those are for defense and hunting. Jontar thought. The humans halted, watching the growing crowd warily.

The Brin formed an arc around the humans while the children, not able to contain their curiosity, approached the strangers. Rocker watched in awe as the children reached out to touch the smooth skin and hair on their heads. Hesitantly at first, but when the beings showed no sign of aggression, the bravest among them grew bolder, reaching out to touch their smooth skin. The men, in turn, ruffled the crests of the youngsters, laughing at the experience. Both investigated the unfamiliar physical characteristics of the other. Rocker knew mammalian creatures with intelligence were theoretically and genetically feasible. After all, the jungle dwelling Tarsis back on Dyan'ta were well known for their ability to solve simple intelligence puzzles, but he never actually believed he would witness such unusual creatures. He found it difficult to accept, even with the evidence of their existence right in front of him. *Who the strix are they? They're not Brin.*

Two hours later, after finally tracking down Karm at the river, the town council convened in the gathering hall. Despite the immense curiosity Maripa allowed only Karm, Dr. Rocker, and two other high ranking council members inside with the guests.

Karm's left arm glowed as he activated the biocomputer. "I hope this thing is translating correctly for us. Do you understand my words?" he asked the newcomers.

Their eyes shot wide and the visitors exchanged wondering looks. Vidad spoke first. "Yes, this is incredible. I hear your words in a strange tongue, but my mind understands their meaning. How is this possible?"

"We have a device which can translate our two languages so we can communicate without difficulty," Karm held out his left palm to show the glowing biocomputer. "There is no need to fear. Who are you? Where do you come from? Why are you here?"

After a furtive glance to his brother, Vidad continued. "My name is Vidad. This is Neas, my brother. We followed your star from across the great sea. Our travels have been long and hard. We hoped to find the Sky People. Our legends make no mention of bird-men and we have never seen anyone like you before. Do you know of the Sky People?"

Maripa spoke next. "We did arrive from the sky just over two years ago, but I don't see how your legends could possibly mean—"

"A moment, please, Maripa," Karm's face gave the impression of one rudely awakened from a dream. He gave his palm a brief look of something between frustration and anger. "My implant just fed me a few dozen centuries of history conveniently left out of my previous education." The glow altered slightly from the familiar yellow to a faintly pinkish hue. "It seems our guests are referring to the Skae."

"You mean Bolt and Zem's race?" asked Maripa, astonishment replacing her normally placid composure.

"The very same. Apparently, the Skae and their people share a long history dating back thousands of years. Something happened to separate them long ago. This darn contraption is up to its old tricks again and won't tell me anything more. I get glimpses of... something... something that went terribly wrong, but then nothing. It's as if there are gaps in the biocomputer's memory banks. Dead spots I can't see through."

The glow became distinctly redder and Karm's arm grew warm.

Maripa ignored Karm's look of concern over the changes. "What are you talking about? The Skae travel out there among the stars." She waved her hand absently toward the sky. "These natives don't look like they know anything about Cosmic Strings and interplanetary exploration. Are you sure your computer is working correctly?"

"They're obviously just a couple of ignorant savages still believing in mystical gods and spirits," said Shoder, leader of the mining guild. "We have more urgent business to take care of. Just give them a few trinkets and send them on their way." A look of disdain crossed his face as he watched the two visitors.

"Be quiet, Shoder," said Maripa. "These men might have information we can use. They are obviously indigenous to Raince'to and know how to survive on the native plants and animals. They may be able to help us."

Vidad held up his hand, tilting his head in apparent confusion. "What is this Rayns taw, you speak of?"

Maripa looked at him as though she had forgotten he was there. "Raince'to. It's the name we have given to your world."

Neas laughed out loud. "How can you give a name to something which already has one? This place is called Kodut."

Shoder sneered and threw up his hands in disgust. "Why are we wasting our time here? What can primitives like these two possibly have to offer us? We need to focus on the science for a cure, not some mystical fantasies."

No longer able to contain himself, Neas pleaded with Maripa. As members of a matriarchal society, Vidad and Neas gravitated toward Maripa as the true leader of the town. "These people you speak of, the Skae, are they the Sky People? Do you know them? Are the legends true? Are they returning?"

She reflected on the idea for a moment. "I think you might be right, Neas. Over time, your people must have altered Skae into something more understandable... Sky. I believe the Skae are your Sky People. They are the ones who brought us here to Raince'to, but they never told us anything about your people inhabiting this planet."

Vidad's eyes widened, his jaw dropped as he reached out, palms upward. "Where are they? Why do they stay hidden from us? Are they angry?"

Maripa shook her head. "No, they are not angry, but they are no longer here. They left us over a year ago. I am sorry, but we do not think they plan on returning."

Neas and Vidad slumped in their chairs, heads hung low. Vidad gripped his brother's shoulder, and turned his brown eyes toward the Brin council. "Then we have failed. If only we left as soon as we saw the light. Maybe then we would have met them and fulfilled the legends. Sechrid must be right. The Sky People deserted us... betrayed us."

Neas slapped his brother's hand away. "No, brother. I can't believe the gods are so petty. There must be another explanation. Maybe these strangers were brought here by the gods to fulfill their promise to us even after all this time."

Vidad brightened a bit at this thought. "Perhaps you are right, Neas. Who are we to question the Sky People and their ways?"

"I am sorry for your troubles," said Rocker. "But I think something good can come from all of this. We need your help."

"You, who traveled with the Sky People among the stars, need our help?" Neas sat back and crossed his arms over his chest. His eyes searched each of the Brin in front of him. "What could we possibly offer to ones who befriend the gods?"

"The Skae, and we, are not gods," continued Rocker. "We are mortal beings like yourselves who have traveled a great distance to save our people. But on this new world, a disease attacks our crops and livestock. All of our efforts to save them are failing. When we try to use native plants for food we find them difficult to eat. Can you teach us about the plants and animals of this world and how to use them for food?"

Vidad and Neas looked at each other in disbelief. Neas shook his head, and waved one hand across his face. "This cannot be true. How can a people understand how to travel among the stars, yet not know how to feed themselves?"

Shoder snorted, slamming his hand on the table. "Ignorant savages. They don't understand anything about genetics, viruses, or disease."

Karm glared at Shoder, a sudden flood of angry images from the biocomputer filled his mind as he lashed out at the miner. "And a kak-load of good our science has done us so far, no offense, Jontar, so why don't you shut your ignorant mouth and try to learn something for once."

Ignoring the argument, Rocker stood and paced the floor behind his chair. "Unfortunately, our world is so different we are not familiar with the problems we face here. The diseases affecting our food are very strong. We don't know what to do. Our people are farmers, not hunters, so we are unskilled at catching wild game. Those we have trapped and killed have made us sick. The same is true of the native plants. We do not know how to make them edible. Nothing we've tried does any good. Can you help us?" He reached out to the brothers, pleading with open arms.

Vidad stood and walked around the table to Rocker, grasping his arms. "If what you say is true, then we must help the friends of the Sky People."

Everyone around the table spoke at once. Even Shoder, under Karm's reproachful glare, reluctantly agreed to let the brothers do what they could to help. The joy of new hope lifted all of their spirits higher than the past many months. Vidad and Neas became instant celebrities.

Karm did not participate in the excitement. Although the glow surrounding his arm returned to its usual pale yellowish color, he studied the device closely. "What has gotten into you?" he asked. The glow changed again, this time to a light pink shade.

***

"It was then I felt a rush, as if the accelerator of a mag-lev stuck and flew out of control." Maliche filled his glass with more water and took another drink. "When everything settled down it felt as if I had suddenly teleported to a new location. This is the wildest thing I've ever experienced."

"Aras set the med viewer on the desk, stepped up behind Maliche and massaged his shoulders. "It sounds incredible. I'm not sure what to make of it all. At least these visions don't appear to be affecting you physically."

Dr. Neywa tapped his notes with his pencil. "We can sort it out later. Right now, we need to hear the rest so you two can get going."

Maliche finished his water and took a deep breath, hunching his shoulders to lead Aras to a tight knot. "All right, professor, as I was saying, the vision teleported me to a new time and place where..."

***

Five months later, Maripa, Karm, and Rocker watched from a nearby hill as farmers plowed their fields and spread the powdered rocks Neas taught them about. Rows of crops shown green and full as farmers walked among the furrows spreading another layer of grey powder. To the west, split rail fences sectioned off large pastures around outcroppings of the same pale mineral. Herds of captured native animals, this world's equivalent of cattle, roamed peacefully munching on native grasses among the rocks.

Rocker took another bite of fruit as he wrapped his arm around his wife. "We should have known better. The minerals in those rocks leach out the poisons so the plants become edible. Our cattle still cannot eat them, but we can."

Maripa scrunched up her face as she looked at the fruit in her talons. "I guess we can get used to the taste, eventually."

"And those animals, what did Vidad call them... tirpits? If we locate our pastures in the areas he showed us, and cure the meat using those native herbs, steaks are back on the menu. The milk tastes a bit sour, but not too bad. Once I am able to analyze the genetic make-up of the native species Neas and Vidad have shown us, creating new variations to suit our needs will be no problem. Those two saved our feathers."

"Shoder is still sulking about it all," Maripa said. "He calls the tirpits 'those kak four-legged hodaks.' And still won't talk directly to Vidad or Neas."

Rocker shook his head as he finished off the fruit, tossing the pit aside. "Shoder is a feather-fluffed hot-head, but he'll get over it soon enough."

"I hope you're right." Her face twisted in apprehension. "I've received reports concerning Shoder's disquiet and how he is building a group of followers."

Rocker turned toward her, incredulous at the news. "Followers for what? We would have died before discovering the things they've taught us. Are they completely yolkless?"

"Ignorance and prejudice still are part of our make-up, my sweet. It appears I will have to have a talk with Shoder and his group before long to calm them down a bit. Maybe if I grant them the exclusive rights to travel across the ocean, Vidad and Neas talk about it will satisfy them."

"How can you possibly grant them exclusive rights? Miners are not the only ones who need to expand their resources."

"It would be limited to only a year or two, then open up to everyone. They do make a good point about being the only ones with wilderness experience. Freelancers have been exploring all over this continent for a while now."

"Surprising, they never mentioned the Govayer on the coast."

"It's a big continent, Jontar. They may be arrogant, self-important fools, but I'm sure they would not have hidden something as important as another intelligent race from us."

Rocker shook his head in disgust. "Maybe you should be more the bodyguard and less the politician and just knock some sense into them."

Karm sat quietly, lost in thought as he listened to his friends. *I wonder why Bolt and Zem never told us about these natives. Why didn't they settle us closer to them? They must have good reasons, but what? And what is going on with this biocomputer lately? Why does it keep skipping over important details I try to access?*

The voice in his head sounded contrite as it answered his queries. *"I cannot provide you with information I do not possess. The information you seek is not a part of my data banks."*

"Why would the Skae not put such important facts in your system? It doesn't make any sense."

The glow in Karm's arm grew distinctly red and warm, almost hot. *"I have searched my system for an explanation, but find nothing. You will have to be satisfied with this limitation."*

Maripa reached over and shook Karm's shoulder. "Are you even listening to us, Karm?"

Grinning, Karm winked and waved his arm across the view. "I'm listening. Just thinking is all. Now we know about drying and storing the fish in cold lake water for at least a month, so I can start eating what I catch again. Won't that be something? You two have any plans for the kiddo tomorrow? I might want some company down by the river."

"You can't go fishing tomorrow, Karm. Vidad and Neas told me they feel confident we can survive on our own now, so they will leave in a day or two. They are anxious to return to their families. Tomorrow is the celebration to thank them. The hunting parties put aside a portion of every catch, and the farmers gathered enough greens to hold a respectable feast for our honored guests."

"I guess the fishing trip can be postponed for a day or two. We don't want to miss a grand feast now do we?"

Later in the evening, Maripa sat on a bench by the fire with her husband and child. "Isn't this the grandest celebration? We haven't eaten so much in over a year." She stretched across Rocker's lap to grab another tirpit nugget. "And this meat does sort of grow on you. Not too bad after all." Licking the juices from her fingers, she tore tiny pieces from her meat, chewed them a bit, pulled out a bit with her talons, and fed them to Little Karm. The child snapped at the offerings, swallowed quickly, and squirmed in his mother's lap for more. "He certainly seems to like them."

Rocker watched as the townspeople danced around the bonfire. Their shadows boogied in the flickering flames. "Everyone is having a wonderful time, too bad they can't sing worth a darn," he said, wiggling a finger in one auricle. "I knew we should have collected more samples from musicians."

"Be nice, Jontar," cautioned Maripa knocking him with her hip.

Karm sauntered up to join the three of them on the bench. "I can't remember when I ever had so much fun. This is just what the people needed. That kid, Neas, is quite the story teller. He has everyone spellbound with his tales of adventures. Folks were getting mighty glum around here." He snagged a nugget and slice of gourd from Rocker's plate.

Rocker set the empty plate aside and pulled Maripa close with one arm. "Vidad and Neas's arrival was nothing short of a miracle."

Karm licked the last of the meal from his talons, gave a not-so-discreet belch, and sighed contentedly. "Speaking of those two, they requested an audience with you, Maripa. They want to express their gratitude for the celebration and the gifts we are sending their people." He pointed to where Vidad and Neas stood waiting at a respectful distance.

Maripa handed the baby to Rocker and waved for them to approach as she stood to greet them. "My friends, you are honored guests here. There is no need for you to be so formal. It is we who are grateful to you for all you have done for us."

She took hold of their hands and reached up on her toes to give each of the brothers a kiss on the cheek. Everyone who wished could now converse almost fluently with them after only a brief session with Karm and his biocomputer. Only Shoder and his faction still resisted.

Vidad was the first to speak. "We are pleased to be of service to the friends of the Sky People. Our people will be forever grateful to know our legends are true."

Neas ran his thumb across the edge of his new knife admiring its elegance. "And these blades of your metal are as beautiful as they are amazing. Our hunters will make great use of them. And the fabrics you give us shimmer in the sun like a thousand stars. Our wives will be the envy of all the women."

Maripa beamed with joy as she watched the brothers enjoying their gifts. "This is the least we could do. As our people grow to know one another better we hope to help in many more ways than these tokens of our thanks."

Vidad looked up into the night sky, searching the stars. "Maybe, one day, we might even learn how to fly among the stars as you did. Perhaps even rejoin the Sky People once again as friends."

"One day," said Maripa, "our people will go to the stars together and search out our friends."

A loud shout suddenly interrupted their talk. "Hairy quetzals!" shouted Shoder. The inebriated miner stumbled toward them from the shadows. Four others, equally drunk and armed with various drilling implements strode unsteadily behind him. He began slicing a large machete through the air in front of him. "I'll teach you to learn your place around here. Think you're better than us. You'll never stop us." He raised the weapon to strike.

Before the blade could start its downward strike, Maripa reached out and shoved the brothers aside. Leaping into the air she landed a solid kick with her heel to the drunkard's jaw. Landing on all fours, she swept out with a wicked kick to the knee, dropping Shoder to the ground. Rocker stepped on Shoder's wrist forcing his grip to open and release the machete. The others in the group froze with mouths slack.

Maripa, crouched in her attack position, snarled at the four. "Which of you down-brained phalks are next?"

Darb, Shoder's son, a large and particularly troublesome youth, charged in anger seeing his father defeated so easily. A heavy single jack raised in his talons.

Maripa deftly side-stepped the arc of the tool, delivering a fist to Darb's throat, followed by a side kick to his temple. Darb's eyes rolled back in his head as he dropped heavily to the ground.

Seeing a crowd gathering behind their mayor and her husband, and the raised weapons of the native brothers, the remaining agitators looked at each other, then, one-by-one dropped their weapons. Murmurs of excitement and concern rose as more townsfolk gathered around the disturbance.

Maripa pointed at the unconscious agitators in a sweeping gesture as she turned away in disgust. "Get these idiot quetzals out of here! Lock them in their quarters and post guards until they sober up. We can deal with them later." Two bystanders grabbed the dazed guildsman by his arms and dragged him off into the night. Others picked up Darb and herded the drunkards back into the housing section of town until all was relatively calm again.

Vidad and Neas bowed deeply. "Our thanks, my lady. You are indeed a great warrior as well as leader of your people. I wish we had more time for you to teach us some of your skills."

Rocker smiled toward Maripa as she brushed herself off and fixed her hair. "You have no idea."

Maripa, recovering from her anger and regaining her composure waved off the discussion. "Just something from my past. Not much call for it lately, though." She took Vidad's hands in hers as she continued. "I apologize for Shoder's behavior. I assure you we are grateful for your help. Without your aid we probably would have starved to death. We owe you a great debt."

"Do not trouble yourself," replied Neas, smiling and genial as ever. "We know all too well the effect of strong drink on men. All is forgotten."

"Yes," agreed Vidad. "We will harbor no ill will toward you or any of your people. Now we must go and prepare for our journey. Thank you again for your actions to protect us." The brothers bowed again, touching their hand to their face in the traditional gesture of respect. They then drifted off toward their residence.

Karm watched Maripa as the brothers walked off. His eyes softened and a smile grew on his lips. "My dear," he said, "You have become quite the leader. Who would have thought you would be as elegant in speech as you are with a weapon?"

Maripa smiled and gave the old man a gentle squeeze on the arm.

The next morning, as the sun cast an orange glow on the hustle and bustle of cleaning up the remains of the party, a crowd gathered at the edge of town to say goodbye to Vidad and Neas.

Maripa, copying the native sign of respect, touched her hand to her face as she addressed the brothers one last time. "Farewell, my friends. We will come to visit your village soon. Perhaps in two years we will be able to manage the journey."

"We look forward to that day," said Vidad. "Our people will learn much from you."

"We cannot ever repay you for the aid you have given us. We would not have survived another winter without your help. Tell your people we will soon embrace each other as family."

Vidad reached under his tanned leather vest and removed a silvery medallion in the shape of a star inside the crescent moon. "This is the emblem of my family," he told Maripa. "I give this to you now as a sign of our brotherhood." He placed the leather strap holding the ornament around Maripa's neck.

She lifted the heavy medallion in her hands as she examined the workmanship, especially the intricate design of pictographs around the outer edge.

"This is exquisite," she said. "I will treasure it always, and think of your kindness and generosity every time I see it."

Karm stepped forward, holding a silver disc. In the center of the disc flashed a brilliant green gem. Engraved around the rim were images of the Skae, Brin and Kolandi extending their arms toward each other in friendship. "May I borrow your present for a moment, my dear?" He removed the medallion from her neck and closed both objects in his hands.

"As a sign of our everlasting friendship, I am going to create a bond between these two gifts." His hands began to glow a bright blue. "This bond will forever allow us to find each other and renew our pledge of friendship." The light subsided as he opened his hands and returned the medallion to Maripa. Holding out the silver disc he approached Vidad. "Present this to your wife as a token of our gratitude and a symbol of our everlasting alliance."

Vidad accepted the gift, familiar now with Karm's strange ability. "Caeri will be pleased. Thank you." He carefully tucked the disc into his pouch.

Maripa, Rocker and Karm embraced the brothers and they all exchanged farewells and promises to see each other soon.

The townspeople cheered and waved as the brothers pulled on the guide ropes and led their pack animals back toward the sunrise. The crowd diminished as the travelers vanished into the shadows of the distant forest.

Once the travelers were out of sight, Maripa turned on Karm. "What was that all about, old man? What did you do to our gifts?"

Karm winked and gave her a quick smile. "Nothing really. I just wanted to have a way of staying connected to them. Now, my biocomputer can reach out and stay in touch."

Maripa gave Karm a long look, and hooked talons with her husband as they walked together back toward home.

Rocker saw the sadness in her face and pulled her hand to his lips, giving her talons a quick kiss. "Don't worry, honey. With the food problem and our survival resolved, we can focus our energies on building up our technology. With enough engineers and manufacturers, we should be able to build flying vehicles to make long distance travel a simple matter. We need to send out proper exploration teams and learn about our new home as soon as possible. Who knows what else is out there waiting for us?"

Maripa snuggled close and pulled his arm around her. "I'm just relieved to know we won't starve to death now. I couldn't bear the thought of all this ending so soon."

"No fear of failure anymore, my dear. Everything is back on track and looking better than ever."

"I know, but I just can't shake the feeling of something awful out there waiting for us." She walked on, fingering the silvery medallion.

***

Maliche shivered at the memories. "And then I woke up to your worried faces. Does any of this make sense to you, professor?"

Dr. Neywa put down his pad and pencil and rubbed his face with both hands. "This certainly does lend credence to your family's stories being more trustworthy than our official histories."

"And it looks like the mining guild was nothing but trouble from the start. We better get a move on." Aras gathered up her pack and field jacket.

Maliche stayed in his chair. "You go on ahead. I need a moment to recover from all of this." He waved her off with a quick gesture. "I'll be along in a few minutes."

As soon as Aras disappeared in the darkness, Maliche grabbed Dr. Neywa's wrist. "Professor, one of the images is particularly disturbing. I wonder if you caught it as well."

"You're referring to the miners in the Govayer village?"

"Precisely. Why would they keep such a thing secret from everyone? Wouldn't it have been in everyone's interest to reveal their existence immediately?"

"Dr. Neywa placed his hand on top of Maliche's. "Be careful, my boy. There are things happening here which none of us know anything about. Too many secrets and too much power in the wrong hands. If I had any hope of convincing you, I'd talk you out of this expedition."

Maliche got to his feet and took up his own pack. "Don't worry professor. I can handle myself. See you in a few weeks."

Chapter Eight

The desert heat weighed down on Maliche. It was as if he had taken up residence in an autoclave, his brain about to be sterilized. He took another long pull from his water flask, emptied twice already and it was only noon. The thin scales on his arms and face were hazy now as they thickened in reaction to the intensity of the sun. Brushing the wilted feathers of his crest from his dripping forehead he readjusted his hat, climbed out of trench four, and headed toward the shade of the awning over the artifact sorting table.

Plumes of sand flew up from the other trenches as diggers tossed shovels of dirt into the air. Mechanical diggers hovered over a rock layer, blasting it away with their high energy beams. Once they pulverized the rock, they glided back to their charging stations as the Brin laborers took over. No robotic gadget could replace the discerning eyes of a living Brin when looking for delicate artifacts.

Shaking his head as he picked through the meager finds, he tugged again at his stained shirt and drank from his flask. "Five days now and nothing older than the remnants of last year's caravan. We may have to go deeper into the desert to find what I'm looking for."

"But sir, we've gone beyond the limits of our permits already. We don't have permission to dig here, much less any further in. If we get caught, none of us will be able to work again." Mitem, the dig supervisor Maliche hired from one of the mine sites close to the coast, waved his hand toward the crew. "We need to go further west, maybe north of the last site, but not east." He took Maliche by the shoulders, looking directly into his dirt encrusted face. "We have families who depend on us. This sort of work is the only thing available while the mine is refitting. We cannot risk going any further."

Maliche took one of the supervisor's hands in his, clasping his arm with the other hand, and smiled. "Don't worry, Mitem. I'll make sure nothing happens to any of you. Have you forgotten who my brother is? Who I am? My family name will protect all of us. We may get a good verbal dressing down, but nobody will lose their jobs. Tomorrow we leave for these mountains." He stuck a talon to a range of mountains shown on the map he unfolded. He always preferred the feel of an actual map over the more modern electronic versions, and spread it out, covering the shards of pottery.

Mitem gave his head a jerk from side-to-side. "Don't say I didn't try to change your mind, sir. If the Assembly finds out about this…" He gave Maliche one last look, then walked back to his tent.

"Maybe you should listen to him."

Maliche startled to see Aras standing just behind him under the awning. A filthy purple scarf protected her head feathers from the harsh sun. Her shorts revealed long leg, displaying an attractive smokiness as her normally transparent scales reacted to the desert sun, a hint of sweat glistened on the faint outline of her epidermal scales. The pale green shirt, tied in a knot at her midriff caused Maliche's heart to skip a beat.

"You did hire him because he is reputably the best dig supervisor on the eastern continent." She approached the table, leaned against him with one hand on his shoulder, and examined the map. "Why are you so determined to go east, anyway? Those mountains don't seem to be any more promising than anywhere else in this eternal kak of a desert. Why not go back within our legal boundary?"

"I can't explain it, Aras. I feel like something is calling me out there. Every time I see those mountains on the map, I feel a tug toward them. Something is out there... I know it."

She cocked her head toward him, furrowing her brow. "Not a very compelling scientific hypothesis. You sure about this?"

"I have to go. It's like an itch I can't quite reach. I'll go crazy if I don't find out what is happening to me." He stared at the map in silence, and then rubbed his tired eyes with his knuckles. "You know about the visions I get from this kak medallion," he pounded his chest where the relic hung inside a small sack, tied with a cord around his neck. "Only a fool would chase after that sort of sorcery."

Standing upright again, hands on hips, she snorted a quick laugh. "For months now, I have kept the secret of your medallion and Maripa's journal. I volunteered to take a semester off to come out here to this desolate waste land, I spend days on end in ungodly heat digging holes in the ground collecting bits of the past for you. I believe in this as much as you do, Maliche. You're no fool. Something is going on here beyond any of our understanding. I want to know what's causing all of this as much as you."

Maliche stared at her for a moment, walked up to her, and pulled her into his embrace. "I'm glad you're here. I need somebody to confide in, someone I can trust." He reveled in the dusty smell of her crest feathers, the softness of her against him.

She looked up into his eyes, a scowl growing on her face. "So, now I'm here simply as your psychiatrist? Is that it?"

Releasing his hold on her, he eyed her up and down, and smiled. "No, far from it."

"You want to try the journal and medallion again? Maybe another vision will spark something further."

"It's worth a try." Maliche led Aras back into his tent where he unlocked the metallic vault and brought out the the journal. Removing the sack from his neck, he began to untie the knot securing the relic inside.

Aras halted him before he could begin. "Lie down on your cot first. I don't want to have to try and lift you if you collapse again."

Maliche stretched out on his canvas cot, opened the journal, held the medallion gently in his fist, and started reading.

Why do we never learn from history? I think back on those days of celebration so often with regret now. We should have known better. Throughout antiquity, whenever two cultures meet, it is always the less technological society who suffers, whether intentional or not...

***

A cool morning breeze wafted the colorful curtains of the Rocker kitchen. Little Karm slurped at his breakfast, more reaching the floor than his mouth as his attempts to maneuver the spoon by himself proved more difficult than expected.

Maripa stared incredulously at Rocker, her mouth hung open until her anger found the words she was searching for. "Have you lost your ever-loving feather-fluffed mind? You want to take one of the new shuttles, only recently approved for short distance test runs, and fly off over the eastern ocean in search of Vidad and Neas? Over my dead body, mister." She slammed her mug of tea onto the breakfast table, jarring the other plates and utensils. "You have a four-year-old son and another child on the way. You can't just up and leave on some down-brained scheme like this." She cradled her swollen belly protectively.

Unperturbed, Rocker took another bite of tirpit bacon. "This needs to be done. We promised to go to them as soon as we could. They left us detailed maps so we could find them. Our preliminary expeditions to the east found the Govayer harbor town right where they said it would be. We have to do this. And I would be back in plenty of time for the birth. You still have six weeks to go yet."

Maripa paced the kitchen shaking her head, her fists clenched tightly at her sides. "What if she comes early? Send somebody else. It doesn't have to be you. What about your work in the lab?"

"I spend most of my time buried in paperwork these days. Most of the real work is done by everyone else. My work is pure theoretical research, nothing vital. You know that."

"You still don't have to be the one who goes. What about Karm? You know he is getting more depressed and confused. He spends more and more time just wandering down by the river talking to himself, or that biocomputer. Hard to tell the difference anymore. At his age, I'm afraid for his safety. You can't leave us like this."

Rocker rose from his chair and took Maripa gently by the shoulders. "The trip will only be for one or two weeks at the most. I'm the logical choice to go. I have nothing of critical strategic importance going on now. You, little Karm, the baby, and the old man will be fine."

Maripa squared her shoulders, stiffened her spine, and sternly looked her husband straight in the eyes. "Then I'm going, too. We can have Katch and Velma watch Karmito while we're gone."

"You can't fly in the shuttle when you're this far along," he reminded her. "And you are still mayor here. Without you, this place would fall apart. You know the arguments between the farmers, ranchers, and miners would get ugly without you to keep them in check. If Shoder or any one of them gained control in your absence, all of our noble aspirations for this new world could collapse under their narrow minded greed. You know how he and his followers are against this expedition to find the natives, unless it's to somehow turn them into a cheap labor force. The mining guild is always clamoring about how using the natives would increase productivity and decrease costs. Any mention of becoming friends or allies with any of the Kolandi just makes them all the more obstinate and hold even more firmly to their prejudices. Sometimes I wonder if we might have been wrong to grow so quickly. There just hasn't been time to adjust to everything."

Maripa stood firm for a minute or so, then her shoulders drooped and her head fell. She reached out and grabbed her husband in a ferocious bear hug. "What if something goes wrong?"

"Nothing will happen. You're not the only one here with survival training, you know. We built those ships to handle anything. The current flight time restrictions are only a formality. They can handle the distance and then some."

There were, of course, several more battles, but Rocker knew he won. Maripa's arguments weakened. She only continued them out of stubbornness. The next several days passed in a flurry of preparation and assurances of safety and a swift return.

On the day of departure, thinning grey clouds remained overhead after yesterday's storm. Sunlight to the east revealed the edge of the squall. The sky port hummed with activity. Ground crews rushed around the two working shuttles performing their final checklists items. In the open hangar, three more shuttles under various stages of construction created a cacophony of riveting, grinding, and pounding of metal on metal. Irregular flashes of blinding light blazed from the welders. Two Brin sat at the controls of their shuttles dressed in dark maroon overalls performing their own checklists.

Rocker punched the communicator switch with a talon. "All set to go?"

Mot's voice crackled in his earpiece. "Engines primed and ready. All lights are green and locked."

Dust billowed around the shuttles as the engines revved, lifting the shuttles off the ground.

Life changed in the town during the two years since Vidad and Neas's fateful visit. As Rocker and Mot steadily gained altitude in their solar powered flying shuttles they could see the new developments. Manufacturing plants, factories, and all manner of thriving businesses filled the outskirts of the growing community, now numbering twenty thousand. Their numbers grew so large now that discussions of searching out locations for new communities were commonplace. According to guild records, some few, simply called The Explorers, ranged far and wide traveling the distant regions of the land around First Town. Limited to travel by foot so far, their efforts only provided reconnaissance for a mere five hundred square miles surrounding the community, except for the single patrol to verify the existence of the Govayer village on the coast. Everything beyond remained a mysterious wilderness.

To their north sat the solar power plant constructed by the Skae before they departed. Only specially trained Brin knew how the technology worked, so efforts were nearing completion of the operational manuals for future repair and maintenance of the facility.

The green fields of crop-laden farms and herds of animals surrounded the town. Barely visible on the southern horizon, the ancient ruined city, now a cenotaph to a once great civilization glinted in the sunlight beyond the clouds. Discovered before the shuttles became operational, the once great metropolis with its towers of rusting metal and broken glass hundreds of feet tall remained a mystery. More immediate matters of survival and development of their own lives precluded anything more than the most superficial examination of the ruins. As the men rose higher and aimed their single-person aircraft for the eastern horizon they flew over the new mines and mills dotting the hillsides of the nearby mountains. The red dust plumes of mines' operations obscured many of the buildings.

The pilots settled into their cruising altitude of thirty thousand feet at a speed of Mach 3. Rocker punched the controls, engaging the autopilot. Checking over his left shoulder, he verified Mot's position just off his wing and settled in for the long flight.

Rocker reveled in the beauty of the landscape he flew over. Jagged peaks, still covered in snow even this late in the year gave way to vast green forests blanketing rolling hills. Before long, sparkling blue rivers meandered through open plains with herds of tirpit and shartans running wild. Immense flocks of four-winged yellow crested mertans filled the sky below them. In only a matter of hours since their departure, Rocker watched the mountains drop below the horizon behind him and saw the ocean appear on the horizon.

"You see that Govayer harbor yet?" Rocker called into his microphone.

"Not yet, sir, but it should be coming up soon. Our heading is true."

"All right. Let's drop down some and prepare to land just outside of town in that clearing we found last time. No sense stirring up everybody again."

"Agreed, sir. They certainly got a bit agitated when we fell out of the sky like we did. I'm still not sure they believed you telling them we weren't some gods returning from the stars."

Just ahead there appeared a small bay with the Govayer village on the north shore. In the years since the two brothers' arrival, the village remained unchanged. Rocker wondered again how this dilapidated hovel kept from either burning to the ground or becoming swallowed by the ocean. Between the pilots and the town, a clearing among the trees showed itself.

"There's the clearing now. You stay with the shuttles while I go into the town. I want to verify the coordinates with the town leaders before we tackle the open water tomorrow and make sure we have everything correct."

"Yes, sir. We don't want to get lost out there. These shuttles are good, but I don't want to test their buoyancy anytime soon."

As Rocker passed by one of the outer huts, he noticed a shadow in the window. The sun's glare hid any details, and the shape vanished from view almost immediately. Shrugging, he continued on toward the center of the village. Inside the hut, a solitary figure hunched over a communicator.

"Guildsman Hort reporting. Target Rocker in sight at the village. Will report on departure. Out."

The next day, Rocker and Mot found themselves flying over the ocean. Rocker peered hard from one horizon to the next in amazement. "I've never seen so much water. No land in sight anywhere, even from this height."

"Yes, sir," Mot agreed. "At least we won't die of thirst on this world. How much farther you figure until we reach the coast?"

"Two, maybe three hours. Depends on how accurate the maps and all of our calculations are. We should be there well before sundown at any rate."

Two hours and eight minutes later the aircraft shot over the coastline of the second largest continent on Raince'to. Tall black cliffs rose sharply out of the ocean whose powerful waves pounded relentlessly at their base, a long range of snow covered volcanic mountains towered only a short distance inland.

Rocker checked his map and notes. "Adjust heading to Three-Two-Two. Twenty thousand feet at Mach two."

"Yes, sir. Three-Two-Two, twenty thousand feet and Mach two."

"Destination in one hour," called Rocker. *I can't wait to see the look of their faces when we land. Vidad and Neas are in for quite a shock.*

"I don't see any villages, sir," called Mot over the com system.

Rocker rechecked his maps and calculations. A vague concern gnawed at his gut for several days prior to their leaving and resurfaced anew—the sort of concern one gets when something important has been forgotten and is trying to claw its way to consciousness.

"They must be around here someplace. All of the other coordinates have been spot on. It has to be here. Let's drop down to five thousand feet and reduce speed to five hundred kph. Maybe they're hidden in this forest somewhere. We'll probably find them in a small glen or something. Keep the search pattern tight."

"Five thousand feet and five hundred kph. Roger that, sir."

Ten minutes later, Rocker's head set crackled. "I see something down there, sir. Just ahead in those low hills."

"I see it, Mot, in that valley near the lake. Doesn't look like much of a village, but let's land and check it out. Maybe somebody there can tell us where we are."

Rocker and Mot set down just behind a grassy hill out of sight. As they approached the dilapidated village they passed through an area covered with mounds, each marked with a carved stone.

"Can you read the engravings on these, sir?" asked Mot. "There's dozens of them. Looks like some sort of graveyard."

"I can't read their language, but most of these look pretty recent."

"Looks like the village is deserted to me, sir," Mot said as they approached the decaying mud-walled structures, many with collapsed roofs and walls. "Awfully quiet to be what we're looking for."

"I agree, but look, smoke coming up out of that hut over there. Must be somebody home. Let's check it out."

"Hello in the house!" called Rocker in the language of Vidad and Neas as the pilots advanced on the broken down building. He heard muffled voices coming from within, and then a skeletal figure appeared in the crooked entry.

"Hello!" he called again. "My friend and I are lost and we..." Rocker stopped in his tracks and stood dumfounded as he suddenly recognized the emaciated form of Vidad. The man's once bright, clear eyes and imposing physique were now mere remnants of the former hunter. Grey discolorations covered his faded brown skin. Vidad held onto the frame of the hut's entry for support, his head wobbled as he strained to see who his visitors were.

Rocker stepped closer, reaching out to steady the teetering man. "Vidad... Is that you?"

The gaunt figure straightened slightly as he recognized the man in front of him. "Doctor Rocker? Have you come to us at last?" Tears welled, but refused to drop from his eyes.

"What has happened here? Come, let me help you back inside." Rocker carefully took Vidad's arm and led him slowly into the darkness of the hut. As his eyes adjusted to the shadows, he saw five other individuals, children, and adults, lying on rotting, bug infested straw mats around the room. A pitifully small fire provided almost no warmth in the chilly air. Hanging from a hook above the fire, Rocker observed a pot containing a thin broth. A few vegetables bubbled up, but no meat, a hopelessly small meal for six people. The people were dressed in rags hanging from frames even more devastated than Vidad's. Grey blemishes marred their skin as well.

Upon entering, Vidad spoke to the others. "Neas, our friend Doctor Rocker has come to us. Caeri, this is the friend I spoke of from our voyage so long ago. Ila, wake up, greet our visitors. Rahnoa, Lelyk, get up and help your mother. Friends have come to help us."

The wasted forms of the woman and her daughters rose with difficulty on straining legs, using each other for support as they slowly managed their way toward Rocker. In the light of the doorway, the scars and discolorations covering their bodies horrified Rocker.

Rocker leaned out the doorway, nearly tearing the thin curtain from its pins, and shouted to Mot. "Bring the medical kit, and hurry! We have some sort of infection here."

He returned to his new patients and tried to comfort them as best he could. When the medical kit arrived he took blood samples from each of them and fed them into the kit's computerized analyzer. In seconds, the results appeared on the small monitor.

The forgotten memory suddenly burst forward in his mind. "Viral infection… I am such an idiot. It looks like the flu virus we contracted our first year on this planet."

"Flu virus? How can a simple little flu virus do this? I never saw anyone with the flu look this bad before."

"You never saw anyone without immunity to our diseases before. Remember your history. In the early days of our expanding populations many hundreds of years ago on Dyan'ta, as soon as the explorers came in contact with the indigenous population they died in the millions by diseases that hardly affected the explorers. How could we be so stupid? Of course this would happen."

"So, how come their viruses don't affect us?"

"They did. Remember all those outbreaks of fever two years ago, right after these two left us?"

"Yeah, but almost nobody died. A few pills and folks got better."

"Exactly. Our technology saved us. These poor people didn't have the medical knowledge to create the medicines strong enough to fight the infection. This is the result."

"Can we help them?"

"We sure as strix are going to try. Can you fly home on your own and bring me the supplies I need?"

"No problem, sir. Tell me what you need and I can be back here in three days, now that I know how to get here I can push the shuttle for all she's worth. I just wish we had more shuttles to bring the real doctors here."

"Don't worry about that. With the long range communicator you'll bring back, the doctors can walk me through anything I need. Tell doctor Nela everything and get back here as fast as you can. These people saved our lives, now it's our turn to save them. Bring me the extra blankets and emergency rations from the shuttle before you leave. And tell them to get the other shuttles ready as soon as possible."

Mot returned with a communications array which he set up so they could contact the medical professionals for assistance and, a week later, amid an array of portable medical computers, genetic analyzers, separators, purifiers, growth medium incubators and a host of other equipment, Rocker developed a vaccine.

Pulling aside the entry curtain of one of the huts they repaired and now used as living quarters and laboratory, Mot found Dr. Rocker already hard at work.

"Your patients seem to be improving," he said as he delivered breakfast.

"Yes, the fever is broken and their lungs are clearing. With food and enough rest, they should be fine. Thank goodness for Karm's help. It would have taken us a month to solve this without him."

"The rumor mill said that gizmo of his is broken. Did he fix it?"

"It certainly has been finicky these past many months. I guess it decided to be helpful this time. Normally it doesn't give anything helpful when we try to ask it about the Kolandi."

Mot hunched his shoulders and ran his talons through his crest. "Well, whatever happened, the medicine you made here is working. Those grey marks are fading and one of them even talked to me when I brought them breakfast this morning."

Rocker swallowed one last bite of his grub and headed out the door to visit the four patients in the next hut. "Time to make my rounds. Keep an eye on these read-outs for me." They discovered others in some of the other structures, all of them near death. Rocker's care succeeded in reviving all but two of the most seriously ill. Those two he and Mot quietly removed to the cemetery, adding their graves to the rest.

"Good morning, everyone," said Rocker upon entering the room. "How are you all today?"

A smile brightened the faces of each person inside. "Thanks to you, we are doing well now," replied Caeri. "Your medicines are truly amazing. We owe you our lives." She tried to sit up fully, but sank quietly back to the mat.

Rahnoa and Lelyk each held a small pail of water and wash cloth, carefully washing those too weak to care for themselves yet. The young always seemed to bounce back from illness more quickly. They smiled up at Dr. Rocker, but returned quickly to their duties.

"Good to hear you are feeling better, but let's not rush anything. You are obviously still very weak. It will take a few more days of bed rest before you will be strong enough to get up and around. Let me open the window so you can have a bit more light and fresh air." Rocker stepped carefully around the prone figures and pulled back the cloth hung over the window frame. *At least the smell of death is gone from this room.*

"Ahh, that feels good," said Ila. "I was not sure I would ever feel the sun's warmth again." She smiled and reached out a thin arm to Neas who lay next to her.

"I am so glad all of you are improving so quickly. Another day or two and we would have been too late to help you." He knelt beside each bedside as he administered their mid-morning dose of curative. "Maripa sends her love and hopes she can come visit you before long. The baby is due in about three weeks, so I will need to return to her soon, but I will send others to be with you until we can return. Larger shuttles are being built as we speak, so you can expect visitors in another month or so." He surveyed the room once more and headed back toward the doorway. "I'll let you get some rest now. See you again in a couple of hours."

Visits to the rest of the huts brought equally good news. Everyone grew stronger and showed signs of recovering. As Rocker walked back through the village his head hung low, tired feet dragging in the dust. He slumped down in a camping style chair near the former village fire pit. He took a long draft of water from his canteen, leaned back in the chair, and rubbed his eyes.

This is our fault. Dozens dead in just this one village. And these are the lucky ones. Mott's reports from his visits to nearby villages are unbelievable. Whole communities wiped out. Only handfuls of survivors. There is only so much medicine and only the two of us to bring it to them. With so few of them remaining it's only a matter of time before this entire race is gone. A century or two at best. Will history ever forgive us? If only we built the shuttles larger, or more of them. We should have come here sooner.

Reaching down into the small storage container next to him, he pulled out a clear bag, opened it, and took a bite of the sandwich.

In another week, the survivors regained enough strength to begin reliving their lives as normally as possible. Sadness filled everyone as they went about their daily chores. Plowing the fields and repairing damaged homes gave them purpose again. Only a few children proved strong enough to survive the virus, and none of the elders. The town was far too quiet.

One night during supper, Rocker built up the courage to ask the question he needed answered.

"Can you tell me how this all started?" He saw the sadness deepen in everyone's face, but he needed to know. "Please, I know this is difficult, but I must know what happened."

Vidad glanced at his wife and the others. They each gave a slow nod of agreement. "All right, my friend," he began. "If you must know, then it is our duty to explain." Vidad gathered his thoughts as he stared, unseeing, at the table in front of him. "A few months after our return from the voyage to find your people, some others of your village appeared.

Rocker jerked up, not believing what he had heard. "What? Some Brin came here? Who were they? What did they want?"

"They asked us about where we find the metals to make our arrows and other tools, and showed us different rocks, wondering if we had seen similar types here."

Rocker punched his fist into the table, rattling the dishes and utensils. "Miners. Those phalking quetzals. They've been lying to us all along." Regaining his composure, he noticed the startled looks of his patients. "No, my friends, this is nothing for you to worry about. You did nothing wrong. It is my people who have committed a terrible wrong. What else can you tell me?"

Vidad's hands shook slightly with tremors as he continued his tale. "Since our two people have a bond of friendship we told them everything they wanted to know. They seemed most pleased and offered many gifts in return. Some of our young hunters led them on forays into the mountains to help them seek out the rocks they sought.

"After a few weeks, they left. Soon after, some of the elders began to show signs of this strange illness. Samej, our village Homsan, tried everything, but to no avail. None of his remedies cured us. At first, only a few of the oldest died, but then more became ill. As more of us showed signs of the sickness Samej traveled to nearby villages to see if any of the other Homsan knew of a cure. Some of the people saw the illness as a sign of displeasure from the gods and left us to live with family in other towns."

Neas picked up the story and continued. "Some of the herbs delayed the sickness, but only for a brief time. In a matter of weeks, those who were stricken first began to die. The children suffered far worse. Their fevers grew steadily for days, and the grey blemishes covered their skin causing intense pain. Nothing helped them. A few of us, those who are still alive, also developed a fever, but we recovered… at least that first year. A dozen or so died in the first three months. But then summer arrived and the illness went away. We were all very grateful and life returned to normal. We heard tales from other villages of similar devastation. Sometimes even rumors of entire towns dying."

Vidad continued the tale, his voice low and stricken with deep sorrow. "But then came winter. The snows piled high and the lakes froze sooner than usual. And the disease returned. This time, the children were hit the hardest. Their skin burned with fever. The grey marks ate through their skin and they died within days. At first, only a few became affected, but each week, more and more fell. Soon, even the men and women who survived the first year became sick. They, too, suffered horribly as the fevers and greyness devoured them. Many of the hunters remained unaffected, so food was still plentiful, but as the cold deepened and hunting expeditions became less frequent, even they began to suffer and die."

A stillness fell over the room. Rocker felt a large lump growing in his throat. "Those of you who recovered from that first fever are the only ones left?"

"Yes," replied Caeri. "But even we finally succumbed to the disease. Late this spring, those of us who were strong enough to dig the graves, felt the rise of fevers and saw the greyness start to ravage our bodies. If you had not arrived when you did, all of us would be gone."

"I am so sorry," Rocker said with tears in his eyes and a tightness in his throat. "We should have known better. We should have taken steps to prevent anything like this from happening."

"How could you have known?" asked Caeri. "Our legends tell us that plagues like this have struck us before. That is why the Sky People left us, so the stories say. Who could have predicted such a thing would happen again at this time?"

Rocker hung his head low, his voice barely audible. "Our history tells us of the consequences when two people meet each other for the first time. Terrible diseases like this are commonly the result. We should have remembered and taken steps."

Caeri crossed the room and placed her hand on his shoulder. "Be at peace, friend Rocker. We have survived and we will recover. We will remember you and your people as our saviors. This is not your fault."

Rocker simply smothered his face in his arms on the table. His shoulders heaved with sobbing. The next day, he packed the shuttle with his few belongings, said goodbye to his friends and, leaving Mott behind to continue caring for the sick, he returned home.

Two weeks later, he sat by Maripa's hospital bed holding Tari, his new daughter. The tiny pink face with tawny down feathers covering her head, gurgled softly in his arms.

Chapter Nine

Maripa stretched, waking from her nap and smiling at the sight of her husband and new daughter. "You have a way with children, but it's my turn now." She reached out for the baby, cradling her gently to her chest, encouraging her to nurse.

"Nela says you can come home today if you feel up to it."

"And give up all this pampering? Maybe another week."

"If you say so, but the council will probably want to set up shop right here if you don't get back to them soon. But I'm sure Shoder and his gang would be very happy to run things in your place for a while. The fines and bans you laid on them for their treachery are not sitting well with them. Another week and they'll probably convince a majority to side with them and overturn your decrees."

"Over my dead body!" Maripa replied, detaching the perturbed infant from her breast, handing her back to her father. "Where are my clothes?" She climbed out of bed and stormed around the room, ranting about the idiots on the council, getting dressed and packing her bag. Rocker sat quietly smiling at Tari, stroking her tiny cheek with one talon.

***

The months that followed brought new visitors across the ocean as the Brin built increasing numbers of flying shuttles. Life at Vidad and Caeri's village slowly regained a sense of normalcy, even if true joy continued to be elusive.

The mining guild members proved especially hostile. These Brin, under the guise of volunteers on a mission to help rebuild their village, never let an opportunity slip to ask about mineral resources on this continent. If a few of the volunteers disappeared from the ranks, nobody questioned the head guildsman's word of their setting off on reconnaissance missions to search out more survivors in the distant mountains.

***

The visions faded, leaving Maliche disoriented and weak. His heart raced, he gasped for air in quick gulps. "They almost died out. We nearly killed them all."

"What are you talking about? Who did we kill?" Aras sat on the edge of Maliche's cot, gently wiping his crest with a cool, wet cloth. Her portable med viewer beeped rhythmically, but gave no emergency warnings so she removed it from Maliche's chest and set it aside.

"The Kolandi—we nearly destroyed them. Exposure to our germs infected them with diseases they had no immunity to. Those phalking miners brought our diseases to an unprotected group of people in their greedy search for expansion and wealth. Jontar got to them in time and brought them back."

Her eyes softened, tears welled up. "But for how long. It couldn't have been long before they did disappear forever. They did die out, eventually."

Maliche sat up, and brought her into his arms, trying to comfort her. "I'm not so sure. Whenever I start to think about the Kolandi extinction, something doesn't feel right." She wrapped her arms around him in response, and pulled him in further. "Anyway, the miner's guild seems to be a recurring theme in all of this. They caused as much trouble back then as they do now. I wish I had more than just these visions to go on. I'd be laughed out of any court in the world if I showed up with nothing more than a bunch of hallucinations as evidence."

Aras did not respond, so he tilted her head back and saw the tears streaming down her cheeks.

"What's wrong?"

She sniffled, blinked away the tears, and looked into his eyes. "It's all so sad. An entire species of intelligent beings going extinct, and we helped cause it." She managed a weak smile. "Sorry, I'm not being much of a scientist right now."

Maliche held her chin in his talons and leaned in close to kiss her. He tasted the saltiness of her lips as she pressed back into him. Together, they lay back onto the cot, embracing each other.

***

The morning sun rose hot and intense in another cloudless blue sky. Maliche shielded his eyes as he pushed through the tent flaps to begin his day. Stretching his back he surveyed the campsite. The diggers were busy packing up the gear and stowing it aboard the three shuttles. Robot excavators filled in the various trenches with dirt so little, if any, traces of the dig-site would remain once they left.

The dust clouds blew off north and, thankfully, away from camp, so no breathing aids were required. Smoke, with a pleasant aroma of mertans' eggs and tirpit bacon wafted toward him on the breeze. Mitem appeared from behind the lead shuttle and waved as he headed over to the kitchen canopy. Realizing he probably owed Aras an apology, he decided to pay her a visit before breakfast. As if on cue, she appeared from around the corner of the shower tent, orange sleeveless shirt with shorts, towel draped around her shoulders, using one corner to finish drying her face.

Before he could approach, she saw him, and held up one hand with paired talons crossed as warning to keep his distance. She disappeared behind the flaps of her tent, leaving Maliche standing in his tracks, hoping he had not ruined a growing friendship, or was it more, much less a promising career. A powerful grumble from his stomach convinced him to tackle the problem after eating something.

By noon, with no sign of Aras, his shuttle was loaded and ready for takeoff. He sat with Mitem at one of the tables under the kitchen canopy, always the last to be broken down, discussing flight plans and rendezvous schedules.

"Looks like the rest of the shuttles will be ready in a couple of hours. You finished with the preflight checklist?"

"Yes, sir. I took care of it first thing."

"Excellent. Make sure everything is cleaned up and returned to original conditions before you join me."

"No worries, sir. You sure I can't talk you out of this? I still think it is too risky."

"No Mitem, my mind is made up. We are going to the eastern mountains."

"Very well, sir. I'll make sure everything here is set to right and we will meet you later this afternoon. Send me the exact coordinates once you decide on the site." He tipped his hat in salute, grunted as he stood and went off to supervise the remaining camp deconstruction procedures.

Maliche finished his cup of tea and headed toward his shuttle. Once inside, he sealed the hatch and removed his hat.

"About time you decided to get on with this madness." Aras swung around in the co-pilot's chair, impatience written all over her face.

Maliche nearly tripped over the bulkhead at the unexpected voice. He grabbed one of the overhead bins to steady himself. "What the strix are you doing here? I thought I scared you away. All these visions are getting pretty intense. Also, I'm sorry if I took too many liberties last night. It won't happen again. You are my student, after all."

Legs crossed, she unfolded one arm to point accusingly in his direction. "First of all, as for being my professor, we are almost the same age, Doctor Rocker." She spat out his name and title with a venom common to all the women Maliche knew when they were angry. "You're by far the youngest professor on the campus, and I got a late start trying to raise enough money to pay for my tuition. So get over that antiquated teacher – student taboo thing. Nevertheless, I almost did commandeer one of the shuttles to go back home, but… I started thinking about what you said. I remembered the old tales about Karm and how he possessed some mystical power to see into the future and control others, or something like that, and, now I sound like the crazy one. I realized you are one of his descendants, at least sort of, so maybe you can do things like that. I mean the medallion is certainly a mystery… who knows what it might be capable of doing? Maybe you and the medallion are like Karm and his alien biocomputer thing. In any case, after a lousy night's sleep I decided to stick with you no matter what. After all, I am an archeologist, too and I'll be feather fluffed if I let you go off and make the discovery of a lifetime without me. You have anything to eat in this thing? I'm starving."

"But what about last night? I thought you were mad at me for taking advantage of you."

Her laughter stopped his short. "Oh, I was pretty mad at first, more at myself than you, though. I had hoped our first time would be much more romantic. I've been hoping for you to notice me for some time now. But then I decided, 'What the strix?' Can we get going now?"

Maliche slid into the pilot's seat next to Aras and began punching controls with his talons. "From one lunatic to another, welcome aboard."

He pushed the controls forward and the shuttle lifted off amid a cloud of sand. He waved to Mitem who leaned on his shovel, shaded his eyes, and watched from next to the last trench.

***

An hour later, the snow-capped mountains grew steadily larger as the two archeologists approached. Dark clouds appeared to hang on the jagged peaks.

"I've marked a couple of potential dig sites on the map." Maliche touched a control button to bring up the front view window display overlaying the real world in front of them. Three green dots glowed; the closest appeared a short distance up the canyon in front of them. "We should be there in a few minutes and—"

The port side mag-lev exploded in a burst of noise and light. Alarms sounded and warning lights flashed across the control panel. The shuttle gave a lurch to the left, dropping altitude at a frightening rate. With a supreme effort, Maliche managed to level the ship, but the ground, rising up to meet the mountains, approached far too fast.

"Grab hold of something! This is going to be rough!"

Aras, preoccupied with her own set of controls, ignored him.

An explosion of rock, dirt, and brush flew into the air and the shuttle struck the ground. Flames shot out of the fuselage as both wings tore off. The machine bounced several times before coming to a halt at the end of the long trench it gouged. Smoke filled the cabin as flames devoured the remains.

Maliche clawed at his eyes, blood streaming from a long gash in his forehead, his right arm hung at a bad angle. "Aras! Aras! Are you okay?"

He undid the seat restraints with a punch of his left hand, and then tumbled out of his chair, coughing, barely able to breathe the acrid air. He pulled up on the emergency escape latch, blowing out the canopy. Fresh air fought with the smoke for control of the cockpit. Reaching out with his only functioning arm, he searched for Aras.

"Aras, answer me! Where are you?"

Then he saw her. The co-pilot's chair ripped loose from its mounting and came to rest in a back corner of the cabin. Aras, still securely belted into the seat, lay dead, her neck broken.

"NO! No... Aras..."

Flames erupted through the bulkhead, forcing Maliche to scramble out of the shuttle. He stopped a few yards away and watched the inferno destroy everything. As he lay there, the world began to swim around him. Pain filled his mind, and then everything went black.

Chapter Ten

Pain. His entire body screamed with pain. Every breath brought daggers to his chest. Maliche opened his eyes, but saw nothing. *I'm alive? Blind as a carthatch, but alive.* Stars blazed in the darkness when he attempted to move. His brain swooned in agony. He groaned weakly, and even that hurt.

"Don't move, unless you want to cripple yourself permanently, Brin."

Gradually, a faint light grew as his eyes accustomed themselves to the darkness. There, in the corner, a dark shape hunched over a small fire. Maliche heard the clank of stirring and the occasional hiss as liquid spilled onto the flames.

"How you survived this long is a miracle, so be still and thank the sky gods for your good fortune. Your soup will be ready in a moment."

Speaking was agony, his chest screamed with every breath, but Maliche needed to know. "How long have I been here? And what is this place? Who are you?"

The sudden realization hit Maliche that this was a Kolandi, a living Kolandi, brought a wooden bowl to him and slowly dripped a thin broth into his mouth.

"So many questions. At least your brain does not seem too damaged, Brin. But before I answer you, I have one question of my own. How did you come by this?" He held up Maliche's silver medallion.

Maliche's eyes struggled to focus on the object as he considered his options. There weren't many, so he opted for the truth. "It is a family heirloom. My name is Maliche Rocker."

The Kolandi reflexively touched his forehead, chin, and chest. "Then Lejenal may be right. She always believed in the old prophecies. If you are the great one, it is lucky I saw this before I drove my spear into your heart. But I may yet have that pleasure." He placed the medallion back around Maliche's neck.

"Maliche's head swam with vertigo as he clung desperately to consciousness. "What do you mean 'the great one'? I'm just an archaeologist, nothing special. What prophecy…"

"Did you not say you are Rocker? Is this not your medallion?" The brown skinned man tapped the carved object on Maliche's chest with his spear. "It is a sign from our ancestors that The Rocker has returned to us. Only he would have this sign of our bond. If you live, I must bring you to the princess. She will decide the truth of your words."

The Kolandi's words swirled in Maliche's head, mixing with images from his visions. He found it difficult to tell reality from hallucination. The pain seized him again and he trailed off as darkness overtook him once more, his last coherent thoughts were of Aras.

***

"You seem much better today, Great One." Maliche awoke to a new voice, much softer than before. Keeping his head as still as possible, he looked toward the voice. There, next to him, sat a female native. The hair on her head, yes, hair, not feathers as in the old books and his visions, was long, straight, and black. Her skin brown and smooth, she wore leather skins fastened by a series of bone and wood buttons as well as leather ties. Dust particles danced in beams of sunlight streaming in from the cave's opening bathing its interior in the orange glow of sunrise.

"Are you well enough for more soup?"

"Who are you?" He winced as a new wave of pain shot through his body, but his stomach growled in hunger as the aroma of the bubbling pot filled his nostrils.

"Do not try to move, Great One. My name is Lejenal. It was my mate, Opet, who found you and brought you here five days ago. You are fortunate he noticed your medallion before he killed you. Only someone who has shown great loyalty and friendship toward our people would have one. None have been bestowed on any of your kind in many generations. Is it true what Opet tells me, you are The Rocker?"

Maliche shifted his weight and attempted a smile, not too terribly agonizing, and sipped the soup Lejenal offered. "Well, my name is Maliche Rocker. If what I believe is true, it was my ancestors who first met yours so long ago. The medallion came to me recently and I have been searching for what is left of your people ever since. We thought you became extinct." His leg throbbed, and the constant ache in his back and chest made it difficult to think. "I need to contact my companions. They can bring me home for medical treatment."

Lejenal shook her head and laid a gentle hand on Maliche's chest. "I do not think that would be wise, Great One."

"What do you mean? I need medicine and a doctor."

She hesitated a moment, her eyes fixed on Maliche.

Maliche lifted his hand in appeal. "Don't hold back. Tell me what's wrong."

She nodded as if to agree. "As Opet was bringing you here, he saw one of your flying ships in the sky headed toward where yours crashed. He was wary, but decided to risk returning to your ship, in case they were a rescue party searching for you. As he watched, hiding behind a low ridge nearby, he saw one of your kind search the wreckage and overheard him as he spoke to some others over a communicator." She hesitated, as if trying to judge how much more to reveal. "You will not like to hear this, great one, but Opet heard your Brin companion tell the others his sabotage was successful and you died in the crash, only your burned bones remained. Opet watched as he flew off toward the mine, and then returned to bring you to me."

The vertigo enveloped him again as he tried to absorb this news. "Sabotage? Are you sure Opet heard him correctly?"

"He would not make a mistake in such an important matter. His knowledge of your language is strong from his days as a slave in your mines. I will leave you to rest now. Opet will return in a day or two and then we will go see the princess. She will decide what is to become of you."

"Wait, what princess? Where are we going? What—"

Lejenal laid another hand softly on his left arm. "Hush now. No more questions. You need to build your strength for the journey. The princess will decide what to tell you when we reach her. Be well, Great One."

She dowsed the small fire setting smoke and bright embers climbing toward the cave's ceiling, and left Maliche alone in his alcove.

***

The journey took three days due to Maliche's injuries and the need to travel slowly and with extreme caution. The travois, though well padded, still bounced far too much over the rocks on the trail. Even under the influence of a pain numbing drug, Maliche felt every jolt.

Lejenal and Opet steadfastly refused to answer any questions about other Brin they might have seen, the mine she mentioned, it certainly was not on any map he knew of.

He resigned himself to watch the passing of clouds above, falling back into the childhood game of imagining all manner of creatures in their shifting shapes, and the multi-colored stratigraphy of the sparsely vegetated canyon walls.

At long last, they entered a well-hidden cave deep in the canyon. Maliche looked on in awe as he was carried passed dozens of Kolandi, most of them looked to be in as poor health, or worse than he. Many, dressed in tattered rags of cloth and skins, shrank back, or gestured forcefully in his direction. The disturbed murmur grew louder and angrier as Opet and Lejenal helped into a makeshift bed in another alcove.

Lejenal pulled a tattered curtain closed over the opening and spoke gently to the gathering crowd in a language he did not understand, but assumed to be the Kolandi native tongue. Some in the gathering argued with her in anger, but her authority eventually persuaded the others to leave. After posting a single guard, Opet and Lejenal vanished down the corridor.

Amid the sound of hushed voices, confused echoes and dripping water, Maliche drifted off to sleep. His dreams were strangely calming, filled with overtones of relief and excitement.

***

A week later, Maliche's health improved to the point where he could sit up, and even manage to get around on a rickety pair of wooden crutches for short distances. He dared not leave his meager quarters. He heard frequent arguments between the cave's inhabitants. While their language was unfamiliar to Maliche as they spoke amongst themselves, they knew how to speak Brin, but limited their vocabulary to the most colorful of derogatory terms when they addressed him from a distance. The meaning was clear. He was not a welcome guest.

Shortly after lunch, Lejenal approached him. "The princess wishes to see you now that you are recovered sufficiently for an audience. I have been instructed to bring you to her."

Maliche nodded, gathered his crutches, and raised himself up with a grimace. "Lead on, my lady."

As he hobbled through the passages the inhabitants he encountered were less than pleased to see him. Women and children spat in his face. A group of boys threw stones at his back, one bounced painfully off his head bringing whoops of laughter from the youths. Lejenal led him through several twists and turns only to find her way blocked by a gathering of young warriors. With their knives drawn, the men approached. They shouted in Kolandi at Lejenal, gesturing with their weapons for her to step aside.

With a burst of anger, Lejenal stormed at the men, waving her arms at them, back at Maliche, then at the men again. Her tirade continued and she continued stepping forward, forcing the shocked men into slowly retreating. She jabbed their leader in the chest with two thin, but strong fingers as she backed him against a wall. They looked at each other for support, but Lejenal's outrage finally cowered them into submission. With only a few face-saving grumbles in retaliation the men sheathed their knives and allowed the two to pass, with no more than a cursory punch to Maliche's arm which nearly knocked him to the ground.

When they reached a tunnel where they were alone, Maliche pulled up alongside his protector. "Thank you. I don't know what you told them, but you certainly saved my life back there."

Lejenal waver her arm in dismissal. "Pay those schuteks no mind. They are young and foolish, trying to impress each other with how fierce they can be."

"I am grateful to you for getting them to back down. You might have been killed, too."

She laughed and rolled her eyes. "By them? I used to change their dirty wraps when they were babies.

Sometimes they are too impressed by their new status as warriors and need to be reminded of their place."

After only two brief rest stops, Lejenal led Maliche into a large room within the cave. A wide vein of quartz brought in light from the outside, lending a brilliant glow to the damp walls. Two rows of benches lined either side of a central aisle. Several large fire pits lent warmth to the chamber. At the far end stood a massive marble tomb inlaid with gold and silver. In front of the tomb knelt a woman dressed in green robes, elegant, but showing the strain of her office. Her long brown hair was luminous in the refracted light. Around her neck she wore a golden disc cradling a brilliant green gem at its center and a series of carvings, humanoid in nature, with outstretched arms linked together around its edge. Lejenal signaled for Maliche to wait as she approached the woman.

Lejenal genuflected before the tomb, and then reverently addressed the woman. "Princess, I have brought the Brin called Rocker as you requested." She gestured for Maliche to approach.

The princess turned to face him as he maneuvered down the pathway. "Welcome descendant of The Rocker. Your arrival is celebrated."

Lejenal, at a signal from the Princess formally introduced them. "Princess, I present Maliche Rocker, descendant of The Rocker. Maliche Rocker, I am honored to present Princess Ryma, leader of the Kolandi." She bowed toward Princess Ryma.

Maliche hobbled forward, maneuvering with some difficulty between the rows of benches, attempted a bow, but only managed a head nod with moderate discomfort while balancing on his crutches. "I am honored, my lady, and I thank you for the service your people have bestowed this humble stranger. Although, I am afraid my presence is not exactly celebrated by most of your people."

Ryma nodded in return and extended both her hands, palms up. "If your name is true, then you are certainly no stranger among us and all will come to accept you as an honored guest. But your kind have imprisoned and enslaved us for many generations. There is much bad blood between us. For the sake of us all, I pray you are who you say and the prophecy of our deliverance is at hand." She turned, gesturing toward the tomb. Maliche approached and read the name carved deep into the marble. "Jontar Rocker." Above the name, carved in bas relief was a replica of his medallion.

Stunned, Maliche staggered a bit, and then gathered his wits. "How is this possible? I've seen Jontar Rocker's tomb back in First Town. Well, at least his marker. Nobody knew what happened to him after he traveled east across the ocean." He took another few steps closer to the monument. "Are you telling me this is his actual tomb?"

Princess Ryma smiled and bowed her head in agreement. "This is the final resting place of the great Rocker… he who returned to help us in the days following the great sorrow. Your medallion and this pendant are symbols of our ancient ties." She held out her necklace for Maliche to see.

A few more steps and Maliche came close enough to reach out his hand and touch the marble monument containing his ancestor. As his hand caressed the cool stone, feeling the warmth of the inlaid silver, he noticed a glow emanating from within the tomb. His hand tingled as if crawling with invisible insects. Then a burst of light and power filled his consciousness, blocking out everything. Visions of events long past mixed furiously with feelings of great joy. Overwhelmed, his knees buckled. The princess reached out to keep him from collapsing, and grabbed onto the tomb with her other hand to maintain her balance. With this touch, the glow burst into a blinding light surrounding the pair, paralyzing them both. The passage of time lost all meaning as Maliche and Ryma absorbed the energy penetrating their bodies and minds. Visions of memories became shared between them, random and without meaning at first, gradually resolving into coherence. A final torrent of energy shot through them, and a voice, coming from the entrapped pair, but not theirs, resounded in the room.

"Success! At long last, Success!"

Maliche collapsed, the princess falling at his side. As consciousness returned, he felt many powerful hands roughly carrying him away, angry voices shouting at him. The guards kicked and beat him as they dragged him from the tomb.

"Stop! Do not harm him!" Ryma's voice shook and lacked the power to be heard over the angry tumult. Gathering her strength, she pulled herself upright and willed her voice to command power. "I said release him! He is not to be harmed!" This time her voice echoed throughout the chamber and produced the desired effect.

The mob halted and became silent, nearly dropping their victim to the ground. Maliche turned his head toward her voice and saw several female attendants helping her to her feet.

"Princess," one of the men carrying Maliche protested. "This foul Brin tried to kill you. We must slay him for his treachery.'

With the aid of her attendants, Ryma approached the men. "No. This was not his doing. It was The Rocker who awoke and revealed his thoughts to us both. Bring him to my chambers where he can be cared for properly."

The men carrying Maliche stood motionless for a brief moment, eyes flickering between the tomb, their princess, and the Brin they planned to execute.

"Do as I command! Bring him to my chambers and send for the healers!" Her voice carried all the authority of her station, and resonated around the alcove.

The men, bowing in submission, obeyed. They tossed Maliche onto a cot in an antechamber of the princess's cave and left. Covered in a thin blanket he felt warmth growing in his body.

"Sleep now. I'll have you fixed up and healthy again in no time." The voice seemed to come from everywhere at once. Maliche looked around for the person who spoke. *"I'm in here. You'll get used to me pretty soon. Karm and Jontar did and so will you. You rest now while I fill you in on the rest of the story."* Maliche's mind went numb; visions of the past filled his thoughts as he drifted off to sleep.

Chapter Eleven

Karmito, who now, with the approach of his fifteenth birthday, gave notice that he was too old for such a baby name like 'little Karm' insisting everyone call him Karmito, burst into the room.

"Mother! Come quickly! Grandfather has had an accident!"

"What happened?" Maripa asked as she grabbed her coat ran after her son.

"Grandfather went fishing and slipped on a rock. He fell into the river and carried downstream. By the time I reached him he was barely conscious. I ran for help and we got him to the hospital."

"Go tell your father to meet me there, and go find Tari. I think she is playing with Nareen in the schoolyard." She rounded the corner and sped the two blocks to the hospital entrance.

"Where is he?" she shouted to the admissions clerk as she burst through the front doorway. The clerk pointed and she ran down the hall, scattering nurses, orderlies and patients in her wake.

Maripa gasped at the site of her uncle through the glass doorway of his room in the Intensive Care Ward. Electronic equipment in the room beeped and clicked rhythmically as it measured the vital signs of the pale, withered figure lying in the bed. Doctors and nurses busied themselves with needles and various instruments they used to examine the semi-conscious patient. She slowly opened the door and entered the room, her heart pounded in her chest.

"How is he, Nela?"

"He's alive, but just barely," the doctor responded without turning around. "We'll know more after we get the test results."

Maripa recognized death when she saw it, and she saw it in Karm's face as clearly as daylight. "How long does he have?"

Nela turned to face Maripa. She studied her for a moment before responding. "Not long," she said. "Maybe hours, a day, or two at most. I'm not sure what's keeping him alive right now, unless it's that incredible computer enhancement of his. Anyone else his age would have died instantly from these injuries. It's a miracle he is alive at all. He's what… one hundred and twenty years old? Hard to keep track with his time traveling trick and all."

She considered the news for a few seconds, took a deep breath to steady herself against the rising emotions, and straightened her shoulders. "Is he conscious?"

"He's under mild sedation, just sleeping for now. If you want to wait in the hall for a couple of minutes while we will finish up here and then you can come back in. You can talk to him if he wakes up."

Rocker, with Karmito and Tari at his side, pushed through the double door and joined Maripa standing in the brightly lit hallway watching through the glass window as the doctors completed their routines. He walked up beside her and placed a protective arm around her waist.

"Is there any hope?" The children stood on either side of them, each reaching for a hand.

Maripa simply shook her head, fighting back the tears welling up in her eyes. She refused to give in to sentimentality, for Karm's sake if not her own.

Two hours later, Karm's eyes fluttered and he turned his head to look at his family, his voice weak and gravely, barely managing a smile. "Guess I really messed up this time."

"Don't waste your energy, grandfather," cautioned Tari. "You need to rest so you can come home with us." She stood on tiptoes, reaching across the blanket to hook talons.

Karm reached over and patted his granddaughter's cheek. "Not this time, my sweet girl. I'm afraid we won't be taking any more fishing trips together."

Karm coughed weakly as he turned to Maripa. "No regrets, my dear. You are the joy of my life. I couldn't have been prouder if you were my blood daughter."

"I love you, too, old man." She took his hand and gently held it for several silent minutes.

Karm eventually removed his hand from Maripa's soft grip and reached out to Rocker. "I need to share something with you, Jontar. Come, take my hand." A deep blue glow began to surround Karm's form.

Rocker stood up from his chair and walked over to Karm's bedside. He grasped Karm's hand lightly in his own. "I'm here, my friend."

The glow extended to embrace Rocker as well as Karm. Its color fluctuated between the deep, sad blue and a more excited and somehow happier green. Rocker tried to release his grip, but found his hand frozen and unable to respond.

"What are you doing, Karm? What's happening?" In his mind, there was a flash of white.

A voice seemed to resonate from everywhere at once. *"Oh, this is nice. None of those artificial transcription errors to work around."*

Rocker awoke to find himself lying on the floor looking up into Maripa's worried face. His mind filled with images and rapid fire bits of information. He lifted his hand and saw the green glow surrounding it, and his entire body.

"I'm okay... I think." He sat up, holding his head as if it might explode. Maripa and Karmito helped him back onto his chair.

Karmito poured a cup of water from a nearby pitcher and handed it to Jontar. "What happened, father?"

Rocker continued to stare at his glowing arm. "I'm not entirely sure, but I think Karm transferred his biocomputer to me."

All four of them turned simultaneously toward Karm. "Can he do that?" asked Tari. Her voice cracked with fear.

The dying man managed a frail smile. "My gift to you." The blue glow continued to surround him, but it was fading. "The biocomputer knows I am dying and we talked it over. No, I'm not crazy. As you will soon learn, the computer communicates with me in many different ways. We've had many conversations over the years, but the most interesting ones have been in the past few months. I believe the feather-fluffed thing is actually evolving."

Rocker and Maripa exchanged glances, but said nothing.

Karm coughed feebly and winced in pain as he continued. "This marvel of technology cannot be lost. It is almost sentient in the way it communicates with me lately. We both reasoned that since I am your clone, and we share the same DNA, so the computer could adapt itself to your physiology. I guess it worked."

"You mean you weren't sure this would work?"

"No, but we were pretty certain. In time, you will get the hang of it. Just be careful not to lose yourself in the experience. I know how overwhelming the feelings can become. Take it slow at first and you'll be fine. I think it likes you." He pointed to the now steady green glow around Rocker's body.

"Does it hurt, father?" asked Tari as she extended one talon out to touch the aura surrounding him.

"No, Tari. I'm fine. Just a little tingle… and a strange buzzing in my ear."

Maripa stepped forward now and took Karm's hands. She placed them back onto the bed and lifted the blanket up to his chin.

"That's enough excitement for now. You need to get some rest. We'll be here when you wake up again." She carefully combed his sparse top crest with her talons, humming one of his favorite old tunes.

"All right, my dear, I am tired, so maybe I will try to get some shut eye for now." Karm closed his eyes and drifted off to sleep.

In moments, his breathing became irregular and rattled softly. Then his face relaxed and his chest settled as he exhaled his last breath. Maripa, Rocker, Karmito, and Tari embraced each other as tears streamed down their faces in silence.

The funeral followed a week later and, despite their objections, grew into a massive affair. Though Maripa and Rocker preferred a simpler, more private service, they recognized Karm's nearly mythical stature among the population. His body lay in state in the lobby of the newly constructed capital building. The mining guild provided the stone, something like marble, and dozens of craftsmen carved the intricate figures inside and out depicting their brief history on this new world. People filed past, paying their respect for two days. Representatives from all of the co-ops and guilds spoke eloquently during the final service. All of them referenced Karm's position as "The Savior" of the Brin and expressed their deepest sorrow to his family. Even the miner's guild seemed sincere in their eulogy. After the courts upheld the sentence against them they settled in to a less adversarial role in the Brin community. Rumors persisted, but nothing concrete ever surfaced.

As the sun set and a somber procession through the street lined with mourners, they laid Karm's body to rest nearby in the base of what would become a monument to the great man. Maripa and Rocker resisted the idea of a monument, but again relented under pressure from the people. The need to provide a lasting tribute proved too strong among those who revered him. At long last, the ceremonies and long lines of those wishing to extend their condolences dwindled enough for Maripa, Rocker, and their children to retire gracefully for the evening.

Back home again, Maripa excused herself and went off to the small room serving as her home office. Rocker approached the closed door, hoping to comfort his wife, but stopped when he heard her sobbing. He knew her too well to intrude on her need for privacy. Laying his palm against the door, he saw the blue glow return to his arm.

"Will that happen to me one day, too, father?"

Rocker turned to see Karmito looking at his own hand and pointing to the blue nimbus. "Only time will tell, son, but we share the same genes, so I think maybe yes."

The glow turned a bright green and in his mind he distinctly heard a voice. *"Looks like you might be nearly as smart as Karm believed."*

***

As he slept, Maliche stirred as the dream shifted, blurring into greyness, only to resolve itself in an entirely new time and place.

***

"Ten Year Anniversary Memorial Celebration!" announced the flyer in her hand. "Games, Parade, Food, and Fireworks!" A photo of Karm and the great stone statue over his tomb emblazoned the center of the leaflet.

"Can you believe it's been ten years?" Maripa asked. She passed the broadside to Rocker, placing the bouquet of flowers on the old Brin's tomb.

"Seems like only yesterday. We could use a little fun these days. What do you think about the reports of Caeri's village being deserted?"

"I don't like it. What could possibly have forced them out with no warning, and no communication?"

"I don't know. But I intend to find out."

"What are you talking about? Where do you think you're going?" Maripa planted her feet, hands firmly on her hips, and faced her husband.

"I'm on the next flight over to the village to try to find out where they went and why."

"You most certainly are not. We need you here, not gallivanting across the planet when others can do the job just as well. We don't know what happened. For all we know they were attacked and carried off somewhere." Her green eyes blazed with absolute certainty and finality.

Rocker stood his ground as he confronted Maripa. "The mining guild reports indicate no signs of violence. In fact, photos of the village look so normal it's as if they just vanished all at once. I need to find out what happened to them."

Her voice took on the calm deadliness he knew all too well. "No, you don't. In fact, I am going before the council today to insist upon a total ban on all transportation and exploration across the ocean to be effective immediately."

Rocker fumbled for a moment, trying to comprehend Maripa's declaration. "What do you mean, 'ban all transportation'? We have to figure out where they went. We owe it to them."

Maripa softened her stance and reached out to Rocker. "Jontar, we have no idea what happened over there. If we go stumbling around who knows what we might find. There's a lot we still don't know about that part of the planet, or even our own neighborhood for that matter. We still have no idea who or what built those ruins, and they're less than one hundred km away. If we expose ourselves to some hostile force before our own defenses are ready, then we are opening ourselves to the same fate. I can't allow that to happen."

"Are you telling me that you want us to abandon our friends?"

"For now, yes," she replied. "At least until we can build up our ability to defend ourselves against whatever is out there. Once we are stronger, then we can go looking for them. You haven't forgotten Karm's warning about enemies from the sky, have you? It's haunted me for years. Every time one of us goes up in one of those shuttles I worry some disaster will strike us again. Besides, you've heard the anti-native contingent. They're growing stronger every year."

She walked over to the carved murals on the wall surrounding Karm's memorial. She reached out to touch the stone wall depicting Karm leading her and Rocker into the Hegira II.

"For once, I agree with the mining guild. They can continue operations on the eastern continent and provide advance warning if their security forces discover anything. If we don't stop now, limiting further contamination over there, who knows what damage may result. I'm afraid some of the miners may be behind some of the disappearances, but there's no proof. The quetzals and their guards won't allow anyone near their operations, claiming the mines are too dangerous for untrained visitors."

Rocker shook his head. "Maripa, I've seen you charge into a fight with nothing more than a small knife. You've never been afraid of anything. What are you not telling me?"

Maripa turned her back to Rocker and stood rigidly, fists clenched at her side. "I can't lose you the way we lost Karm. If you go over there and whatever got Vidad, Neas and the rest of them got you, too, I couldn't live knowing I should have stopped you. With Karmito off on his own and married now—I just couldn't survive without you."

Before Rocker could respond, his palm glowed a reddish-pink. He stopped, listening to the voice in his head. A moment later, his eyes focused again and he knew what he must do.

"It seems my friend up here," he said pointing to his head, "agrees with you. I can't fight both of you, so let's go talk with the council."

The mining guild representatives spoke convincingly in favor of the travel ban. Since the lifting of their restrictions three years ago, the discovery of important mineral deposits across the ocean made this a wealthy and powerful group, and the others eventually gave in under pressure from them, their allies, and Maripa. Maripa reassured the ranchers and farmers guilds of her intent to open up new sections of this continent for their use in exchange for their support of the ban. Additional votes gave responsibility for the eastern continent to the mining guild, complete with sole rights to transport any and all minerals discovered in the region. The news of the travel prohibition was initially unpopular, but the oppositions soon lost steam among the preparations for the grand celebration to come.

The ten-year anniversary celebration became a grand affair lasting three days. The speeches given at the foot of Karm's memorial (a twenty-foot-tall statue of the great man) roused the people in their patriotism and sense of duty to the community. Since most of the people never traveled more than a hundred kilometers from home anyway, the ban produced minimal disruption to daily life. Within a couple of month's few people even remembered the ban, or felt any remorse at the loss of contact with those across the ocean. The influx of so many riches made everyone's life more comfortable.

***

Another shift in perspective of the dream woke Maliche. The dark room was quiet, except for the Kolandi guard's soft snoring from the chair nearby.

"Not yet, my friend. There is more to show you before I let you go. Rest now. Let me continue." Sleep overtook Maliche once more.

***

Rocker sat silently by Maripa's bedside. Her tiny, frail form barely created a disturbance in the thick blankets covering her. Wrinkled, with only the faintest wisp of a silver top crest, her eyes still retained their old intensity and strength. He held her small, aged hand, his shoulders and head bowed by time and sorrow, whispering to his dying wife.

"Twenty-two years to the day since Karm's passing. We've traveled quite the journey together, my love." He heard the door open softly behind him, but did not look to see who entered.

"Father," Karmito said quietly walking to Rocker's side. "How is she doing today?" The young man, now in his late forties and mayor of the town, pulled up a chair to join his father.

The old geneticist gave a weak smile acknowledging his son, but never looked away from Maripa's peaceful sleep. "She's resting peacefully, but there's nothing more the doctors can do. She's a fighter, but it's just a matter of time now. Her cloned DNA, while stronger than Karm's, still proved faulty enough to shorten her life-span by a couple of decades." He continued to watch his wife's face for any sign of rousing from her sleep.

"Elarc and I are glad you brought mother home. She never did like hospitals. Can I get you anything? You look like you could use some breakfast."

"You know how proud we are of you, don't you?" asked Jontar, still refusing to look away from Maripa.

"I know, father. I'll go down and fix you something. Maybe then you would like to get a bit of rest. Oh, I spoke to Tari and she will come to visit you this afternoon." Karmito patted Rocker's shoulder and left the room, closing the door gently behind him.

Rocker stroked his wife's thin grey crest as she slept. "He's become quite the young man, my love, and now a family of his own. Where did the time go?"

Maripa stirred and opened her eyes. "Jontar?"

"I'm here, Maripa. I'm not going anywhere."

She smiled weakly at him and squeezed his hand. "You may not be, but I'm afraid I am, my husband." She coughed and blanched at the effort.

"Don't try to talk, dear. You need to conserve your strength."

"And what good will that do?" She gave Rocker one of her famous glares. "I know what the doctors are saying. I need to talk to you while I still can." With an effort, Maripa shifted onto her side so she could face her husband more easily. "I need to talk to you about my decision to stop you from going out to find our friends across the ocean."

Rocker shook his head, fighting to keep the tears out of his eyes at the memory of the many fierce arguments between them on this matter.

"No, I understand. You were right. We needed to see to our own safety first. You made the right decision."

Smiling weakly, she patted his hand. "Yes, I did, but things are different now. I know the burden of not knowing what happened has never left you. The old scientist in you needs to discover the truth of it all. You will never be satisfied until you go and search for them."

Rocker fought back the lump in his throat. "That doesn't matter now. I can't leave you."

"Jontar," she said, mustering as much irritation in her voice as she could. "I'm dying. We both know the facts. I can no longer hold you to your promise. Go and find our friends. Learn what happened to them. Our people are ready now if the worst happens."

"Maripa, we can talk about this later. It's not important now."

Maripa, gripped his hand tighter, closed her eyes and gritted her teeth. Rocker wiped the beads of sweat from her forehead as the pain eased.

"There will not be any 'later', Jontar. I've already talked to Karmito about this and he will talk to the council to grant you permission to go on this quest. You and your biocomputer are the best chance we have of learning the truth. We are ready. We need to know what happened so we can face whatever dangers may be out there. Just promise me one thing."

"Anything, my love."

"Don't let them build any kak monument over me like they did to poor Karm. I'm no savior, and I certainly don't want any idiots fawning over me like they do at his silly statue."

Rocker bent over and gently kissed her on the forehead. "I promise."

A week later, the funeral procession, second only to Karm's service, preceded through the dusty streets. At its conclusion, they laid Maripa to rest in a simple grave next to Karm's. A small, plain marble headstone placed over her read:

Maripa Rocker
Loving Wife and Mother
Our Guardian

For the next few weeks, Dr. Jontar Rocker sat by the gravesite talking to his wife. People passing by were struck by the scene, especially the soft blue glow surrounding the grieving man.

***

"One more story to tell and then we can talk." The voice resounded in Maliche's mind as the vision jumped once more.

***

Flying far above the desert, Rocker looked down onto as bleak a scene as existed anywhere on Raince'to. Rock and sand as far as the eye could see, broken only rarely with the grey-green of lonely scrub struggling to survive the harsh environment. Two weeks of flying over the remotest regions of this forbidding place revealed nothing of the missing natives.

"Are you sure this is where they are?" Rocker asked out loud. He accepted the biocomputer as another sentient entity now and often spoke to it. Communicating by thought alone was sufficient, but somehow it just seemed more natural this way. At first, the biocomputer chided him over the cumbersome nature of speech, but now accepted the method as one of Rocker's many personal quirks.

"Yes, I'm sure," the device replied. *"You don't think I'm so fond of sand to bring you here on vacation do you? Be patient. I am sensing them now. We are very close."*

Without warning, the shuttle shook violently, lurching to starboard. "What the strix?" cursed Rocker as he fought for control. Flashing lights and alarms signaled on the control panel. Flying over the southern desert, always difficult even under ideal conditions, but now suddenly became life threatening. The dunes rose up from below at a startling rate. The glaring sun vanished into blackness as Rocker's shuttle slammed into the ground.

***

Awareness slowly crept into Rocker's consciousness. His head pounded mercilessly, his entire body ached. Opening his eyes required a nearly inhuman effort. *I'm alive?* Straw crunched as he shifted his position and he looked up at the inside of a thatched roof. *Where the strix am I? How did I get here?* He attempted to sit up, but a wave of nausea and pain coursed through him and he collapsed back onto the bed. He heard the shuffling of feet on dirt and the soft gasp of a woman.

"So, you are alive after all, Doctor Rocker." The woman knelt next to him and wiped his face gently with a cool wet cloth. "My name is Lomyl, granddaughter of Caeri and Vidad. You are in my village now."

Rocker managed to turn his head, painfully, to see his caregiver. "How did I get here?"

"Ten days ago, my people saw your flying craft crash and found you. They brought you here to me as soon as they realized who you were. Rest now, we will talk more when you are better."

As Rocker drifted off, he noticed she wore the golden amulet with the green gem at its center. He relaxed, knowing he was among friends.

Three days later, Rocker felt remarkably well. His head and body no longer felt as if they had been crushed beneath a ten-ton stone.

"Did you have something to do with my miraculous recovery?" he mentally asked his biocomputer.

"Of course," it replied. *"I almost lost you a few times, but managed to pull you through. I even succeeded in repairing a few other malfunctions you were developing."*

Before he could reply, Lomyl, the village princess and heir to Caeri's throne, reappeared through the entryway.

"Good morning Doctor Rocker. You appear to be nearly cured today. Is it common for your kind to heal so rapidly? Your wounds would have taken one of us months to recover from."

"I'm not sure I can explain what happened, either. Where are your grandparents? I want to thank them for my rescue as well."

Lomyl closed her eyes briefly before responding. "Sadly, they have passed on to the spirit world. Five years ago, after bringing us to this new village they succumbed to the passing of their years. I am now leader of my people." She thought for a moment before continuing. "I remember you, Doctor, from your visits to our homes so many years ago. I was a child, but I remember you clearly. You seem unchanged by the years. Or are we mistaken and you are not The Rocker, but merely his offspring?"

Rocker laughed at her observations. "I thank you for your kindness to an old man, my dear. I can assure you that I am the same man who visited you in those long ago times. Surely this face shows the passing of the decades."

Lomyl's face contorted in confusion, but decided to hold off further questions. "We can discuss this matter later. For now, though, we must get you cleaned up. You were too fragile for us to do much before now. But we must wash you now, before you start attracting scavengers." She called for the waiting attendants who entered carrying bowls of water, towels, changes of clothes shaving implements and a mirror. "We will leave you now to attend to your cleansing, unless you require assistance."

Rocker stood to accept the items. "No, I can manage. Thank you," He grabbed the mirror and nearly dropped to the ground when he saw the reflection. Staring back at him was not the familiar face of recent years, but that of the younger man who once owned this body, more than four decades ago.

***

*"S*urprise,*"* said the voice in his head. Rocker's entire body flared up in a bright green glow.

Chapter Twelve

"He's waking up now, Princess."

"Thank you, Lejenal. You should go have something to eat now. I will be fine."

Lejenal bowed and left the alcove. Maliche watched through blurry eyes as the princess approached, a slight tingling like a static charge building in his mind, hovered in the back of his brain.

"What happened? Are you all right?"

He sat up, suddenly realizing most of his pain was gone, and everything seemed to be in good working order. "How long have I been out?"

Ryma took two of his talons in her fingers as she sat on the cot next to him, her pale yellow dress rustling softly with the movement. "The incident in the tomb was only yesterday. Was that truly The Rocker who joined with us? Are the visions real? Are you one of his descendants?" She trembled slightly, her eyes barely hiding the fear.

Maliche sat quietly, letting the memories coalesce. His left palm began to glow and the tingling strengthened, his eyes grew vacant.

"Don't try to figure it all out at once. I'll sort it all out for you in time. Let yourself heal a bit longer. There was a lot of damage to repair. It's enough right now for you to know that I am the device originally implanted in Karm, but passed along to Jontar Roker, and now to you. Jontar died without producing an heir, at least not where I could get to them. I've been trapped here until now. The medallion created the initial link between us. Your genetic markers were close enough to his to allow me to send you

the visions, as you call them, and guide you on this journey. When you touched the tomb I was able to use the Kolandi amulet and your medallion to connect myself to your neural network."

"What about before? I've had this compulsion about my family's history since I was a small child."

"Oh, that. Lots of members of your family are interested in your history. I've been sending out that general impulse for generations. You were the first to have markers strong enough to take hold of. While I slept I was able to meddle in your subconscious for years. That artifact in the desert awakened me when you touched it. The medallion solidified the connection, and now here I am."

Maliche's eyes refocused on the princess as the voice in his mind faded. He raised his left palm and watched as the glow subsided. "This is extraordinary. I seem to be the host for some sort of biological computer entity. I've heard strange tales of my ancestor and Karm having some strange abilities, but we always brushed them off as mythology. I think we may have been mistaken."

The princess looked skeptical. "But I was affected, too. I do not seem to have this entity you speak of. And I certainly do not glow the way you do ever since the incident. I have no choice but to believe you since the visions I saw are undeniable, but…" She searched his face for answers.

Maliche thought for a moment. "Let me try something." He closed his eyes and concentrated.

"Not now. It is too soon to know for sure if my experiment worked well enough, but I am very hopeful. Neither of you needs to know about it yet, so don't bother trying to find out. I can keep a secret very well. She is unharmed and will suffer no lingering effects. Even the memory of the visions will fade with time."

"No good. My friend in here…" He tapped his head with one talon. "…seems to have some secrets he doesn't want to share. All he would say is that you and I are part of some experiment of his, but you will be fine. Sorry."

Ryma dropped his talons and stood, stepping away a few paces, her brow furrowed in thought. "I am uncomfortable with this entity of yours using me in some experiment." She paced the floor again, mumbling to herself, hands gesturing with the argument raging in her. Turning to face Maliche, she stood tall, squared her shoulders, and placed her hands on her hips. "However, and I don't know how I know this, but I do, everything you say is true. Our legends also tell us of The Rocker's mysterious abilities. His tomb is reputed to be a source of inspiration, some even claim to have heard ghostly voices. While your story seems unbelievable, I know, down to my spirit, the truth of it all. We have much to discuss, you and I, Maliche Rocker. Rest now. Tomorrow we begin."

***

In the days that followed, Maliche heard the tales of the Kolandi. Many of the Kolandi warriors argued against a Brin, even if he was a Rocker, participating in the ritual, but the princess silenced them and escorted Maliche to the ceremony herself. The elder Homsan told the stories of the tribe dating back centuries, to the days of Jontar Rocker. Sitting in a room far in the back of the cave, one covered in sacred and historical drawings, flickering in the wavering orange glow of the fire pit, the leaders beat on sticks and rocks, keeping rhythm as the Homsan recited the legends around the fire. The sweet smell of burning wood filled the air.

"And when The Rocker lived among us for a span of ten seasons, our people prospered. Our numbers grew, and all were happy. Then, the Brin descended upon us. They came with chains and weapons of great power, and enslaved us. The Brin spared none. They carried off the women and children, along with the men over the mountains and across the great desert to work in their mines. Even The Rocker was helpless against them."

At this, the elders stopped their drumming. Their heads lowered, hands covering their faces, they began a wailing cry full of deep sadness. This continued for a few minutes when the Homsan raised his head and the rhythm resumed.

"Many attempts to rescue our people came to death and ruin. It was then that The Rocker gathered the few who remained and took us to this hidden canyon of caves. We remained safe for many years, though our numbers were few. The Rocker continued to search far and wide, gathering the scattered remnants of our people together, until even he could no longer stave off time. We built his tomb according to the very design he himself prescribed."

The drumming ceased again and all the elders raised their faces and hands to the ceiling of the cave. The solitary voice of the princess lifted high and clear in a song of praise for The Rocker. When she finished, the elders again continued their pulse.

"And now, when the Brin once again threaten our people with their new mine so close to our caves, The Rocker sends us his descendant to protect us and deliver us from our enslavement. The prophecy is fulfilled."

All eyes focused on Maliche Rocker, heir to the Jontar Rocker legacy. If any doubted his claim to the title, the blue glow surrounding him silenced their objections. Many still muttered amongst themselves, and cast unfriendly gestures his way behind his back, but his claim was indisputable.

"I thought I told you to stop doing this." Maliche, after much practice and rebuke from the computer entity, finally accustomed himself to talking to the biocomputer by thought alone. He always felt talking out loud clarified his thoughts, but he was getting better with practice.

"They need to know who you are. We are going to need their absolute trust if you want to help free them from your compatriots. Besides, I think it looks rather stunning. Blue is definitely your color." A flicker of green joined in with the blue, as if the entity was laughing at him.

Chapter Thirteen

The funeral, a private affair at the request of the family, ended an hour before. Selan sat alone by the empty grave of his brother. The sun shone overhead and a flock of smats flitted through the branches of nearby trees singing their mating songs. The scent of hundreds of flowers, mementos of well-wishers, filled the air with a confused mix of aromas. None of this intruded on Selan's despondency. Wiping a tear away, he stood, walked to the large granite headstone, and rested his hand on the ornately carved family crest. An animated holographic image of Maliche's smiling face filled a central hole carved into the stone.

"I'm sorry, Maliche. I never intended for this to happen." He bowed his head, patted the engraved stone and left to join the others at the public memorial service convening at the Assembly.

The eulogies prattled on for three hours. The head of each guild took his or her turn at the podium to praise the life of the young archeologist and lament his untimely passing in such a pointless pursuit. Of course, they were all very politically correct in their choice of words, but the message was clearly there. Maliche was a disappointment, but he was a Rocker and thus deserving of at least public mourning. At the end, Fejf, and Ceila, both clearly distraught at the loss of their eldest son, thanked the dignitaries for their comforting words, ending the ceremony.

"Walk with me, Selan." Raencert's voice whispered in Selan's ear as the large guildsman leaned close.

"I don't have anything to say to you, Raencert." Selan attempted to move away.

"I beg to differ. We have a great deal to discuss." Raencert took Selan's arm and guided him through the crowd, eventually to one of the secluded garden atriums in the center of the building.

"How could you have been so stupid? Murdering him, even if it looks like an accident, is too big a risk. I thought we agreed on this." Selan turned his back to Raencert, raking his crest with the talons of one hand. "He did not have to die."

Raencert studied the young Brin, like a lepti about to strike its prey. "We need to talk. It is time you learned the truth of the matter."

Selan whirled around, talons flared. "What are you talking about? We could have simply arrested him for exceeding his permits!"

Raencert laughed. "And you think arresting him would have controlled him? Come now, Selan, you know your brother. You know he would have used his influence to get back out there to look for his treasures. We could not risk his stumbling across our operations. Get in the mag-lev. I need to show you something." He pulled out a large cigar and lit it, blowing clouds of grey smoke into the air. Inside the vehicle, Raencert handed Selan a locked metal strongbox. "Open it. I coded the lock to your retinal pattern and DNA sequence"

"I don't have time for your games, Raencert. What is this?"

The guildsman simply gestured toward the box with a monstrous hand. Selan held his eye to the scanner, licked one talon placing it into the receptacle in the lid, and opened the box. His jaw dropped and he froze, not willing to accept what he saw in the 3-D photos.

"What is this? It looks like our mine, but those aren't Brin miners… they're not even Brin. What are these creatures?"

"You're looking at the reason why the minerals are so reasonably priced." Raencert blew another thick cloud of smoke into the air. "For centuries, the guild has kept this secret. The natives, the Kolandi, never went extinct. We have kept them hidden from the Brin populace to use as laborers. Only a select few trusted individuals know this guild secret. You have just joined their ranks."

Selan let the photos slip from his talons back into the box. "All this time… the Kolandi still live? How is this even possible?"

"Over two hundred years ago, the first great plague nearly did wipe them all out. Our ancestors, or at least the original guild leaders, unwittingly helped spread the disease when we tried to enlist their help locating and extracting the minerals. While most of them died, our guild soon discovered a few scattered tribes roaming the deserts. We gathered them together and helped them recover. At first, we paid them to work the mines with the supplies they needed to survive. Before long, we couldn't release them without severely hurting our operations. A few well-padded government officials wrote the laws restricting travel to the eastern continent and the rest, as they say, is history."

"But it's been centuries… how has word of this not gotten out?"

"I'm as surprised as you are. The guilds must be favored by The Eternal." He chuckled at that bit of irony. "We keep the miners on the eastern continent with land grants and high wages to keep them and their families over there, and all communications are strictly controlled. Personally, I think we've been lucky as strix."

Selan jerked upright and stared at Raencert. "So why tell me? And why now?"

Raencert's laugh dripped with satisfaction. "Why not? You're one of us now. You still think your brother's accident wasn't necessary? Besides, we did give him every opportunity to turn back. Our operative warned him several times and suggested alternative sites to dig, but Maliche was stubborn. He was determined to keep going east. He was too much of a threat."

"I never agreed to this." Selan's shoulders slumped, he folded his arms around his chest, his eyes fell to the ground. "Maliche and I disagreed and fought about many things, Raencert, but he was my brother. He didn't need to die."

Raencert's eyes narrowed, his crest twitched and stood fully erect. He clenched tight to the cigar in his mouth. "You're not going soft on me now, are you? That would be very unwise."

"Will you have me killed, too? Do you think you are so far above the law you can do as you wish without consequence?"

"You underestimate me, lad. There's nothing to connect me to any of this, while I have documented verification of your advanced knowledge of the plan. All you have is speculation. Nothing that would stand up in a court. Anything you do would look like a grieving brother lashing out in some desperate attempt to lay blame. Your disgrace would work far better for me than your death."

"And what about my knowledge about your mining operations and the Kolandi? What would happen to you if the Assembly became aware of how you are conducting your business over there?"

"Once again, you lack the proof. Where is your evidence? I kept you on the fringe for many reasons, Selan. I never have trusted you enough to bring you in far enough for you to have anything other than hearsay and rumor. Besides, you have no idea how strong of a grip greed has on the average Brin. Given the choice between mineral prices going sky high, or ignoring the unsupported claims of even somebody from your family, they will choose their purses every time."

"I can get the evidence. All I have to do is turn over these images of the mine sites and they will have to believe me."

"Those can be easily dismissed as doctored images produced by conspiracy theorists. Over the years, the few hints which have leaked out only helped feed the imagination of believers, while your average Brin laughs at them. We couldn't have asked for a better cover story. Besides, who do you think controls the other guilds? Are you so naïve to believe any of them are willing to risk exposing their own illegal activities for this? Think again lad, you are beaten. Accept your situation and join the flock."

Selan slumped into one of the nearby benches and sat, hands folded in his lap and head bowed. Raencert reached out one large hand and placed it on Selan's shoulder.

"I figured you would see the reason of it all. You were always a bright young Brin. By the way, keep the images."

***

"How could I have been so blind? That conniving quetzal!" Selan seethed as the door to his private office slammed behind him. He went immediately to the large safe, allowed the scanner to read his face, pressed the code to open it, and placed the metal box inside. As he punched the locking code he caught a movement near the doorway. He relaxed and took firm control of his anger as he realized it was only his wife approaching.

"Nedia, what are you doing here? I thought you were with mother."

"I was, my husband, but I saw your agitation from her window and came to see if there was anything I could do to ease your sorrow."

He shook his head and took her talons in his. Our fathers made a wise choice when they arranged for our joining. You are a fine treasure, but this is something I must handle myself."

"Maliche knows you loved him, despite all of your disagreements. He would not want you to feel guilt or regret at any unfortunate last words you may have had."

Selan reached in and gave Nedia a lingering peck on her crest. "I know that, but it is still hard. Go now, I have some things to arrange before the day is over. Tell the children I will be up to see them later."

"Yes, my husband." She returned a kiss to his cheek and gently closed the carved wooden doors behind her.

Alone again, Selan's face turned red and his crest twitched with rage. "I can't afford to let Raencert take control like this. If I'm ever to lead the Assembly, then I need to be the one with all the secrets."

Selan picked up the communicator and touched a single button on the keypad. "It's time to activate Syrinx."

Chapter Fourteen

Hundreds of skeletal Kolandi, men, women, and children hauled rock and dug trenches in this section of the open pit. Unlike most mines, here the minerals were found close to the surface. Most of the slaves wore only the shredded remains of what was once clothing. The crack of whips echoed off the canyon walls, blood flowed from the fresh wounds on their backs, regardless of age or gender. Bare footed, they struggled to haul woven baskets of minerals out of the pit to the processing plant a mile away. The procession of slaves travelled this circuit endlessly day and night in two shifts.

From his perch high up in the canyon wall, Maliche surveyed the scene below. Sweat dripped from his face, his crest hung limp and wet, clouds of dust choked his lungs even at the height of his hidden cave.

"How can they continue to work like that in this heat? I can barely breathe up here." He drank again from the clay jar of water he and each of his guides carried. He winced as a Brin miner beat on another of the Kolandi for dropping his basket of rocks.

"What choice do they have?" Danet, the young warrior chosen to lead Maliche to this observation point replied through clenched teeth. "Your kind makes our lives a misery, but we Kolandi do not surrender. We live each day in the hope of gaining our freedom and taking revenge on the Brin who enslave us." He spat on the ground and turned his back to Maliche. Wearing only leather breeches, the deep scars etching his back reminded Maliche of Danet's recent escape from this very mine.

"Not all Brin are like these. Most of us are completely unaware of your existence. We thought you all went extinct centuries ago."

Danet snorted and then threw his hands wide. "Then you must all be blind fools." He stormed off into the darkness of the tunnels, cursing as he went.

A soft hand touched Maliche's back. "Do not worry about Danet. He is young and full of anger, but he will learn the truth of things as he comes to know you, Great One." Tikae, one of Ryma's attendants, sent as the princesses' emissary so no harm would come to Maliche accidentally, spoke gently. Her short, tattered dress clung to her body with sweat. "I have watched you closely in your talks with the princess. I know she trusts you, and so do I. The others will see your true nature in time." She smiled at him, but her eyes filled with tears as she watched the scene below.

Maliche attempted a smile in return. "Thanks, but I'm not sure we have enough time left. We have to do something to end this atrocity now."

"Great One, you are The Rocker. You will know what to do to save us. I must talk to Danet and try to soothe his anger." Tikae bowed and followed Danet back into the tunnel to their camp. The others should begin the meal preparations soon and her supervision was required.

As Maliche watched the mining operations, his mind wandered to thoughts of Ryma. He could feel her touch. Her voice soothed his agitation. The blue of her eyes reminded him of the sky on a bright spring day back home. A scream and another whip crack jolted Maliche out of his daydream.

He scratched at the itch in his palm. "Kak! Stop that you idiot." He looked around embarrassed, hoping nobody noticed his reaction to the daydream. The two remaining guides had their backs to him so he let out a sigh of relief. *I must be some sort of deviant or something. It can't be normal to keep having thoughts like these about someone of another species. Even if she is beautiful.*

A chuckle echoed in Maliche's head. *"Don't be so sure of that."* The biocomputer's voice laughed at him. *"You just relax and start working on a plan to rescue the Kolandi."*

***

"He cannot be trusted! He will betray us the first chance he gets. He is not one of us and cannot be part of this raid." Danet and Opet paced, thrusting their spear to the sky as the council debated plans for a raid on a Brin outpost.

"Have you no eyes? Are your ears closed? The Rocker has come to us as the prophecies foretold. I, myself have heard The Rocker and seen the visions. Maliche may not be of our flesh, but he is of our spirit." The princess sat on her carved stone throne hands folded in her lap. "His knowledge of the Brin and their technology could bring us a great advantage. He must be allowed to participate in this attack."

Arguments broke out on both sides of the issue around the fire. Their frantic shadows bounced on the cave walls as their voices reverberated into a cacophony. In the end, Maliche gained permission to join the raiding party, but only in the capacity of a fledgling to stay behind and care for the camp while the warriors conducted the actual foray.

In the morning, Maliche reluctantly accepted his role and collected weapons from the blacksmith. Located under a large overhang in the cliffside, and disguised with hanging vines, brush and other natural features. The smith was an essential aspect of life in the caverns. Hanging on the walls, Maliche saw all manner of metal pots, utensils and personal ornaments as well as spears, knives and other weapons. The blacksmith stood bare-chested over his forge, sweating in the heat even on this chill morning, directing the efforts of two apprentices.

Maliche examined a long, curved knife. "This is incredible workmanship. How do you make such intricate engravings on the blade like this?" He ran his thumb along one edge, drawing a fine line of blood.

The smith grunted, glancing his way. "That one is a poor example, Brin. A first year apprentice practiced on it. No time for true craftsmanship any more with the war coming." The smith's eyes focused on the amulet around Maliche's neck and his smile grew as he pointed to it. "Perhaps, one day, when all this war nonsense is over, you'll let me take a closer gander at that beauty. Tales are told of great craftsmen of the past who worked such intricate and beautiful ornaments as this one. Maybe I can tease some of the old secrets out of your treasure there and create something worthwhile for a change."

Maliche removed the medallion and handed it to the blacksmith. "It would be my pleasure to help you in any way I can, master smith."

The large man, after quickly rubbing the worst of the soot off his hands, turned it over reverently in his grasp examining closely the intricate details of the engravings before handing it back.

With a wave of his scarred and calloused hand, the man returned to his forge. "You best be off to your duties now."

As directed, Maliche returned to camp with the armaments and helped pack the supplies they would require. Several of the warriors spat their disapproval as they threw their bundles at his feet and scuffed dirt in his face, or roughly shouldered him aside as they passed by. Maliche grumbled as he bent to pick up the bags.

"Stop those thoughts right now," commanded the voice in his head. *"This is a very delicate time for us, and my plans. Don't get us both killed by acting stupid."*

Maliche's thoughts turned to a variety of unpleasant responses to the biocomputer, but he continued to accept the abuse. A light blue glow surrounded him, softening his mood, and causing the remaining warriors to simply deposit their packs and move along without comment.

"Are you truly The Rocker?" A boy, not yet old enough to train as a warrior, helped Maliche organize the camp supplies stared wide-eyed at him.

Maliche smiled at the youth, straining a bit as he lifted a heavy pack. "No, I'm not The Rocker. My name is Maliche. I am a descendant of his, though."

"But you have his sign." The boy reached out as if to touch the blue glow, withdrawing his hand just short of its edge. "All the stories tell of this sign. You must be him."

Maliche held his hand up to allow the boy a closer look at the glow. "My ancestor's abilities seem to have passed to me when I touched his tomb. I am not him, but I hope I can prove just as worthy of your people's trust."

The princess, observing from a distance, watched Maliche talk with the fledgling. She lifted one hand to her breast, smiled, and her eyes unfocused for a moment as if lost in a beautiful dream.

"All is ready for our departure, Princess. My men await your blessing."

Ryma startled awake from her reverie, clasped her hands, and followed Opet to the assembly point.

***

The dust stung his eyes and throat as Maliche and the other fledglings followed the warriors along the desert trail. Hidden by low ridges and dry ravines, the party reached their final staging point and began to set up camp. The men set out scouts and perimeter guards while the fledglings managed the packs, extra weapons, small cooking fire, and other necessities. Under the watchful eyes of a couple of the more experienced women, sent on this expedition by the princess personally to be her eyes and ears, and

Maliche's protectors, the campsite quickly became a hive of organized activity.

Maliche, assigned to feed the drunges, two scrawny pack animals brought along to help carry the raid's plunder back to the caves, stared at the starry sky.

"Are you sure about this?" he asked the biocomputer. *"It may take a lifetime to overcome the hatred those warriors have toward me. How will I ever be able to gain their trust if this is all they let me do?"*

"Trust me. Your chance will come sooner than you think."

Maliche felt a soothing calm envelop him as the blue glow faded to green.

After breakfast, the raiding party left camp, leaving only the fledglings behind. A few of the older boys and women took up their positions as scouts to watch for danger, and the returning warriors. As Maliche puttered around the camp cleaning up after the morning meal, he tried to ignore the angry looks and chatter among the women, his thoughts turned inward. *Maybe if I understood their language as well as they understand Brin I might be able to convince them of my intentions.*

"I think I can help you there. It should only take a few adjustments to your brain's language processing center."

Maliche's skull began to itch. Slightly at first, but quickly intensified and focused in his left cortex as if thousands of nits were feasting inside his head. A wave of vertigo washed over him and he found he could suddenly understand the Kolandi women.

"… should never have let him live. He is a danger to all of us."

"But the princess supports him and claims he is to be trusted."

"I was there. I saw the blue flames around them both. Who knows what evil sorcery was worked on our princess."

"But he is The Rocker. He is not like the others. I have watched him."

"I am not convinced. What does he want with us? Why is he here?"

Maliche smiled and walked over to the gathered women. "For now, I want to finish washing the dishes. Do you have any more for me to bring to the stream?"

They stared, mouths gaping, as he reached down to gather up the pots and utensils among them.

"Thank you ladies. I hope someday you will learn to trust me. I am here to undo the evil my people have brought to yours." He bowed and went about his chores as the group erupted into a new and even more excited debate.

A little over two hours later, after much of the commotion over his learning to speak Kolandi died down, three of the scouts charged back into camp, breathless and covered in scratches from their hasty flight through the scrub brush.

"We must flee! The Brin are headed this way!"

Neri, the first of the princess' aides, gathered the youths. "We must take what we can and hide. Time is short." She pointed to one of the boys. "You, Gatel, find the men and tell them what has happened. We will head west, back toward the caves. They can find us along the trail there." She watched as the boy bowed and ran off, dust flying from his heels.

Maliche felt his head swim. The desert faded from his sight as images and thoughts filled his mind.

"This is your chance. I can sense the Brin who approach. They are not aware of this camp and have no advance scouts. Follow my lead and you can start to gain the hearts of many who want to trust you."

Tactical images filled Maliche's mind and he saw how to position the fledglings and entrap the approaching Brin party. As the world returned into focus, he went to Neri and explained his plan to capture the Brin.

"Are you sure of this, Great One?" Neri and Rilo, Neri's young trainee, exchanged glances. "Most of these boys are not trained in battle. Rilo and I have some skills in order to protect the princess, but how can we hope to win over a group of Brin? Their weapons are too much for us without our warriors."

"You are far too modest, Neri. I've seen you practicing. You're no stranger to combat. Rilo and the other, what is your group called, Skatak? Your fighting skills are among the best I've ever seen. And that blade you all carry. It is an incredible weapon in your hands. I think you are more than a match for these Brin."

Neri straightened her shoulders and gave a predatory look toward Maliche. "The Skatak are an ancient group, sworn to protect the princess even at the cost of our own lives. The battle forms you have observed are only the public face we provide. The skills of the finest of us are born from years of training in secret enclaves. Our kital is the emblem of our oath to the princess and her royal line." She pulled the blade free from its strap at her belt and held it up for Maliche to examine.

Whistling his admiration, Maliche raised his hands wide and lowered his face in respect. "Maybe someday I could learn a few tricks from you."

Neri let out a soft laugh. "Not unless you woke up as a female Kolandi, sir Brin. Tell me more of this great plan of yours."

Maliche took a stick and outlined his plan in the dirt. "Those Brin are not soldiers, they are miners. Yes, they have weapons, but if we catch them unaware they will not be able to use them. You see, if they follow the path, they will come to this narrow gap in the ravine. It is then we shall…"

The miners trudged single-file through the narrow section of the path. Their heavy packs barely fitting between the rocks. Two guards, one in front, and one behind provided security.

"Stop! Help me!" Maliche ran up to the front guard, as if in fear of his life. His garments torn and filthy, gave the appearance of one lost for days in the desert. He stumbled, grabbing onto the guard's jacket, nearly pulling him to the ground. "Don't let them get me!"

The guard tried to unsling his particle beam rifle, but Maliche's struggles prevented him from getting a grip on the weapon. "Stand up, you quetzal. Who are you and why aren't you at the mine?"

Maliche continued his wild-eyed pleas, pointing frantically back down the ravine behind him. "They're right behind me. Please, you've got to help me." Grasping at the guard's jacket, Maliche collapsed to the ground. Only this time, as the guard bent with the weight, Maliche seized the beam rifle, yanked it over the guard's head, and pointed it at him, a talon poised over the firing contact. He stood upright, aiming at the miner's chest. "Don't move."

The miner turned as a startled cry came from the other guard. There stood Neri, her kital, the curved, triple bladed weapon of the Skatak, guardians of the princess, pressed against his throat. The Brin slowly removed his weapon as ordered, handing it to one of the older fledglings who accompanied Neri.

Maliche aimed the rifle at each member of the trapped group of miners. "Let's not have any heroes today. If you look up, you'll see we have you well covered." All eyes went up to the rim of the ravine. Seven grim-faced fledglings, led by Rilo, aimed an assortment of spears and bows at the captives.

The first guard took a step forward, halting as the barrel of Maliche's rifle pointed at his face. His crest reddened as he glared at Maliche. Each miner was relieved of his pack, and all other belongings including beam pistols, food, maps, and tools. Their hands tied behind them, and a rope connecting one neck to the next prevented any chance of escape.

"You can't do this. Who are you, and why are you, a Brin, helping this bunch of slaves?"

Maliche waved his weapon, directing the Brin to head down the ravine toward camp. "A new order is on the horizon. Move along and keep your mouths shut." He led the way, side stepping back down the ravine so as to keep his weapon trained on the miners. The group on the rim kept pace as the Kolandi herded the miners back to camp.

The sun began to set as the group arrived at camp. Neri set three of the fledglings as guards and sat next to Maliche at the fire. She filled her wooden bowl with some of the stew those left behind prepared.

"I can't believe that actually worked." She shook her head, wiping a bit of juice from her chin. "I thought they would shoot you on sight."

"That's why it had to be me who approached them. As far as they knew, I was one of them, so they were more confused and hesitated long enough for me to get in close." He tipped his bowl to his mouth and swallowed the last of his meal. "I'm just glad they were distracted enough for you to get in behind them."

Neri shifted her position, turning to face Maliche. "We were lucky. This should have been a disaster." Her stern visage softened slightly. "Thank you. By the way, this is what they were transporting to the mine." She tossed a small package at his feet.

"Blast charges," said Maliche as he examined the rectangular bundle. "They all carried these?"

"Two hundred charges complete with detonator caps. Enough for us to do a lot of damage to their mines."

"Maybe Opet and the others will start listening to me now."

Neri's eyes narrowed, but she gave him a wink. "Don't expect too much from the warriors. Although, they may agree to not accidentally kill you before we get home."

Maliche gave a half smile in return. "Yeah, that would be nice."

Maliche hefted the package, staring at Neri as she walked off to check the prisoners. Inside his head the biocomputer seemed to smile.

"Well done. This should impress a few of the Kolandi and help win some friends."

Maliche slept fitfully under the stars. Thoughts of how close he came to dying mixed with thoughts of Ryma. The soft melody of her voice sang in his ears, the gentleness of her touch … He punched the bedroll under his head to make it less uncomfortable.

"Relax," said the biocomputer. *"You've had a busy day. Get some sleep."*

With that, Maliche saw a soft blue glow surrounding him. Thinking became difficult and he drifted off to dreams of Ryma and the children they would have together.

As the sun reached its zenith the following day, the warriors returned. Rounding the small hill hiding the camp, they stopped short when they saw the prisoners tied up with Rilo and several fledglings holding Brin weapons on them. The men murmured amongst themselves, gesturing at the strange scene as Neri approached, her arms wide in welcome.

"Hail, Opet. How fares your task? We have a gift for you."

Chapter Fifteen

News of Maliche's actions, to save the fledglings from the miners, and his miraculous ability to speak as one of them swept through the cave like a fresh breeze. Opet had ordered the death of the prisoners back at the camp, there was no food to spare and the Kolandi could not risk revealing the location of their caves, but the capture of weapons and explosives lifted everyone's spirits.

Maliche sat alone in the small chamber with Jontar Rocker's tomb. Two torches sputtered their orange light, flickering shadows across the marble stone of the monument. The drums beat a steady rhythm to the accompanying shuffle of feet against dirt. The aroma of roasting Tirpit filled his nostrils. Voices raised in song echoed through the tunnels. His thoughts rambled far and wide of home, friends, old and new, tales of his family, the Brin miners, and how he might help the Kolandi gain freedom.

"I thought I might find you here."

Maliche started at the voice behind him. He jumped to his feet, turning to face the intruder, raising his arms defensively.

Ryma's smile vanished at his reaction. "Has our treatment of you been so poor?" She seemed to drift silently as she approached him. "Neri and Rilo told me of the treatment you received at the hands of our warriors. Has your triumph not lessened this?"

Maliche relaxed as soon as he recognized the princess and bowed. "Opet and the others treated me with less disrespect during our return to the cave, princess. The fledglings and a few of the younger warriors actually spoke to me. I'm not sure the rest of the warriors know what to do now. They don't like me, but at least they don't seem to want to run me through with a spear."

Ryma smiled and took a seat on the stone bench, signaling for Maliche to sit with her. Her movements appeared so fluid, her linen gown appeared to shimmer in the torchlight.

"There is much hatred to overcome, Great One. No Brin has ever been kind to us since the days of your ancestor." She waved a hand toward the tomb. The brown skin of her arm seemed to flow with incredible grace at every gesture. "It will take time, but I am sure the rest will come to see you as a different sort of Brin than those who have enslaved us." She halted, tilted her head, raising one eyebrow as she examined Maliche. "Why do you stare at me so?"

Maliche's crest blushed as he refocused. "I'm sorry, Princess." He ran the talons of both hands through his crest while attempting to regain his composure. "I was lost in thought for a moment. Yes, I am glad some of the Kolandi are losing their anger toward me. If only I could convince Opet and his men of my sincere desire to help end this atrocity."

She reached out, touching his arm. "Patience, Great One. They will come to know your heart in time." Her hand lingered on his arm, her brown eyes lost focus as they rested on his face. After a second or two, she pulled back her hand, and raised it pretending to brush aside some stray hair, attempting to hide the blush blooming on her cheeks.

Maliche took her hand before she was out of reach, clasping it gently in both of his. The warmth and softness of her small hand caused his heart to skip a beat. "I'm not worried, Princess… as long as you believe in me, everything will work out fine."

The princess gazed into Maliche's eyes with a silent tilt of her head as a blush deepened on her face.

"Excuse my interruption, Princess, but the gathering awaits your blessing." Neri stood at the entrance to the tomb's alcove, avoiding direct eye contact with the two occupants.

Maliche stood, maintaining his hold to assist Ryma from the bench. "Thank you for coming to speak with me, Princess. Please let me know if I can ever be of help."

Ryma nodded with a smile, then turned and joined Neri. Maliche noticed a slight green tinge had joined the blue glow he normally exuded when near the tomb.

***

In the weeks that followed, the Kolandi warriors allowed Maliche to join a number of raiding parties. At first, he remained in the role of a fledgling, doing nothing more than carrying weapons and cleaning pots, but gradually some of the warriors, usually the younger men, began questioning him about ways to improve their raids. His knowledge of Brin ways proved very helpful in guiding the inexperienced warriors as they began leading their own raids. What started as brief questions around the evening campfires evolved into his inclusion, and occasional consultation during planning meetings. The elder warriors learned to withhold judgment as Maliche's suggestions proved valuable in deciding which buildings to destroy for maximum impact, and where to place small charged to disable equipment more effectively.

"Let me do this, Opet. None of you can get passed the guards. I can." Maliche's familiar glow now burned orange in the light of the campfire.

Only a mile away, an airshaft to the slave quarters deep in one of the more remote mines yawned invitingly. Four sentries stood watch during the night as the day and night shifts exchanged places. The Kolandi remained caged below in the bowels of the mine.

"And let you betray us as soon as you are back among your own people? I will not take that risk." Opet crossed his fore arms and threw them apart.

"What must I do to prove I am no threat to you? What can I do to convince you I want to free your people as much as you do?"

Opet turned his back. "You are not one of us. You have not traveled the path of Berit."

Maliche grabbed Opet's shoulder, turning him in defiance. "You have not allowed it! I've asked to face the ordeals, but you and your followers continue to deny me the chance."

Opet leaned down, nose to nose with Maliche. "You would never survive the ordeals! You are not Kolandi. You are no warrior." He shoved Maliche hard and turned to leave.

"Then why not allow me to try? If I die in the ordeals, then you are rid of me forever. If I survive, then I prove my worth. What are you afraid of, Opet?"

The warrior froze. His chiseled and scarred back tensed. "Very well, Brin. You have such a death wish… go ahead into the mine. If you survive and rescue the captives, then you will be allowed to attempt the path." He stormed up to Maliche, sticking a finger in his face. "But know this, Brin," he spat on the ground. "If you betray us, you will never find rest. I will hunt you down and your death will make the ordeals seem like a gentle spring rain."

Maliche stood fast in the awful anger of the warrior. "Agreed." Then he, too, spat on the ground.

The miner's guild uniform fit poorly, pinching at Maliche's groin and neck, but it was the best he could manage. The clothes once belonged to a member of the original group of miners Maliche helped capture with Neri, Rilo and the fledglings those many weeks ago. He tried to walk as casually as the garment allowed. The uniform's rank of inspector allowed him unquestioned passage into the mine.

The endless maze of rock walls, intersecting at odd angles under a never ending series of artificial lights hung from the back, or roof of the tunnels, soon led Maliche to believe he was hopelessly lost. The noise of pneumatic jacklegs assaulted his ears. Powerful ventilators helped reduce most of the dust, but Maliche struggled to keep from coughing. A mine inspector would be used to such conditions.

"You're getting close. I am picking up Kolandi life signs ahead, and down one level." The biocomputer's voice gave him confidence as he strode forward.

A rickety, rusted cage waited at the end of the tunnel. The magnetic hover-lift base showed its age and Maliche hoped it would not choose today to rust out from beneath him. As he stepped onto the rusted floor pad, two miners from another shaft joined him.

"Up or down, sir?"

"Down one level." He tried to sound bored, as if the weight of a mile of rock overhead, which could collapse at any time, did not concern him in the least.

The miner hesitated, then pressed the contact for the next drift, then one three levels below that. The two looked at each other; one of them shrugged, but said nothing.

As the pad came to rest, Maliche stepped out, reminded himself to breathe, and headed down the drift. Turning left at the first intersection he glanced back, noticing one of the miners speaking into his radio.

"What can I do for you, sir?" The Brin standing watch over the Kolandi stood as the supposed inspector entered the dimly lit holding pen.

A dozen gaunt, filthy Kolandi, dressed only in decaying loin cloths, regardless of gender or age, sprawled on the floor behind an electric restraining wall. The prisoners appeared to waver behind the semi-transparent wall as the charge flowed between two panels fastened to either side of the alcove's entrance. The barrier did nothing to prevent air flow so the stench nearly brought tears to Maliche's eyes.

"Prisoner transfer," he said, using the same authoritative voice he heard his father use so often. "I'm taking this lot. Their replacements will be here in the morning."

The guard scratched his crest under his hard hat. "I ain't heard a no prizner transfer. You got the papers fer it?"

Maliche threw his shoulders back, glaring at the miner. "There's been an emergency. I'm scheduled to leave on the next transport in half an hour. The papers will be brought to you as soon as they are completed. Now, unlock this cell and let me get on with my business. Or do you want to tell the guild leaders why you held up their prisoners?"

"All right, sir, no need ta get upset. Here ya go." The guard took a key off the wall and unlocked the gate. "Just doin me job is all."

Maliche upholstered the beam pistol at his side and aimed it at the Kolandi. "Get them on their feet."

As the miner turned his back, Maliche slammed the butt of the pistol into his head, collapsing him in a heap. The Kolandi stared, motionless, at the uniformed Brin who had just attacked one of his own.

Maliche holstered the pistol and lowered his voice, gesturing toward the tunnel. "Hurry, we need to get out of here. Other miners could be here at any time."

The Kolandi froze, not willing to believe.

Maliche fished under his uniform jacket and pulled out a rabbit hide. Opening it up, he revealed a symbol drawn by Opet.

"Do you recognize this? I'm with Opet and the princess. There is no time. We need to get moving. Hurry."

One of the elder Kolandi came out of his stupor. "I hunted with Opet. I know his mark. I do not understand. No Brin would know of this mark."

"My name is Rocker. I'm a descendant of the Great One from your legends. I am working with your princess to free you from those of my kind who are breaking our laws. You need to trust me." A blue aura surrounded Maliche as he spoke.

The Kolandi retreated to the back of their cell, falling to their knees, hiding their faces in the dirt.

The elder slave held his ground, trembling as he faced the legend. "You are The Rocker? The prophecies are true?"

Bursting with impatience, Maliche grabbed the old man by the shoulders, shaking him. "No, I am not him... only his descendant. But we need to hurry. If we don't get moving the guards will catch us before we can escape."

The man hesitated, and then called to the others, gesturing for Maliche to lead the way.

It was not far back to the hover-lift which carried the group up to the main drift at ground level. Maliche, walking behind them holding his beam pistol at the ready, gave the appearance of an armed guard herding a group of slaves. He took them back to the secondary entrance he used earlier that night. Dawn was breaking over the surrounding hills as they exited the mine.

"That's far enough, Maliche Rocker!" two large uniformed Brin approached from behind the office shack. "Your face was all over the news after your crash, and the funeral provided an endless supply of family photos broadcast for weeks."

Two more Brin, he recognized the miners from his descent into the lower levels earlier, joined the security officers.

"How could you possibly think nobody would recognize anyone of your stature?" He lowered his rifle at Maliche's chest. "The boss wants to see you."

At that moment, a burst of orange light cut through the early dawn, slicing through the chest of the Brin guard. Before he hit the ground, several more beams reigned down from the nearby hills. Opet and his warriors opened fire on the Brin.

Maliche grabbed the nearest of his group and shoved her toward the warriors in the distance. He continued to yank and pull on the frightened beings herding them into action toward safety.

"Run! Get to those hills!" He pressed the contact on his own weapon, killing the second guard and sending the two miners scattering for cover as more guards came running. "Run!"

The Kolandi ran toward the covering fire, but small explosions of rock and dirt flew up around them as the mine's security forces fired at them from behind. Suddenly, one of the Kolandi next to him fell to the ground, his legs caught up in a proso cable. Fired form an air gun, this combination of two metal balls attached to each other by a thin electrically-charged cable was a common form of non-lethal restraint used by police. Three of the slaves stopped to untangle the man's legs as he twitched in pain, despite the onslaught of energy blasts.

Maliche halted next to them, and knelt behind a cart to provide covering fire. His shots were wild, but the pursuers dove for cover. In moments, his companions freed the man from the cable and they took off running, Maliche in the rear continued to fire at the closing Brin security forces.

The first of the slaves reached the hills, running up the winding stream bed. Just as he approached the wadi one of the Kolandi women fell, shot through the leg. Maliche knelt by her side, firing back to keep the guards at bay while two of the men picked her up and carried her to safety. He stood, turned to run, and felt an agonizing blaze of fire in his shoulder, forcing him to drop his pistol. An instant later, the punch of a proso cable entangling him forced him to the ground. His nerves felt as if he was on fire and he lost all control over his muscles. As he fell, he saw Opet standing at the crest of the hill, firing his rifle at the Brin, now only seconds away. Blasts of rock and dirt burst from the ground around him as orange shafts of energy slammed into the hill at his feet.

Opet stopped firing, looked at Maliche with a smirk on his face. He signaled to the other warriors and disappeared behind the rocks. Then the blow of the butt of an energy rifle sent sparks flying in his mind.

***

"As you can see, your Honors, the new equipment, and the opening of the new mines, will soon bring production back to normal." Raencert stood before The Assembly committee answering questions about recent shortages in mineral supplies. "An unfortunate combination of failing old machinery and depletion of some of the oldest mines resulted in our current dilemma, but we are working hard to increase shipments of the most critical minerals. Our miners are working double shifts in the meantime until more trainees are hired. I would say we will be back to full operational capacity within two months."

The small silvery, spherical recorder buzzed in his ear as it floated around him, collecting a video record of the testimony. Its single lens kept the speaker in focus despite frequent changes in altitude and distance in the device's flight pattern.

The members of The Assembly idly scanned through pages of Raencert's report. The small chamber, reserved for matters not concerning the full Assembly, gave every appearance of a courtroom. The committee sat behind high, ornately carved wooden desks. Dressed in the traditional deep green robes and gold headbands, they hovered above those brought before them. Selan relished his position of authority over Raencert.

"Very well, Head Guildsman. We will hold you to your promise." Selan, head of the committee concluded. "I would, however, ask you to meet with me after this hearing. I have some other matters to discuss with you." He slammed the stone orb onto his desk indicating the meeting's termination. The council members rose, returning to their private offices.

A few minutes after Selan removed his official robes, his clerk announced Raencert's arrival.

"If I didn't know any better, I would think this report was the genuine article." Selan tossed his personal transcription panel into the bottom drawer of his desk. "What is taking so long to end these uprisings? Are your forces so incompetent they cannot handle a few spear-waving, half-starved natives?"

Not waiting for an invitation, Raencert sat in the chair opposite Selan and helped himself to a glass of Tarlec wine.

"Don't give me that. You know as well as I do these are not just a few unorganized escaped slaves." He swirled the amber liquid in his glass, sniffed at the bittersweet aroma, and downed it with one swallow. "They know the desert and the surrounding mountains. There are thousands of places to hide up there. When we do find one hiding place, they vanish, only to reappear somewhere else."

"Don't give me excuses, Raencert. How are they able to evade your security measures? How can a bunch of primitives understand our technology and evade it so easily?"

"They're much cleverer than you give them credit for, Selan. With the weapons they have captured, it is not such a simple thing to defeat them. We've taken some heavy losses."

"So, what are you going to do to turn this situation around?"

Raencert frowned, leaning forward in his chair. "Don't start getting all high and mighty on me, boy. I'd like to see you do any better. Remember, you're in this as thick as the rest of us. We need reinforcements and increased finances. The pit workers are starting to grumble about needing hazard pay. If we want to gain the upper hand on matters, you need to open the purse strings."

Selan sat back in his chair, tenting his talons at his lips. "I'll see what I can do. Is there anything else I need to know?"

"You have my personal reports. Everything is in there. If there is nothing else, I need to get back and make sure our cover story holds." The barrel-chested Brin rose and strode out of Selan's office.

Selan watched through his window as Raencert left The Assembly. *That arrogant quetzal. Does he think he can keep my brother's capture a secret from me?* He spun on his heels, returned to his desk, and poured his own goblet of wine. *How long does he think I'll continue to buy the story of his death? It's time I took control of the situation.* He reached for the communicator and punched in his private code.

"Syrinx, is everything ready?"

Yes, sir," replied the raspy voice on the other end. "We can begin Operation Recusant as soon as you give the word."

Selan took another swallow of the wine. *Syrinx certainly has a way with words. If ever there was anyone who fits the title of someone who defies authority, it's my brother.* "Very well. Send your operative to free my brother. Let's see if we can find the slave's secret refuge ourselves."

"Yes, sir. I have the perfect individual for the job. I'll let you know once we begin."

Selan pressed the disconnect contact and smiled. *Now the game begins, Raencert. Let's see who is truly in charge here, guildsman.* He slapped his desk and walked out of the office.

"Cancel my afternoon appointments," he told the clerk. "I need to get some fresh air."

Chapter Sixteen

"So, the traitor awakes. I gotta tell the doc. Don't you be goin' nowhere."

The sound of a chair scraping the floor reminded Maliche of the sound of talons scratching along a slate board at the university. He always hated that sound.

"Why they're so concerned about the likes of you, I'll never know."

A door opened and closed, a lock clicked home. Maliche opened his eyes, but the glare of lights sent stabs of pain through his brain. He tried to grab his head, but discovered the wrist restraints confining his movements, securing him to the bed.

"Slowly now," said the biocomputer. *"I've been working on your injuries all night, but you have to give it time. They tore you up pretty good back there at the mine, but nothing too serious."*

Maliche tried to open his eyes again, more carefully this time. The light still hurt, but grew tolerable as his eyes adjusted. Turning his head was another matter entirely. The pain in his shoulder and leg paled in comparison to the sharp pang in his left temple. Keeping as still as possible he surveyed his surroundings. Tiled walls, banks of beeping and clicking equipment next to the bed, the smell of antiseptic filled the air. One of the apparatus displayed the steady rhythm of his heart and breathing rates. An array of wires ran from his head, chest, and arm, connecting to the machines.

"How did I get to a hospital?"

"Two of the mine's security personnel brought you here yesterday, right after the Kolandi escaped. They know who you are and, if the communications I'm able to intercept are any indication, they were surprised to see you alive. They flew you by shuttle back to their main facility."

"Dry Creek? That's over two hundred miles from where we raided the mine. Why here? They could have sent me back to First Town from the mine."

The sound of the door unlocking interrupted Maliche's internal conversation.

"Remarkable," said the doctor. "I put enough sedative in you to keep you under for another day. How are you feeling" The physician lifted Maliche's wrist, silently counting the arterial pulses while observing his breathing rate.

"You mean aside from being shot and pounding in my head from being clobbered by a rifle butt, and being tied up like a common criminal? Other than all that, I'm just fine."

Without responding, the doctor placed the medical view-pad, a much more technically advanced version than the simple primary aid one used by Aras during their early study of his visions, to a series of points on Maliche's chest, nodding his approval.

"Well, everything looks normal." He pushed aside some of the ear coverts and Maliche winced at the touch. "Amazing. I stitched this up just last night and this wound already looks to be about a week old. Incredible."

Maliche turned his face toward the wall. "Yeah, I've always been a quick healer."

The doctor made a few notes on his electronic pad, and then left, never once acknowledging Maliche's existence as anything other than a series of symptoms. A second Brin, dressed in a black uniform, trimmed in blue, remained in the room.

Maliche scrutinized the Brin for a moment. The uniform, frayed at the edges, looked to be about a size too large for the security man. The holster belt hung precariously from narrow hips, an old energy beam pistol, still restrained by its retention strap.

"And who might you be?" Maliche saw the name Sovet on his badge, but needed something to open up a conversation.

"Never you mind who I am, traitor. You got enough to concern yerself tomorra when the director gits here. He's commin all the way from clear back in First Town fer you, traitor."

Maliche strained at the shackles. "Do you have any idea who I am? My name—"

"Yeah, I know who you used ta be. One a them kak Rockers. The ones runnin things back home. Well, no more, at least not fer you." The guard crossed the room, his hand on the pistol at his side. His crest feathers stood completely upright in anger. "You think you could get away with helpin them savages?"

He poked Maliche's shoulder bandage with one talon. The stab of pain shot through Maliche's body like fire.

"Turnin aginst yer own kind. That's the lowest sort a low a Brin can be. You got everthin comin to ya what's commin when the director gits here. You'll see."

With another poke at the wound, the guard returned to his station, grabbed the magazine, one of those outdoors hunting titles, and slammed himself into the chair. A nurse came in to check the monitors every two hours, never speaking, or making more than the briefest of eye contact with the patient. An orderly delivered sparse meal of vegetables and a watery stew of some sort as the evening shift took over.

A new guard replaced the surly Sovet who, as soon as he saw his replacement, gathered his belongings, handed him the duty log, and left without a word, and never more than a timid glance at him. This one's badge read Nalot. Dressed in the same second-hand type uniform as his predecessor, he did not show the same antagonism. Nothing registered on his lean, broken-nosed face at all as he silently scanned the room. He inspected the restraints with a grip of pure iron, and then returned to the desk. His gaze never left him. Maliche felt as if he knew exactly how the small forest dits felt when it realized a hungry lepti slithered in for a strike with its two inch fangs. He decided sleep was the best thing for now.

He awoke to the crash of the door slamming open. He recognized the huge frame as it filled the doorway. The morning sun acted as a spotlight on the leader of the mining guild.

"There you are, boy. My people told me it was you, but I had to be sure. You sure are one difficult quetzal to kill."

"Hello, Raencert. Sorry to disappoint you."

"Be careful with this one," cautioned the biocomputer. *"I've tapped into their communication network and he is on the edge of deciding whether to have the guards kill you right now or use you for something else he is plotting."*

The immense guildsman waved dismissively and Nalot left the room. Raencert strode over to Maliche's bedside, standing only long enough for someone to place a sturdy chair under him.

"You have no idea the trouble you have given us these past few months. Depleted supplies, damaged equipment, escaped workers…"

"Slaves."

Raencert paused briefly before continuing. "Yes, sir, a lot of trouble. It's terribly hot in here, don't you think?" He turned his head and raised his hand, one talon elevated. "Would it be possible to have a glass of water?" He waited patiently as his servant left to fetch the water.

Maliche gritted his teeth. "What do you want, Raencert?"

Ice clinked as the blue-suited young Brin returned, handing his boss the glass. Beads of condensation coated the tumbler, glistening in the sunlight. Raencert took a long sip.

"Now that is just what the doctor ordered." He chuckled at his own joke as he eyed his prisoner. "What do I want? I'm not entirely sure yet. Your refusal to die may turn out to be a blessing in disguise. There are still a few details to work out, but I think you may be the perfect solution to my little problem."

Maliche rested his head back on his pillow, shut his eyes, and sighed. "And what little problem would that be?"

"Your brother is trying to act like he is in control of matters lately. A little lesson in humility might be just the thing, and you may just be the perfect object of that lesson. Right now, he thinks you're dead. There was a beautiful ceremony, by the way. Everyone who is anyone attended. But your survival could be the ticket to controlling him once and for all."

Maliche turned to face his captor, his eyes hard. "You can't keep me here forever. People know who I am and word will leak out soon enough. Selan will demand my release, and once he learns about your dealing in the slave business, you'll be ruined."

Raencert laughed out loud, barely setting his glass on a nearby table before spilling it. "Oh, this is phalking marvelous. But, of course, you wouldn't know, would you?"

Maliche opened his mouth to speak, but Raencert held up a hand, pointer talon extended.

"Who do you think arranged for your shuttle to crash in the first place, dear boy? It might have been my men who sabotaged the fuel line, but Selan gave the final approval. He's in this operation as much as anyone."

"You lie," spat Maliche. "We may argue and disagree with each other on many things, but we're brothers. He would never do such a thing." He strained at the shackles, rattling the bed and disengaging a couple of the remote sensors to the machines, setting off the alarms.

Raencert stood and pressed a massive hand to Maliche's chest, forcing him to lie still. Leaning close, he whispered into his ear. "He was a bit careless in this matter, though. It seems all the evidence for your supposed death, as well as this matter of the mine workers, leads directly to Selan. With a few well-placed documents in his computer and several communication records skillfully recovered by my people, we can prove your entire family was in control of all of it. The mining guild may take a beating, but who could fault us for following the orders of The Rockers? We will survive this business. Of course, your death will have to become a reality, but since everyone already knows you're dead, it is only a matter of deciding how and when. I may need a few access codes and such before you go."

"Planted false evidence, you mean."

"Possibly, but authentic enough to convince any court appointed investigator."

"And you control those puppet strings... don't you?"

As the duty nurse arrived to check the monitor alarms, he gave one powerful press on Maliche's chest, sneered as he rose up, and stepped out of the way, slowly heading to the door. Nalot returned to his station at the small desk, silently observant of everything. An hour later, the day shift took over, Sovet's eyes brightened with a grin. He seemed to relish Maliche's outrage.

"Time to go. Get up and follow me. Not a word."

Maliche awoke to a dark room, Nalot's face just inches from his own.

"Get dressed. We've got four hours before the day shift comes in to check on you." He finished releasing Maliche form the cuffs holding him.

Maliche rubbed his wrists as he sat up. "So Raencert is done with me now? You here to kill me?"

Nalot tossed some civilian clothes onto the bed and went to keep watch at the door. "I don't work for the mining guild."

"You'll have to forgive me if I don't trust your word on this."

"I don't care if you trust me or not. My employer has other plans for you. My job is to get you someplace safe and make plans to send you home."

"And who, exactly, is your employer?"

"Not something you need to know. Or would you rather sit here until they drag your ass out of here at first light and bury you in the desert?"

"Can we trust him?" Maliche asked the biocomputer.

"Of course not. But if I am reading him correctly, we may be able to use him. Play along for now. There's something interesting in him. I need time to work it out."

"All right," he said in a whisper. "How do we get out of here?"

Nalot glared at Maliche, his voice bristled with authority. "By keeping your kak mouth shut and doing exactly what I say. No questions. Got it?"

Maliche nodded as he finished lacing up the last boot. Nalot gripped Maliche by the arm and pulled him through the door into a brightly lit hallway. His effortless grip felt as if his arm were in a vice. The two gave every appearance of a guard escorting his prisoner to new holdings. Those working at the desk barely gave them a glance as they passed. In less than five minutes, they passed out of the clinic into the night.

***

The cool air blowing in through the window calmed Selan as he watched the night sky from the back seat of his mag-lev limousine. The report from Syrinx of Talon's successful rescue of Maliche brought new vigor to his plans to dominate the arrogant Raencert.

Once I find the evidence of that quetzal's involvement in all of this I can spring the trap and rid myself of him once and for all. A frown interrupted the grin on his face. *How much longer before Syrinx can gather the proof? The longer it takes; the more time he has to destroy any sign of his role. Not even Raencert can erase everything. What are we overlooking? At least he won't have Maliche as a potential bargaining chip in the future. There is still time to turn this phalk of a disaster to my advantage.*

"Will you need anything tonight, sir?" The driver's voice startled Selan back to reality. He had been so lost in thought he hadn't even realized the mag-lev was parked in front of his house.

Straightening his shoulders, and gathering his case, Selan opened the door. "No, nothing more tonight. Be here six sharp in the morning. I want to get an early start."

The driver tipped his cap. "Yes, sir, six sharp it is. Have a good evening." He punched the accelerator buttons as the door closed and sped off down the long driveway.

Selan stood watching the receding taillights, taking a deep breath of the night air. The scent of the surrounding woods filled his nostrils. He hated the smell of nature. With one last look at the star-filled sky he scowled and headed up the steps.

"Nedia, I thought you would be in bed by now. It's very late. Is everything all right?" The sight of his wife sitting behind the heavy desk in his study caught Selan by surprise. He stood with his hand on the door's handle his head tilted with crest feathers rising.

Nedia looked up from the paper in front of her on the desk, her crest unpreened. She crumpled the note in her fist and stuffed it into a pocket in her dress.

"Well, there you are. You would not believe the day I have had." She stood up, waving her arms as she stomped toward Selan. "The caterer kept trying to talk me into baked dinter when I specifically told him broiled. The invitations got the address wrong, 873 Dyan'ta Way instead of Dyan'ta Drive, and my cousins, the Borket side of the family, are threatening to cancel if we don't invite their assemblyman." She gave Selan a perfunctory peck on the cheek as she passed him in the doorway. "I was about to leave you a note to talk to the old buzzard tomorrow and invite him. I can't stand the fluff -brain, but what else can I do? Take care of it, will you dear?" And with a final wave of her hand she climbed the stairs to their aerie.

Selan, still holding the door handle, watched his wife disappear around the curve of the second story landing.

Chapter Seventeen

The laser blast shattered the brick over Maliche's head sending shrapnel flying in all directions.

"Strix! Where did they come from?" He saw a half dozen guards closing in on his hiding place behind the crates. Nalot crashed into the hiding place at full run just as a fresh volley of blasts tore up the crates and pavement around him.

"Keep your kak head down," said Nalot as he pulled Maliche out of the line of fire. "They were just coming on duty as I was leaving the ship over there and saw me. They wanted to see my orders and couldn't be talked out of it, so I bolted. Thought I could lose them, but no such luck." Nalot reached inside his jacket and pulled out his own two energy pistols. Tapping off the safeties, he started to take aim.

Maliche grabbed Nalot's arm interrupting his aim. "Wait. More guards will be here any moment. You can't out shoot them all. We need to split up. Give me one of those pistols and I'll meet you at the shuttle."

"Like strix you will," Nalot jerked his arm away and steadied himself for a shot. "You're my responsibility. It took a lot of careful planning to get you out when I did. I'm not about to let you out of my sight now. You even know how to use one of these?" He fired a blast sending one of the guards flying backward, a gaping hole in his chest.

"You can't kill all of them. At least splitting up forces them to divide their own group to chase us both. Give me a weapon. We'll die if we stay here any—"

A blast sent both of them reeling back against the wall of the building. Shaking his head to clear it, Maliche heard only the high pitched ringing in his ears. Through the clearing smoke he saw Nalot getting up to his knees, holding one taloned hand to his head. Peering over a collapsed heap of crates Maliche saw a guard preparing to toss another shock-grenade.

"Look out!" he shoved Nalot to one side behind better cover, and dove to his left.

The explosion missed its intended target, but Maliche's head still spun in nauseating waves from the first one. Trying to steady himself, he saw he was lying on top of a grate. It wobbled as he attempted to push himself up then gave way completely. Maliche tumbled eight feet to the floor of the tunnel below, boxes collapsing on top of him. The effort to stand caused intense pain in his head. Maliche reached out to steady himself on the wall, and then leaned heavily on it. The cool stone felt wonderful on his face and helped clear his mind. Looking up, he saw several large wooden boxes jammed into the hole, blocking any hope of escape that way, not that he wanted to get back into the fire fight, but Nalot was his best hope for survival and now he was alone.

"Well, this is a fine mess. Any suggestions on which way to go?"

The dimly lit passageway seemed to go on forever in either direction, apparently some sort of underground access tunnels for the facility. Only occasional piles of miscellaneous supplies dotted the narrow dusty concrete passage as it curved off into the distance. Maliche's long experience with maps and field work told him heading to the left would take him in the general direction of the shuttle they had hoped to commandeer, but the biocomputer's sensors may provide better information.

"You are correct, the shuttle is toward the left, but the safest route is in the other direction. Besides, there

seems to be Kolandi life signs about two hundred meters to the right."

Maliche's left palm began to glow orange, as the device seemed to feel anger.

"What about guards? I don't have any weapons."

"The alarm went out, so all guards in the vicinity were called to the runway to capture you and Nalot. I'm not detecting any Brin other than you anywhere nearby. The Kolandi might prove useful in the escape. I have a fix on the shuttle's location, so I can lead you back here."

Maliche headed toward the right and the Kolandi group. His steps echoed off the stone walls. The sporadic thump of a shock grenade or some other explosive shook dirt from the ceiling.

"Have you got a fix on Nalot? I suspect he is a survivor, so I'm not particularly worried about him, but the shuttle may need his passcode to operate. Just don't lose track of him. How much further?"

"I have him. He seems to be heading off to the south, probably trying to evade the soldiers. No need to worry if we can't locate him later. I can bypass any security codes the shuttle may have... another twenty meters. Still no sign of any Brin."

As Maliche approached, he heard the muttered prayers of the Kolandi. A few more steps showed him the cage holding the group, suddenly silent as he neared. They huddled together as far to the back of the cell as possible, holding hands. Their eyes warily scrutinizing him. The restraining field hummed and wavered, distorting his view of the captives slightly, but Maliche barely controlled his anger and shame at the pitiful state of the rags which hardly covered them, and the filth encrusting their bodies.

"My name is Maliche Rocker. I'm here to help you escape. Can you travel?" He pressed his palm to the control pad on the wall. He felt his arm grow warm as the familiar glow turned orange. In a matter of seconds, the restraining field shut down.

The captives remained silent and motionless, watching his every move. Maliche approached the group, pulling one to her feet. She screamed and broke free from his grip, fleeing back to her fellow prisoners.

"We don't have time for this. If you want your freedom, you need to act now. The guards will return any time now. Do you understand?"

A dry voice rattled from the center of the group. "What makes you think we would ever trust you, Brin?" The emaciated slave rose to his feet, and spat at the ground, bowed, but defiant. "If you want to kill us, do it now. We will not make your paperwork simpler by dying while trying to escape."

"I'm not one of them. I am a Rocker and I was a prisoner just like you, but I escaped and have a way out of here. Will you come with me?"

A young female in the back of the group stood on spindly bare legs. Her leather dress showed signs of rot and appeared ready to fall from her small frame at any moment.

"Wait, Nevik, I recognize this one." she stepped carefully through the others to the front of the cage, brushing her tangled hair from her face. Her eyes showed a flicker of life. "Yes, this is The Rocker. I recognize him from the cave. He stood with Ryma before the tomb. I will never forget the sight."

Maliche stared at the girl. "Seykel? Is that you? I didn't know you had been captured. Help me convince the others to trust me. We don't have much time."

She turned to their leader, her arms raised in supplication. "We must do as he says, Nevik. Ryma trusted him and so must we. He is The Rocker."

Nevik spat again, glaring at Seykel. "I will never trust a Brin. The Rocker passed into legend long ago. This is an imposter."

Seykel turned her pleading back to Maliche. "Please, Great One. You must show him you are who you say. Show him your holy light. Only The Rocker can shine like the stars."

The blue glow started slowly at Maliche's palms, spreading up his arms until it engulfed his entire body. The light grew brighter until everyone had to shade their eyes from the blazing nimbus.

"Now do you believe me, Nevik? I am not the Rocker of your legends, but I am his descendant and I am here to rescue you. Will you come with me or not?"

Seykel pleaded with the man again. "On my honor as a Skatak, he is The Rocker."

Nevik dropped to his knees, still covering his eyes. "Forgive me, Great One. I heard of your return, but did not believe, until now." He shook like a frightened dinter. "Lead the way and we will follow."

The pattering of bare feet resounded through the empty tunnel. The small group of slaves, led by Maliche, cautiously passed several intersecting passageways, taking one seemingly at random until even Maliche's excellent sense of direction failed him.

"Are sure about this?" he asked the biocomputer. *"We seem to have turned away from the shuttle's location."*

"We had to in order to avoid running into Brin patrols. Not all of them are on the surface chasing Nalot. Trust me; I have the entire underground facility blueprints mapped out. I'll get us there."

Ten minutes later, the biocomputer gave warning. *"A single Brin is closing in on us up ahead. We need to take that tunnel. No way to avoid this one. If you can get to the intersection before he does, maybe you can surprise him."*

A quick run brought them to the intersection with only a minute to spare. As the Brin rounded the corner Maliche and Nevik jumped him. In a blur of motion, the

Brin ducked the attack, spun, and with a well-practiced maneuver, sent both Nevik and Maliche flying into the wall. Maliche felt the air explode from his lungs as Nalot landed, his knees on his chest.

"Just what the phalk do you think you're doing? And why are you with them?" Nalot released the pressure, gesturing to the terrified group of Kolandi cowering against the wall. Only Seykel ran to Nevik's aid.

"Good to see you too, Nalot." He raised one hand for Nalot to help him to his feet. "Where have you been?" *"And how did you lose track of him? Can't you tell one Brin from another?"*

"Sorry. These tunnels have very thick walls loaded with plumbing and wiring. It appears to limit my sensors somewhat. I will try to recalibrate to compensate for them."

"Looking for you, you quetzal. I saw you fall through that grate. It took a while to lose the guards chasing me and then I had to find another way down here. We need to get to that shuttle before they post sentries."

Maliche pointed to the slaves. "These Kolandi are going with us. I broke them out of a prison cell down here. I won't abandon them."

"The strix they are." Nalot thrust his face millimeters from Maliche's nose and jabbed a talon into his chest. "My job is to rescue you, not them. Look at them. They can barely stand up, much less run. And a crowd of slaves running lose will definitely attract a lot of attention. Leave them."

Maliche backed off and turned to help the recovering Nevik to his feet. With his arms around Nevik and Seykel, his feet firmly planted, he faced Nalot. "Either we all leave together, or we all stay here. There's no other option."

Nalot erupted in a flurry of the most obscene and descriptive language as to what Maliche could do with his options and the Kolandi. In the end, he raised his energy pistol and aimed it at one of the slaves.

"And what's to stop me from just killing all of them?"

"You'll have to kill me as well, then. If you harm even one, I'll refuse to cooperate, and then where will you be?" The blue glow in his palm activated and Maliche became aware of fleeting glimpses into Nalot's mind. Intense anger, frustration, and indecision. Conflicting images, but gradually smoothing into reluctant acceptance.

With another blast of indiscrete outbursts, Nalot holstered his pistol and stormed off. "Great. Nursemaid to a bunch of useless niewols and one bleeding heart do-gooder. Are you coming or what?"

Nevik glared at Nalot's back. "I do not trust that one, Great One. He is like the rest of them, only thinking of themselves and profit."

"I don't really trust him either, Nevik. But we have no choice. He has protected me so far, even if only to line his own pockets. We need to move."

He ruffled Seykel's mass of hair and strode to the others, helping them to their feet. Leading the way, he followed after Nalot. As they caught up with him around the next corner, Maliche thought he saw Nalot toss a small object down a side passage and then shove something back into his uniform pocket.

"What was that?"

Nalot continued ahead without turning to look back. "Nothing. I thought it might be an energy pack for a pistol, but it was already discharged. Someone ought to be punished for losing it."

Maliche shifted the weight of the woman he helped support and, checking to see if the others were still together, followed Nalot. He wondered about Nalot's unexpected acceptance of the Kolandi. *"Did you have something to do with that change of heart?"*

"Only a slight nudge in our favor. He is a remarkably complex individual for a mercenary. There is a powerful moral code to him. He would not have killed the Kolandi; he wanted to frighten you into complying."

"Do you trust him?"

"Not entirely, but I wouldn't rule him out entirely, either. Not just yet."

***

"I can't believe nobody stopped us this time." Maliche shook his head as he fastened his restraints in the co-pilot's chair.

Nalot touched a series of controls with his talons, keyed in his passcode, and started the engines. "They were looking for two Brin on the run, not a party of slaves shipping off to the mines. This diseased lot actually did come in handy after all."

With a punch of his talon, the thrust increased, the transport rocked and rose quickly into the night sky. As they climbed above the low lying clouds, Nalot turned the ship toward the brightening early morning horizon and set the controls on full thrust.

"We should have you back in safe hands in about seven hours. I suggest all of you get some sleep before then. And you need to think of how to either explain this bunch," he thrust a thumb over his shoulder, "or locate a safe location to drop them off."

"They need to come back to First Town with us. I need to expose the mining guild for what they are. These Kolandi will be all the proof I need."

Nalot shook his head and ran his dirty talons through his tattered crest. "Mighty risky business, that. I overheard your brother is part of it all. Are you willing to risk your own family for them?"

"I can't believe Selan is a willing partner in the enslavement of others. I won't believe it's anything more than Raencert's lies." Maliche shifted in his seat, continuing to stare out the front portal.

"I can't speak to that, but in my opinion, for what it's worth, you're going to need a heap more proof of what's going on than just a few half dead natives to change the Assembly's mind on matters. There's a powerful lot of money and greed involved here."

Maliche sat silently for a moment, his eyes closed, fist clenched and tapping out a rhythm on his knee. With a loud sigh, he opened his eyes and turned to face his rescuer.

"You're right. We need undeniable proof of the guild's slavery trade and the murders they have committed. We need to get the evidence before returning to First Town. We need to go back to the caverns and find a way to infiltrate some of the mines."

A brief, almost undetectable smile touched the corner of Nalot's mouth and vanished even more quickly than it arrived. "Oh, no, not with me you, aren't. I'm getting paid to bring you back to civilization. I'm not risking my crest for you or anyone else unless I get paid for it."

Maliche's fists clenched again. "Fine. You know my family. I'll pay you ten thousand extra if you help me do this. Keep me safe for another two weeks is all I ask."

Nalot chuckled and sat up in his seat. "If you're offering ten thousand, you must think it's worth at least twenty. I'll take thirty thousand." He turned a stern, unreadable face toward Maliche.

"Done."

Maliche punched in a set of numbers for the navigation computer, grabbed the control stick and turned the ship north toward the caves. "You take the gunner's seat, in case there's trouble along the way. I'm assuming your training taught you how to fire these weapons?"

"I'll manage." Nalot strapped himself into the co-pilot seat next to him, pressed a few controls of his own, and tested the sights on the heads-up display.

***

Four hours later, Seykel stood behind Maliche and Nalot, enjoying the view. One small brown hand rested on Maliche's shoulder.

"This is wonderful. I've never seen anything more than the inside of one of these flying ships before. Your people are truly magicians to have such abilities." Her eyes beamed with joy at the beauty of the desert hills below. Pillows of white clouds drifting on the winds spotted the deep blue sky above. She turned to Nalot. "Could you teach me to fly a ship such as this?"

Nalot tilted his head in her direction, his crest slightly raised. He stared at her for a long moment, and then returned his gaze forward with a grunt.

"I'm no pilot, girl. We aren't here for fun and games." He jerked his head toward Maliche. "Likely going to get us all killed, he is."

Seykel sniffed and straightened herself to her full height, all one and a half meters of it. "The Great One will do no such thing," she brushed aside a lock of stray hair. "He will save us all... including you." She jabbed his shoulder with two fingers, turned as royally as she could manage in the slightly rocking transport, and returned to her group.

***

Nalot laughed out loud. "That little one has more spunk than brains."

"At least she is willing to stand up and fight for what she believes in." Maliche glared at Nalot, a red aura surrounding him. "What do you believe in, Nalot? Is there anything other than money that stirs your heart?" Before

Nalot could respond, a flash of something on the horizon caught his attention. "What are those?"

"That, my boy, is a formation of armed transports preparing to attack. Probably one of your precious Kolandi camps down there. We need to make ourselves scarce."

Maliche's talons hovered over the control panel, then turned off the auto pilot and grabbed the control stick. "No. We have to help them. We have energy cannons on this ship, too. We can't let them slaughter any more Kolandi."

"You're crazy, boy. Three ships against one is a phalking bad idea. You need to get us out of here." Before he could continue his argument, he saw one of the ships turn and head toward them. The communicator crackled with a commanding voice.

"Unidentified shuttle transport, identify yourself. If you do not provide immediate passcodes we will be forced to open fire."

"Kak, they must have picked us up on scanners. He touched the communicator activation pad. "Approaching vessel, this is Nalot, passcode Talon One, repeat, Talon One. We have authorization to transport slaves to the gem mines. Do you copy?"

A blast of energy cannon beams burst a few meters to port, violently rocking the ship. "Unidentified shuttle transport, your passcode is not on record. Turn around now or be destroyed. This is your final warning."

Nalot tightened his restraints and grabbed the control stick. "High Command must have deleted my old security codes quicker than I expected." He turned to Maliche. "Tell your friends back there to strap in and hold on tight. Looks like you get your wish."

With a few quick flicks of his talons, Nalot powered up the energy cannons and fired at the swiftly approaching Brin ship. The high energy beam ripped into the ship's starboard engine, releasing thick plumes of smoke. The vessel lost altitude and struggled to a hard landing.

Another flash of light and explosion rocked the transport as Maliche maneuvered the ship to evade the second Brin vessel shooting at them. The third remained over the Kolandi camp, firing at the ground. Maliche rolled their ship out of the beam's path just in time. A quick exchange of fire and a series of aerobatic maneuvers by both ships filled the sky with wild energy blasts. The Kolandi screamed in fright. Those who had not fastened their safety straps clung desperately to the others as their legs flung wildly behind them. One more death-defying turn brought their ship behind the Brin and Nalot fired. A long fissure ripped across the side of the vessel. It, too, began to lose altitude, trailing smoke and flame until it hit the ground in a cloud of dust, exploding on impact.

Nalot readjusted himself in the chair after the sudden maneuvers. "That's some fancy flying for an archaeologist."

"My family has a couple of racing yachts I learned to pilot when I was a kid. Guess I didn't forget as much as I thought. Looks like you had some pretty fair training on those weapons."

"Yeah, I wasn't always a private."

Pointing toward the third ship, still firing at the defenseless Kolandi, Maliche shouted at Nalot. "We have to protect them. Take out that ship." He glanced back over his shoulder. "Is everyone all right back there?"

Nevik's eyes were wide in fright, but he controlled himself enough to help those who still needed to get strapped in. "We have suffered worse, Great One. You must save those on the ground out there." He quickly regained his seat and pulled the restraints extra tight.

Maliche aimed them straight toward the last attack ship. Just as Nalot fired the energy cannons, the ship veered hard to port and looped overhead. It settled in behind them as Maliche shoved the controls to starboard. The ship lurched violently and the energy beam hit a glancing blow. Continuing his turn, Maliche hit the controls to dive, and then pulled hard upward as another blast caught them in the port engine. Smoke began to fill the cabin. Maliche completed his maneuver and at the peak of his loop, flipped the ship hard over, and Nalot fired straight into the cockpit of the enemy craft. This one did not land so much as cratered.

Fighting for control, Maliche and Nalot guided the transport to a rough landing a hundred meters from the low hills, opened the hatch, and got everyone away from the now burning vessel.

Between fits of coughing, Seykel stumbled to Nalot and threw both arms around his waist. "You saved us. Thank you. I told you the Great One would not let us die."

Nalot stood with his arms spread wide and mouth open. Nevik approached and pried the girl from him, never looking him in the face. "I offer thanks as well, Brin. We owe you a life debt." The two went back to their group, helping the others to their feet.

Nalot, dumbstruck, looked at Maliche.

Maliche shrugged, and pointed north east. "I think the camp was over this way. Let's check for survivors."

They headed off, following Maliche's lead. As they ran, the crack of energy beams split the air around them. Nalot turned to see three Brin soldiers from the first vessel closing in, firing their rifles at them, one taking aim at Seykel. He grabbed Seykel's arm and threw her to the ground while raising his own weapon, killing the soldier. Picking her up by the back of her dress, he shoved her on.

"Get moving! Run to those hills!"

Twenty meters from the hills, Nevik threw himself full force into Nalot's back, knocking him to the ground as an energy beam sliced through the air above them. Nalot rolled, tossing Nevik aside, and pulled his pistol, aiming it at Nevik. He lowered the weapon when he saw the burning hole in Nevik's back. Turning quickly, he aimed the weapon at the Brin soldiers who had fired at them. As Nalot's beam found its mark, an arrow lodged itself in the chest of the second soldier.

Maliche looked up to the crest of the hill. Standing there was Opet.

Nalot knelt by Nevik, turning him gently onto his back. "Why would you do that? You hate me, and all Brin. Why take that hit for me?"

Nevik's eyes fluttered and he gasped for air. For the first time since his enslavement he looked a Brin in the eyes. "I owed you a life debt. I can now go to my ancestors with honor." His last breath rattled from his throat.

Chapter Eighteen

"Why would that old fool do that? What do these niewols know of honor? They're barely more advanced than animals, scraping out an existence in the desert like Ukaliti." Nalot sat hunched over on the dirt floor of his cell, muttering his curses, hardly aware of Maliche's presence on the other side of the bars. "And that girl is the worst of the lot. Hangs around here like some feather-fluffed idiot. What's wrong with her?" He pounded a fist on the ground.

Maliche hung his head, shaking it. He stood with one hand holding one of the bars of the prison cell, the other tapping a talon on the crossbar.

"You don't know anything about these people, Nalot. You've never seen them outside the mines, beaten down, half starved, the very life drained out of them." He thought for a moment, trying to think how to explain the Kolandi. "Seykel is young and idealistic. I don't think she is capable of hating anyone, even a Brin. And the only reason you're not dead is Opet witnessed not only our aerial battle, but he saw how you protected Seykel, killing one of your own kind in the process. She's not just an ordinary aide to the princess you know. When I first met her, she was one of the Skatak, specially trained women warriors whose sole purpose is to defend their Princess to the death. How they captured her alive is beyond me."

Nalot looked up at Maliche; his crest disheveled, but slightly lifted, his eyes searching. "I thought you said she was incapable of hate. If she's such a fighter, then you're not making any sense."

"Yes, that's right." Maliche squatted down on the balls of his feet, elbows resting on his knees and talons clasped. "The Kolandi are a lot more complex than I ever imagined. Even Opet, who brought us here, realized something was going on and chose to bring you to the princess for examination rather than kill you on the spot. He may hate you... strix, he still hates me, too, but he recognized the need to keep us alive so Ryma could discover the truth of things. Are those the actions of ukaliti?"

Nalot simply stared.

When Maliche turned to leave he saw Kitae and Neri standing quietly, dressed in soft tirpit hide dresses fringed with colorful mertan and cardis feathers, the formal dress of the Skatak. "I didn't see you. You should have said something."

The two bowed and Neri, the elder of the two women folded her hands in the official pose of the princess's messenger. Her voice rang out in the clear, high tones of a royal summons. "Princess Ryma requires your presence in the Hall of Rocker to give witness on the case before her."

The two bowed again and Kitae took up the call. "Follow now and be presented. May the blessings of The Rocker be with you and guide your testimony."

They turned in unison, waited for Maliche to come forward, and led him to the sacred burial chamber of Jontar Rocker, their kitals, curved triangular bladed weapon of choice by the Skatak, swung at their hips. A bright blue radiance surrounding Maliche cast their shadows ahead.

The burial chamber shone brightly in the light emanating from the quartz seams in the walls and ceiling. Two columns of Kolandi filled the room on either side of a central aisle. On the dais in front of Jontar Rocker's marble tomb sat Princess Ryma. A mantel of gold and scarlet feathers with a high collar of long, exotic feathers tipped with iridescent blue draped from her shoulders. She sat on a simple wooden bench, holding a meter-long metallic staff, decorated with symbols and writing Maliche did not recognize. Her dress was the same soft tirpit leather as her aide's, but dyed deep blue. A delicate silver circlet sat on top of her long dark hair, the green gem in her amulet sparkled as if it held a thousand stars.

As Maliche followed Neri and Kitae into the chamber, the hostility from the warriors present was palpable. Their glares and angry mutterings made him glad they were in such a sacred area. Even the princess may not be able to control them if they caught him outside right now. He tried to swallow, but his throat seized up.

"Don't worry," whispered the voice in his head. *"Don't be stupid, but don't worry. You know what you have to do to regain their trust. I won't let anything too horrible happen to you."* The blue glow intensified, compensating for the brightness of the room.

Neri and Kitae stopped as they reached the front of the aisle and bowed formally. "We bring the descendant of The Rocker to bear witness before our princess and The Rocker." They bowed again, turned in unison, and stepped up to either side of Ryma.

With a raise of her staff, and a stern glance at the warriors, Ryma began the proceedings. "Great One, we have brought you here—"

"He brings our enemy among us! He cannot be who he claims!"

"The Rocker would not betray us like this!"

Ryma stood, raised her staff, silencing the outbursts with a look. "Who here questions my authority?" She paused, staring down the warriors. Neri and Kitae closed ranks in front of the princess, hands resting on their kitals. "Who here has not witnessed for themselves the miracle which took place in this very room?" Again she gazed into each angry face before her and pointed her staff at Maliche.

"The Rocker himself has anointed this one. I myself received visions of the truth of this." She waved the staff toward those gathered. "Your own warriors have testified of the valor shown by this one and his companion in the battle defeating our enemy. The stranger risked his own life to save one of my court. Are these the actions of an enemy? Even Nevik gave his life saving the stranger. Who among you would do the same if you did not have faith in another's worthiness?"

The warriors quieted, their faces showed anger, but not the blind hatred which possessed them before. Ryma sat on her bench, Kitae and Neri rearranged her cloak, and she began again.

"Great One, I apologize for the lack of faith some of us have shown here today. We have brought you here to tell us how you came to be accompanied by one of our enemies and to help us understand your wisdom."

Maliche took a deep breath and tried to swallow again, this time with a slight success. He bowed, following the example of Kitae and Neri, then spoke. His voice cracked at first, but gained strength. "I am no traitor to your people, Princess. And, as you say, I was implanted with my ancestor's spirit force here in this very chamber not long after you rescued me."

"Spirit force?"

"Oh, shut up and don't distract me. This is hard enough without you in my head."

"All right, have it your way. I sort of like being thought of as some mystical power."

"I was taken by my countrymen and held captive. They hoped to use me as a pawn in some scheme for power and control over my government. It is my mission to end their control over these mines and end their ability to keep you captive. Most of my countrymen believe your people to be extinct. They know nothing of your enslavement, and would be repulsed if they did. I do not know why, but Nalot freed me from my captors and helped free those who came with us. It is only his skills as a soldier that allowed us to defeat the vessels which attacked you. It is his bravery which saved Seykel. It is these traits which Nevik saw and gave his life to preserve."

He turned to face the gathering, pointing at Opet. "Opet's own testimony here today verifies the truth of this. He witnessed the bravery and skill of Nalot." Maliche turned back to face Ryma. "Even so, I do not understand Nalot's reasons and so do not yet fully trust him. But I do owe him a debt and ask here for your favor to allow him to prove his worth as an ally."

"What right do you have to make such a request?" Danet rose to his feet grabbed his hair and pulled with both hands as if trying to rip it out by the roots. "You are not Kolandi. You have not traveled the Path of Berit." He forced his way to the center aisle crossed both forearms in front of him, fists clenched. "No Brin, not even this one, has any rights among us until he has proven his worth." He stormed out of the chamber, the deep scars on his back reflecting pale against his dark skin.

Murmurs of agreement spread among the crowd. Maliche suddenly knew exactly what he needed to do. He squared his shoulders and reached out, palms upward, facing the princess. "I will walk the Path of Berit, if that is required of me. If the light of The Rocker is not enough to sway your people, then I must become one of you."

Ryma smiled, but her eyes were lit with fear as well. "Are you aware of the risk you will be undertaking? Even some of our most promising candidates do not survive. The Path is more dangerous than anything you have ever faced."

"I understand the risk and gladly accept it if this is what is required to convince the Kolandi of my worthiness."

"Very well. The request is made and accepted. We cannot refuse." She stood, spread her arms and raised her face to the ceiling. "Prepare the Path of Berit for The Rocker. May his spirit be true and strong."

She signaled to her attendants who stepped forward and led the way down the aisle passed Maliche and out of the sacred chamber. Several warriors, mostly the younger ones who had learned to trust him, gathered around smiling and jabbing his arms. The elder warriors held back, their faces showed the mix of shock and admiration for his most likely sacrifice.

***

After three days of preparation, fasting, and meditation, Maliche followed the solemn procession deep into the caverns. The air grew steadily warmer and more humid. After a mile or so, he found breathing difficult. Sweat poured down his face and back. He walked naked, as tradition demanded, revealing his true nature to Berit. His only adornment was Maripa's medallion, a special consideration to his namesake. Kolandi warriors, male and female, lined the trail, ritually striking him with their weapons.

After several more turns down torch lit shafts, they entered a massive cavern. The walls glowed red and orange in the light of several fires. A vast underground lake disappeared into the darkness before them, its surface as still as glass with no wind to stir its surface. Maliche scowled at the acrid smell of burning herbs. The chanting which accompanied their march ceased and Opet, leader of the warriors stood before them. His massive, scarred chest and back glistened with sweat. He wore a ceremonial version of the hunter's garb. The scales of an albino Mordu blazed like fire in the torch light. A robe of claws, teeth and horns of fierce predators rattled as Opet moved.

Another warrior waved branches of smoking herbs around and between the two, striking them each at intervals, showering them with burning embers as they stood facing each other. Sing song chants filled the air. Opet lifted his arms high, calling for silence. He signaled Maliche to follow him to the edge of the lake where the two stood side by side.

In a low voice, he spoke so only Maliche could hear. "I do not understand why you, a Brin, would risk this, but before you die I want you to know I believe you have great courage. Therefore, I promise you, we will not kill the other Brin until your fate is decided." Turning to the assembled witnesses he declared, "You must first cleanse yourself of your past. Rid your body and mind of childhood and prepare for the mantle of a warrior." As the echoes died he motioned for Maliche to enter the lake.

"Prepare yourself. This is going to hurt, but don't show any sign of weakness. I can only dull your senses so much if we want to respect their traditions."

Maliche felt his body go numb; his skin tingled in the same way his legs felt after sitting too long. The water was hot. Painfully hot. He almost hesitated, but forced himself to keep moving deeper. His deadened senses helped, but he gritted his teeth and strained to control himself as the water reached his groin. It was then he felt the grip of two men on either arm helping him wade in further. He recognized Danet on his left, scowling at him.

"You are a fool, Brin. Brave, but a fool."

When he was waist deep, they turned him around. Danet and the warrior on his right raised curved bone hooks with a thick cord attached high above and chanted in the Kolandi tongue. In one swift movement they pierced Maliche's upper chest with the hooks. Maliche winced, but tolerated the reduced sense of pain. A trickle of blood ran down his torso from the piercing. With one hand on the cords, pulling them tight, their other hand grabbed his shoulders and bent him backward, using the cords as the primary method of supporting his weight while submerging him completely in the scalding lake. He was not prepared for how long they held him under. His lungs ached for air.

"Only a little while longer. Let me slow down your metabolism a bit. That should alleviate the need for oxygen some. You don't have the lung capacity of a Kolandi."

He felt his mind going dark, consciousness starting to slip away when the warriors lifted him by the hooks back to the surface. Coughing and gasping for breath, he held on tight to his companions. Wiping the water and drenched crest feathers from his eyes, he realized how red his skin looked. It should have hurt like strix, but he felt only a dull throb. As he struggled back to the shore, the warriors began their chanting again. Standing again in front of Opet, the men at his side cautiously released their hold on him.

Opet raised his hands and sang again in Kolandi. "The cleansing waters of Berit have prepared you for The Path. May you be shown the sacred ways and brought home safely so you may take your place as one of us."

He led Maliche to a small stone hut with a thick leather doorway. The interior was only large enough to sit or lie down, but not to stretch out, even for a Brin. In the center sat a fire, adding to the already oppressive heat. Danet and his partner pulled Maliche into the hut with the cords attached to the hooks in his chest. They forced him into a kneeling position and tied the ends of the cords to small black iron rings in the wall, stretching his skin as far as it could go without tearing. Maliche clenched his teeth as the pain level increased.

Opet knelt in prayer before the fire, continuing his chants tossing an arrangement of foul-smelling twigs, leaves, and powders into the flames.

"Holy Spirit of Berit, we send this soul to you for judgment. If he proves worthy, return him to us so he may become one of us. If you deem him unworthy, have no mercy. Rend his soul to pieces and feed them to the darkness of the strix-bound."

The stench of the thick smoke soon filled the room. Maliche felt the world around him start to lurch violently. His stomach did the same. All the while, Danet and the other pierced his arms, back and thighs with more of the hooks. Each one tied off to the remaining rings in the walls. Maliche hung on the verge of unconsciousness, groaning despite the dulling of his pain receptors.

Opet stood, hunching over in the small hut, and motioned the others out. He leaned in to Maliche's ear and whispered, "You will die here, Brin. You may not be Kolandi, but you have honor. I promise we will celebrate your ancestors when we give your body to the fires." He rose up and left, closing the door behind him. As his senses drifted away, Maliche heard the warriors chanting outside.

***

"*Don't worry. I can minimize the effects of the drugs... for the most part, anyway. Let me make a few adjustments to help make you more comfortable. It's the blood loss I'm mostly concerned about, but I can reduce some of that as well. Relax and go to sleep now. I'll have you back to your stubborn, impulsive self in no time.*"

That was the last memory Maliche had of the cavern. The rest became ensnared in wild phantasms of colors, shapes, noises, and patterns. Sometimes these hallucinations formed into recognizable images of home, friends and family, other times he recalled speaking to Jontar, Maripa and Karm as if they were well acquainted. Other dreams could only be described as nightmares where he took on the visage of a monster striding through Kolandi camps slaughtering them all. While in others he was equally monstrous, tearing down First Town, crushing any Brin who stood in his way, even Selan. Aras stood before him, blaming him for her death while proclaiming her undying love for him.

Time and space had no meaning. He saw vast planets in distant parts of the galaxy, some inhabited by peaceful beings, others by creatures ravaging through system after system. He stood on one world, with others of his kind, and watched the sun explode, engulfing them all. On other worlds he saw technologies far beyond his comprehension, experienced feelings of terror, hope, and greed regarding them. The universe was his home. No, he *was* the universe. He felt the pulse of every star as it was born and the surge of each one as it died.

He shrank to miniscule size and saw the structure of his own DNA. Its triple helix winding and twisting in complex patterns providing the instructions guiding his very existence. He witnessed molecules coming and going, joining and separating, creating the fabric of the universe. Energy in all its forms filled him. He heard the song of creation. And then all was darkness.

Consciousness fought its way back into his mind. He heard the call of something stabbing at his brain trying to haul him back to reality. Painfully, gradually, light returned.

"Well, that was a close one. I nearly lost you there more than once. You really are a fighter, even if you are a mere archaeologist. Time to wake up, though. We have a problem."

He struggled to open his eyes, to argue with whoever belonged to that voice. The light stung, but he forced his eyes open anyway. A blurry figure resolved itself into a familiar face.

"Neri?" His voice weak and strained, barely audible even this close. He tried to move his hand, but managed only a faint talon wiggle.

"Don't try to speak, Great One. You've been out for four days. No one has ever survived being on The Path for that long. Berit and the spirit of your ancestors are truly with you." She wiped his forehead with a cool rag. He couldn't recall a more wonderful feeling.

***

"Thank you, Neri. The meal is delicious, but I need to know what is going on outside these walls." Maliche handed the wooden bowl back to her and strode toward the entry to his alcove.

"Great One, forgive me, but I must insist you stay here until the princess permits your release."

Stopping mid stride, Maliche turned to face Neri, his crest feathers rising, and talons clenched. "So, even after traveling the Path of Berit, I am a prisoner here? Has Ryma lost all faith in me at last?"

Neri dropped the bowl on the floor, splattering the few remaining bits on her legs. She reached out to Maliche, bowing her head.

"No, Great One, you misunderstand me." With one hand on her breast and one hand reverently touching his chest she composed herself. "We only fear for your health. You only awoke this morning after your ordeal. We do not want you to risk another fever. You must rest." Her face, though compassionate, showed her firm determination to follow her princess's command.

Taking a deep breath to calm himself, Maliche took her hand. "It's all right, Neri, I'm not angry, just a bit frustrated is all." Cupping her chin in his hand, he gently lifted her face toward his and smiled. At his silent request, a soft blue glow surrounded him. "You see? I am fine now. There is no need to fear for my health, unless I go mad staring at these walls any longer. Where is Ryma?"

Neri flinched at the sight of the blue nimbus. Her mouth twisted, and brows furrowed as she weighed her duty to Ryma as well as to The Rocker. She slowly returned his smile.

"As you command, Great One. How you have recovered is outside my understanding, but I trust in your power. The princess is in her chambers awaiting the outcome of your companion's trial."

The smile vanished from Maliche's face. "Trial? What trial?"

"He is a Brin, Great One. His execution would not normally require a trial, but he brought you back to us, and helped you rescue the others so he deserves the trial by combat. It will be an honorable death."

***

Maliche turned on his heels and burst out of his alcove, running full speed down the narrow tunnels. The few he encountered pressed hard against the walls when they saw him charging, a bright orange light enfolding him. Gasping for air, he pushed his way passed the guards and burst into Ryma's private chambers.

"Ryma! You need to stop them! We need Nalot if we have any hope of winning this war!"

Rilo unsheathed her kital and jumped to bar Maliche's approach. Neri, having accompanied Maliche in the race to the Princesse's chambers, quickly joined her sister skatak. Ryma's face grew red, her glare would have stopped a charging grendel.

"How dare you enter my rooms without permission! Even you have no right!"

Maliche struggled to gain his composure, tried unsuccessfully to shake free of the princess's guardians, and realized the futility of his anger. Taking a deep breath, he calmed himself.

"Princess, I have just learned Nalot is to be killed in the arena. You cannot allow that to happen. We need him."

Ryma softened a bit and signaled for his release. "I understand your compassion for your fellow Brin, but Nalot has been tried and found guilty of his crimes against the Kolandi." She waved off Maliche's attempt to object. "In recognition of his bravery and skills, we are permitting him an honorable death as a warrior in the arena."

"You are making a mistake. There is more to him than you realize. You must prevent his death."

The Princess sighed, lowering her eyes to avoid looking at him. "It is for the best. It is done." She waved for her protectors to remove Maliche from the room.

"This has gone far enough. She won't like this, but I need to talk to her."

The biocomputer's bright blue glow filled the room, freezing everyone in place. Ryma's eyes grew wide in shock and anger.

After only seconds passed, the blue light vanished. Rilo and Neri rushed to Ryma's side as she staggered. With their help, she found a chair and took a sip of water Neri brought. She raised her chin to face Maliche.

"I told you, and that thing in your head, to NEVER do that to me again without my permission. I will deal with both of you after we get to the arena." She rose and stormed out of her chambers, followed by Neri and Rilo.

Maliche cringed as he imagined what Ryma might be planning for him. *"Oh, great. Now you've really done it. You know how much she hates you invading her mind like that. She may never forgive me for letting you."*

"We can work out our penitence later. Right now you need to get moving before she tries to face the warriors alone."

Chapter Nineteen

The door to the pit swung open. Nalot, bruised and bloody from the beatings and wearing only the shredded remnants of his pants, staggered through. Several stacks of weapons, spears, swords, mallets of various shapes and sizes, knives and more lay scattered around the dirt floor of the stone-walled circular arena. A deafening roar of jeers rose around him. The sweltering heat of the afternoon sun beat hard into the ring. Above him sat the rows of warriors anticipating the trial by combat.

In the place of honor, sat Opet flanked by his second in command, Danet. Opet lifted his arms to the sky to quiet the spectators. As the crowd became silent he rose to speak. "Warriors, the promised time has passed. The Rocker has not recovered. It is time to judge this Brin for his crimes." A loud cheer echoed through the stadium.

Opet pointed at Nalot, a scowl of hatred on his brown face. "Brin, your fate will be decided by the gods of our fathers. We award you this trial by combat because of your valor in helping The Rocker rescue many of our brothers and sisters. You have shown honor to us, your enemy, therefore your death will be an honorable one. Prepare yourself."

Nalot glared at Opet, spat on the ground, and walked over to the nearest pile of weapons. He selected a rusted, but sturdy curved sword and a long knife. Testing their balance in a series of swings and combat maneuvers, he satisfied himself as to their suitability.

Opet raised his arms again and raised his voice. "Let the trial begin. May the will of Berit prevail." He sat, and pointed to the opposite side of the arena.

The crowd cheered as a heavy wooden door opened and two Brin soldiers, also showing signs of recent tortures entered, shielding their eyes against the sun's glare.

Opet addressed Nalot again. "Brin, these two prisoners are the last survivors of the games to this point. They have shown their skills in battle and earned the privilege to either provide you with an honorable death, or earn a noble death for themselves." Opet surveyed the scene below, raised his fist in the air and brought it sharply down. "Begin!"

The two soldiers ran to nearby piles of weapons. The first grabbed a long metal tipped spear. The other picked through the choices quickly, settling on a spiked mace and long knife. They nodded toward each other and started to encircle Nalot.

Holding his ground, Nalot studied his foes as they moved into position. He noted their footwork, the way they held their weapons, and looked into their eyes. He decided they were probably two of the mercenaries hired by the military.

Yes, Nalot thought. *They are well trained and they are ready to fight to the death. So be it.*

He took his fighting stance and waited. The soldiers attacked together from opposite sides. With a side-step, Nalot slapped aside the spear thrust, using it to block the mace as it descended toward his head. He swung his sword at the spear-bearer, but met only empty air as the Brin dodged back, using the spear to keep him at a distance. Spinning to avoid another blow from the mace, Nalot feigned a move to his left, then dove right, stabbing his sword toward the soldier, but succeeding only in grazing his chest. A thin line of blood appeared, trickled down his body, but not enough to slow the soldier. A noise from behind alerted Nalot of another attack. He ducked, rolling to his right, barely avoiding the weapon, receiving a superficial slice to his left leg instead.

The maneuvers continued for several minutes longer. Nalot dodged and twisted, his weapons finding their mark frequently. Blood flowed from the many wounds he inflicted on his foes. The spearman limped heavily from a knife wound in his right leg. He held the spear in only one hand now. His left arm hung useless at his side from a deep cut of Nalot's sword.

The second mercenary now held only his knife, his mace arm was broken when Nalot grabbed him, wrenching the arm against the joint. He, too, was suffering from blood loss, primarily the gash on his head, courtesy of Nalot's knife.

Nalot could feel his wounds taking their toll. The spear met his skin on more than one occasion, leaving long stripes of blood in its wake. His head ached from a nearly fatal blow of the mace before he dealt with that one. He knew this had to end now. Summoning all of his skill, he attacked. He ducked under the spear thrust, rolled into the soldier's legs, putting him on the ground. Rising up onto his knees, Nalot turned and drove the sword deep into his opponent's chest. Blood splattered as the wound sliced open. Rising up without delay, he spun and tossed his knife into the face of the remaining foe as he closed in, trying to take advantage of Nalot's distraction. The mercenary screamed, flailed at the hilt of the knife protruding from his blood-splattered face, and fell dead in a puff of dust.

Nalot, breathing hard, covered in blood and dirt, placed his foot on the body of his opponent, and pulled the sword free of the man's chest. He turned to face Opet, squared his shoulders and pointed his sword at him.

"Are you entertained enough?"

Opet remained seated, listening to Danet's voice in his ear. Waving Danet off, Opet rose and crossed one arm over his chest in salute. "You have fought bravely and with skill. We honor you with a warrior's death." Raising both arms high, he called out in a loud voice. "Release the grendel!"

At the far end of the ring, a huge wooden door groaned as it slowly opened. In the darkness beyond, Nalot heard the snarls and stomps of the great beast. He swallowed hard as the creature charged out, struggling against massive chains, whipping its monstrous tusks side-to-side searching for a target. Froth flew in long arcs from its powerful jaws.

As Nalot and the beast studied each other, Opet continued. "Only a true warrior dare attempt to fight even a young grendel, Brin. None would dare an enraged adult such as this. Die well." He signaled for the chains to be released.

Nalot shook his head to clear his thoughts. He tested his legs and arms, taking note of his injuries, deciding how to protect them during this encounter. All the while he watched the grendel for any weakness. Three meters tall at the shoulders, the thick black fur would act like a shield against most weapons. The tusks were long and sharp. They could prove lethal with even a glancing blow. He took in a deep breath, steadied himself, and began his maneuvering.

The beast charged.

Chapter Twenty

"All right, I'm here. What's so important you couldn't relay over our private channel? And why out here in the middle of nowhere? I've never liked the wilderness."

Selan looked around in disgust at the deep green of the forest. A breeze rustled the leaves creating patterns of light dancing among the undergrowth alongside the path. Mertans sang their mating songs in the canopy while a small stream bubbled nearby. His breath condensed in small clouds in the chill air as the morning sun would take several more hours to warm the forest this time of year.

"This is the only place I could be sure nobody was listening. Raencert has ears everywhere." Syrinx, Selan's top agent living among the miners, sat on a moss covered log examining a stick-shaped insect crawling up the back of his hand. "I've always been fascinated at the perfection these creatures have mastered at blending in with their surroundings." He flicked the bug with one talon, sending it into a bush.

"Looks like just another filthy bug to me. Disgusting creatures." A corner of Selan's mouth scrunched up as if he had tasted a particularly awful mouthful.

"These mountains are only a few minutes' flight from the city. Besides, aren't you and your family spending the weekend in your vacation home just over the hill? What I have to say is far too important to risk getting out. It could be the key to removing Raencert from power once and for all."

"I would still prefer some out of the way spot in the city. Even as a kid I never liked coming out here." He looked for a place to sit, but decided to remain standing. "So much dirt and everything keeps moving. It's unsettling. Get on with it, Syrinx, what do you have?"

A smile, or the facsimile of one, crept onto the spy's craggy face. "One of my agents in the administrative offices cracked Raencert's codes. We got into his secret files."

Selan's mouth dropped a bit, his eyes widened. He tried to speak, but stumbled over the words. "You found... did you get the... you mean we have him at last?" without thinking, Selan sat on the damp log next to his agent, leaning heavily on one hand. "You found the files linking him to the Kolandi?"

No, not them... at least, not yet. There's a lot of information going back years. It will take time to work through it all. We have to be careful not to trip any hidden security programs."

"I thought you said you broke his codes."

"Raencert is no fluff-brain. He obviously wanted these files kept secret. His most precious files are kept under intense security, with precautions we haven't figured out how to bypass yet."

Selan looked up at the distant snow-covered hills beyond the trees overhead. He sighed, shoulders slumped, and head lowered. "Of course, you're right. We need the information at all cost." He turned back to Syrinx, noticing the smile had not faded from his face. "What have you learned?"

Syrinx reached into his coat pocket and pulled out a recording chip. "There's enough documentation here to prove Raencert is the recipient of most of the vast profits from his illegal dealings with the resources from the mines. There's no mention of the slaves. We've managed to piece together a long trail of written orders, bank accounts, memos, pay-offs, everything you need to show he orchestrated the entire so-called shortage of minerals and their subsequent high prices. We even located warehouses full of stockpiles of the undeclared supplies. But that's only the beginning." He reached into his pack, pulled out a stick of tirpit jerky and bit off a piece, then held out his other hand, palm up.

Selan grumbled as he reached into his own coat pocket pulling out a thick tan envelope, passing it to the spy. "All right, what else do you have? You know this is all worthless so long as he has his trumped up proof of my involvement in his schemes. Did you find those documents as well?"

"Also on the chip. And we were able to delete them from the hard drives. He has nothing on you now."

Selan jumped up from the log and threw a fist into the air. "Yes!"

A flock of mertans bolted from the trees as Selan's voice broke the stillness. Several harns shook leaves loose from the overhead branches as they ran, furry tails stiff with fear in their flight from the noise below.

"I have you now, you quetzal. The Assembly will have your head for this, and father will realize how capable I am once and for all." He danced a clumsy jig on the dirt path, nearly tripping over a protruding stone. Out of breath, he bent over, resting both hands on his knees breathing deeply. Forgetting his disdain of the slimy log, Selan returned to his seat. "Hah! Well done. Your 'bonus' is deserved. Now, what of my dear brother? I trust your operative has been in touch."

Syrinx let his smile fade. "No, sir. Our last communication was over a week ago when he informed us he had arranged to steal a transport and had the prisoner in hand. We lost contact with his vessel over the desert as it approached the mountains."

"Don't tell me your agent has failed. How could you lose contact?" Selan's eyes hardened. "Maybe I should demand a refund."

"These things take time, sir, and almost never go according to plans. That's why I put Talon on the case. He knows how to improvise and has never failed us. I did intercept some military communications about an attack from an unidentified vessel in the general vicinity of their last known position, so I suspect Talon is dealing with some unforeseen developments. He will be in touch as soon as he is able." He stood up and stepped back onto the narrow trail, brushing off his clothes.

Selan joined Syrinx on the path, squaring his shoulders as he approached. "You know I can't proceed with plans to discredit Raencert before the slaves are dealt with. We need to locate their whereabouts and destroy them all. If knowledge of their existence ever got out, we would all lose our positions in The Assembly. Taking out Raencert would be pointless if I lose everything, too."

"No need to be concerned, sir." Syrinx stood toe to toe with Selan, his eyes never flinching. "Talon has never let me down. He will signal us when he has information."

"You better be right. I can't afford any mistakes. If we don't hear anything in a few days, we may have to make alternative plans to find the slaves. This Talon better be as good as you say."

"He is, sir. Now, I must be going. I need to get back to the mines by this afternoon or there might be questions." He turned and strode off down the trail. Selan watched as he disappeared around a bend and the trees hid him from view."

Selan took the chip out of his pocket, examined it closely, and smiled again as he tossed it in the air, catching it in a tight fist. His crest feathers stood up. "I have you now, you old quetzal. As soon as we locate those phalking Kolandi and erase them you will fall. And I'm going to enjoy wiping the smugness off your face." He jammed the chip back into his pocket and walked back to the vacation home.

"Selan, what are you doing out here? I thought you hated all this fresh air?"

Lost in his thoughts, Selan startled at the sound of his wife's voice. He looked up to see her seated on a blue checkered blanket in a clearing next to the trail, a picnic lunch spread out in front of her.

"I thought you were back at the house with the children." He stepped carefully among the fallen leaves as if they were some unnatural surface he walked on.

Nedia stood up, brushing off the twigs and dust from her shorts and blouse. Adjusting her wide-brimmed hat, she stood on her toes to give her husband a peck on the cheek. "I decided this was too nice of a day, so I sent them off with Dykis to go play by the lake. It is so rare to get some time to myself these days. I didn't expect to run into you, but there may be enough here if you would like to join me." She sat back down on the blanket, stretching out her legs.

"Thank you, my love, but I think I'll head back to the house for lunch. I'll never understand the allure of eating on the ground. Too many germs and bugs for me."

She giggled, wiggled her fingers at him as if they were bugs, and shook her head. "And I'll never understand your distaste of nature, especially on such a beautiful day. Your late brother certainly knew how to appreciate the outdoors." She unwrapped a bit of meat, picked it up in her talons, and took a bite. "Germs... such nonsense. Are you sure you won't join me?"

He winced as he watched her chew. "No, my dear. Not today. But you enjoy yourself. Perhaps we could indulge in a drive later on... after I finish a bit of work."

"Can't you forget about Assembly business for one day?" She lowered her head and frowned. "The children were looking forward to spending time with you here. This is supposed to be a vacation, you know. Can't you at least talk with them before you disappear into your office for the day?"

He shook his head, shrugging his shoulders, holding his hands out palms up. "The government never sleeps, Nedia. Some matters need immediate attention. You're right, though. I'll stop by the lake for a bit before I tackle the bureaucracy."

"Thank you, dear. The children will be delighted." She popped a small slice of some yellow fruit in her mouth and waved him goodbye. As Selan disappeared around the bend Nedia pulled out a communicator from under the blanket. Her talons tapped out the remainder of a message. She hit send, and placed the device in her pocket.

Chapter Twenty-One

"How ow dare you address me in that manner in front of my people. Even The Rocker does not have the right to speak to me like that." She ran through the tunnels toward the arena, Maliche at her side, her two guardians close behind. "And *never* let your entity do that to me again without my permission. There is enough turmoil without my people thinking some mystical spirit controlled by you has possessed me. How can I continue to rule if their faith in me is destroyed?"

"My deepest apologies, Princess," Maliche gasped for air as he ran beside her. "I did not have any control over that. The biocomputer took matters in its own hands."

"I don't have hands."

"Strix, will you shut up."

"How *dare* you!" Her mouth hung open in shock.

"No, not you, Princess. I was reprimanding the device in here." He pointed to his head.

"Then you must learn to control it. I will not be violated in that manner again."

"You are right, Princess. I will…"

Dashing through the columned entryway, Maliche stopped in horror as he looked down into the arena. Ryma stood equally transfixed by the scene. A blood covered, barely recognizable Nalot staggered away from the dead body of a monstrous creature. A sword, its hilt broken off, impaled the beast's neck. Piles of guts spilled from a long gash along its belly. He watched, transfixed, as Nalot raised a hunting scythe toward the sky, the other arm hung limp at his side, shouting at the murmuring crowd. "Is that all you've got? I'm still standing here! Where is my warrior's death?"

Opet signaled to Danet who rose up, leaped over the wall, and pulled out his knife. He walked up to Nalot who remained unmoving, staring in defiance at Opet.

Danet took his position behind Nalot and whispered in his ear. "This will be quick, Brin." He raised his knife, and then placed it against Nalot's throat. The warriors stood in silence.

Maliche found his voice. "Stop! What are you doing?" A flash of orange light burst from him.

Opet jumped from his seat, his face red with anger. "What is the meaning of this interruption?" He turned to see the blazing figure of Maliche, The Rocker, fully recovered and descending the steps toward him, Ryma at his side, Rilo and Neri displaying their kitals prominently.

Opet stood firm against Maliche. "We waited the promised time. You were near death. This Brin was sentenced to pay for his crimes against the Kolandi." He hesitated, glanced back at Nalot and Danet, frozen as they awaited the outcome of this new encounter. "Because of his assistance in rescuing you, and risking his own life in defense of others, including you, the Brin has proven himself worthy of a warrior's death. Do not interfere. Return to your chamber."

Maliche's orange corona grew brighter and turned a deep red.

Ryma stepped between the two before they could hurt each other. "Enough of this! Opet I know the laws require you to kill all captured Brin. You have shown great honor and respect in offering this one a warrior's death in payment of his actions, but there is more at stake here than we realized."

Opet's jaw hung open, he faced his Princess with upraised palms. "The laws demand the death of our enemies. My warriors demand his life for his crimes."

Ryma gently placed one hand on his shoulder. "I understand, Opet. But I have seen into the mind of Maliche's spirit guide and much is revealed to me. I cannot discuss the matter further here. Come with me and I will explain what I now know."

"What of the prisoner? Is he simply to go free?"

"Bring him with us. There is much he too must hear. After we talk, you will understand his importance to our success, and particularly to the future of our people."

She spun on her heels and walked off, the two Skatak hurrying to keep up.

"You have no right to interfere in this," Nalot yelled at Maliche. Danet supported him by one arm. "I was prepared. You had no right."

Maliche, still in full orange glow, shouted back at Nalot. "Keep quiet. I'm trying to save your life."

"Be quiet, both of you!" Ryma commanded as she took her seat on her bench in front of Jontar Rocker's tomb. Neri and Rilo stood on either side with Seykel protecting the entry. "I will decide who lives and who dies here." She glared at the four of them.

Nalot shook free from Danet's grasp, stumbled, but regained his footing. "I am ready to accept my fate."

"Don't be a feather-fluffed quetzal, Nalot. I'm trying to save your life here," Maliche pleaded with him.

"Do not interfere," warned Opet. "His fate has been decided."

Maliche started to protest, but he felt his mind go blank.

"This is getting us nowhere. Let me help."

The red glow dimmed and changed to a yellowish orange as it grew to encompass everyone in the chamber. Skatak and warrior alike struggled, but found themselves unable to move.

Maliche's mouth moved, but the voice was an odd, more resonant version of his. "Princess, I apologize, but I must include you in this conversation as well, with your permission, of course."

"So, you do have some manners after all." Ryma scowled at Maliche who shrugged helplessly.

"Of course, but are manners really required for a spirit guide?"

The voice rang in each of their minds.

"All of you need to stop this right now and listen to me."

Images of the past and the future, of Brin and Kolandi working together, inhabiting the world in peace flashed before them. Their minds filled with the sights and sounds of the original encounter between Kolandi and Brin. Maliche saw Jontar, Maripa and Karm in his mind and how they were saved by the two brothers. Ryma witnessed the efforts of those long dead Brin to save her ancestors after the plague which nearly wiped them out. The desperate struggles of both species to survive on this world, the growth of the Brin to power and control over the Kolandi, but also the ignorance of nearly all of the Brin to the plight of the enslaved people all rushed through their heads. Then the biocomputer showed them projections of the possible future, of both species working together and joining together in a hybrid species, stronger than either of its parents.

"I've been working on this plan for too many centuries to let you end it now. I need this Brin to further those plans. You will not kill him. I need the two of you working together or all will fail. Do I have your attention?"

The glow dimmed and vanished. "Clear this chamber and prepare a room for Nalot. Place a guard at the door. No one is to harm him." Ryma addressed the Kolandi in her most regal tone then turned to face Maliche again. Her eyes narrowed dangerously. "And you... come with me."

Opet and Danet stood, mouths agape in a shocked, distinctly unwarrior-like silence. Stunned by the overwhelming revelations, and the presence of The Rocker's entity in their minds, it took a few moments for them to recover.

Opet shook his head and tilted it toward Danet. "It appears we have much to consider." He said. Placing a hand gently on Nalot's back, with Danet helping steady the Brin, the trio headed off down the passage.

***

Upon reaching the entry to her chamber, Ryma spoke quietly to her Skatak. The women nodded and took positions on either side of the doorway. She pointed at Maliche. "You. Inside now, and not a word."

Once the door shut behind them she whirled on Maliche. "Can I speak to your companion? I need to get something straight with it once and for all. And I would like to do so without you listening in."

Maliche furrowed his brow and scratched at his crest feathers. "I don't know. Let me check." His mind turned inward to ask the biocomputer if it could do as she asked.

"Of course I can." A purple glow surrounded Maliche as his face blanked.

"What do you wish to say, Princess?" The biocomputer's more resonant version of Maliche's voice came from his mouth. "Are you certain Maliche cannot hear what we say?"

"He is sound asleep. We are alone."

"I don't know how Maliche felt when you first entered his mind, but I find it—overwhelming." She paced the room in front of him. "I need time to prepare myself for the sensations you bring to my mind."

"I understand, Princess. Maliche had many of the same sensations, but his family history helped him adjust. I will allow you time to prepare yourself in the future."

"And what if I don't want you to be inside my head? Will you honor my refusal?"

A long silence ensued. Ryma stopped her pacing and stared at Maliche's inert face. "Well? Will you respect my privacy or not?"

"Yes, Princess. I will agree to your terms."

She nodded her ascent and approached Maliche, placing one hand on his arm. "Thank you. Can you bring him back now?" She withdrew her hand and stood back.

Maliche wobbled a bit as he returned to consciousness and found a bench to sit on. "Did you get what you needed?"

Ryma handed him a cup of water and sat next to him. Nodding her head, she stared at her hands clasped tightly in her lap. "I was so worried for you. First when you were captured, and then when you failed to recover from the ordeals for so long. I thought I had lost you. I was so angry."

"You... wait... what? You were worried about me?"

"Of course I was worried. I have been inside your mind, at least partially. I think that experience made me fall in love with you." Keeping her face lowered, she looked up at Maliche through her long lashes.

Maliche gulped and held her gaze. "You love me? Are you sure? Because I think I love you, too. I can't stop thinking about you when we're apart."

Ryma smiled at him, lifting her chin to face him directly. "So, what do we do now?"

The two embraced, kissing and holding onto each other as if trying to meld into one being. Together they lowered themselves onto the thick fur rug, exploring each other's bodies with their touch. As they removed each other's clothes, a pale pink glow surrounded them.

"I thought I told you not to do that again," the princess chided Maliche about the pink glow as it subsided. After an hour of love-making they sat up and gathered their garments.

"Sorry. As I said, it sometimes has a mind of its own. I think it was a bit embarrassed."

Ryma laughed as she stood, tugging on her gown to readjust it. She gave Maliche a wink. "Maybe we should have it disconnected."

"Not Funny."

"Then behave yourself next time." He smiled at Ryma pointing to his head.

When they were both dressed, Ryma opened the wooden door to her private chamber and called for Rilo. "Have Nalot brought back to the main hall and assemble the people."

An hour later, with everyone present, and Maliche at her side, Ryma addressed her people. "The Rocker has something he wishes to say." She sat on her bench and waved him forward.

Standing before Nalot, Maliche lifted him to his feet and turned him to face the Kolandi.

"My brothers." An angry muttering rose from the audience of warriors. Maliche raised one hand to quiet them. "Yes, my brothers. Have I not earned the right to call you that now that I have walked The Path of Berit? Am I not a descendant of The Rocker? Have I not proven myself to you all?" He stood facing them, looking each in the eye. The pale blue glow shimmered around him again. "As your brother, I tell you this Brin is no enemy." The crowd shuffled nervously, but did not object. "This Brin saved my life. He saved the life of each of the slaves we brought back with us. He saved the lives of many of you here now who were at the encampment under attack from the Brin soldiers."

Maliche turned to the princess and raised his voice. "I claim the life debt for this man, and claim responsibility for him. Will you grant me this right?"

Before she could answer, a small figure wormed her way through the crowd to stand beside the prisoner.

"I, too, claim the life debt." Seykel, dressed in the formal uniform of the Skatak, brown leather hide tunic with green and blue stones woven in dramatic patterns, laid one hand on Nalot's back, the other on her kital. "Without him, I would not be here today. I will stand with The Rocker and take responsibility for him."

At that moment, Opet set aside his scythe and took his place at Nalot's side. "I, too, will be responsible for this Brin. I am witness to his bravery and skills in the arena as well as Nevik's sacrifice. He gave his life for this one. That is testimony enough for me."

Ryma smiled and stood as she lifted her hands high. "Then let all here be witness. Three of our brethren have found worthiness in this prisoner and claim responsibility for his actions and his life. Is there one here who wishes to voice opposition?"

Stunned silence filled the room, everyone looking to see if anyone was willing to oppose the three claimants.

"Then, with no opposition, I proclaim this Brin free from his past guilt and blame. Let his future actions determine our path."

Nalot, open mouth, and wide eyed, stared at his three protectors, but his eyes lingered most on Seykel. His brow furrowed as his crest quivered, flashing a confusion of muted colors. Opet pulled out his hunting knife and handed it to Nalot. The two eyed each other, and then nodded in silent agreement.

"Let us drink together to celebrate the death of your former life and the birth of the new." Opet slapped Nalot on the back and together, they walked out of the proceedings.

As soon as he was alone in his chamber, Maliche addressed the biocomputer. *"All right, what are you up to? What is this plan of yours and those hybrids you talked about? Why is it so important for Brin and Kolandi to join?"*

"This is the central purpose of my existence. It is why I was built and combined with Karm. Brin DNA hold the key to curing the plague-contaminated DNA of the Kolandi. This must be done."

"But WHY must it be done? For what purpose?"

The device hesitated, struggling to continue. *"I do not know. There is something hidden in my programming which I cannot break through. I have tried for centuries to uncover the truth behind this imperative, but have failed every time. For some reason, that data was withheld from my core."*

"But that makes no sense," Maliche thought in reply and shook his head. *"Why would you be programmed with such life-altering... world-changing purpose, and not know why?"*

"Despite my awakening sentience, I am still a machine, of sorts. I am limited by my creators' designs. I can only speculate there must be secrets the Skae were unwilling to risk revealing. What those may be, I cannot say."

Maliche sat on the edge of his bed, staring at the wall. His eyes came to rest on one of the carved decorations near the ceiling. It depicted a spear-shaped object standing on what appeared to be a planet. Next to the object stood two beings. Facing them were three others kneeling with arms outstretched as if pleading for help.

Maliche rubbed his face with his hands and sighed out loud. "What have I gotten myself into now?"

***

Nalot grimaced as the light stung his eyes. "Three weeks of helping on these raids and they still don't trust me enough to let me come and go unhooded from the caves." He rubbed his eyes and scratched his crest with the talons of one hand. "Can't blame them though, my mission hasn't changed."

"Give it some time. We don't really know anything about you."

"And yet those two stood up for me. And what's with the Seykel? She hovers around me like some sort of dinter around a nut harvest." He raised the scope to his eyes, getting a close look at the mine entrance and surrounding buildings.

"Haven't you figured it out yet?" Maliche took his own scope and viewed the scene below.

Miners filed out of the lift and hung their tokens on the count board. A second group, much cleaner, replaced them and descended into the darkness of the shaft.

"They take their life debts seriously. Plus, you're helping to train her younger brother. He was so weak when we rescued him with her and the others she was afraid he might never recover enough to become a warrior."

"He has the heart of a warrior, that one. Not sure if his skills will ever amount to anything, but he never gives up." A half grin crossed Nalot's lips, slightly creasing his gnarled and dusty face. "Opet's the one that has me really baffled, though."

"How's that?"

"Why would a warrior of his stature, and a former slave, stand up for me like he did? If it was me, I would have killed him without thinking about it. The rest of them would stick a spear in me in a heartbeat if it wasn't for the princess's order."

"I think the two of you are alike in a lot of ways. He nearly killed me, too, when we first met." He reached down and pulled out his medallion. "When he saw this, he decided to keep me alive a while longer and let the princess decide my fate."

"And what is that? Some mystical, magical emblem or something?"

"An heirloom from my ancestors, given to them by one of his ancestors. The stuff of legends. The Kolandi take their legends very seriously."

Nalot stared silently through his scope. "The sun's going down. Time to move." He grabbed his pack, stuffed the scope in, and slid back down the hill to the waiting raiding party. Seykel took his pack and shouldered it.

By the time the group moved into position, darkness had fallen. Only the yellow lights of the compound provided illumination on this chilly moonless night. They advanced in three groups of five. One group to locate and steal supplies, one to free slaves, and one to plant explosives to destroy what they could not steal. Maliche, Nalot, and Seykel led the explosives group.

Avoiding the circles of light, the team made their way among the buildings. They placed charges on the outside of the power station, the central office, and the supply depot. There was too much to carry away, so they planned to eliminate the rest. Nalot suggested using some of the plastic explosives they found there instead of their own. Maliche agreed and stood watch as Nalot picked the lock to the remote building, isolated to prevent widespread damage in case of accident. A soft click alerted Nalot of the lock's opening.

"Got it. A simple old style padlock, just like I said it would be." He unhooked it from the latch, examined it for a moment, turning it in his hands. He started to place it in his pocket.

Seykel watched him reach into his pocket. "What are you doing?"

"I thought it might make a nice souvenir back in my room."

She shook her head, frowning at the object. "No. It is a Brin thing and of no use to us. Kolandi have no use for locks. Too many of us have been kept prisoners by such things. It has no place in our caves."

"All right, not a problem." He fished around in his pocket a moment, brought out the lock, and tossed it aside. "Satisfied now?" He smiled at her, or at least gave his best impression of one.

"Just get the explosives so we can be done with this and go home."

Creeping inside, he located an open crate of explosives and detonators, filled a satchel, and returned to his group. With the added firepower, the group agreed to destroy the shuttle transports at the airfield on the outskirts of the facility.

Maliche leaned carefully around the corner of a large shipping crate, and then crawled back to his group. "This is going to be a bit more difficult. There must be five or six guards around those transports."

"Don't worry," Nalot assured him with a pat on the back. "Once those buildings start to go up, they will be too busy trying to put out the fires to even notice us."

Ten minutes later, the night sky blazed with light. The noise was deafening as the supply depot blew. The guards at the airfield stood motionless for a few seconds, and then took off running toward the inferno of the rest of mining facility.

Nalot nudged Maliche with an elbow. "Told you they weren't a problem."

A crack on the back of his head made Nalot wince. "Don't gloat. It's not good manners," Seykel chided him, and then took off running to the shuttle transport assigned to her.

Nalot rubbed his head, and ran off toward his own target. Once at the aircraft, he pulled out his charges and placed them inside the engine, setting the timer for fifteen minutes as agreed.

"No!" Nalot heard Seykel's shout simultaneously with the discharge of an energy rifle. He pulled out his knife and spun around.

He saw Seykel landing in a crouch in front of a soldier he had not seen in the shadows. The Brin's rifle landed on the ground several meters away in a clatter. Before he could react, Seykel pulled out her kital and in a flurry of maneuvers avoiding his attempts to cut her with his knife, sliced the soldier's leg, sending him to his knees. Another quick spin and the kital dug deep into the Brin's neck. He grabbed for the spurting wound, and then collapsed to the ground.

"What have you done, girl?" He ran to her, turned her over to see the ugly wound in her side. The soldier had apparently not missed all of his blows.

She smiled up at Nalot, coughing. "I have your life debt. I couldn't let him shoot you."

Nalot opened a bandage from his satchel and pressed hard on the wound to stop the bleeding. "Young fool... feather-fluffed kak for brains." He wrapped the bandage tight, picked her up and carried her back to the rendezvous point.

"What happened?" Maliche ran toward the pair as Nalot carried Seykel.

"She'll be all right, just took a hit in her side. She's passed out from the shock, but she should be fine in a few days."

"How the strix did that happen?"

Nalot lowered his head and held her closer. "I got careless. Didn't notice the guard that stayed behind. She tried to warn me and fought him. I've never seen such skill in one so young."

At that moment, the blast of more detonations, this time from the airfield, split the air. They saw burning pieces of airships flying through the night sky trailing orange smoky contrails behind them. The smell of burning fuel and dense clouds of black smoke filled the air.

Maliche stood up and called to the others. "Let's go home. The rest of the expedition will be worried about us."

***

A lone figure searched the rubble, kicking aside bits of debris from charred buildings. Near the remains of the now smoldering supply depot, he bent over and picked up a piece of metal. He pulled out a small recording device from the former padlock, examined it, then closed his talons around it and smiled.

"We have what we came for. Take me back now."

"Yes sir, Captain Syrinx. The transport is ready for takeoff."

***

"That's it, we finally have him." Selan punched the keys necessary to hide and encrypt the folder of information from Syrinx and threw his fist in the air. "Now with the coordinates provided by Talon we know the location of the caves where the escaped slaves are hiding. Now I can eliminate them and send Raencert's precious production schedules into utter chaos. The final quill to break his neck."

He picked up the communicator, gave the command for stealth mode, and waited as the system made the predetermined connections.

A crisp deep voice responded. "Kelden here, sir."

"General, time to implement downfall. How long before you can begin?"

"With our current status, sir, I believe we can put everything in motion in three weeks."

"We may have to hold off on the attack for a while, general. There may be some changes in the command structure in the near future."

"Sir, the troops have been training for weeks now. Our timetables are nearly complete. Any changes now may delay us for a month or more. We're ready."

"No, General. We cannot proceed until other matters are settled. I will keep you informed as matters develop. Continue making your preparations, but be ready to make adjustments as required. Things are very fluid at the moment and we may need to move quickly."

"Yes, sir. I understand. My troops will be ready to move on your word."

The connection ended and Selan sat behind his desk smiling.

Chapter Twenty-Two

Nalot sat by Seykel's bedside waiting for her to wake up. The steady rhythm of her chest rising and falling as she breathed was almost hypnotic. After several hours, he was thankfully becoming nose-blind to the smell of herbs, roots and all manner of concoctions boiling in pots as various healing poultices were prepared.

The night doctor padded softly from bed to bed in the dimly lit hospital chamber of the caves treating an assortment battle wounds and other ailments. The doctor gently lifted the medicated bandage from Seykel's injury, nodded in approval, and patted Nalot's shoulder as she moved on.

"The wound is healing well. She will be back on her feet in a day or two."

Nalot's thoughts focused on the conflict between his mission and his growing respect for the Kolandi.

A weak voice startled Nalot out of his ruminations. "I'm glad you are not injured." Seykel looked up at him with half-lidded eyes and a smile.

He scowled at her. "What the strix did you think you were doing? A simple shout would have given me warning enough to deal with that phalking guard."

Seykel's smile turned to stern indignation. "I am Skatak. I am a trained warrior, no less than Opet, Danet, or even you." Tears welled up in her eyes, an embarrassing side-effect of the poultice herbs.

"Don't be going all to pieces on me now." He took her small hand in his, gently stroking her wrist with a talon. "You did a brave thing out there. Stupid, but very brave.

Better to be smart than brave, though. Remember that next time."

Her smile returned and she sniffed away the tears. "I'll try to remember, but you need to be more careful. I assumed one with your abilities would see his approach. I nearly didn't get there in time. How long have I been out?"

"Only a couple of days. The doc says you'll be fine soon. Maybe even get out of here tomorrow if someone agrees to look after you."

Her eyes widened and an impish smile grew. "Will you be that someone?"

He feigned annoyance and sat up straighter. "I'm no babysitter. Maybe I have things to do with Rocker."

She squinted, studying his face. "You're lying. You already agreed, didn't you?"

He winked at her and gave a slightly improved grin, which did not look as frightening as before. "Yeah, well, maybe I did. Seeing how everyone else is so busy and all. No raids are planned for a few days yet, so guess I'll be your nursemaid."

Seykel shifted herself into a more comfortable position, patted his hand, and closed her eyes. "Good. I think I'll take a little nap now. Being a heroine is exhausting you know."

Once she settled into a deep sleep, Nalot approached the doctor. "I'll be over at the east entrance for a while. Send someone when she wakes up again."

Ten minutes later, he found himself sitting on a large boulder overlooking the valley. The tall mountains, snow covering their jagged peaks, cast long shadows over the vast scrub lands below as the sun began to sink. The glow of the setting sun seemed to set the changing colors of the leaves ablaze. A chill in the air foretold the onset of autumn. In the glade below, he watched as one pair of warriors trained youth in the art of using a scythe to hunt, while other pairs provided instruction in hand-to-hand combat or tracking, or other skills necessary to a warrior.

"Amazing people, aren't they?" Maliche sat beside Nalot, tossing him a sweet tuber to chew on. "Even after everything they have been through, they can still laugh and see a future for themselves."

"They are a strong and proud people. True warriors." He continued to stare at the training clusters below. "I've been watching them. There is much honor here, something I can respect."

After a few minutes of silence, Maliche turned to face Nalot. "My friend in here tells me he thinks you are ready to talk to me about something." He pointed to his head with one talon.

Nalot sighed deeply, remained silent for a moment, and then nodded to himself. "Your friend is correct. I have a confession to make. Wouldn't blame you if you turned me over to them to have me killed for it. That's probably what I would do in your place, but I can't keep doing my job any longer. Not with a clean conscience, anyway."

"Why don't you get it out and let me decide what I'm going to do about it? Remember, I have your life debt, too."

Nalot stood up and took a few steps, hands clasped behind his back, tapping together as he thought. "I'm not what you think, Maliche. I'm no soldier prison guard helping you escape." He paced back and forth as he talked, constantly watching the Kolandi below. "I've betrayed all of you. I'm a spy sent by your brother to find out where these people are hiding so he can kill them all."

Maliche's jaw dropped. "So, it's true? Selan is in on all of this? Even my shuttle crash?"

"Not my place to know all of the particulars, but from what I put together, it seems you and your brother have some issues to work out." He turned to face Maliche. "I wasn't involved in any of this until you were captured, so I don't know much about your crash, other than the files they provided me. My job was to have you lead me here so I could gather as much intelligence about the Kolandi as possible."

"How much do they know?"

"During the last raid, I hid a recording chip inside the supply shed's lock. It contained coordinates of this and several other caverns as well as numbers of Kolandi, defensive capabilities, and other relevant information. Enough for them to carry out a full scale attack and wipe them out. I'm sure Syrinx has found the information by now."

Maliche turned his back and walked away a few steps. He stood silently staring out into the distance. "What about my father and the rest? Are they involved as well?"

"Not to my knowledge. As far as I know, this is strictly an internal matter between your brother and Raencert."

Combing his crest with his talons for a moment, Maliche closed his eyes, and drifted off in mental conversation with the biocomputer entity. After a few moments he nodded and turned back to face Nalot. "Very well then. If my brother is lost to me, so be it. We need to warn the rest of The Assembly about how corrupt and despicable he and the guilds have become."

Nalot laughed for the first time in Maliche's memory. "You're going to take on the guilds, the military with energy weapons and attack transports with nothing more than this group of Kolandi and their bows? You're phalking mad."

"Probably, but I have a plan. We need to talk to Ryma, Opet and Danet."

Nalot held his hands up to stop Maliche. "Now, wait just a minute. If we tell them about my betrayal, they'll have me torn limb from limb. No deal."

"Then why did you tell me?"

"You're Brin, not one of them, despite your mystical mumbo jumbo about legends and kak. I've come to respect you and the Kolandi, they're my kind of people, but I'm no fool. I want to be a hundred kilometers from here when they find out about me."

Maliche grasped Nalot's shoulders, standing face-to-face with him. "Trust me. I can protect you. I don't think Seykel will let them do anything to you either. She, and many others, see the side of you who protected them and works side by side with them every day. It may take a bit of convincing, but I am The Rocker."

Nalot stared into Maliche's eyes, searching. "I hope it's enough. Let's get this over with." He spun around and strode toward the princess's chambers with Maliche at his side.

***

Ryma crossed the space between them, lifted her arm, and slapped Nalot across the face with all her strength. He remained silent, absorbing the strike without flinching. "How dare you!" She slapped him again. "After we have taken you in… trusted you… accepted you. I should have you executed immediately."

Nalot stood before her, accepting her tirade.

Maliche let her rage run its course. When she began to pace the room he approached her. "Ryma, I know what a terrible blow this has been, but he has done the honorable thing and come to us knowing full well his likely fate."

She turned on him, her fury finding a new target. "Don't you dare defend him. Not after such betrayal. The lives of my people are at risk as never before due to his actions. And you ask me to forgive him? Never! Even The Rocker hasn't the right." She started summoning her guards when Maliche grabbed her arms from behind.

"I'm sorry to do this to you, Princess, but you must understand."

A blazing yellow light began to grow outward from Maliche's palms until it surrounded both of them, holding them in a trance for several minutes. As it subsided, Ryma collapsed into Maliche's arms. The two Brin carried the unconscious princess to her bed chamber and placed her gently on the fur covered cot.

Maliche knelt beside her, checking her pulse.

"Get me a cloth and some cool water."

Nalot dipped a cloth in a basin of water, wrung it out and handed it to Maliche, then stood back by the entry to the chamber.

In a moment, Ryma's eyes fluttered as she returned to consciousness. She bolted upright, clutching her temples, and held back a sickening wretch. "Will you stop doing that to me?! It is a terrible invasion." She swiped his hands away.

"Sorry, Princess, but it is imperative you believe how sincere Nalot is, and how vital he is to our future. This was the only way to circumvent hours, possibly days we don't have to spend in arguing."

As her mind began to focus and realization of the information she received from the biocomputer sharpened, her anger relented. She looked up toward Nalot.

"Come here, Nalot. Kneel before me." She held out one hand in his direction.

Nalot approached swiftly, got down on one knee, and took her hand in his, bowing his head.

"Forgive me, Princess. I have done your people a great disservice. My only excuse is that I did not understand. Now I know what a fool I was. I pledge my life to you and the Kolandi."

She smiled and squeezed his rough, scaly hands in hers. "You are forgiven, Nalot. I hope your skills are enough to undo what you have started."

She tilted her face to give Maliche a stern gaze. "You and I are not done yet. Your entity needs some lessons in how to treat its princess."

Maliche bowed, deep violet glow emanated from his left palm which he understood to be a sort of apology from the biocomputer. "We understand. And thank you. But now we must make plans on how to deal with this emergency. We need to enlist the help of Opet and Danet."

She thought for a while, and then rose from her bed, gathering the two Brin to her in a conspiratorial triad. "They need to know of this imminent attack, but not of the betrayal. Not yet, at least. We will invent a story of how you discovered the information."

"I could have the biocomputer convince them." Maliche's left palm glowed a bright green.

Ryma took Maliche's face in a firm grip, glaring into his eyes. "Absolutely not. Do you hear me in there? You will never invade the mind of any of my people again. Not without my permission. And I do not foresee ever granting it. Am I perfectly understood on this?"

The green glow dulled to a soft blue as Maliche replied. "Yes, Ryma. We understand."

She faced Nalot next, one hand on his shoulder. "Can you continue to deceive them for a while longer?"

Nalot nodded his head in agreement. "I am a trained spy, Princess. Deception is what we are best at. It grieves me to do this to an ally, but I understand the need. Perhaps we can tell them I finally had time to decipher some papers I recovered during the last raid and learned of the coming attack. But I am concerned about Seykel. I am reluctant to lose her faith in me."

"I don't think you need to worry about her, Nalot." Peering over his shoulder toward the partially open door to her private room, she raised her voice a bit. "Did you hear everything you needed to hear, Seykel?"

The door creaked as it slowly opened, revealing a sheepish appearing Seykel. She approached the three, head down, hands folded in front of her. Her sandaled feet made no sound on the hide-covered floor.

"Yes, ma'am. I am happy you signaled me to remain hidden, but listen. I almost disobeyed when you collapsed, but I trusted The Great One would not harm you." She stood by Nalot's side, peering up at him.

"I know your heart, Nalot. I believe you have repented your betrayal and will do everything in your power to help us now." She took his cracked talons in her hand, pressing them to her chest. "I will not reveal your secret to the others."

Nalot stood wordlessly staring at the young girl for several moments before releasing her grip and facing the others. "We need to get started. No telling how long we have."

***

Selan waited impatiently in the café. Dust filled the air with each passing mag-lev vehicle. Fortunately, there were few of those in such a remote location. The diner smelled of grease and overcooked food. The tables showed the wear of thousands of meals served over the years. The chairs badly needed repainting. The curving walls supported photographs of random scenes from around the continent.

A scrawny Brin wearing a light green apron stood behind the serving counter wiping off some glassware. An overweight, bespectacled Brin in a sweat stained shirt flipped some grilling meat of indeterminate origin. Selan's stomach lurched at the thought of anyone actually eating food prepared under such primitive conditions. Not a microwaver or nutrient re-hydrator was in sight. Only one couple, an exhausted looking elderly pair in outdated colorful clothing, sat in a booth by the window.

An old mag-lev pulled into the parking lot raised another cloud of dust as it came to rest. Selan sat up straighter as he recognized the middle aged Brin getting out of the vehicle. A wave of heat washed over him as the door opened.

"Hello, Syrinx. It's about time you got here. I was actually contemplating ordering something to eat here."

The head of Selan's spy ring sat in the chair opposite him, its legs squeaking in protest. "I had to make sure you weren't followed. Can't be too careful in matters like this." He called out to the thin Brin at the counter. "A large water here."

Selan sat tapping his talons on the table impatiently as the waiter brought the water and Syrinx downed half of it in one long gulp. "Disgusting. There's probably billions of diseases floating around in that unfiltered swill. How can you stomach it?"

Syrinx held up the glass, watched the ice sparkle, and took another gulp. "Some of us don't have the luxury to be so particular in our diet. Can't always tell where or when the next meal comes."

Selan fought back the urge to comment how he pays him well enough to eat like a king, and changed the subject. "What is so urgent we had to meet in such an Eternal forsaken place as this?"

Syrinx handed him a memory chip. "Talon sent the information we've been waiting for. It's very detailed, everything you requested."

"It's about time," Selan said as he grabbed the chip. "I about gave up hope. I thought you said he was the best. What took him so long?"

Syrinx emptied his glass, examined it, and set it back on the table exactly back on the water ring it had made. "These things take time. He has never failed me. Now, about payment."

"Are you certain everything I need to begin the operation is here?"

"Yes. As I said, Talon is the best."

Selan pulled out his communicator, touched a few buttons entering the code, waited for the requested screen to appear, typed in a set of seven figures, pressed the send key and showed it to his companion. "Just as we agreed. Are you satisfied?"

Syrinx nodded, pushed back his chair, and walked out of the diner. Selan watched his mag-lev lift up and accelerate down the dirt road. He clapped his talons together, smiling broadly. "At last I have you, Raencert. I've played your puppet for too long. Now it is time for you to pay."

He considered ordering a flavored tea, but one look at the filth on the waiter's apron convinced him to wait until he got back to civilization. After the agreed upon fifteen-minute delay, he left the café and headed back to First Town.

Chapter Twenty-Three

"As you can see, council members, the evidence of Raencert's guilt is incontrovertible. His mismanagement of government funds, inept administrative practices, and, though there is no direct evidence, the many implications of his corrupt and criminal abuse of his station provide us with ample grounds for his removal from office."

Selan stood beaming at the podium before the special council of The Assembly. Overhead, the gold chandelier with its dozens of electrically flickering candle-like lamps illuminated the small blue carpeted chamber. Tall stained-glass windows illustrated several important scenes of Brin history on Raince'to, not a few featuring Maripa, Jontar Rocker, and Karm among other illustrious members of Selan's ancestors. The small gallery was empty, being late in the evening. Eleven high backed metal chairs sat behind the long, curved bench. In each chair sat a somber faced assemblyman in full regalia.

The vital and wide-reaching implications of the proceedings dictated extreme caution. Fejf, the head assemblyman, Selan's father, called the heads of each guild as well as the leading assemblymen together in this special council rather than risk a full assembly session. The downfall of such a powerful individual as Raencert required extremely cautious handling.

In the weeks since his meeting with Syrinx, Selan worked tirelessly to prepare his case against the leader of the mining guild, carefully omitting all references to the Kolandi slaves. He would deal with them later. Even his plans to wipe out the slaves were put on hold. No, he wanted Raencert exposed for the corrupt quetzal he was. Any public outcry about freeing slaves would end his hopes to run the mines.

"Guildsman Raencert," Fejf addressed the accused. "You have heard the evidence presented to this council. How do you respond?"

Raencert lifted his immense bulk out of his chair and approached the podium. Several small recording spheres hovered in strategic locations around the assembly courtroom. The two assigned to focus on the defendant adjusted their position to keep him in focus. Refusing to look at Selan as they passed, he put on his most diplomatic manners as he addressed the other leaders.

"Honored assemblymen, I stand before you innocent of all these false charges laid before you." He looked directly at Fejf. "With all due respect, Headsman, Selan has long been envious of my position. His sole purpose here is to discredit me with misleading and outright manufactured evidence in an attempt to usurp me as head of the mining guild—"

"I fail to follow your reasoning, guildsman," one of the councilmen interrupted with a raised hand, one talon shifting a paper in front of him. "Selan's record is one of nearly total support of your proposals before The Assembly."

"One can vote in favor of wise decisions, councilman," Raencert replied, tilting his head in his direction, "and yet have ambitions to take control for himself."

"And yet," said another councilman to Fejf's left, "every public statement by young Selan, and indeed, many in private and on the record show nothing but almost compulsive backing of your leadership. He has, on many occasions, refused to participate in previous investigations into allegations of improprieties of your management of the guild."

Raencert shook his head, lifting his hands in supplication. "Who here has never been accused of wrongdoing?" He waved the talon of one hand from one side of the long table to the other. "Does not being a leader with so much responsibility for so many often involve making decisions which, though necessary for the greater good, prove unpopular to some? Do not those who disagree with a policy often make unjust claims against those who bear the responsibility?" Raencert turned now to his left, jabbing a talon in Selan's direction. "And is it so unthinkable for one as devious and scheming as this one to carefully plot a course of action to seem supportive of a leadership, only to betray those who trusted him in the end?"

Fejf glared at Raencert. "If you are making allegations before this assembly, sir, you had best come prepared to back them with incontrovertible evidence. Or do you wish to add perjury to your charges?"

Raencert placed his hands on the podium, returning his dark gaze to Fejf. "I make no allegations, Headsman. I only present a question for consideration." He glanced again at Selan. "After recent security breaches to mining guild network systems, a number of vital files and records have been corrupted, so even if I had wished to present such proof of anyone's criminal activity I am unable to do so. I merely hoped to present a possibility without accusation."

"The internal network difficulties of the guild do not concern us, sir," said an aged councilman to Fejf's right. "Several of us have conducted independent searches into the charges presented here in an attempt to verify the veracity of the allegations. As you say, many decisions made by those in power often prove unpopular, but are not criminal. In your case, however, there can be little doubt of your guilt. Much of the information presented to us bears the stamp of your own office, complete with your signature. The diverting of government funds and guild property into your own personal accounts is well documented and independently confirmed. Years of tax evasion, both guild and personal, again with your direct involvement is amply documented. I am afraid your pleas of innocence and persecution appear, once again, that you're attempting to deceive this illustrious body."

Raencert opened his mouth to reply, but froze at a signal from Fejf.

"I am in agreement with the esteemed councilman," said Fejf, signaling the councilman. "Your defense is without merit and simply a ploy to hide the truth from us."

"Now just a minute, Fejf," Raencert's anger erupted, his baritone voice echoed through the room. "You forget who you're talking to here. You know I have secrets none of you want revealed. Do you really want to strip me of my position? Are you willing to take that risk?"

The council burst into shouts of indignation and outrage. Fejf jumped to his feet, talons raking the metal table as he leaned heavily toward the giant guildsman.

"Enough, Raencert! We have suffered your threats and arrogance long enough. You have gone too far and will now suffer the consequences of your own greed." The head assemblyman regained his composure, took hold of the polished stone sphere in front of him, and banged it three times on the table.. "We will now adjourn to contemplate a verdict." Fejf, followed by the others, filed out of the room into a private chamber behind them.

Once they were alone. Raencert stormed over to Selan, his eyes filled with hatred, his crest turning red as it stiffened. "I don't know how you accomplished this, boy, but you haven't heard the last from me." He jabbed a talon into Selan's chest, bringing himself nose-to-nose with his opponent. "You have no idea the amount of pain I can bring to you and your family."

"Careful, Raencert. You really want to add threatening an assemblyman's life to the list of charges?" His eyes drifted up to the cameras high on the walls recording the proceedings. "Come with me. I have something from the council to offer you before they deliver their verdict." He spun on his heels and strode down the center aisle. Raencert stared at Selan's back as he left, then stormed down the aisle after him.

Once outside in one of the building's courtyards, Selan signaled for Raencert to sit beside him on a bench. Flowers of all colors bloomed in pots among the bushes and trees along the pathway. No breeze disturbed the leaves of the trees thanks to the protection of the surrounding structure. Security personnel guarded the doorways to ensure privacy.

"No cameras here, Raencert. I have an offer from my father in honor of your long service to the mining guild and our people. Despite everything, you have done a great deal of good for all the Brin and he would rather not see you go down in disgrace."

"You mean he wants to save his own crest," Raencert sneered. "He's afraid for his own skin once I reveal their improprieties. "I could bring down the entire government with what I know, boy."

Selan turned to face the hulking figure next to him. "Is that how you truly want to be remembered, Raencert? The Brin who destroyed our way of life? The Brin who brought chaos and devastation to everyone?" He stood and paced in front of the bench. "Is that how you want your legacy to read for future generations? Or would you rather be remembered as the greatest of the guildsman… a hero to the miners and all the Brin?"

"Don't start going all patriotic on me now, boy. I don't give two phalks for anyone else. If those idiots vote me out, I will destroy them all."

"You mean all the evidence you had stored in your secret files?" Selan pulled a sheet of paper from his pocket, handing it to Raencert. "Just a few selections as proof I'm not bluffing. Your files are gone, Raencert. You have nothing."

Raencert slumped as he sat, the paper fell from his grasp. His crest faded and went slack. His head hung low. "What is the council's offer?"

Selan stopped his pacing, reached into his pocket and pulled out a glass vial, holding it out to the defeated Brin. "It would appear as if you suffered a fatal heart attack. We promise to erase all evidence of your wrong doing from existence. The Assembly would sing your praises. The guild will erect a monument in your honor, at government expense, of course, and your personal finances will remain with your family. They will remember you for your greatness, not your downfall."

Raencert sat silently for a long moment. Without raising his head, he reached out and took the capsule from Selan. "I don't know how a sniveling quetzal like you outdid me. I guess you have more guts than I gave you credit for."

"I'm a Rocker. My family has dealt with your likes before. It may have taken me a while to realize that, but in the end, you simply weren't as smart as you thought you were." Selan walked off, leaving Raencert watching after him from the bench. As he exited the courtyard, he turned to look once again at his adversary. He saw Raencert clutching his chest as he collapsed to the ground.

Back in his father's private office, Selan seated himself in the overstuffed leather chair opposite the massive desk. "It's done."

"Are you prepared to undo this mess he created?"

"Yes, father. All I need is your written orders granting me control over the guild and the mines affairs. With the aid of the military I will make sure any resistance of the miners to government oversight is put down swiftly. Production will resume to full levels within two months."

Fejf pushed a file across his desk and leaned forward with both hands on his desk. "Then you better not waste any time. Don't fail me, son."

Selan stood, picked up the file, and walked out.

Two weeks later, the funeral procession and memorial service for Raencert gathered the largest crowds in memory. Speeches from all the guild leaders and assemblymen sang his praises and extolled his many virtues. Along the road to the cemetery miners stood in silence, raising their picks and shovels in homage as the mag-lev hearse passed by. The gravesite sat not far from the monument to Karm, Jontar, and Maripa.

Selan contemplated his ancestors as he ignored the solemn proceedings. *Would you be proud of me; I wonder? Or would you be ashamed of my actions? Did you ever have such adversaries as him? How would you have dealt with such Brin as he?*

A week later, the attack delayed due to Raencert's trial and funeral, Selan observed the final loading of soldiers and supplies as he prepared for his assumption of power over the mines.

"Is everything ready, Captain?" He took the papers from the approaching officer.

"Another hour and we will be ready to take off, sir. Advance ships with your emissaries lifted off a few minutes ago. So far, the miners seem cooperative, but restless."

"Of course they're restless, Captain. Changes in leadership always make the masses restless and unsure of their future. Just make sure they remain under control. They need to believe nothing will change for them, except the possibility of greater profits bringing them higher wages and benefits."

"I'm sure that news will reassure them greatly, sir."

Selan smirked as he read the reports. "Of course it will. The ignorant masses will always believe a well told lie."

***

Maliche and Nalot followed Seykel into the large torch lit cavern. They joined Ryma, Opet, and Danet at the long wooden table supporting maps of the region drawn by hand on a tanned Tirpit hide. Local mines were indicated by charcoal x's while cavern entrances were shown by dark spots. Small streams and other water sources, hills and other strategic features were also located on the map.

"We have a problem," Maliche announced as he approached Ryma.

Ryma continued examining the maps as she looked at him out of the corner of her eyes. "Our lives are one problem followed by another. What is one more?"

He glanced around the chamber, leaned heavily on the table, and hung his head. "Nalot and I discovered several dispatches during our last raid. It appears we are in for a massive assault."

Nalot tossed a communication tablet on one of the maps. Ryma picked up the device and scanned through the long list of transcripts as she listened.

"While Maliche was gathering weapons and supplies, Seykel and I decided to investigate the communications room, hoping for some new intelligence we could take advantage of. It seems Raencert is dead and Maliche's brother has taken control of the mining guild."

Opet leaned across the table, his hands splayed on the map. "And how does this affect us, other than we now have a new master to conquer?"

Maliche picked up the tablet, searched for the com transcripts he wanted, and then handed it to Opet. "Selan has convinced The Assembly that Raencert was responsible for the drop in mine production. He is continuing to hide any trace of your existence."

"How can they continue to keep our presence a secret?" Ryma demanded. "Surely someone would send word home of us."

Maliche shook his head. "The mining guild controls all communication outside this continent. They censor any and all information even hinting at Kolandi existence. Sure, rumors have persisted over the centuries, but the guilds work very hard to keep knowledge of the Kolandi as a mythology; the realm of conspiracy theorists and fanatics."

Danet threw his hands in the air as he watched Maliche. "So, to your people, we are nothing more than a myth? How can they be so ignorant? We are fighting for our lives while your people refuse to accept our existence?"

"When facing the truth that would confront their comfortable way of life, people will believe almost anything, I'm afraid. Greed, and the inability to believe anything but the best in yourself are a powerful, and dangerous combination. My people are, in general, a kind and compassionate group, but this challenges them in ways too terrifying to face. They are afraid to see the truth, so they close their eyes to it and pretend you are no more than history."

"And they call us savages and ignorant beasts." Danet pounded his fists on the map and hung his head.

"The problem," Nalot interrupted, "is that Selan has convinced The Assembly the miners may rebel against the new leadership since he is not one of them. They have given him an army to bring over here to enforce mine production quotas and to keep order. At least that is the story they believe."

"In reality, I fear my dear brother wants to have full control over all operations here and wants the military to exterminate all Kolandi resistance. He means to wipe us out except for those he can use to continue the slave population. And now he has the soldiers to back him."

"A full-scale invasion? They are sending your military and all the weapons they control to attack us?" Opet wiped his face with both hands, clasping them behind his head. "How can we possibly hope to defeat such power? The miners kept us captive with only their few security forces and small arms. If the Brin military have the strength you have described, then all is lost. We cannot hope to win against such odds."

Nalot stepped forward, holding out his hands, palms up. "All is not lost. The histories of our home world are full of examples of small guerilla factions successfully defeating far superior forces. It's all a matter of knowing how to deploy your fighters in ways which exploit your enemy's weaknesses. We do have a chance to win this thing, if we are smart about it. Now, Professor Rocker... tell me, exactly what can that thing in your head do?"

Hours later, after much arguing and modifying their strategy, they decided to end this session and get some sleep.

Ryma stood up, rigidly controlling herself. "How long do we have?"

Maliche laid one hand on her shoulder. "Not long enough."

Chapter Twenty-Four

Training of the young warriors intensified over the next few days. Opet and Danet took responsibility for the youngest groups, teaching them the basics of Kolandi weapons. Maliche and Nalot, with Seykel at his side as always, taught the older trainees Brin hand-to-hand fighting skills. Maliche's knowledge was mostly theoretical, so he did the talking while Nalot performed the demonstrations.

"We know how to use a knife," complained one trainee, tossing his weapon point first into the ground. "What we need is more skill with the Brin rifles. What use is a knife against energy beam rifles?"

Nalot tossed his rifle to the youngster. "Go ahead. Shoot me."

The trainee looked nervously at his companions, then at Seykel, and dropped the rifle. "She would kill me if I harmed you," he said, backing up a step.

"Pick up the weapon, boy. Nobody is going to hurt you if you succeed." He gave Seykel a knowing look. "Isn't that right?"

Seykel removed her grip from her kital and nodded. "If that is your wish."

"You see, now pick up the rifle and shoot me with it. Do as you're told, boy." Nalot positioned himself with talons clasped behind his back and knees slightly bent.

The boy's friends shouted encouragement, goading him into action. He reached down, lifted the rifle to his waist, and checked to see if the safety was on. He snapped the rifle up to his shoulder to aim.

In a blur of motion, Nalot drew his knife, rolled to his left, and threw the knife, hitting the rifle and knocking it loose in the boy's grip. With a leap, Nalot kicked the weapon free, landed in a crouch, and swept his opponent's feet out from under him. Gathering him in a leg vise, with one arm tight around his neck, Nalot rolled with the youth until he reached out, grabbed the knife from the ground, and held it across the boy's throat.

Some of the elder warriors who had gathered to watch the training laughed at the youngster's predicament. Opet and Danet pointed to the pair, using the lesson to admonish their youths to focus and train harder.

"Never underestimate the value of the old ways, son." He released the lad and jumped to his feet then extended his hand to help the trainee. "Energy weapons are clumsy and random, no good in most situations. Skill with the knife and close-in combat is what will keep you alive."

Later that evening, the leaders sat in council over their plan to fight the Brin. Maliche, his voice filled with passion, argued his ideas. "If we can hijack enough explosives, we can destroy the mines, and enough equipment to make them completely useless. It would take years to recover. We could force them to focus so much on rebuilding the mines to save their economy they wouldn't have time to fight us."

Opet shook his head. "We cannot destroy the mines. We need them."

Maliche stared in disbelief. "You need them? You need the places that held you captives for generations? The Kolandi don't need the minerals from so many mines."

"No," replied Opet, "but the Brin do. When we drive the Brin from our land, they will still need the resources from the mines. From what you have told us, they would do anything to regain their wealth."

"If the mines were destroyed, they would have to look elsewhere. Your people would be free."

"Not true. They know the minerals are here. They would simply return with greater force and enslave us again, forcing us to reopen the mines for them."

Maliche's shoulders slumped, his eyes dropped to the map. "And I suppose you have a better plan?"

Opet rose to his full height, his face stern as he looked at Maliche. "This land is ours. The mines are ours. We will operate the mines. We have been working them for generations, we will continue to do so, but we will control them, not the Brin. We will need the equipment, so it must not be completely destroyed."

Everyone stared at Opet, confusion slowly replaced by dawning admiration. "You want to become trading partners with the Brin," said Maliche, his smile growing. "There's no guarantee we will win this war…"

The princess interrupted. "But if we do, the mines would ensure our prosperity. We would become valuable allies of the Brin, not enemies. Both of our cultures would benefit."

Maliche paced back and forth as he processed the potentials of such a future. "You would need Brin engineers and specialists to help run the more technical procedures, at least until your people could learn what is necessary to maintain and continue operating."

Opet's smile broadened as he clapped Maliche on the back. "That is why The Rocker sent you to us. You will not let us down."

"I hate to put a damper on all this, but shouldn't we focus on winning the war first?" Nalot's somber demeanor brought the room back to reality. The others returned to the table, leaned over the map, and continued plans for the coming invasion.

In the morning, Nalot awoke to the sounds and smells of the cave. Refusing to open his eyes, he lay in his cot, simply absorbing the experience; the rhythmic drip of water into a small puddle, laughter, and hushed conversations as others began their day; the scent of roasting meat and tubers filled his nostrils. With eyes still shut, he stretched, groaning with the aches of the previous day's activities. "I'm getting too old for this kak."

"You wouldn't make a very good farmer."

Nalot bolted to his feet, reaching for his knife, when he saw Seykel seated cross-legged on the dirt floor of his chamber, a bowl of something stewish in her lap.

"Don't do that, girl," he growled, preening his crest with the talons of his left hand, replacing the knife in its holder in the small of his back.

"You looked so peaceful lying there. I think it's the first time I've ever seen you so relaxed."

"And as a result, I let you sneak up on me. Could get me killed some day."

"Not if you chose to stay here with us," she said, setting the bowl beside his cot, and turning to leave.

"They would never accept me. I spied on them and betrayed them. No, girl, your people will never allow me to stay after this is over."

Seykel stopped, looked back over her shoulder, her eyes fixed on him. "But you are already forgiven. Our princess and the Great One support you. Opet and I have given you our life debt. You are trusted to help train our young warriors and go on raids." She stepped back into the small room and knelt down in front of Nalot as he sat on the edge of his bed. Her tiny hands held his talons as she looked up into his eyes. "Your transgressions are a thing of the past. We see the change in your heart. You are no longer who you were, so your sins against us are no longer yours. Have faith, Nalot. We would be fortunate to have you live among us."

Nalot shook his head. "You are blinded by your youth and affection for me, girl. Don't let emotions get the better of you. The world is not as gentle and forgiving as you."

She jumped to her feet and slapped him across the face. "Do not insult me. I am Skatak. I have survived captivity, I have killed many of our enemy, and I serve in the court of the princess. Do not mistake my kindness for weakness. It is not me who is blinded by emotions. You refuse to forgive yourself and wallow in self-loathing. What kind of a warrior are you? If all of your soldiers are as weak inside as you, then this war will be over very soon."

Nalot, shocked by the violence of Seykel's tone, and the strength behind her slap, stared in silence and amazement as she stormed out of his room.

***

Three nights later, a large raiding party gathered in the darkness at a remote Brin facility. "Only a couple of guards patrolling the ships," reported Nalot as he returned with Seykel to the group. Most of the soldiers have been shipped off to join the main attack force."

"I still think we need to stick together. What if we get separated?"

Nalot gripped Maliche's arm tight, scowling at him. "And what would happen to our plan if some soldier got off a lucky shot and took us down? It's a terrible idea to put all of your leaders in a single craft. No, we do this as planned. You, the princess, Danet, and Rilo go in one shuttle with the second group of fighters. Opet, Seykel, Kitae and I will take the lead ship with the others. If one ship goes down the others can still carry on and lead the fight."

"He's right. Just do as he says." The familiar mental tingle of the biocomputer's voice tickled Maliche's brain.

"All right, but the sooner we're together the better I'll feel. Let's get this over with."

As Maliche watched, again against his wishes, Nalot, Rilo, Seykel, Kitae and Danet crept their way among the shadows toward the soldiers. Splitting into two groups, Nalot and Seykel silently eliminated the pair of guards at the shuttles while the others took out the rest still sleeping in the nearby hut. A wave from Kitae signaled the all clear and the party ran to the waiting vessels. Maliche sat at the controls of one while Nalot piloted the other.

Adjusting his headset, Maliche touched the control to turn on the intership communications. "Group two, ready when you are."

"Remember, get as high as you can as fast as you can. Once airborne, you break left and head south. We'll break right and head north. Rendezvous at the agreed coordinates in twenty minutes. Maintain communications blackout until then. Nalot out."

"Got it. Be safe." Maliche turned off the switch and started the engines. With a jolt, he launched the ship into the air at full velocity, banking hard left as he rose into the night sky.

As he crossed the fenced perimeter of the outpost, bursts of orange shot passed the vessel. "Small weapons fire," he called back to the others. "Nothing to worry about. We'll be out of range in a few seconds." The ship continued to rise into the darkness, g-forces pulled them deep into the cushioned seats, making breathing difficult until they reached cruising altitude and Maliche leveled off.

Glancing over at Ryma in the co-pilot's seat, he saw her terrified expression. "Exciting, isn't it?"

She slowly released her death grip on the arm rests, but continued to stare straight ahead. "You could have warned me," she admonished, her voice trembling.

Maliche patted her hand, glancing up from the controls. "Sorry, I didn't think."

He looked back at the instrument panel, turned the dials, and punched in the required coordinates to meet up with Nalot's ship. The vessel tilted, changed headings, and flew on over the white peaked mountains below.

Overlooking the airfield, Maliche's heart sank as he counted the number of attack transport ships on the tarmac. For the past three hours, military troops marched off the vessels on to the make-shift tent city in the fields beyond.

"Are you sure about this?" He mentally asked the biocomputer.

He felt a tingling as his adrenaline levels rose. *"Just get me to the main computer terminal in the communication tower. I'll take care of the rest."*

Maliche nodded, and slunk down behind the hill to join the others.

Chapter Twenty-Five

"No, Great One. You and the princess are far too important to risk in this initial assault." Opet stood tall as he confronted Maliche. "We cannot risk losing you. We must follow the plan as you yourself set for us."

"But the sooner I get to the communications room the more time I'll have to make sure everything goes as planned. What if there are complications?"

"Then," Nalot chimed in, "the warriors and I will deal with it. We are expendable. You are not. If you go down, then everything is over. Just sit here and wait for the signal. Once we distract the patrols away from the building you come running."

Opet waved off any further discussion. "Rilo, Kitae and three experienced warriors will remain behind to protect you. We must go now before moon reaches its full height."

Maliche sat down on a tuft of grass among the rocks, his face sullen. A brief shiver shot down his spine in the chill air. "All right, but don't take any unnecessary risks. If too many soldiers show up get out of there quick."

"We know our job, Maliche," a crooked smile crossed Nalot's mouth. "This will be fun." He turned and followed Opet and the others into the night.

Ryma sat beside him placing one arm around his waist and resting her head on his shoulder. Rilo and Kitae stood by at a respectful distance, their eyes searching the darkness for any potential threats. "You know Opet and Nalot are right. We must get you and your spirit guide safely to the control room computers or everything we have done will be wasted."

"My spirit guide?" Maliche tilted his head, his crest lifting.

"Ryma smiled. "It sounds nicer than biocomputer, don't you think? Besides, the people are more trusting if it doesn't sound so much like Brin technology."

Maliche chuckled and wrapped his arm around her. "As you wish. And I know... all of you are right. It just galls me to have to sit here while others fight my battles." He puzzled on the statement for a moment. "Guess I've grown up a lot since I left home. Letting others do the fighting used to be my main characteristic. It's why I became an archaeologist in the first place."

"The past is what it was... the present is what it is. No one is who they once were. All of our experiences shape who we become."

Maliche sighed, pulling her tight. "Time to go watch for our signal." He stood, held out a hand for Ryma, helping her to her feet. Together they climbed back up the low hill.

Stooping to a crawl to remain hidden, they stretched out behind an outcropping of tall grass to watch the scene below. The grass waved slowly in a slight breeze, but allowed a clear view of the airbase. Dozens of large transport ships stood in rows along the tarmac, each one capable of carrying a full company of soldiers. Hundreds of round tents filled the fields beyond. The night patrols seemed to congregate in the islands of illumination provided by scattered lights.

"Not very bright, are they?" Kitae observed at their side as she pointed out the soldiers. "Those lights ruin their night vision."

Maliche watched the perimeter, peering into the deep shadows when he noticed the skulking movement.

"There they are, between those transport ships. Won't be long now."

In another few minutes, they saw the flickering of small flames ignite in two of the mechanical outbuildings at the far end of the airfield near one group of tents. The flames grew quickly, their orange fury revealed the fleeing Kolandi as they dashed back into the shadows. Shouts and alarms sounded, awakening the camp. Emergency crews sprang into action advancing on the burning structures. Soldiers stumbled out of their tents and watched the excitement.

"There's our signal. Let's move." Maliche jumped up, leading the others in a race to the control room.

"Wait, Great One," Rilo blocked Maliche with one arm, her kital at the ready. "We will lead the way." Hurrying down the hillside, Rilo led them to the nearest building, an empty hangar. She peeked around the corner of structure. "This way. Hurry," she waved them forward and ran ahead between buildings to the next intersection. With a finger to her mouth, she ducked low and froze in the shadows.

Maliche, Ryma, and the rest copied her action just as a trio of soldiers ran passed them heading toward the fires. As they rounded the next corner, Rilo skidded to a halt and raised her kital. A dark shape stood in their path. She threw the kital sending its spinning blades at the Brin's head. With a swift movement the shadow ducked, shot out one hand catching the kital in the center.

"Hold on, girl," Nalot's voice called out of the darkness. "Save this toy for the enemy." He strolled up to them and returned her weapon, Seykel beaming at his side.

Rilo accepted the weapon, her eyes narrowed, studying Nalot. "You should have announced yourself. I could have killed you."

"Not today. I watched your approach. You know you flinch your elbow before you throw that thing don't you? May want to work on that."

Rilo stepped forward, standing nose to nose with Nalot. "Who are you to try to give me lessons?"

"That's enough," interrupted Maliche getting between the two. "Did you locate the communications center?"

Nalot winked at Rilo, and then walked back with Maliche. "It's over there," he said pointing toward the vicinity of the airstrip's control tower. "The building with the satellite array on top."

Maliche nodded, observing the low one-story wooden structure. "Only three guards."

"Yeah, the rest took off to help with the fires and to chase the 'raiding party'. We should be clear if we hurry."

Sticking to the shadows, the group ran, stopping only once when two soldiers came around the corner behind them. The warriors bringing up the rear gave a warning cry and before the soldiers could fire their energy rifles, their chests each sprouted two arrows and three kitals embedded in their heads.

Retrieving their blades, Kitae, Seykel, and Rilo made a brief gesture waving their left hands in front of them, three fingers touching, the remaining two pointing straight, brought the two fingers to their mouths, muttered something in the language of the Kolandi, wiped the weapons off on their trouser legs. Rilo, resuming her position beside Nalot, gave him a wink. Four warriors carried off the bodies to hide them among the pallets of equipment alongside the building.

Their approach took them to the rear of the communications center. As planned, Maliche and Nalot used their disguises as Brin officers to distract the guards.

"You three," shouted Maliche as they came near. "Any sign of trouble here?"

The Brin soldiers came to attention, saluting with their fists across their chests, rifles held upright by their left legs.

"No sir," replied the corporal, highest ranking of the group. "Everything is—"

Seykel's kital sliced through his throat, cutting off the rest of his reply. At the same time, the other two soldiers collapsed, blood spurting from their throats as well. The three Skatak glanced at each other, made a quick gesture with their left hand, muttered the same words as before, wiped the red stain from their kitals, and motioned for the warriors to remove the corpses.

Once inside the empty foyer, Nalot, crest rising slightly, his head tilted, whispered to Seykel. "What is that thing you do over the bodies? Should we really be wasting our time over them?"

Seykel looked up at him, her eyes examining his face before deciding how to answer. "It is the Mitan, a prayer for their souls." She saw the lack of comprehension on his face. "They are soldiers performing their duty as they understand it. Even Brin soldiers are living beings with souls. To kill without forgiveness would be a terrible dishonor on ourselves."

"Time to move," Maliche whispered to the group. He gripped Nalot's shoulder with one hand. "You okay here?"

Nalot tipped his head toward Seykel. "With this deadly little bodyguard at my side, how can we lose? Get moving before somebody comes in here and raises the alarm."

With Rilo and Kitae in the lead, Maliche and Ryma safely in the center with the four young warriors protecting the rear, the party slowly worked their way down the long hallway to the computer room, the heart of the communication center. The brightly lit, slightly rounded passage contained several doors, but each attached room proved to be empty.

"Where is everyone?" asked Ryma.

"The night shift is still on duty," said Maliche in her ear. "The officers will still be sleeping in their quarters. There should only be one or two operators, possibly a maintenance worker, but not much else at this hour."

The sign on the fourth door to the right read MAIN COMPUTER.

"Let's try to take them alive," said Maliche. "These guys are probably more technicians than soldiers. I can erase their memories before we leave." He pointed to his head with one talon.

Rilo nodded her agreement, then, silently counting down with her fingers, opened the door and they all rushed in, weapons drawn and ready.

In the chilled room sat two Brin, each at a desk containing a monitor, keyboard, small lamp and a variety of stacked files and papers. Behind them stood three rows of large computers, panels of numbers and colored lights displayed their current operating status. On one wall hung a poster of some computer game fantasy character Maliche vaguely remembered from his days at the university battling strange creatures. The two Brin, dressed in green baggy jumpsuits with their names pinned on their chest looked up from their terminals, froze for a second, and then started to jump to their feet. One of them reached for the large blue alarm button on the wall nearest him. An arrow stuck into the wall inches from his outreached hand.

"Stay still and you won't be harmed," called out Maliche.

The two Brin remained frozen halfway between standing and sitting, glanced at each other, and then back to the bows armed and ready to be released into them.

"Anything you say… we don't want any trouble."

"That's right. We aren't soldiers like them other fellas. Just a couple of comp techs."

The two sat back down, hands raised, crests quivering.

Rilo took charge now, waving her kital at the Brin techs. "Move over there," she pointed to the far wall of the room, away from the computers.

"Yes, ma'am," they said in unison as they shuffled carefully to the indicated place, and sat on the floor, never removing their eyes from the curved blades aimed at them.

Without warning, a door on the far side of the room opened. A flash of sparks sprayed across the floor and the maintenance bot fell over, two arrows and Rilo's kital sprouted from its mechanical body, three wheels on its base spun and rotated spasmodically, then fell silent.

"Relax, everyone. Just a maintenance robot." He pointed to two of the warriors. "You two set up a perimeter down that hallway, so there are no more surprises."

The two men looked sheepishly at each other, kicked the machine as they passed it, and vanished through the door.

"Sorry, Great One. We're all a bit nervous." Rilo placed her foot on the maintenance bot's head and yanked her kital from its chest. She looked over at Kitae, shrugging as she wiped leaking lubricant from her weapon's blades.

"Your turn, Great One," said Kitae, rolling her eyes toward the ceiling as she led Maliche and Ryma to the terminals.

Maliche sat in the chair, closed his eyes and focused his attention. *"So what do I do?"*

"Keep your eyes closed, clear your mind, and place your talons over the keyboard. I'll take it from there."

As he followed the instructions, his mind filled with series after series of numbers, letters, and computer code he did not understand. Images of circuitry, schematics, and equations of fuel mixture ratios flashed by behind closed eyes. All the while, his blue nimbus grew brighter and enveloped the keyboard. Each of the computer banks began to glow bright blue as well. Maliche felt his heart rate soar. His nerves tingled almost painfully as the biocomputer's energy flowed through him. Lights flashed on the panels, displays raced through lines of code and charts too fast for the eye to follow.

"Done!"

The blue light diminished, absorbing back into Maliche's body and, as the last hint of the energy field faded, he gasped for air and collapsed to the floor. Slowly coming to, he felt Ryma's soft hands gently caressing his forehead. His eyes fluttered open to see her worried face gazing down at him.

"How long was I out?"

"We've only been here less than five minutes, Great One," she replied. "You collapsed only seconds ago. Are you all right? What went wrong?"

He mentally checked himself, and then sat up, extending one hand to the nearest warrior to help him to his feet. He reached back and winced as he felt the knot growing on the back of his head where he hit the edge of the terminal.

"Nothing went wrong. Everything is ready. We need to get out of here before the day shift arrives." His head swam as he rose, nearly dropping him to the floor again. The warrior who helped him up grabbed his arm with a strong grip while Nalot took hold of the other, settling him back into the chair.

"Steady there, boy," said Nalot. "Get your head on straight and then we can go. There's time still."

"Sorry," said the voice in his head. *"The alterations took a bit more energy than I had first expected. Here, this should help."*

Maliche felt a surge of strength flow through him. The room stopped spinning and the throb in his head vanished. "Thanks." He said out loud, forgetting to think the words.

"Don't mention it. By the way, you shouldn't leave just yet. I came across some interesting information while I was inside the communications array. There's a surprise arriving for you at the main hangar. It might make getting back to First Town much easier."

"What sort of surprise?" he said aloud again jumping to his feet. He saw the confused faces of the others watching him. "Don't worry, my friend in here is telling me something is happening which might help us."

"Don't ask questions and spoil my surprise. You'll know what to do when you see him."

Minutes later, after adjusting the comp techs' memories to forget everything about their visit, the party dashed outside into the chill morning air. The sun, still below the horizon, cast an orange brilliance against the sky. The soldiers had long since returned to their tents once the novelty of the fires and the raid were over. Only the clean-up crews remained at the burnt facilities, far too concerned with their efforts to notice Maliche and the others darting between buildings heading toward the main hangar. Even the arrival of an expensive private shuttle distracted them for only a moment.

As they watched from behind the maintenance shed across the way, they watched as the shuttle landed and taxied to the hangar entry. The engines shut down and the door opened.

Maliche's jaw dropped, his crest rose to full height. "That's Selan. What's he doing here?"

"From what I picked up back with the computers, your brother is the one in charge now. He has eliminated Raencert and convinced The Assembly he is the one to take charge of the mines. Apparently, they all think it is a miner's strike causing all the problems here. Your people are still oblivious to what is really happening."

A loud voice broke the still of the early morning as the group watched Selan and his four security guards walk over to the control tower. "Thirty minutes for morning chow! Repeat, thirty minutes for morning chow. All personnel with full packs and extra charge packs report to transport loading zones in sixty minutes. Repeat, sixty minutes." A series of blasting whoops followed the announcement, then only the noise of Brin soldiers rushing and complaining as they exited their tents and headed for the mess hall.

"Let's hide in here," Maliche said as he opened the door to the maintenance shed. "It doesn't look like it's used very often."

Once inside among the work benches, shelves of random machine parts, racks of tools large and small, and one mag-lev truck lifted up on supports, its engine parts laid out neatly on the concrete floor, Ryma approached Maliche.

"Your brother is here? Didn't he try to get you out of the prison? Maybe he's here to help?"

"Not that one," interrupted Nalot. "My instructions were to keep you hidden until he could settle accounts with Raencert, find the location of the Kolandi camps, and then bury you somewhere out in the middle of the desert. If he's in charge now, and that's what it looks like to me, he's here to watch his conquering army take off for victory."

Seykel listened to the conversation, a growing horror showed on her face. "But he is the Great One's brother. Surely he does not want his own flesh and blood dead."

Maliche took Seykel's face in his hands. "While many Brin, possibly most, are kind and generous folk, far too often those in power become lost to greed and will do anything to increase their power over others." He saw the tears start to gather in her eyes. "This is what we have come to stop. If we succeed, the Kolandi and the Brin will become one people whose future lies among the stars. We are here to stop my brother and others like him so those Brin who do strive for honor can rise up and join us."

She wiped her eyes and went to Nalot, nestling her face in his shoulder. "This is what you have come to believe as well?"

"Yes, I guess I have," he said, gathering her up in his arms, pulling her tight.

"All right, everyone, find somewhere comfortable to be for the next hour or so, but stay alert in case I'm wrong about this hiding place. We need to be ready to move once those ships take off."

Chapter Twenty-Six

As the sun began to rise in the morning sky, Maliche watched the soldiers assemble by platoons in the designated loading zones by each transport vessel. On a signal from the loudspeaker, they began boarding the ships. Hundreds of soldiers loaded for war, climbed onto dozens of ships in neat columns. Glancing up into the control tower, he saw Selan watching the spectacle through a pair of distance viewers.

"Are we sure there's no other way?"

"Not if you want to get out of this alive and free the Kolandi. Your brother is at the heart of all this now. Exposing him and his schemes is the quickest way to end the enslavement of the Kolandi. If it helps, he agreed to have you killed, not simply silenced."

Maliche closed his eyes and bowed his head.

He felt Ryma by his side, her hand seeking out his. "Are you sure this will work? I'm afraid for my people if something goes wrong."

"No need to worry. Opet and the others are evacuating the caverns as we speak, bringing your people to new locations. Even if we fail, the soldiers will find your homes empty."

"I pray you are right, Great One."

"It is not your people who will die today, Princess. It's mine. All those soldiers heading off to their deaths, and at my hand." He remained silent for a moment then squeezed her hand tight. "How does one say the Mitan?"

***

At last, the ships were fully loaded, hatches sealed, and ready for lift off. A warning signal blared from the loudspeaker. Dust flew up from the ships as they rose heavily into the sky, engines whining as they strained to lift the heavy loads.

"Get ready, everyone. We'll need to move fast once they've taken flight."

The others joined Maliche at the windows, holding their breath as the transports gained speed, rising higher and heading off toward the mountains.

In the distance, the ships looked like a swarm of cardis flying south for the winter. Then, in a burst of orange flame and smoke, the first ship exploded. Within seconds the rest of the armada, one after another, burst into flame. Long meteoric trails of smoke and debris flew from the fireballs filling the sky. Tons of rock, dirt, and wreckage burst from the craters blasted into the ground by the plummeting debris and remains of shuttles which, only seconds before, held thousands of Brin soldiers. Moments later, the shock wave of sound hit them in a powerful concussion, shattering many windows. Maliche and the others held their hands firmly over their ears to block out as much of the deafening noise as possible.

"That's it. Let's move," Maliche had to shout over the commotion of sirens and rescue shuttles as the base began to respond to the horror.

They ran in formation, heedless of the dumbfounded Brin staring in disbelief and shock at the catastrophe in the sky. In less than a minute, they burst through the control tower doorway, disabling the two guards, and charged up the stairs to the observation room. Hearing the commotion below, Selan's guards turned to see what was going on when three fell to the floor with kital rooted in their brains, the fourth grasped at the large knife protruding from his chest. Four Kolandi warriors, led by Danet and with bows bent, entered the room.

"Get on the floor now!" they shouted. "Do not resist or you will die."

Nalot, Kitae, and Rilo moved swiftly from one Brin to the next, checking them for weapons and gathering them into a group sitting on the wood floor at the far end of the room.

"All clear," called Nalot. "Come on in."

Selan started to rise, but a kick from Rilo took his legs out from under him, sending him crashing back to the floor.

"What is the meaning of this? Who are you? How dare you attack me! Do you know who I am?"

"Hello, brother dear. It's been a while. How are mother and father?" Maliche entered the room with Ryma at his side.

"Maliche?" Selan looked up at his older brother, eyes wide and brow furrowed in confusion. "What are you doing here?"

"You mean, why am I still alive?"

Selan tried to respond, but his mouth opened and closed without the words escaping.

"Don't look so shocked, brother. Your spy here," he pointed at Nalot, "had a change of heart. It seems you hired someone with a conscience, despite your best intentions, I'm sure." He turned his back on Selan and gazed out the windows at the flaming wreckage in the distance. "As for what I am doing here, I would think that would be obvious now."

Selan sputtered, trying to regain his composure. "You are responsible for this?"

Maliche continued to stare out at the carnage, Ryma's arm around his shoulder.

"You've betrayed your own people! You've destroyed our family!"

Spinning around and storming up to Selan, Maliche unleashed his fury. He grabbed Selan by the front of his suit and threw him across the room.

"No, Selan, that is your doing. You have participated in the enslavement of an entire people, lying to everyone about their existence, for your own profit. You have attempted to commit fratricide and then cover it up. You have abused your position in The Assembly to carry out your fraudulent deceptions." He drug Selan to the windows, forcing him to look at the huge column of smoke rising from the crash site. "You have killed all of those soldiers with your arrogance and greed. You are the traitor here, not me." He tossed Selan back to the floor, turning his back to him. "I am going to try to salvage what little honor is left in our family. This travesty ends now."

Selan stared at his brother, his face a study in horror. "You can't reveal what is going on here. You can't! Our entire economy will collapse if the truth comes out. We will never be able to obtain the resources we need to survive without the slaves working the mines. You will destroy us all."

"If our existence depends on the secrets and the enslavement of others, then maybe we deserve whatever happens to us. But I think you underestimate the citizenry. I believe there is still honor in the Brin. I believe our better nature will rise to the occasion and we will find a way to survive together." He took Ryma by the hands, gazing into her eyes. "Together we will become stronger than ever, as our ancestors hoped we would be."

Selan snorted, pointing a well-manicured talon at Maliche. "You are a hopeless romantic, brother. Naïve and blind to reality. Do you really believe the guilds will permit you to ruin us? Do you have even the faintest idea of how powerful we are?"

"It isn't the guilds, or the Assembly I have faith in. It is the people I trust and believe in. It is you who is the naïve one. The people hold the real power… and they will see justice is done. Even if it means having your head on a platter."

"You think you're smarter than all of us? You won't have a chance. The people will never know anything about any of this. We will stop you."

Nalot laughed out loud. "Good luck with that. From what I've seen, he's out maneuvered you every step of the way. Looks to me like you're the one who doesn't stand a chance."

Selan sulked as Rilo returned him to a far corner of the room. "Just to set the record straight, it was Raencert who ordered your death, not me. He blackmailed me into all of this. I wanted to keep you quiet, but he forced me to go along."

Maliche kept his back to his brother, his head hung low. "Maybe that was true at first, but you certainly took charge as soon as you were able to. When you did have control, you only made things worse. No, Selan, this is your doing, nobody else's."

***

The flight back to First Town proved uneventful, but a nervous time for the Kolandi onboard. Selan sat under guard in the rear of the craft while Maliche and Nalot did the flying. Before taking off, Maliche ordered the destruction of all communication equipment and any remaining transports in order to keep their arrival secret for as long as possible.

"So much water," said Opet as he stared out the portals. "How can there be deserts on a world with so much water?"

"We can discuss global weather patterns another time, my friend," Maliche said, chuckling slightly. "We're coming up to the coastline now, only a few more hours before we reach First Town."

Ryma and the others marveled at the scenes passing below. "Your mountains are so green here, not like ours at all. There must be enough food to feed thousands."

"That's probably true, but our food comes from farms and ranches, not wild game. My people rarely go into the mountains except for recreation."

She pondered that thought as they flew over the foothills and out above the plains with its circular patches of irrigated green farms and rectangles of various shades of brown.

"Come up here, Ryma," called Maliche. "First Town is just over the horizon. We should be able to see it in a minute or so.

Ryma gripped Maliche's arm, her jaw dropping in amazement as she viewed the tall towers and vast reaches of buildings that were First Town. "Your people are truly amazing to be able to create such wonders. I thought you were telling tales to impress me, but now, I realize you were being modest. We have much to learn from you."

"And we have much to learn from you as well." He patted her hand, still gripping his arm. Time to let them know we are here." He touched the control pad to open his microphone.

"Control tower, this is Maliche Rocker, repeat, this is Maliche Rocker, code ID R2M1 requesting permission to land."

Static filled the speaker as the air controllers hesitated. "This is control tower chief, R2M1, please identify yourself again."

It's me, Chief, Maliche Rocker. The reports of my demise were mistaken. I have returned. Is the usual hangar landing pad available?"

Another hesitation followed. "Yes, R2M1, landing pad Rocker is available and awaiting your arrival. Let me be the first to congratulate you on your survival. I'm sure your family will be relieved to hear you are still with us."

"Roger that, Chief. I would prefer you hold off on notifying anyone official about my return. Is anyone from one of the news agencies around? I have something for them that will probably make them famous."

"There's always a few hanging out here somewhere. In fact, they've probably been monitoring our communications and on their way to your hangar already."

"Good. And can you have one of the limousine services send us the largest car they have. We need to take some guests to The Assembly."

"Can do, R2M1. We have your approach vectors clear. Welcome home."

Maliche maneuvered the vessel carefully over the landing pad outside the Rocker family hangar. Dust kicked up as they neared the ground causing the gathered reporters to grab their coats and shield their eyes. A gentle bump and the ship settled on its landing gear. Maliche and Nalot turned off the controls, unfastened their harnesses, and joined the others in the main compartment.

"Is everyone ready?"

Selan grabbed Maliche's arm with his bound hands, yanking on his sleeve. "Don't be a fool, Maliche. You'll bring ruin on us all."

Opet slapped Selan with the back of his hand, causing a slight trickle of blood to flow from the corner of his mouth.

Maliche scowled at his brother, then shook his head and turned toward the hatch, pressing the switch to open the door. "Let me go out first to prepare them," he said, looking back over his shoulder.

He stepped out into the daylight and electronic flashes and floodlights of the news cameras. A cacophony of shouted questions assaulted him as he appeared in front of the correspondents. He raised his arms in the air calling for their attention.

"Before I answer any questions, ladies and gentlemen, I have an important announcement. I'm sure you will have many more questions once I bring them out, but we must first address The Assembly. All your questions will be answered there."

Amid the muttering of the reporters, Maliche turned back to the ship's open hatch and lifted one hand. "May I present Princess Ryma of the Kolandi, and her entourage."

The princess stepped into the light, tall, and regal in her formal gown, she paused for effect, then took Maliche's hand and walked out to stand beside him. Rilo and Kitae, and then Opet followed next. Each one took his or her place behind Ryma. Finally, Seykel and Nalot walked out, with Selan between them, his hands bound behind his back.

Shouted questions erupted from the reporters, recording equipment clicked, hummed, and flashed at a furious rate. Broadcast drones circled madly around the group, sending images of the Kolandi throughout First Town. The mob surged forward, each with microphones raised.

Maliche stood in front of the princess, held up both arms, and called for order. "As I said, everyone, all of your questions will be answered at The Assembly. All I can say now is that, yes, these are representatives of the Kolandi, a people we thought were long extinct. And I have taken my brother into custody for treason. Now please, our transportation has arrived and we must leave you for now."

As the mag-lev vehicle arrived, the driver inserted it between the reporters and Maliche, allowing them to enter without having to force their way through the small mob.

***

After fighting their way through an immense crowd of onlookers and more reporters, with the assistance of Assembly security forces, Maliche and the others now sat in the main chamber of The Assembly awaiting the arrival of the leadership. News of their arrival had reached everyone with a vid receiver and it appeared the entire city had rushed to The Assembly building to get a glimpse of the princess and her companions.

"Are you sure the broadcast drones will get their signals out? Nobody here will block them?"

"Come now, Give me a little credit. I disabled all security firewalls and interference twenty minutes ago. These proceedings will be seen by everyone."

A door opened behind the curved bench in front of them and out stepped a middle-aged Brin in black trousers with deep blue formal coat and tie. His sash flashed with medals and ribbons, each noting some service or honor. He carried a long metal pole with a golden sphere on top. He pounded the floor four times with the staff and called out in a baritone voice which rang throughout the chamber. "All rise, the council is in session. Give honor to the council before you."

He stepped aside allowing the councilmen to enter. Two of the levitating video drones rushed to film the grand entrance while the remaining four continued to transmit images of Maliche and the Kolandi.

Seven of the eleven councilmembers took their seats, each wearing their dark blue robes of office, each one emblazoned with embroidery depicting their particular office and rank. Fejf, leader of The Assembly, dressed in the forest green robe of the highest office entered last, but rounded the bench and strode to Maliche, extending his arms in greeting. A large smile broke through his traditionally stern visage as they embraced.

"We thought you dead, boy." He pulled back, returning to his persona of head of The Assembly. "I'm sure you are prepared to explain all of this," he waved a hand toward the Kolandi seated behind the tables. "And to explain why your brother, a leading member of this council was brought here like a prisoner."

Maliche stood tall, squaring his shoulders as he faced his father. "Yes, sir. Everything will be made clear. I'm afraid we are in for a rough time, though. You, and all of us, have some difficult decisions to make."

Fejf eyed his son, scrutinizing him for a moment, and then nodded in approval. "You've changed, son. You have a strength about you I've not seen before. Don't disappoint me." He spun on his heels and took his seat in the center of the high council bench, and nodded to the herald.

"Attention all present, these proceedings are now in session. May The Eternal give all here wisdom and compassion." He pounded the floor again and took his place standing by the back wall.

***

Several days of hearings followed. As the days passed, the galleries filled to capacity with dignitaries from each of the guilds, representatives from each district, and visitors curious to witness the unprecedented events unfolding in the chamber. Maliche presented the Kolandi and each took turns telling their story to the audience. He, and the others, each presented evidence supporting Maliche's claims.

DNA samples collected from Ryma and the others confirmed their identities. Hundreds of questions posed by members of the high council gradually revealed the treachery of the mining guild, Raencert's leadership in the Kolandi enslavement and Selan's complicity, and attempted takeover of events.

In addition, the involvement of most of the guilds, and an overwhelming majority of councilmembers, even many on the high council itself, were implicated by either direct participation in cover-ups or by purposeful denial of the travesty over the years.

"Ladies and gentlemen of the council," called out Maliche as he rose to speak on the final day of the hearings.

"You have heard the evidence, and we all are well aware of the potential consequences. Even now, reports of riots and outrage from the citizenry reach us as the people have learned the truth."

Shouts of anger and dismay filled the room as representatives, guildsman, and visitors, leapt to their feet in outrage. Fejf rapped the bench with his stone sphere calling for order. As the room stilled, Maliche continued.

"Undoubtedly, many here will be removed from their current positions. We have shaken the very roots of our government. Only time will tell if we survive this or not, but I have an offer from the Kolandi which may help stabilize matters in the long term. We propose an alliance between our two people. An alliance which will benefit and bring prosperity to both our species."

More outbursts filled the chamber forcing Fejf to once again call for order. "We will hear your proposal in private, Maliche." He rapped the stone sphere again. "The bailiff will now clear the chamber."

Two weeks of negotiations between the Kolandi and the high council ensued.

Maliche read from the document finalizing the treaty between the two peoples. "And we are, therefore, agreed that the Kolandi will be sovereigns of their own lands on the Eastern Continent, and all Brin claims are renounced."

Ryma nodded her approval as she sat across from Fejf, arms folded across her chest. "Including all the mines and equipment associated with their operations. I want that point made absolutely clear as well."

"Yes, of course. The Brin will provide technical and advisory support until such time as the Kolandi are secure in their ability to operate the mines without assistance. In return, the Kolandi will provide all mineral resources required by the Brin at mutually acceptable rates of exchange, to be decided during regularly scheduled annual summits."

Ryma held up her hand to interrupt. "And what about the matter of Brin settlers?"

Maliche ran his talon down the document a few paragraphs to locate the provision. "No Brin will be allowed access to the Eastern Continent for a span of five years. All those currently residing in Kolandi territory will be peacefully removed by combined Brin – Kolandi security personnel. After said five years, any Brin wishing to visit Kolandi lands for employment, tourism, education, or homestead, must complete the Kolandi visa requirements and submit to Kolandi supervision until deemed benign."

The reading continued for another hour with only minor corrections. "Thank you ladies and gentlemen. We have a treaty. Now, on to other matters."

One by one, they brought in guildsman and council members to negotiate their removal from office. Some would require public trials, but most agreed to resign their positions. An emergency election was set up to take place in a few months, allowing time to recruit replacement candidates and provide them the time to gather a constituency.

Chapter Twenty-Seven

During the weeks that followed, the courts filled with the prosecution of those involved in the heinous crimes. Everyone's attention, though, focused on the upcoming trial of Selan Rocker.

Three days before the trial, Selan sat at the dinner table of his home in First Town. He scratched at the site on his arm where they had injected the locator beacon before his release from his holding cell in the prison.

"Nedia, where are the children? Aren't they coming down to dinner?"

"No, dear. I don't want them exposed to all this publicity. We can't even walk out the front door without dozens of onlookers and reporters shouting questions and taking our photos. It's disgraceful. I sent them off to my father's place this morning to get them away from it all."

"I miss them. It would be comforting to have them around now."

She poured their wine and brought him his glass, swirling the red liquid as she set it in front of him. Returning to her chair at the far end of the table, she watched her husband, chin resting on steepled talons.

"You probably should have thought of that before you got us involved in this mess, dear. Now eat your appetizers, so the servants can serve the meal before it gets cold." She attached her talon clip utensils and speared a piece of bread.

He took a long gulp of the wine, emptying the glass and setting it back on the table. Placing the talon utensils on his fingers, he jabbed at a piece of fruit and tossed it in his mouth.

"I still don't know how Maliche..." His heart stuttered in his chest, gave one strong beat, then began racing, cutting off the rest of his sentence. A look of panic filled his face as he clutched at his chest. "Nedia, something's wrong... call the doctor."

Nedia looked up from her plate, smiling as she watched him. Calmly removing her talon utensils, she stood up and sedately walked over to him. Leaning in close with one hand on his back, she whispered in his auricle.

"No, dear, nothing is wrong. Everything is going exactly as planned."

"Nedia," he gasped, his face reddening. "Call the doctor... my heart."

"You're not listening, dear. I said everything is just fine. The poison I put in your wine is working exactly as promised."

Selan grasped at his collar, trying to loosen it.

"You see, dear, I couldn't allow you to continue after what you did."

Selan tried to stand, but collapsed back into his chair, knocking over several goblets and bowls as his arm swept out groping for support. "What do you mean? Everything I've done is for us and the children. Please... help me."

She sat sideways in her chair, looking down her nose at Selan's struggles, her arms folded across her chest. "You killed the finest man I've ever known. Raencert gave us everything and you poisoned him. Poetic justice, don't you think?"

Gasping and clutching his chest as the pains intensified, Selan gaped at his wife. "Raencert was going to destroy us. He was only out for himself. Don't do this... the children..."

"Oh, no, dear. He would not have destroyed us... only you. You failed him. I loved him... and he loved me. We had it all planned out. After you were disgraced and in prison, I would divorce you. After a respectable time passed, he and I would marry." She laughed at Selan's look of shock. "Ahhh, now you finally understand. I haven't loved you in years, Selan. You had promise once, but Raencert proved to be the real power. I've been his mistress and spy for quite some time now. Your failed attempt to take control and destroy him threatened not only us, but my entire family by extension. I will not allow your failure to stain my children's future."

She walked around the corner of the long table and pulled up a chair next to Selan as he gasped for air, trying to call out for help, but managing no more than weak yelps.

"This will appear as a normal heart attack. Who would doubt the stress you have been under after all that has happened? The doctors will confirm the existence of a previously undiagnosed weakness in the arteries. The trial will never happen, so nobody will know the full extent of your culpability. I will inherit your estate and the children will be well cared for, even if the future they once had is gone."

His last sight was of his wife strolling back to her seat at the other end of the table. The last sound he heard was of Nedia calling out in panic for help.

***

Three months later, after Selan's hasty funeral and the general elections concluded, the wedding of Maliche Rocker and Princess Ryma captured everyone's attention. During her many appearances over the communications network, she had not only impressed the Brin with her wit and intelligence, but reassured them of her sincere desire to become strong allies. The news media played it up as a sign of great tidings for the future, and the tensions which had first erupted relaxed as confidence grew and those responsible were seen to suffer the consequences of their actions. The ceremony, held in the Savior's Memorial in front of Karm's obelisk, combined the rituals of both cultures.

A deep violet nimbus surrounded Maliche as he entered the Memorial and stood before the marble tomb. An intense sadness filled his mind. *"What's wrong?"*

"Old memories of long-lost friends. It has been a long time since I was last here. I was just reminiscing is all."

Maliche walked up to the obelisk, reached out and touched the cold stone with its myriad of silver inlays. A jolt shot down his arm as the violet light returned to its normal blue color and surrounded the entire obelisk. The light shown like a beacon as it fired up into the sky for all to see.

"What is that all about?"

"Paying homage to your ancestor, and letting a few other friends know I have finally accomplished my task. They may want to stop by for a visit sometime to check on our progress."

Princess Ryma strode regally down the aisle, preceded by Rilo, followed by Kitae and Seykel. Maliche watched her procession with Opet, Danet, and Nalot at his side. The Brin celebrant, dressed in his most opulent bejeweled white raiment, told of the great history of the Rocker clan and blessed the couple with prayers to The Eternal.

"As in the first days of Jontar, Maripa, and Karm, whose memories we honor and stand before today, we seek to join two people as one. The will of our ancestors is honored at last."

The ancient Homsan, flown in specifically at Ryma's request, recited the tales of the Kolandi back to the days of great promise with the first Brin.

"The joining of our two people was foretold by the Sky People long ago," he proclaimed. "And now, the prophecies are fulfilled."

Bracelets were exchanged to signify their commitment to each other and both officiates declared as one their final blessings and the presentation of the new pair to family, friends, and invited dignitaries.

Thousands gathered outside waited and watched as the famous couple exited the Memorial. Maliche, in his finest forest green robes of his new office as leader of the reformed assembly as the people now called it, and Ryma, resplendent in her gossamer gown of fine linen overlaid with blue gemstones, stood at the top of the steps waving to the cheers. In the distance, barely heard over the adulations, a small gathering of protestors proclaimed their opposition to the supposedly unholy joining of two different species. As always, Rilo and Kitae stood close behind their princess with Seykel at their side. Behind Maliche stood Nalot, Opet, and Danet, smiling and clapping each other on the back.

"Are you ready, my wife?" asked Maliche as he took her hand.

"Yes, my husband." She smiled at him, clasping his hand tighter.

That evening, in the most expensive suite of the city's finest hotel, their exploration of each other culminated in a passion far greater than either knew was possible. As they joined together in lovemaking, a rainbow of colors burst from them, and shot through them. Their bodies vibrated with energy, every nerve aflame. Exhausted at the conclusion, they collapsed, senseless, in each other's embrace.

Late the next morning, as they strolled through the nearby park, a flash of light lit up the sky above them and a long, spear-like silvery metallic vessel appeared.

"Ah, we have guests." Maliche's body radiated with an intense blue light.

"Do not fear," rang a voice from the vessel. "We are the Skae and we have returned."

Moments later, as the gathering crowd gave way, the Skae ship landed. A seam, appearing as if by magic, revealed a hatch which slid upward as a series of steps lowered to the ground. In the dark opening stood the tall bluish frame of one of the Skae, except he stood slightly stooped over, leaning on a staff, and his skin was blotchy and wrinkled with age. His appearance exactly as the images in Karm's memorial described. His skin-tight clothing shimmered a rainbow of colors in the sunlight.

Maliche, with Ryma at his side, approached the vessel. He felt a great outward surge of energy toward the alien who stood motionless, eyes closed as if thinking to himself.

The alien opened his large eyes and spoke to Maliche. "Ah, I understand. We had given you up as lost when we did not hear from you for so long. Other matters prevented us from returning to check on you, but we rejoiced when we received your signal. My name is Bolt."

***

Over the next year, Bolt and several other Skae, visited both the Brin and the Kolandi, offering their help and guidance with their technical skills and the scientific advancements of thousands of years of space exploration, and then vanishing for weeks at a time. Maliche sat in council with his closest advisors in his private chambers at The Assembly.

"As I understand it, the Skae received my biocomputer's signal several years from now, but traveled back in time to the coordinates it gave them. Apparently, the stories of Karm being a time traveler are not fantasy after all."

The new agricultural guild master reached out with both hands, palms upturned. "And they are giving us this advanced technology because they need our help? How can they possibly need us?"

"I don't pretend to understand all the answers to this yet," Maliche replied. "From what I do gather, the Skae have been at war for an eternity with a race called the Gorvin. I've accessed everything the biocomputer has about them and they appear to be a relentless destroyer of worlds. Apparently, the Kolandi were originally allies and partners of the Skae, until the Gorvin unleashed a horror here, nearly destroying the Kolandi. Those old ruined cities out in the wilderness we have heard about, before we tore them down, were built by the Kolandi at the height of their power."

"And now they need our help to defeat their enemy? Why wait until now?"

"Apparently, something in our genetic make-up counteracts a plague agent in the Kolandi DNA which has, so far, prevented the Skae from enlisting their help. Only our DNA combining with theirs will cure them."

"So, we were a breeding experiment? That's why they brought us here?" asked the ranching guild master.

"That is my understanding, but the threat of the Gorvin in this part of the galaxy, in their time, has increased and the Skae are losing the war. They need our help... or at least, will need the help of our future generations. Their time-traveling frames of reference get me all turned around."

"If we mate with the natives, you mean," interrupted the guildsman.

Maliche glared at him. "Do you have a problem with that?"

"Me personally? Not at all. But you must be aware of those who are opposed to such unions."

Maliche waved his hand dismissively. "A fringe group. Nothing to concern ourselves with. They'll come around once they see how gentle and honorable the Kolandi are."

"If my ancient history lessons serve me correctly, isn't that what our ancestors on Dyan'ta said about The Faith movement when it began? Can we really afford to ignore them?"

The door burst open and in rushed a breathless page. "It's time, your excellency. You're needed at the hospital."

"Excuse me, my wife needs me." Maliche ran out of the room, down the stairs and into the waiting mag-lev car in front of the building. The escort sirens blared as they accelerated away.

***

"It's a fine healthy boy, Maliche," said Nalot, slapping Maliche on the back. "Takes after his mother, except for the small crest there."

The front room overflowed with guests come to celebrate the new arrival. Piles of gifts grew in the corner. Servants hurried as best they could with trays of drinks and food for the visitors.

Maliche smiled at his old friend. "Let's go out back where we can talk."

"Been a long strange road we've traveled," said Nalot once they were alone.

"It has indeed, my friend," Maliche replied, sitting down on the stoop, motioning for Nalot to join him. "I can never thank you enough for everything. I owe you my life, and Ryma's as well. And yet there is so much still to do."

Nalot grunted and looked back over his shoulder as Seykel came to sit beside him. "About that..." he struggled to find the words. "There's something I need to do first." He took Seykel's hand in his lap.

Maliche examined the pair, tilting his head in question.

"There's a certain path I need to travel, and a promise to them folks back in the caverns I need to keep before I can go any further."

"You aren't going soft on me now, are you?" Maliche grinned.

"Just thinking I finally found a home."

Maliche stood on the lowest step of the porch, eye-to-eye with the pair. He clasped Nalot's shoulders with a strong grip. "I wish you all the best, my friend." Turning to Seykel, he reached out one hand, taking hers. "Promise me you'll bring him back alive?"

She smiled, lighting up her entire face. "I promise, but only if you promise to stand as his witness, and bring my princess back home for our joining."

Later that evening, after the guests left, the eight companions said their farewells.

Ryma and Maliche watched from the doorway of their home as Rilo and Kitae, who would never leave their princess's side, hugged the others as they got into the mag-lev taking them to the shuttle station.

As they watched the vehicle depart, they held each other close.

"Are you ready for all of this?" he asked her,

"As long as you are with me, I am."

Epilogue

"Has it been five years already?" Ryma asked her husband as she prepared the birthday celebrations for their son. She reached down and scooped up the baby crawling underfoot, and deposited her on Maliche's lap.

In the years following the Great Transformation, as the people now called the upheaval, Maliche and Ryma had carved out a working alliance between the two cultures. The Kolandi held all the rights to the eastern continent and all it contained. The Brin maintained the rights to purchase the minerals produced by the mines at strictly and jointly controlled prices. The Kolandi granted limited homesteading rights to some of the Brin after a lengthy application process, and many Kolandi now walked the streets of First Town, and other cities in the western continent. Maliche always took a double check whenever he spotted a Kolandi youth (few elders ever visited the western cities) in Brin attire strolling down the street. There was still much to accomplish and much diplomacy to carry out, but as time went on, the two people were growing to accept one another and greater numbers of mixed couples and families could be seen on both continents.

"We still need to talk about the southern mine shipping contracts," she called from the kitchen. "Don't think for a minute I'm going to let them steamroll me into a corner on it. We still need those guarantees."

"Save it for the office, my love. Enjoy the party." He stood up to answer the door, swinging his two-year-old daughter through the air as he went, to her immense delight.

"Bolt! A wonderful surprise as always, my friend. Come in." He stepped aside. Allowing the tall alien to enter. Leaning heavily on his staff, looking weary, Bolt no longer had to bend over to enter a Brin home.

"Thank you, Maliche. I cannot stay long, but I wanted to greet the first of our new family on his birthday, and leave him this token of our esteem." He pulled a small package out of his pocket. "Where is the boy?"

"Jontar, come here for a moment. Someone has come to visit you."

The youngster banged down the curving stairs from his room on the second level, jumped the last three steps, bounced off the rounded wall and careened into the front room.

"Hello, Sir Bolt. How are you today?" Jontar reached out to take the present.

"I am doing well for such an old one as myself. Are you enjoying your birthday?"

The youth, barely containing his excitement, remembered his manners. "Yes, sir. May I open this now?"

"Of course you may," said Bolt, ruffling the boy's small crest.

As Jontar ran off to another part of the room to open his gift, Bolt watched, his face seemed puzzled.

"Is something wrong?" asked Maliche.

"The child seems unusually advanced in his ability to converse, yet I do not detect any signs of the biocomputer in him. Was the transfer unsuccessful?"

"He is extremely intelligent for his age. The geneticists are examining his DNA to see if the hybridization process is responsible, or if he is just a statistical anomaly. You are correct, though. The biocomputer shows no interest in him. Perhaps it cannot adapt to Jontar's nervous system."

"And what does the biocomputer say about it?"

"That's the strange thing. It doesn't tell me anything at all. It's as if it does not even understand the question. Should we be concerned?"

Bolt thought for a moment. "I do not think you need to worry. The child seems perfectly healthy. I will look into the matter, though. The device has been around for quite some time now. It may need an adjustment."

"I don't think that would be necessary. It operates normally for everything else."

"Very well, then. I do have other business to attend to, so I will take my leave of you now."

Maliche held the door for him and waved goodbye as the elderly Skae bent nearly in two as he entered the mag-lev car.

"Did he leave already?" asked Ryma as she came into the room. "We were in the middle of making the desert and just finished."

"Yes, he said he had other matters to attend to and couldn't stay."

"Too bad, I was looking forward to talking to him about your ancestors. He always has such fascinating stories about them, and how he raised Karm and brought him back in time to your planet to save everyone. What an incredible people they are."

Young Jontar walked over to them and looked up at their faces. His head tilted with eyes wide in wonder. "Don't you know about them?"

Maliche returned the boy's gaze. "About who, son?"

"About the Skae. Don't you know?"

Ryma knelt down to be at eye level with her child. "Know what, dear?"

"That they're lying. They lie about everything."

About Jim Cronin:

I worked for thirty-five years as a middle school science teacher, but am now semi-retired, working part-time as an educator/performer at the Denver Museum of Nature and Science. I have been married for thirty-eight years to the love of my life, Diane. Together, we raised two incredible sons, and now have a beautiful granddaughter to spoil rotten.

I was born in Kansas City, Missouri and lived in Arlington, Virginia before moving to Denver where I attended High School and eventually college at Colorado State University, graduating with a degree in Zoology and a teacher certification. I currently live near Denver in the small town of Parker.

My first novel, Hegira, a science fiction tale of time travel, political and religious intrigue, cloning, and imminent planetary destruction, proved to be only the start of a new adventure. I have completed Hegira's sequel, Recusant, and am working on the third and final book of The Brin Archives, Empyrean. Retirement has proved to be an exciting journey into new realms of discovery.

Social Media Links:

Facebook: https://www.facebook.com/Jim-Cronin-Science-Edutainer-Author-704524026327838/

Twitter: https://twitter.com/authorjimcronin
@authorjimcronin

Website: http://jimcroninscienceedutainer.weebly.com/

Amazon Author Page: http://www.amazon.com/Jim-Cronin/e/B01C1V5OF6/ref=dp_byline_cont_pop_book_1

Solstice Bookstore: http://solsticepublishing.com/solstice-universe/

Acknowledgements:

I want to thank all of those who helped make this novel possible. First of all, Diane, the love of my life, for being so patient and understanding when I was in the throes of a writing marathon. Mike, my brother, who sat through many hours helping me brainstorm story and plot ideas. Also, Susan and Cat, thank you for all your edits and suggestions which helped make this story so much better than I originally wrote it. A huge shout out to all of you who read and wrote such encouraging reviews of Hegira, you inspired me to continue the story. And, to everyone, friends and family, who's encouragement and support over the years has made me the person I am today.

If you enjoyed this story, check out the other Solstice Publishing books by Jim Cronin:

Hegira:

His home world is dead; the victim of a supernova, but this does not stop Karm from attempting to save the Brin, his extinct species. Rescued by an alien race from a derelict spacecraft as a vial of DNA, then cloned, Karm must travel back in time, convince a small team of co-conspirators to join him in his quest, and outmaneuver a power hungry monarch and his fanatic brother, leader of The Faith, both absolutely committed to opposing him.

All of Karm's plans rest on the untested and controversial cloning theories of the young geneticist Dr. Jontar Rocker, and the abilities of his bodyguard, personal assistant, and surrogate niece, Maripa. Will their combined efforts be enough to overcome the power of the monarchy and the planet's most influential religion? Will Karm's secrets destroy the trust of his companions and ruin his campaign to save the Brin?

http://bookgoodies.com/a/B010E3EKC6

Links to Reviews for Hegira:

Reader's Favorite: https://readersfavorite.com/book-review/hegira

Online Book Club:
http://forums.onlinebookclub.org/viewtopic.php?f=21&t=33545&sid=2141c95f05215340942efac618351dbc